A Season of Sons

Black Spiral – Book 1

Rob Tucker

Printed in the United States of America

A Season of Sons is a paranormal thriller of deception, illusion... and murder.

The year is 2012. While investigating the heinous death of a prominent evangelist, FBI agent, Leon Safullo is unable to identify the killer through traditional methods of forensic analysis. Simultaneously, Leon learns of the sudden disappearance of Paul Evans, CEO of a major corporation.

Leon is a pragmatic realist whose career is based on interpreting symptoms of aberrant human behavior. The killer contacts Leon with the purpose of challenging the validity of his investigation. Leon perceives the threatening direct communication as a masquerade using digital technology, but fears for the safety of his family.

With the help of an illusionary alter ego named Pearl, Antonio Guzman claims to be a macabre combination of man and spirit, who has infiltrated society as a normal human being. He uses advanced technology combined with microbiology, drugs, and hypnosis to invade his victims' minds and manipulate their unconscious desires. Guzman is in search of "candidates" to possess and convert those who embody "the perfect light."

Paul Evans is a preferred target for Guzman/Pearl. Once a considerate and responsible husband and father, he has fashioned his life according to how he believes others perceive him, which exposes him to the influence of corporate greed, destroys the life of his business partner, and damages his own family.

Guzman invades and breaks down Paul's resistance to acknowledging that dark powers have created his success, and now they want Paul's only son, Matt, in a Faustian exchange. Matt and his sister, Jenny, possess the resistant strain of "Perfect Light." Struggling to reclaim shreds of his identity incrementally taken and possessed by Guzman, Paul and his son flee into a mountain wilderness.

In the midst of a violent winter storm in the remote Rocky Mountains, father and son fight for survival against the forces of darkness whose sole objective is to possess them and extinguish the light wherever and in whomever it may exist.

The unfolding evidence and trail of mayhem and murder force Leon to confront his disbelief in paranormal activity as something more than the imagination and projections of a psychopathic killer.

Prologue

New York 2012

"A conversation with the Lord will help to clarify the muddy theological waters that lie ahead," Reverend Lawrence Livingston said.

"I know you would enjoy a stroll but is it safe in the city at this time of night?" asked his wife.

"God is always with me. God is my bodyguard," he said with a chuckle. "There's a church just a few blocks from the hotel, and it will help me prepare for the summit tomorrow morning."

"Well, if you're gone more than an hour, I'm calling the police."

"You worry too much." He gently reached down and touched her lightly freckled cheek. He loved her freckles. They were a feature that had caught his attention twenty years ago during a conference in Columbia, South Carolina. She had that sun fresh southern look with gray-blue eyes that bespoke a deep emotional sincerity and faith in God. The long blonde-tinted brown hair that draped back over her shoulders then was now worn in a shorter mature style, but her natural beauty remained. He marveled at how youthful she appeared, even after bearing and raising four children.

Married life had been difficult during their early years. Beth had worked two jobs as an accountant while he was building his ministry. He had visions of one day heading a world-wide network. Ten years ago, that dream came to fruition thanks to a generous financial gift from a wealthy venture capitalist among Larry's ardent admirers, one who was dying of cancer.

Although Larry denied he possessed "star power," his wife and other followers convinced him that he had a special charisma that attracted people to him. From the pulpit, the stadium stage, and on television, he projected a calm but forceful intensity when he delivered a sermon. He had the lean Nordic face, challenging blue eyes, and muscled body of an Olympic athlete that many women in his audience perceived as a natural and acceptable sexuality for a religious leader.

There were those among them who pretended intimacy and called him Larry, rather than the formal Reverend Livingston. By nature, he promoted a casual, personal reference, but he tactfully discouraged the numerous suggestions of availability and advances by smitten young and middle aged females. He took the precaution of always leaving his private office door open when women came to seek his advice on personal matters. Visitors were aware that his secretary could see what transpired and, for the most part, hear what was said. Reverend Livingston had no use for scandal and lawsuits.

As he stepped off the elevator and walked briskly across the expansive hotel lobby, he was followed closely by a well-dressed businessman wearing a dark suit and solid color tie. He carried a laptop side bag slung over one shoulder and conversed earnestly into a headset attached to his left ear.

The businessman was only a few steps behind Reverend Livingston when the green liveried doorman grasped the brass handle. Lawrence diverted his glance from the elaborate hotel monogram on the glass door to nod his appreciation as he passed through onto the canopied entrance. While turning at the sidewalk and setting out in the direction of the church five blocks away, he briefly overheard the man request assistance of the doorman in getting him a cab. He had no reason to pause or glance back and notice that the man declined the cab when it pulled up, but continued to follow him at an unobtrusive distance.

The church signage of St. Stephens engraved in granite and on a wall plaque at the front entrance did not deter him. Lawrence was not a Catholic. He was famous for encouraging and promoting the acceptance and value of all religions, since they all had the purpose of trying to explain and understand man's existence in a spiritually meaningful way. There were many of his own constituents and other ordained religious leaders who profoundly disagreed with him. They believed in the exclusivity of their faith and relationship with their named God.

What was at issue and was the underlying reason that Lawrence had organized the summit conference of religious leaders of all faiths from around the world was the abuse of religion for personal, political, and economic gain. His opening remarks the next morning would be that God in any manifestation was not on anybody's side. During these times of Islamic and

Christian fundamentalist radicalism, he placed himself and his career at great risk. He knew that a summit conference would do little to change diverse cultures and societies and the greed and intolerance that pervaded the world overnight, but someone had to start somewhere. He felt it was his calling to do so.

The conference drew the attention of the media as a prospective target of a terrorist act, another of the mindless programmed incidents of violence that only perpetuated religious conflict and animosity and accomplished nothing. Lawrence believed that man was a sufficiently high-reasoning being and that he would find the ways and means to prevent the exploitation and ultimate destruction of the planet. New technologies could provide the resources the world needed to sustain life and alleviate the continual competition for land and food and water and sources of energy. Promoting the mutual acceptability of different belief systems was ten times more difficult.

The church's imposing hand-carved oak door opened with a slight effort at his touch. It remained unlocked for late worshippers until midnight. He noticed a few older people seated or kneeling and praying inside the cathedral. In deference to the Catholic ritual, he dipped his fingers into the font near the entrance and appropriately crossed himself, then walked up the central aisle to the altar and knelt.

He did not immediately set his mind into the meditative act of prayer, but studied the architectural structure and milieu of the church interior. The vaulted ceiling under the dome spread like an octopus to the buttressed heavy gray stone that enclosed the nave and transepts designed to block out the world beyond the walls. Detailed stained glass scenes of saints allowed filtered light to penetrate the holy sanctuary and inevitably drew one's gaze to the sculpted rendering of Christ on the cross extending high above and to the rear of the gold filigreed altar. The two gothic spirals of the church towers seized an onlooker with the impression that these were elevator passages for one's soul to ascend heavenward.

As Lawrence closed his eyes and bowed his head in over his hands folded against his chest, he heard and sensed the presence of an individual kneeling beside him. He did not open his eyes, but focused his mental energy on an appeal to the Lord in guiding him during the problematic days ahead.

The prayer spoken by the man to his right was sufficiently audible that it intruded on his thoughts and caused him to listen, at first with curiosity, then a deep chill.

"I am speaking to you now, Lord, so that you will understand my acts are according to Your natural laws and that you not mistakenly condemn me, for you created me to do your will. I know your true existence. You brought me into this world and my acts are justified. I lift my voice to you in prayer to bless me as the son you created.

Understanding the essential privilege of privacy in communal prayer, Lawrence nevertheless sensed that something was drastically wrong. He opened his eyes and stood and the man who had followed him into the church rose with him shoulder to shoulder. He quickly glanced at his face, but the man continued to stare straight ahead at the figure of the suspended Christ. Lawrence wondered if his sudden clutch of fear was unwarranted, except for the bizarre message of the man's prayer. The close proximity of the man raised a second premonition.

The man then turned his head and looked past Lawrence at the bald figure only he could see. Translucent milky blue eyes, pale skin, and his shaved head provided Pearl an other-worldly appearance. At six feet five inches tall with a body like iron, he exuded a lethal aura that discouraged casual conversation.

Lawrence looked over his shoulder and saw that the few people who had been seated in the pews were now gone. He was alone with this man whom he now sensed meant to do him harm.

The sudden pin prick of a sharp needle penetrated the side of Lawrence's neck. He lurched away with a cry and snatched at the invasive instrument, but it had been immediately withdrawn.

The chapel slowly began to spin. His eyes blurred and he clutched at the air as he collapsed on the steps. He watched the man remove a glistening razor sharp machete from his computer bag and place it on the altar.

He thought he must be dreaming as the wavy vision of the man disrobed in slow motion and stood naked above him.

Just before he died, Lawrence Livingston experienced a burning sensation from his heart to his groin. He felt no pain watching the man pull his entrails from his body and ritually drape them over the altar. Or when the man smeared blood over his chest and abdomen and coated his erection with blood. He watched the slow rhythmic strokes of the hand and the explosion of semen that desecrated the altar Bible.

As he lay on the steps, arms and legs spread wide, Lawrence's dimming gaze watched the blue and gold stain-glass rendering of Mary Magdalene that dominated the transept wall under-lit by flickering candles blur and fade to darkness.

The blood flowing from Lawrence's body down over the steps evaporated and was gone. Guzman wiped the blade of the machete clean using the altar cloth.

* * *

Chapter 1

Even when he had his office computer disconnected, the messages continued to appear on the screen as though some unexplainable presence were at work within its electronic circuitry. Paul Evans did not have the computer and laser printer removed, because he was compelled to discover the source of the diary entries that invaded his daily email. By that time, IT had branded the whole affair a hoax probably perpetrated by someone who held a grudge against the CEO. They suspected his IP address had been hacked. They disassembled the computer, but were unable to find the source of the problem.

Paul pretended to go along with them, but was terrified that his disconnected personal computer at home continued to create files of the diary.

No one else had ever read the diary. No one else knew about it with the exception of IT. So he deleted the files as they appeared in his spam filter, but they kept on appearing and reappearing like clones of themselves. Every morning when he opened his Email, a new one confronted him.

He was the president of Helix, a multinational corporation and he didn't get there by being a mental case. He got there by being smart, forming alliances, making acquisitions as a corporate raider, and divesting himself of others.

Paul wrestled with the fear of becoming a victim of some hallucination or cerebral anomaly.

Despite his achievements, he had never realized how dependent he was on how others perceived him.

He believed now someone might be stalking him or trying to manipulate him through a bizarre form of blackmail, but he was reluctant to go to the police or call the FBI because of the elaborate tax evasion schemes in which he participated with the assistance of his lawyers and a financial investment organization, The First World Corporation.

Not a believer in superstition, he resisted an impulse that seemed to take over and control him during the past two months, especially when the unknown source spoke to him through the diary, its medium of communication. Paul did not believe he could have written the messages as an aberration of his thoughts. Much like personal notes, they advised him on how to lie and cheat and exploit individuals and other companies to further his own profit. They were business strategies. But lately, a troubling message appeared.

It informed him of the price.

Now he was going back in search of clues as to the source's existence and reality.

You are drifting from the path and are being called to task. You must return to the fold of those who guide your life. Through the diary you will clearly understand that I exist and what you must do for me. You will attempt to deny me what I am seeking, but to keep what you desire, you cannot disbelieve in me.

I will talk to you in your dreams and you will believe that they are strange and awful dreams, because that is what you want to believe. But they are real and my voice speaking to you is but a reflection of you.

Although you have never seen me before, you will soon. Every time we write in this diary together, you will come to learn more about me. The words here are your own. They come from your thoughts. They represent who you are.

Soon you will learn more about your contract.

Paul scanned the next few pages of the diary. He rejected that he had written any of it, even after a particular passage jumped out at him as a response to his rejection.

"I'm not writing this god-damn diary," Paul shouted to an empty room.

He struggled with the malaise of disorientation that clouded his brain. His ability to rationally consider and work through problems had markedly diminished. The results of a physical exam one month ago showed that his blood pressure was much higher than normal, that his cholesterol level was elevated, and he was experiencing sexual dysfunction.

He had previously been diagnosed with sleep *apnea,* that limited an appropriate amount of oxygen to his brain due to his slightly overweight condition and excessive consumption of alcohol. The lack of consistent deep sleep affected his perception.

When Paul questioned the possibility of a tumor, the brain scan was negative. The psychiatrist explained that a chemical imbalance of the brain could cause psychotic episodes. He believed this could be happening to him, because of the vast distortions he was experiencing in bizarre dreams and scrambled memories of his past social, business, and family life. To his dismay, the prescribed medication had no effect on him other than to make him momentarily high. He feared he was losing his grip on reality, and stabilizing himself was finally up to him.

*   *   *

When he first met his wife, Moya, their relationship happened sweet and quiet, like her, a sense of falling into place without effort, the two of them excluding the rest of the world.

The memory of music and warm rain recalled the moments as he had experienced them.

Paul remembered the umbrellas and slick wetness of coats in the moving crowd coming from the concert music inside the hall, shuttling into the slap and splatter of rain.

Their relationship had been too ideal from the beginning. He was not aware at first that the romanticism stemmed from Moya's projected fantasies and how he met her expectations.

Having always been admired by women, he coveted her image of him, the special admiration, her ingratiating shyness, a withdrawing intimacy that frustrated and fascinated him.

He remembered her heels clipping along the wet walk before him. She walked with a tall trench-coated swinging stride. Hoping she would stop at the corner, he lengthened his own step to keep pace.

He was concerned that she would not remember him, especially in the night and driving rain. When she did stop, he was nearly too embarrassed to glance sidewise at her.

No such trouble with other girls, but with her, he had to force himself to look. She flicked a bare glance at him. Within that brief moment, she conveyed the warmth and intrigue of her aloofness. There was an invitation in that glance, he was sure of it, and fear of encounter, as well, for she hurried on, skirted the parking area walking quickly to the wrought iron campus gate. Well, at least she recognized him.

He hurried to his car. Driving quickly in the direction she had disappeared, he found her walking down the dark wet street. She turned and was suddenly gone again. He sat in his car, motor idling, at the curb. Approaching headlights ballooned in the wipers skimming the windshield and passed quickly into the wet night.

Disappointed, he cruised along hoping to catch sight of her. He guessed at the turn and there she was three blocks down a side street, a neighborhood of boarding houses, about to walk up the sprawling wooden porch in the fractured glow of yellow light.

He pressed the horn and she turned at the top step, edged back in beneath the lip of the sloping roof and peered at the Plymouth through the curtain of rain.

She was out of focus standing there in the porch light. He honked again to make her image clear. She stopped and turned, but she wondered if he were honking for somebody inside the house. Leaving the motor running, he leaped out of the car and ran through the rain to the porch. She was opening the apartment door.

"Moya!"

She looked back as he thumped up the soggy steps. She did not answer, only questioned with her enigmatic eyes. She talked in silences.

"I'm Paul Evans. You remember? From Mervis's English class." She simply nodded.

"Would you like to have a cup of coffee or hot chocolate with me?" he asked.

She hesitated, pondering, looking past him at the car, nodded again, let the apartment door fall closed. Going down the slippery steps, he supported her by her willing arm.

Being within the moving car isolated them from the rain and the night. The flicking elegant dash and lazy sweeping rhythm of the wipers mesmerized her. He felt compelled to fill the silence. "How did you like the concert?"

"I did very much."

He nodded with a compressed grin. "You a music lover?"

"I don't play but I enjoy listening."

"Same here. You'd think this rain would stop after two weeks. Gets to be tiresome."

"Yes, and awfully wet."

He caught her twinkle.

"This your last semester?"

"Yes."

"I never saw you around campus before the class."

She shrugged. "Different departments."

"Business and economics. You're humanities, right?"

She nodded.

"So what are your plans?"

"Probably teach somewhere."

"Looked yet for a job?"

She shrugged. "Not yet."

"Where are you from?"

"Wisconsin."

"City?"

She shook her head. "No, I was raised on a farm."

He cocked his head in interest. "Well, this is my hometown. It's not bad as far as cities go."

"I used to visit my aunt here when I was a small girl, especially in summer. Guess that's why I picked this campus."

"Nice in summer on the lake. Gets a little humid."

"What will you be doing?" she asked with detached interest. He glanced at her. "After this year, build a financial base, find a partner, investors, and start my own business," Paul told her assuredly.

"What kind of business?"

"Electronics and related technologies. There's a forecast that in the next ten to twenty years, everything will be run by computers and robots."

"Oh, I don't know the first thing about them," said Moya.

"My roommate does," said Paul. "Jim Owens is a genius. With his brains and my business sense, we can become very wealthy."

They pulled into the parking lot of a cozy Italian bistro. Paul requested a corner booth and ordered wine. Coffee was forgotten.

"Smoke?"

She declined.

"Do you mind?"

"No."

He lit his cigarette in a studied manner that amused her. He noticed. "You're smiling."

"You must see a lot of movies," she said.

He hesitated, grinned, nonplused, then realized what she was referring to. "Oh, yes, that and a lot of practice handling a cigarette in front of the mirror. Am I a fool to admit it?"

"Everybody uses mirrors for one thing or another."

The wine was delicately served. The waiter left menus.   "Hungry?"

"A Little."

"Do you ride?" he asked.

"The bus?"

"No, camels."

"Camels!"

He laughed. "Horses. A friend of mine has horses. He's a very wealthy friend. He's going to invest in my business."

"I've ridden bareback as a girl on my dad's farm, but --"

"Tomorrow at eight, I'1l pick you up, then breakfast. They throw a fantastic spread. His mother is unbearable though. A hell of a snob. Always knows what's best for sonny boy. That kind." He winked and flicked an ash from his cigarette.

They read their menus. The waiter returned. "Have you decided?"

Paul looked at Moya's light brown hair rolling in soft waves to her shoulders, the somber eyes.

"I think I'11 have. . ."

Chapter 2

If you try to ignore me, you will suffer. Your children are trying to interfere with what you do and who you are. Do not concern yourself with them. Listen only to me. You are not responsible for what happens. Your soul is clean.

Paul closed the diary on his computer. The more he read, the more confused he became. He decided that the only way he could discover the source, would be to test its existence. He picked up the phone and called his son.

"Hello." A nervous tremor crept into Paul's voice. "Matt, some things have been happening to me lately, strange things. I need to talk to you."

"I'm working on my thesis. I have to submit a draft to my Masters committee in four weeks. Can you call back after that? I'1l have time to talk."

Paul coughed. "This can't wait. It's urgent. It's an emergency and this is not something I can discuss over the phone. It involves you and me," he paused, "and your sister and your mother."

"Dad, I really don't have the time. Why don't you call Jenny."

"Because I have to see you. I need to see you. I need your help."

Paul sensed Matt's silent impatience at the other end of the line. He heard the click of computer keys underscoring a tone of irritation. "Help? What kind of help? If you're in legal trouble, you should be talking to your attorney."

"It's nothing like that," said Paul desperately. "It's me. It's just me. Please, son, we've got to get together and I've got to talk to you. We have to get away."

"What do you mean get away? What do you mean we? Get away from what?" The anger in Matt's voice panicked his father.

"I mean I have to get away and - and so do you." At Matt's prolonged silence, Paul glanced at the phone display to see if he had disconnected.

Matt's resigned voice returned. "Where are you calling from?"

"My New York office."

"When are you flying out?"

"Tomorrow. Not to California. I want us to meet in Great Falls, Montana. Something is drawing me to that location. Just an instinct. I have a plan."

"You're not making sense."

"If I can see you and talk to you, you can make something come clear in my mind. But we have to go away, be off alone where no one knows where we are, where no one can find us."

Again, a long silence.

"Matt, are you still there?"

"Yes, I'm here. What the hell is going on? This is too strange, what you're asking me to do. Have you been drinking? Are you drunk? You on meds?"

"No, none of those things. It could be something far worse."

"What could be worse? Whatever it is, I'm not even sure I want to hear about it." Matt repressed the impulse to hang up on him.

"I need you to help me discover the thing that could be worse."

"Discover?"

"Get it to reveal itself. Bring it out into the open."

"It? What do you mean it? What's it?"

"That's what I don't know. But it's there."

"Dad, go see a shrink. You're talking crazy."

"I'm not crazy. I know I'm not crazy. Whatever it is, it's real. It follows me."

"Is someone stalking you?"

Paul hesitated. "In a manner of speaking, yes."

"Who?"

"I don't know who, or even what it is."

"Then why don't you call the police?"

"To be honest, they would probably think I'm delusional."

"I think you're delusional," said Matt. "You sound delusional."

"I'm sorry, but this is the only way I can explain it. I've been made some kind of target and it involves you."

"This is getting too weird, Dad. You need to call the police."

"We're not that kind of target. What is stalking us is not physical. It's demonic."

"Dad, no one is stalking us," he emphasized the 'us.' "Especially some demon. This is all in your head."

"It's not just in my head. It's not. Strange things are happening to me at home and here in my office. That's what I mean about being followed. It's not just some mental aberration. I'm not losing my mind. At least I don't think I am."

"You really should see a psychiatrist. It sounds like you're having a breakdown."

"If that were true," the tremor in Paul's voice intensified, "I wouldn't be calling you. You've got to believe me."

"How many days are you talking about?"

"Just a few. A week should be enough."

"Enough for what? I still don't get what this is all about."

"To figure out what is happening to me, to us."

"Nothing is happening to me but a deadline for my thesis."

"Whatever this is touches you. We're both targets."

"Dad, you're losing it, all right. The only reason I'll meet you is because you deny you need professional help. But when we meet and talk, that's what I want you to do, get professional help. A week is all I have."

"What? What did you say?" Paul broke into a cold sweat. "I'm just feeling a little disoriented right now. I'm under a lot of stress. What I need is to just walk away from everything here for a while, but there's something trying to prevent me. It has to do with you and your sister."

"Jenny? What does she have to do with this? Do you want me to call her?"

"No, no, you don't have to call her. Considering what she thinks of me, this will just make it worse. If I could explain, I would. So please don't judge me by what I'm telling you over the phone. None of this can possibly make any sense to you."

"You've sure got that right. All I said was I can spend only a week with you. I'll bring my computer so I can get some work done."

"You'll have to excuse me, son. I'm grateful to you. I'm feeling out of sorts."

"Yeah, Dad, I can tell. I know. You buying my plane ticket?"

"Yes, yes, of course. You make your own flight arrangements and let's meet in Great Falls at noon tomorrow at the airport, the Avis desk. And you said you'll have your computer?"

"Yes."

"That's good. I have some files to show you."

"Files? What the hell? Okay, don't say anymore." said Matt, "I'l1 see you there."

"Thank you, son. Goodbye."

"Bye."   Matt switched off his phone.

Paul stared at the thumb drive containing the diary.

His secretary looked up from her computer as he passed through the front office. "Take any messages.   I'll be out for a while."

Assuming he was going to the health club, she said, "Have a nice afternoon," and phoned the parking valet.

He took his private elevator from the fortieth floor down to the parking lobby where he placed a call on his iPhone to American Airlines reservations.

His chauffeur waited with the limousine door open.

<h1 style="text-align:center">Chapter 3</h1>

Jenny paused in her supper preparations to listen to her two and three old playing in the sandbox on the patio. She had not heard any outcry during the last ten minutes, a sign that neither child had thrown sand or hit the other.

They had awakened from their naps a half-hour ago, so they were still rested and even-tempered. She had also fed them a snack. Maintaining their blood sugar level was important to controlling what she called "the squall factor".

She had wanted to live where the climate was warm and people were anonymous. She had wanted to escape the memory of her mother hospitalized in a psychiatric ward, where, as children, she and her brother, Matt, had been taken for infrequent visits.

The visits had left her sad and shaken to see her mother staring vacuously through them as though they didn't exist.

They told her what they were doing at their grandfather's farm, in school, and about the river. "Grampa said he used to take you to the same place he showed us," Jenny's childhood voice echoed in memory.

After several visits to see her mother, Jenny had tearfully begged to be left at home. Her grandparents had not forced her to go.

She assembled an entourage of pets who followed her about. She fed them and talked to them like a mother to her children. She cared for them and loved them and they loved her back

Her school years seemed to pass quickly. She developed only a few playground friendships. Her grandparents' farm was a great distance from town.

She spent long hours alone reading, talking to her animals, and practicing what she called The Light.

She would concentrate on a ray or a patch of sunlight and, through her own meditative process, draw that light into her. She would fill her mind with the image of light from the serene backwater their grandfather had shown them. She discovered that sometimes, she believed, she could project the light into the mind of another person.

The effort required her absolute concentration. She wanted desperately to believe she could heal others.

When she decided to visit her mother again, she no longer attempted to talk to her. She focused her inner energy and what she believed to be her healing power, within her mother's mind. But her imagined light was not absorbed. She rationalized that her mother's emotional darkness repelled it.

The phone rang as she was watching John Morley's news story about the grisly murder of Reverend Larry Livingston. When she answered, she sensed the urgency in Matt's voice. Their occasional courtesy calls on weekends caught them up on what was happening in each others' lives, an emotional need originating during childhood.

"Hi, Sis, how you doin'?"

"I'm doin' diapers and puke and poop."

"Sounds like the kids are okay then."

"They're absolutely perfect little beasts."

"And Jeff?"

"He still has a job. He's proud of his promotion to chief software engineer."

"Are you proud?"

"Of course I'm proud, dufus. He's my husband. As long as he gets a paycheck and provides benefits for his family, I'm proud. If not, different story. I love talking to you, but I'm sure you didn't call to hear about my domestic bliss. What's up?"

"Something's happened to dad."

Jenny paused stirring a sauce pan of oatmeal. "We don't talk about him. Remember?"

"I know. I know we agreed, but this time it's different. Weird different."

"We've always known he's weird. In a good way or bad way?"

"I don't know. Not so good. He's acting strange. I just got off the phone with him. Out of nowhere, he wants me to meet him in Great Falls, Montana."

"You've got to be kidding. Why?"

"He wouldn't say, but he sounded really desperate, like he's losing it."

Jenny snorted. "Whatever it is, he never had it."

"He sounded like he might be having a mental breakdown."

"You know, Matt, that doesn't concern me. He shouldn't concern you either. We left him years ago."

"That's what we wanted to believe, but I'm not sure that's how things are."

"They are for me, dear brother. I'll never forgive him."

"I'm not saying I forgive him either, but people do change."

"It sounds like you're going. Are you?"

"I really don't have the time."

"But are you going?"

"I told him I would."

"Why?"

"I'm not sure."

"We don't owe him anything, not even a response."

"Well, I still think of him as my father." Matt braced himself for a tirade.

"I don't. I blotted him out. He doesn't exist for me," Jenny's voice came across clipped, exasperated.

"I was going to turn him down, but something he said changed my mind."

"What did he say?"

"He said he needed to talk about what happened, the way he treated us."

"It's too late for that."

"I know," Matt shrugged apologetically. "Nothing can be reclaimed. We can't go back. But I got the sense he needs to absolve himself."

"Try a priest. Try a fucking psychiatrist. How old is he now, anyway?"

"I don't know. I lost track. Fifty-five, fifty-six maybe."

"He's probably having a mid-life crisis. He'll just earn all the money he possibly can and then die. And no one will care. No one will miss him. He'll just be a rich man in the graveyard."

"That's pretty strong."

"That's how I feel, dear brother. There is no healing for him."

"I know. I used to feel that way, but I've outgrown it, outgrown him."

"You forgive him for all the shit he did to us? Mom will never recover. She'll live out her life in that hospital afraid to come back into the world, because she's afraid she'll meet him and others like him."

"Well, you have to remember the doctor said mom also had other symptoms."

"Oh, yes," Jenny sneered. "She didn't have the ability to handle what dad was doing to her. None of us knew that he had this other personality. I still get nightmares over it. That's the only connection."

"He asked for a week."

"I don't think you should let him lure you out there."

"He's not luring me."

"It sounds suspicious. My intuition tells me that it's not right."

"We're not kids anymore," said Matt. "I can handle dad."

"Nobody can handle him. Who would want to. He's a monster."

"He must have some regrets."

Jenny sputtered into the phone. "You're too good for him, Matt. He doesn't deserve a son like you."

"It's not all that important to me."

"I'm serious, Matt. You're a wonderful person. It's almost unbelievable that he's our father."

"I guess mom gave us our good traits."

"She did that for sure."

"I have to pack a few things, but I wanted to let you know. I can still get some work done out there, in the great outdoors."

"I appreciate your calling me. Is he paying for your ticket?"

"Yeah, I'm E-ticketed."

"You be careful, Matt. And I mean that seriously. Outside of Jeff and the kids, you mean more to me than anyone else in this world. I include mom, of course, but mentally, she's not in this world."

"I'll be careful."

"I love you, Matt."

"I love you too, Sis." He listened to the click, as she hung up the phone.

Chapter 4

Sigmund Safullo thrust his nose upward and snuffled along the edge of the desk and discovered what his keen olfactory senses told him was there. But it was out of reach. Not intimidated by any obstacle, he reared up on his hind legs and firmly planted his front paws on the desktop blotter and stretched his head toward the blue plasma-filled stress ball that eluded his drooling mouth by mere inches. He bounced slightly on his hind legs to get closer, but the effort wasn't enough. Throwing caution to the winds, he took a swipe at the ball with his right front paw and succeeded in knocking over and spilling a cup containing pens and pencils. A small bronze bust of the great psychiatrist, Sigmund Freud, the dog's namesake, jettisoned off the edge of the desk and crashed to the floor followed by the plummeting stress ball that bounced twice and was snatched from the air on the third bounce and firmly deposited into the left jowl of the triumphant Golden Retriever.

Sigmund romped out of the room with a swish of his flagging golden tail and bounded down the hall to a far corner of the house to hide and hoard his treasure with seven other like stress balls he had stolen from his master. Just moments before, Sigmund had heard his car coming down the street and turning into the driveway.

Satisfied that the stress balls were concealed, Sigmund raced back through the house and leaped into the living room just in time to see his master coming through the front door. He "woofed" in greeting.

His master patted him affectionately on his golden head and tugged gently on his large floppy ears. "Hi, Sig, where's your mom?"

Leon Safullo was squeamish about reading the newspaper or watching the reported news on television. Every morning, the headlines reached out and grabbed him by the throat with their horrific renderings of what had transpired somewhere in the world the day or the night before. Yet, each morning, he was compelled to at least briefly scan some editor's impression of what was meant to shock the average reader's attention. Leon was an above average reader. He was intelligent, well-educated, and, given his profession, understood the dynamics of all forms of communication.

"Maybe I just want to see how low they're willing to stoop," he conjectured several years ago. "Or maybe there's actually some gem of credible information buried somewhere in the newsprint that might influence my thinking in some way. The news is not thorough like it used to be. Whatever became of in-depth analysis?"

He felt the same about commercial television news. But he could detect the biases coming faster, the vitriolic shallowness and grandstanding of certain pundits in place of intelligent commentary, the one dimensional treatment of people's lives and events in order to fit in between the commercial time slots. What bothered Leon was that people had stopped thinking for themselves. They believed the sound bytes and ping-ponged from one throw-away opinion to another.

He believed people were so influenced by the media, they tried to live by what they saw on television and read in newspapers or, these days, on computers, iPads and cell phones. They tried to be like the models, the stars, the politicians, the villains, the heroes, and the killers. Pick their favorite celebrity and emulate. Forget about trying to be unique, different, an individual. Become one of them, a stereotype who is all shell and no substance, an electronic image that is momentarily on the screen until the series is over, to be replaced by yet another of endless derivative concepts. People had become a society of electronic clones -- and clowns.

He didn't understand how his wife could waste nearly an entire Sunday morning reading not one, but two newspapers, while drinking her fresh ground decafe.

"I enjoy reading," she told him following one of his remarks. "I will read just about anything." She rattled the newspaper at him. "There is so much information and I learn about so many things that are happening."

Leon picked up a front page from the papers scattered on the coffee table. "But how can you be sure they are actually happening and they weren't just made up by some schmuck who has to meet a deadline?"

"They aren't made up. They did happen and a journalist wrote about them." Her slender nose lifted with a smug wrinkle.

Leon dropped the paper back on the table. "But they are selective about what they write about. They slant the story to favor their point of view. They sensationalize to grab the attention of people like you," he pointed at her, "so you will read their lousy newspaper. Television commentators are the modern electronic age version of the ancient Greek chorus. They tell us what we're looking at, even though we can plainly see it. Then they tell us what we saw. Then they tell us what we just saw is supposed to mean, as though we can't think for ourselves. Admittedly, a lot of people don't these days."

"The problem with you, Leon, dear, is that you don't know how to relax."

"Reading the newspaper or watching a newscast causes me stress. How can you relax reading about daily catastrophes. You have probably become desensitized to catastrophes. That's the problem with the world today -- overexposure to catastrophes. Everyone is desensitized. They're walking around like zombies." He removed his suitcoat.

"Everyone except you, you sensitive creature you." She blew him a kiss. "You're too compulsive for your own good, Leo. If you don't relax and enjoy life, you're just going to turn in to a grumpy old man."

"I need a drink." He dropped his suitcoat over the back of an armchair and walked to a service cart. "What is this sudden preoccupation with getting old? It's in everything we read." He scooped two cubes from an ice bucket and dropped them with a clink into a cut-glass tumbler followed by a healthy pour of single malt scotch. "We hear about it constantly, see it, breathe it, try anything to postpone it. It is the most talked-about topic in the world today." He turned to face her. "Why? I'll tell you why. Because there's so much of it. We don't have to be reminded."

"You're taking what you read in the papers much too seriously. Look at it as -- entertainment."

"Entertainment? Do you realize what you just said? The world is in chaos, coming apart at the seams and you call it entertainment!"

"The world is not coming apart. The world is just fine. The world takes care of itself."

"What is that supposed to mean?"

"It means, Leon dear, that when things go sufficiently awry, Mother Nature will assert herself. She will take charge. Notice my gender reference.

She will restore the ball to its original position. She will rebalance. Man destroys. Woman creates."

"That kind of balance is only in the long term, eons of time, dinosaurs and evolution and Darwinian frogs and amphibians."

"Amphibians?"

"Amphibians. It's stress, Julie, stress. I know too much. I get too much information and it sticks right here," his right finger tapped his head. "All of it. I have a huge mental capacity for absorbing information."

"That's what makes you so good at your job, Leon. The trouble is, you're obsessive. No, not just obsessive, compulsive. You can't separate yourself from all the baggage. So how was your day?"

He sipped his scotch. "Not bad. The usual, but not bad."

"So what was bad? I'm sure you're dying to talk about it."

"I don't like to bring my work home."

"But you do anyway. You carry it around like a shroud. It makes you grumpy and negative about life."

"I'm not grumpy and negative about life. I'm positive about life. That's why I do what I do, because I'm positive, not negative. I work against the negative. My attitude is also because I'm growing older. I don't have the energy I used to."

"You aren't happy, Leon. You can't truly say that you are happy. Now me, I'm fun-loving. I want to love and have a good time. But lately, Leon, you're like a cloud of gloom descending over us. Sometimes, I feel like I should raise an umbrella in case there's a cloudburst. Are you sure you don't have a health problem?"

"I'm okay. I'm fine. I'm healthy. My cholesterol level and blood pressure are slightly above normal is all."

"But you're not happy, Leon. You're moody. You seem depressed. That's not good."

"Well, I am happy. This is who I am. This is how I'm happy, by being concerned."

"You are really confused. You need to loosen up, Leon. Why don't we go out on a date?"

"We do go on dates," he scowled. "We go to the grocery store together. I enjoy going with you to the grocery store. It's a pleasant experience."

"Leon, going to the grocery store is not a date."

"It's nice if you just listen to me, not tell me about my…infirmities."

"Have you considered maybe it's time to retire?"

"I like what I do and I've achieved a level of competency that has resulted in success and some recognition."

"So you're a guru, Leon. You deserve the recognition. But more importantly, do they pay you more money for being a guru, or do they just massage your ego?"

"Money is not the only reward for competence."

"You have two college educations to pay for in addition to maintaining the lifestyle to which we have all grown accustomed. Although not lavish by any stretch, it is comfortable. You're a good provider, Leon. Together, we are good providers."

Leon moved away and stared out through a picture window that overlooked a large green trim back yard that gently sloped toward a wooded area shared with a neighboring five acre tract. He and Julie and their two children had lived there for twenty-one years -- rich enjoyable years. Now, their children were gone, past. He felt like an empty hole gaped before him -- the future. Even if he immersed himself in his work, he felt like an emotional amputee.

He recalled that, as a child, the future was always something there ahead in the black, or maybe it was the bright, void of life that was singularly un-definable and unreachable, that present pleasures and enjoyments would just go on and on uninterrupted. There would always be mom and dad and brothers and sisters and friends, endless rounds of playing. Now, his eldest daughter was getting married in six months, and he had been changing her diapers and reading her bedtime stories when? Not so very long ago.

"Maybe you're right," he said. "Maybe we do need a date. We share many things in common, but I feel saddened."

"About what?"

"The passage of time. That we'll never have that time again that we had with our kids."

"Oh, that, Leon, it's just one of those things about life. You know. It moves on. Time goes by." Her voice rose into a pleasant mid-soprano range.

"You must remember this. A kiss is just a kiss. A smile's just a smile. The fundamental things apply, as time goes by."

"I have to sort this out."

"Sort it out later." She watched him squeezing the blue stress ball that he usually carried in his left pants pocket. She had told him that particular bulge in that position on his thigh looked obscene, but he had ignored her as he always did when she commented on his compulsion to squeeze stress balls. He kept a collection of at least a dozen that she knew of in as many places around the house, in his car glove compartment, and at his office downtown. In fact, she was the one who encouraged the dog, Sigmund, to take the balls and hide them. Sigmund loved the game of trailing after his garrulous sputtering master in search of the missing balls. Although he couldn't prove it, Leon suspected and accused his wife of being in collusion with the dog. She had laughed uproariously and had told him she had better things to do with her time than assist Sigmund in stealing and hiding his precious stress balls. When he would discover them, they were invariably slimed with the dog's saliva, which Leon found disgusting.

"That's what I'm trying to do," he said, "but you keep interrupting me."

"Then go off someplace and squeeze your stress ball and cogitate so I can read in peace. Your endless thinking renders you inert. When you think too much, you don't do anything. You don't act. You just stand there or sit there and think."

"I don't mean to bother you. I'm confiding in you," Leon raised his half-empty glass. "And why do you hate my stress balls? If you actually tried using one, you would discover its soothing therapeutic properties."

Julie tucked her chin down to hide her smirk of amusement. "I find reading the newspaper is soothing and therapeutic."

"You're impossible."

"Maybe you should go to church. Maybe you should take up religion," she laughed at their inside joke.

"You can't be serious."

"Am I ever serious?"

"Sometimes, I'm not sure. You make a joke out of everything I say. I'm a confirmed atheist. I was religious once, when it was programmed into me as a child in Catholic Italy."

"When are we going to take a trip to Italy?"

"Then I grew up and began thinking for myself instead of believing in what doesn't exist. Religion plays a significant role in many of the problems of the world. In fact, it's the cause of far too many problems, both directly and indirectly."

"That's just your opinion."

He patted Sigmund's head as the dog sidled up to him. "It's not just my opinion. It's what the trends show."

Julie spluttered. "Hey, here. Here it is, Leon." She laughed and smacked the open newspaper with the back of her hand. "Just what we've been looking for to perk up our lives."

"What's that?"

"Ballroom dancing."

"Oh, come on, Julie! In your dreams! We're not in shape for that kind of thing. Can you see me picking you up and throwing you around like a sack of potatoes?"

"No, that's swing. You're thinking of jitterbugging. This is not jitterbugging."

"We don't know the first thing about it anyway."

"We can learn. We join this club and they give lessons. Then we go to other dance clubs. It'll be fun, Leon. Meet people. Make new friends."

"I don't like to mingle like that. And I've never been comfortable expressing myself on the dance floor and I don't want to make new friends. You and Sigmund are all the friends I need."

"A complement like that will get you nowhere. Little attitude adjustment here, Leon. Fix this in your mind. We're going to do this, Leon. I'm going to sign us up. It's for your own good. It's for our own good. Don't be such a curmudgeon."

"When I come home after a hard day at work, I don't want to go out dancing. I prefer to swim or jog or putter around in the yard. Jiggling and dancing just isn't me."

"Ballroom dancing is not jiggling. It's smooth. It's transporting. You might be surprised how much you enjoy it."

"It's not a good idea. We'll figure out something else to do together."

"Ballroom dancing, Leon. Get used to the idea."

"Absolutely not. No appeal. It has no appeal for me."

"Face it, Leon. You're in. We're in. You and me, babe." She laughed.

"You know, I've been giving a lot of thought lately to behavioral patterns. Adaptation is a mechanism for survival. Work, school, all of it. Even crime. Especially crime. Whole societies. Committing crimes is how one can get ahead in life."

"Fancy that, since you work in it," she laughed. "Have you ever considered what job security you have? There will always be a market for crime and crime solvers. Why are you going back to societies again?"

"Now, consider this. Fish and insects, for example, reproduce trillions, but most of them die or get eaten. The forces of nature and behavior are to restore balance, not to distort and disperse it. We are always being pulled back into alignment or realignment."

"Like car tires, Leon. We get realigned by the forces. And do you realize that's what you do for a living? You realign."

"I guess so." He looked back through the window. "There are a lot of leaves on the ground out there."

"Better out there than in my house."

"They're scattered. They need raking. I'm going to rake them up." He finished his cocktail with a rattle of melting ice cubes.

"You do that, Leon. You go rake up those leaves and realign them in neat piles."

"Concurrent thoughts. How long has Blanche been taking birth control pills?"

"About a year, why?"

"I read that cancer can be a side effect of taking birth control medication."

"Another side effect is not getting pregnant."

"She should stop taking them. When is the next time we're going to call her?"

"Her doctor won't let her take them any longer than is safe."

"How do we know he's even monitoring her?"

"It's in her medical record. When she goes for a checkup, he'll tell her. She's a smart girl, Leon. She's our daughter. She's up on these matters."

"I'm not so sure."

"Your leaves are calling you, Leon. Go align them."

"We need to caution her."

"Ballroom dancing, Leon."

He noticed Sigmund eyeing the ball in his hand and quickly jammed it into his left pocket as he exited to the garage to find a rake. Sigmund bounded after him.

At the same time, a strange and chilling email arrived that would change his life.

Chapter 5

Early the next morning, Leon left the house to stop by the bank for cash. He then pulled into a gas station, since the dash indicator veered toward empty.

Leon drove a blue BMW 530i. He extolled its virtues, its quality of design and manufacture, and the fact that after sixty-thousand miles, the only maintenance the car needed was one tune-up and a few oil changes, along with two tire rotations and wheel alignments. Although, he had to purchase one full set of new tires, a fault of the tires, not the vehicle.

"Adaptation," he thought. "The American automotive industry didn't adapt, so they lost business. They're barely surviving. Competitiveness, that's what strategy's all about. People want quality, value for their hard-earned dollar. So give them quality and you stay in business."

While he pumped gas, he had to endure glam tunes played over the P.A. speaker system. "There was a lot of whining and crying and self-absorbtion in those old songs. They must have sold a lot of Kleenex in the 80's," he thought. "Waa Waa Waa! Poor suffering me. Those same singers now are probably complaining about hemorrhoids instead of heartaches."

The "Waa Waa's" stuck in his mind like an unwanted mantra that refused to go away. After he paid for the gas and returned to the BMW, he filled his own speakers with orchestral thunder which blotted out and replaced the "Waa Waa's." Driving on, he tuned in to his favorite station, catching the opening triumphant strains of the Toreador Song, from Bizet's Carmen. "I'm a toreador out fighting the bulls. I love classical music because of its complexity," he conjectured. "The quiet power of Mendelssohn, the lyric spirit of Mozart, the emotional inventiveness of Chopin." Leon especially appreciated piano, since he had taken lessons as a boy from a retired concert pianist who had arthritis. "I should have maintained the piano for the last twenty years. I need to take it up again, not ballroom dancing."

He and Julie had a vast collection of classical music, records, tapes, and CD's. Julie liked string instruments, especially the violin.

"Complexity," he thought. "The joy of violins -- and ballroom dancing."

His cell phone warbled. He hated the cell phone, even the blue tooth jammed into his left ear like an oversized robotic beetle boring into his brain. The perception of being attached to an electronic leash aggravated him.

The intense voice of Roy Waterman, the Special Agent In Charge, leaped into his ear. "Leon, have you seen the morning news?"

"I try my best to avoid watching it for personal reasons. It has a negative effect and makes me feel depressed."

"What the hell are you talking about? It never ceases to amaze me how the newsies get to the crime scene before we do."

"I understand there's a serious communication problem between the various law enforcement agencies," said Leon.

"I don't know what the local agencies think they can do without us. They are getting better about calling us in. We have the technology. That's changing everything."

"I'm missing something."

"What?"

"The purpose of your call."

"Reverend Lawrence Livingston was murdered last night."

"The evangelist?"

"Yes, the evangelist. Only this is not any ordinary murder."

"I never considered murder ordinary."

"This happened late last night in St. Stephens Catholic Church."

"And Livingston isn't Catholic."

"No, he's an eclectic Christian. He accepts all faiths, all religions."

"That could be career limiting these days," said Leon.

"It was for him. When I say this was no ordinary murder, this one has got to rise to the top of the list."

"What happened?"

"He was eviscerated."

Leon remained silent registering the image in his mind.

Waterman cut in. "Leon, you still there? You still with me?"

"I'm here."

"There's more, much more."

"We're on an open line. Wait 'til I get to the office. I'm ten minutes away."

"CNN has a continuous instant replay on this. It's been going on for the past hour."

"The Greek Chorus."

"What? The Greek what? Are you sober?"

"Nothing. Nothing. Just a personal observation. I'll see you in ten minutes."

"Right."

Leon disconnected the blue tooth. It suddenly occurred to him that the microwave signal might cause a cancerous growth in his brain. That would be the final insult, death by blue tooth.

When Leon arrived at the Bureau office, he found Waterman in a state of agitation watching the CNN newscast. "You're here. That's good. That's fifty percent. Where's Berzinsky?"

"He's usually at the gym working out at this hour."

"Call him and tell him to get his ass over here. I swear if someone didn't tell him the difference, he'd wear a jockstrap for a necktie. You know what I think of body builders? Underneath, they're all fruitcakes."

"Ed hardly fits that profile. He's very active heterosexually. He's married and has three children."

"Don't matter. Anybody who spends as much time on his body as he does has a fruitcake orientation. Here, use my phone." Waterman shoved it across the desk toward Leon, who picked up the receiver and dialed Berzinsky's pager number.

Berzinsky was in the middle of a counterweight routine for his upper arms, latissimus dorsi, and shoulders when the pager vibrated. He paused long enough to check the number and turn off the pager, then resumed his repetitions. A few minutes later, he grabbed his Iphone and returned the call. He didn't expect Leon's voice on the other end of the line and expressed his dissatisfaction. "You in his office?"

"Yes."

"He called me about an hour ago when I was starting my workout. He does it deliberately. I told him he didn't have anything that urgent that it couldn't wait for an hour. Now he has you calling me. Tell him I'm going to take a shower and I'll be there in twenty minutes." He wiped the sweat off his forehead back into his dark crew cut.

"Okay, I'll tell him." Leon turned the phone aside. "He says twenty minutes. He wants to take a shower."

"Tell him to take a fucking shower on his own time," Waterman raised his voice. "Did you hear that, Buttinsky? Take a fucking shower on your own time. I can stand your stink. What I can't stand is your insubordination."

Leon moved the receiver away from his ear at Berzinsky's response, then handed it back to Waterman. "He's going to take a shower first."

Waterman shouted into the phone, "Make it a cold one, you bastard!" then hung up.

"I really should have him transferred out of this unit. I'm thinking seriously about it. A fucking four bagger. That's what that son-of-a-bitch needs -- censure, transfer, suspension, and probation. Berzinsky's a glorified slingshot," Waterman took a sip of coffee, freshly poured by his secretary from his personal sterling coffee pot. "He should have stayed with SWAT. He likes to dress up and play ninja."

"You know he's one of the best when it comes to field work. His investigative instincts have proven accurate time and time again," Leon supported his associate. He understood that Waterman never would appreciate a maverick like Berzinsky.

Berzinsky did not think twice, when it came to risking his life for a fellow agent. He did not conceal his feelings for Waterman, not even for the sake of appearances. True to his word, he walked through the door twenty minutes later.

"Well, Jocko," Waterman greeted him. "You ready yet to compete in the Mr. Universe contest with all the other steroids?"

Ignoring the remark, Berzinsky pulled up a chair. "Okay, sir, I'm here. What is it?"

"See for yourself. It's on T.V."

They watched the attractive news announcer, with just enough revealed décolletage, read her lines from the teleprompter. There were no direct images of the grisly murder, only exterior shots of the crime scene and the on-camera commentary of the broadcaster. Four police units, a dozen motorcycle cops, two fire engines, a fire paramedic ambulance, and an AMR ambulance filled the yellow taped-off boundary of the street and wide stone steps to the massive doors. Uniformed officers stood guard along the tape line to block gawkers with their cell phone cameras and members of the media.

"Do you have anything from the first responder?" asked Leon.

"Zone search photos and contact with the first responder." Waterman pulled up a collage of digital images taken at the crime scene. "Notice anything unusual?"

"No blood spatter," said Berzinsky.

Waterman nodded. "Not a drop."

"That's impossible," said Berzinsky. "The victim was eviscerated."

"There should be blood all over the place, pools of it. The responder described it as looking like all the blood evaporated."

"Blood doesn't evaporate," said Berzinsky. "Whoever the perp is had to have an accomplice to help him clean up. What about body fluids?"

"Have to wait for the medical examiner on that. The responder said forensics couldn't raise any fingerprints or footprints. But they did find dried semen. See there in that photo? On the Bible."

"It's characteristic of a ritual murder," said Leon. "The absence of blood is baffling."

"Sicko is what it is," said Waterman. "Some nut who didn't like the Reverend's sermon. He was supposed to chair a major conference of religious leaders from around the world today to address all the chaotic shit that's happening."

"Where's the body now?"

"The medical examiner ordered it removed and taken to autopsy."

"Have they started yet?"

"Not your normal procedure, but because of the unusual circumstances the ME wants you to observe. He called and said he'll wait."

"CSI file a report yet?" asked Berzinsky.

"Still gathering evidence or trying to find evidence. Checking who else was in the church at the time of the murder. So far, no witnesses," said Waterman. "The place was deserted. No tourists at that hour. No visitors. No service. Not even a priest in the house. Forensics checked the janitor supplies. No chemicals were used. No blood stains. No odor of bleach. They would have had to use bleach. All we have are the photos. A homeless man was questioned. Said he saw Livingston go in and a few minutes later, another man."

"They have a description?"

"The man who followed the victim was wearing a business suit and his head was shaved. He was carrying a leather briefcase."

"Probably contained the murder weapon," said Berzinsky.

"Did the homeless man see the second man come out of the church?" asked Leon.

"He said no. The perp must have left by a side or rear exit."

"Any signature?" asked Leon.

"Yes, a black pearl in the palm of the Reverend's hand."

"A black pearl."

"As of an hour ago, that was all forensics could tell me."

"Okay," Leon rose from his chair.

"Autopsy."

Leon and Berzinsky quickly left the office.

Chapter 6

Leon spent twenty-five years in police work as a forensic psychiatrist and criminal analyst. He thought he had seen and heard just about every abnormal behavioral possibility that one human being could perpetrate against another. Although he had long ago intellectually and emotionally distanced himself with professional detachment in studying murder victims, he always experienced a profound sadness at the brutal destruction of human life.

During his career, he dealt with psychiatric cases that had their basis in a combination of psychological and physiological factors including drug and alcohol abuse, disease and trauma, depression and bipolar disorder, and schizophrenia that caused or influenced perverse behaviors.

He understood the relationship between mental illness and criminal acts, the loss of contact with reality and the inability to cope. He had usually been able to conclude why someone took the life or lives of others. He considered the ritual butchering of the Reverend Lawrence Livingston the killer's statement made against religion. This gave Leon a starting point. Determining the underlying cause would not be easy. Psychosis was a symptom of a range of mental illnesses. With the bizarre nature of Reverend Livingston's murder, Leon gravitated toward the killer having a delusional disorder, the inability to recognize and cope with reality. To Leon, the pearl was more than a signature. It was symbolic of a fixation in the killer's mind, the representation of a surrogate. He appeared to be schizophrenic.

During his residency in psychiatry, a particular case involving a prison inmate had motivated Leon to join the FBI. The former patient suffered from dissociative identity disorder. The thirty three year old man claimed he heard disembodied voices talking to him. He believed he was possessed by a demonic spiritual power that made him strong. He had been severely abused as a child. His delusional alternate identity of being able to dematerialize and escape into a dark safe place in a cave, the basement, had evolved as a means of self-protection.

A different personality carried over into his adult life. In stressful social situations, his third identity would emerge and, believing he was invincible, he would become aggressive. People avoided him. His violent assault against a fellow warehouse employee who had insulted him put him in prison.

Through psychotherapy, Leon had deconstructed the three personalities into one.

Working with prison inmates opened the world to him of aberrant criminal and psychopathic behavior.

The killer's written email statement indicated that he had created an alternate reality to Leon's own. For Leon, this communication from the killer provided the beginning of an investigative trail.

The initial photographic information from the crime scene provided evidence of an extreme psychosis. The absence of blood posed a condition he had never encountered before. The logical cause for a bloodless crime scene related to the killer or killers cleaning up the area and removing the body, usually burying it where it could not be found or weighting and dropping it into a deep body of water like a river, or lake, or the ocean. But the bloodless corpse as a flagrant display left Leon with an inexplicable crime.

Of course, when word finally reached the media, especially the anchor John Morley, the sensationalism he promoted as news would take front and center in titillating and appealing to the paranormal fear factor of his ardent fans. He considered Morley a conspiracy theorist, a latter day purveyor of updated diabolic spirits, dwarves, elves, trolls, fairies, and goblins with origins in European and Celtic folklore. Such characters and stories and ritual executions of heretics branded as witches were early historical attempts to explain and confront madness and fear of the unknown.

Leon considered the belief in pseudoscience a source for authors of horror novels and the platform of self-proclaimed ascended *New Age* gurus who made personal fortunes by appealing to the imagination of the unexplainable. A huge audience of cult followers existed whose desperate passion to *know what awaited them in the beyond* made them an easily accessible and profitable market to manipulate by claiming to have *the answer* but withholding it just beyond reach.

He observed the profiteering among television evangelists. The extreme example was one who stared into the camera while smoking a cigar and willed viewers to send him money. And they did, making him a multimillionaire through an incredible con.

Leon suspected there could be a link in the killer's mind to organized religion's primary function of political control of others using the promise of spiritual redemption and salvation. Psychopaths expressed control and denial by taking life.

* * *

Leon and Ed pulled on white lab coats and latex gloves before entering the autopsy room. They introduced themselves to the lead detective attending at his request and to the medical examiner who would perform the autopsy. He began by referring them to several key photos displayed on a large computer screen.

And so the thought process began with something more that was demonstrated with the careful study of each successive photograph. They revealed behavioral evidence that contributed to an impression of the killer's possible identity or at least narrowed the focus. All deductions would be evaluated through the forensic reconstruction and crime scene analysis linked to an assessment of the victim.

The second unusual feature of the photographed crime scene was the absence of splattered blood. Either the killer had murdered Reverend Livingston at another location and brought him into the church, or had been confident enough to take the time to chemically clean up after himself. Something seemed very strange and unexplainable about the murder without blood.

"Did you determine if anyone else was in the church at the time of the murder or just after?" Leon directed his question to the detective who had been at the crime scene. "Isn't it customary for a priest to be available for confessions at that hour of the night or at least in his office or living quarters?"

"We questioned Father O'Neal. He was visiting a family in bereavement. He discovered Reverend Livingston's corpse when he returned and called the police. In his statement he said he believes this is the work of Satanists."

"It has the characteristics. So you think there's more than one of them?"

"We don't know. It hasn't been determined yet."

"Did anyone see them leave the church?" asked Ed.

"So far, the only witnesses is a homeless man who said he saw them go in, but not come out."

"The layout and general architecture for access and egress. We have an extensive description of the scene and investigation on tape."

"Either someone knew the church was vacated or it was random chance."

"Have you talked with the victim's family?" asked Leon.

"Only to inform them. No details were given out, of course. They're in a state of severe shock and being comforted by friends."

"I'd like to interview his wife at the first opportunity," said Leon.

The detective nodded. "The conference he was to lead today has been canceled. There's concern that other religious leaders might be targeted."

The next photo was of the corpse's slightly opened hand clutching the black pearl.

"Calling card. Historically, the first time we've seen it used in a homicide. We ran a systems check for a pattern. Hasn't occurred anywhere. We dusted it for prints. It was clean. Our gemologist identified it as a specimen typically found in the South Pacific."

Leon picked up a small labeled plastic bag containing the signature evidence. He would research its symbolic significance later and formulate an association with the behavior.

The detective jotted a note on his pad.

Leon and Ed turned their attention to the body on the stainless steel examining table. Leon nodded to the examiner to begin.

"On an initial examination of the body, I discovered a puncture wound on the left side of the neck probably made by a needle injected into the carotid artery. I'll check fluid from the heart, lungs, and brain to determine whether a chemical injection occurred," he spoke into an overhanging microphone describing in detail each step of the procedure.

The autopsy continued through the rest of the morning and well into the afternoon. In the meantime, the black pearl had been X-rayed and the film provided to Leon and Berzinsky. They viewed it on a wall-mounted backlight. Of itself, the X-ray did not reveal a physical characteristic that lent itself to symbolic interpretation.

"We need to have a gemologist examine this," said Leon. He turned off the backlight and reinserted the film into its brown envelope.

They went into the lab office where Ed sat at the computer, logged onto the internet and keyed in *black pearl*. Leon looked over his shoulder as a variety of website choices came up.

An attractive scenic photograph of an island lagoon in Tahiti loomed onto the screen.

"Want me to read this?" asked Ed.

"Yeah, the print's kind of small."

"One of nature's magnificent creations grows in the turquoise-colored lagoons of these South Pacific islands. The Tahitian black pearl, called the jewel of the sea, is a living symbol of purity and perfection. Long before Westerners discovered Tahiti, the black pearl had a reputation for exceptional value and rarity, enhanced by its use in Jewelry of the world's Royalty and Nobility. As such, natural black pearl was known as the *Pearl of Queens* and the *Queen of Pearls*, its wonder inspiring many questions among people, centuries ago. But their lack of scientific precision led them to improvise with legend and poetry. Thus, ancient Chinese believed that Pearls were conceived in the brains of dragons.

"Luster is the most important factor in choosing pearls. The inner glow of the pearl combined with the surface brilliance defines luster. The higher the luster, the thicker the nacre or secretion from the oyster and the stronger the glow."

As Ed continued to read, associations between concepts and symbology of light and dark began to emerge in Leon's mind. The reference to the ancient belief that pearls germinated in the brains of dragons provided a folkloric association.

"A Tahitian pearl has many thousands of layers of aragonite, depending on the length of time the pearl spends in the oyster. Each one is extremely thin and has the appearance of a transparent film.

"Reflection is the phenomenon of light bouncing off the surface of the pearl, which acts like a mirror. The smoother the surface, the brighter the pearl will appear.

"The transparent aragonite acts like a prism, refracting or bending the light as it passes through the pearl. The more transparent these layers, the easier it is for the light to pass through and reach deeper into the pearl. Reflection and refraction combined produces interference, causing the pearl to radiate iridescent light."

Ed continued scrolling through the photos of various pearl shapes, sizes, and colors along with criteria for market value. "What do you think?"

"It makes for an unusual signature, but I'm beginning to see the symbolic connection with the murder of a clergyman taking place in a church and the ritual display on the altar," said Leon.

Amy Jacobi, a genetic analyst with an explosion of curly red hair stepped into the office from the neighboring histology lab. Her blue eyes seemed to be in a perpetual squint from hours of peering into a microscope, although the majority of her work involved the use of a computerized genetic analyzer.

"Hi, Leon. We have an unusual sample of material taken from the crime scene that will be of interest to you."

"What kind of material?"

"There was an abundance of dried semen smeared across open pages of the Bible on a stand next to the rostrum."

Leon and Ed followed her into the lab. The over-sized massive volume lay open on an examination bench. They approached it and peered down at the stained pages turned to John: Acts. A particular quote had been circled with black ink.

I am the light of the world: he that followeth me shall not walk in darkness,

but shall have the light of life.

"How soon can you get me a DNA analysis?"

"Thirty-six hours. Can't speed up the process."

"Call me as soon as you have the results. We're going over to the church to look around. Call me on my cell regardless of the time."

Amy nodded. "Good hunting."

Leon and Ed walked out of the lab and back to Leon's car.

"Getting weird, isn't it?" said Ed.

"More than challenging," said Leon.

They paused just inside the massive front doors of St. Stephens Catholic Church and surveyed the interior. The first ten rows of pews and the entire area around the altar had been taped. Although the physical evidence had already been removed to the forensic lab, not all indicators were typically found during the first phase.

"Let's check the office," said Leon. They walked around the left back row of the nave and took a side hall in the direction of a small brass sign with black lettering posted on the wall, *Church Office*. The door was blocked with a single ribbon of yellow tape but was unlocked. Ed removed the tape as they pushed the door open and entered.

Desk drawers had been left pulled open after a search. The computer screen was dark. The hard drive had been confiscated and was now at the lab for analysis.

"Nothing unusual. They wrecked enough havoc at the altar," said Leon. "Maybe they didn't feel it necessary to come in here."

"Report should be ready by tomorrow," said Ed. "We'll see if anything was taken besides the computer."

"How 'bout the back door."

"Floor plan shows one as a basement entrance."

"I'll look."

"Photographs sequenced their likely exit."

"This was carefully planned. Maybe after tomorrow, we'll get some insights from his wife," said Leon. "At that hour, it seems he just left the hotel on an impulse. That being the case, the killers were probably waiting for an opportunity."

"I'm going to walk the distance to the back door," said Ed.

Leon nodded and began reading some of the written correspondence on the priest's desk. He took a small note pad from his coat pocket and jotted a series of impressions.

When he pulled into his driveway that evening, Leon noticed the curtain fall into its original position at the front window. *Julie must be waiting about something,* he thought. The automatic door rolled back and he pulled his blue BMW into the cool confines of the three car garage. He entered the house through the connecting kitchen and family room door and discovered Julie waiting next to the stove. A small open box and a squiggle of black silk ribbon lay on the adjoining white tile counter like a snake. He paused at her amused expression.

"What is it? You're smiling."

"And I always thought you hated jewelry. Couldn't be bothered with it. Just a bunch of stones of artificial value."

"That's right. I haven't changed my opinion."

"Then what's this?"

At the sight of the Tahitian black pearl in the small velveteen box, Leon felt a sudden surge of his blood pressure. His mind reeled to the point of near dizziness.

"Leon, dear, are you all right?" Julie grasped his arm.

"No, I'm not. Not at all. Where did you get this?"

"You sent it to me. See. Here's your note."

Leon grabbed the gift note. "I didn't send this to you. This is not my note. Did you see who delivered it?"

"UPS. The driver came to the door and I signed for it. I was pleasantly surprised when I opened it. It's okay that I opened it, wasn't it?   It was addressed to me."

"Oh, shit! Oh, shit!" Leon's left hand pulled the stress ball from his left pocket and he began to repeatedly squeeze it vigorously and rapidly.

"Leon, what's the matter? What's going on? You're scaring me."

"It's not a gift and it's not from me. Can you remember what the delivery person looked like?"

"A very pleasant handsome young man, not unlike yourself about 30 years ago."

"What color was his hair?"

"His hair? What difference does it make."

"It makes a difference, a big difference. How about his eyes?"

"All right, my powers of observation are just as good as yours, if not better. He didn't have any hair and swimmingly deep brown eyes."

"Swimmingly?"

"You want a description, I'm giving you a description."

"Okay, swimmingly deep brown eyes. What about his physique?" "He looked like a body builder."

"Did you watch the news today?"

"The Greek Chorus?"

"What did they have to say?"

"Oh, about the war in Afghanistan, the latest suicide bombing, the Senate investigation of corporate tax abuse, drug wars and gang killings, immigration issues, more cases of child molestation by Boy Scout leaders and Catholic priests."

"There was a murder of a high profile Christian evangelist," said Leon.

"Yes, the bright young teleprompter readers read to us about that too."

"I'm investigating the case."

"From your reaction, I surmised as much."

"Reverend Livingston was butchered alive."

"The Greek Chorus didn't give the audience those explicit details."

"The point is, whoever committed the murder knows that I'm trying to find him and I just got started on the case this morning. That is significant." He took out his cell phone. "I'm calling in now for twenty-four hour security for Kit and Blanche. I need to call them too. Talk to them. I don't want them to be alarmed, but they need to be alert to whatever is going on around them, whoever might be watching them. We need a unit here, as well."

"Leon, you're really frightening me. What is going on?"

"I'm dealing with a psychopathic killer. I don't know who he is or where he is. But he knows who I am."

"The pearl?"

"It's not from me. It's from him or them. It's possible there's more than one killer."

Fear contorted her face. "Why would he send a pearl to me?"

"It's not for you." The reality constricted his voice. "It's for me." He swallowed hard. "The black pearl is his signature, his calling card. Some killers like this game of cat and mouse. He's leading me on. He wants me to try to figure out who he is and to test how skillful he is at avoiding discovery."

"I need to get protection for you and Kit and Blanche. Then I need to identify who this psycho is and take him down."

Leon immediately called Reese Waterman, his SAI, and explained the situation. Waterman dispatched six agents and arranged the shift watches for Leon's wife and son and daughter. Leon expected he would be getting calls from his children during the night wanting to know what was happening. Their bodyguards could tell them only so much.

Julie clutched his arm. "What can we do? What can you do? Are we in great danger? How vulnerable are we?"

"He came to our door, Julie, and handed you the pearl."

Chapter 7

John Morley lived most of his waking hours in a world of glass and refractive light images, including his own. He saw his face and heard the words he read from a teleprompter on a multitude of screens and monitors throughout the studio. Over the years, his televised existence had merged in his mind with the few hours of his life he spent outside the studio with his wife and now grown children. His average nights' sleep was four to six hours and was enough to sustain him, considering the demanding routine of his work. The extensive news story research and production preparation required of him left little time for his wife and children. His career was his first and foremost priority, to the detriment of all else.

His seasoned good looks, a must for a male anchor, and deep modulated punctuating voice guaranteed him a position in prime time news for the past ten years. He earned over six million a year and was a recognized star personality of the network. However, lately he had noticed the political maneuvering of young up and coming television and communications majors fresh out of college and intent on forging careers just as he had twenty-five years ago.

His producer and news director were both skilled and competent women who had displaced their male counterparts within five years of moving up in the studio ranks. They, in turn, had also influenced the hiring of attractive and intelligent female television journalists to cover stories on-site linked to the central news broadcast. It didn't take industry insiders long to refer to them as Morley's harem, which prompted the producer to hire three men as consultant reporters to assist in the coverage of political, defense, and health-related news.

Morley was a proponent of hard journalism, stories of the day that dealt with coverage of breaking events involving national and international leaders and major issues that he could spin into conspiracies or significant disruptions in the routines of daily life, such as wars, hijackings and bombings and natural disasters.

His career as a journalist was earmarked by mature logic and insightful in-depth analysis and reporting of significant world and national events. He eventually came to believe that reality, for most American people was what they saw and heard on television.

The personal Email that he opened that morning set him back on his heels.

I reside in the dark spaces of the universe.

By putting a biological life form to death, I cause the vibration of energy, atoms, and the soul is set free. Lawrence Livingston is now one of us.

The sender stated that Morley was the only one to be sent the message. He usually ignored such nonsense. But one of his field reporters had covered the crime scene at St. Stephens church during the regular news hour. Even though the police barred the media from entering the church, there had been glimpses and snatches of description gleaned from the investigation team. The most graphic depiction of the grisly murder had come from Father O'Neal, who discovered Reverend Livingston's eviscerated body and the absence of blood.

Morley's responsibility to his viewing audience and the social impact of his reporting concerned him. The murder would be broadcast by other news stations regardless. What they didn't have was the direct and exclusive message he received from whom he suspected might be the killer himself, unless the message was from some other nut job.

From a level-headed perspective, such claims were absurd pseudo-science with a little spiritual hoobajoob thrown in. But the messenger impressed him with an explanation of spirits and dark energy. He reread it for the tenth time.

Energy, such as light, is given off and absorbed in tiny definite units called quanta or photons. Light appears to be in a steady stream or continuous flow, but is a series of many small actions. Radiant energy is transmitted in waves in ranges of certain frequencies called spectrums. When the atoms of a substance are disturbed, such as in a metal or in a biological form, the death of an animal or a human, all the atoms of that substance begin to vibrate and the energy radiates outward and escapes just as a vapor dissipates into the medium of air from boiling water. It becomes dark energy. I am one of the Spirits who reside in these dark spaces of the universe.

Reverend Livingston's murder created fodder for fundamentalist crusaders to stir up their own brand of media rampage. This was the fabric of moral corruption that propagated witch hunts and resulted in the persecution of innocent people.

Morley did not want to precipitate conditions of panic and emotional unrest, but, on the other hand, he was the exclusive recipient of a powerful dramatic news story that would titillate and frighten, and audiences thrived on fear mongering. If he didn't go forward with it, there was a strong likelihood the killer would select someone else.

John Morley's newscast featured expert pundits on the subject of ritual killings. They included a sociologist, an anthropologist, a detective, and a psychiatrist.

The psychiatrist corroborated Leon Safullo's position and confirmed that Satanic practices were occasionally used to explain away or justify criminal activity, but there was no valid connection between mental illness, deviant behavior, and Satanic influence.

Several on-camera interviews with men, women, and teenagers divulged claims of ritual abuse by Satanic cults. The discovery of mutilated pets on gravestones in one community struck a universal chord of fear that a Satanist was living among them. The incident had increased church attendance and sermonic diatribes against the materialistic evils of society, occult video games and heavy metal music. Others commented on the political and distorted moral positions of pro-choice and pro-life commentators who accused doctors who performed abortions of being agents of Satan.

An evangelical minister proclaimed to the camera, "Those of us who are true Christians and believe in the goodness of God work for God. Satanists are out in the world working to undermine the goodness of God," he said.

Leon thought that putting a panel of experts on the national media only gave credibility to the paranormal and supported fundamentalist agendas of moral propaganda. Both ignored scientific investigation and analysis. The audience didn't have access to factual data, only emotionally loaded blanket statements of the prevalence of cults and practices. They were selling fear.

Leon recognized that the media broadcast of the killer's horrific act invaded everyone's psyche. Raising the specter of fear and loathing they repressed was part of the killer's intent and gave credibility to his existence. The murder was a sign that he was coming and he was real.

Morley made attempts to gain an exclusive interview with the FBI and was repeatedly refused.

*   *   *

Hiram Bean was incensed at what he had just seen and heard on John Morley's news cast.

"What does Guzman think he's doing?"

He turned to his staff. "Can anyone get in contact with him?"

"We've tried, sir, but without success. He's very elusive, even to us."

"He had no authority to contact the media. We don't want some investigative journalist sniffing around thinking he's associated with us. We have enemies in the media."

"You recall your order to him was to be creative."

"He's out of line. It's a distortion of what we stand for. Get a message to him to stop."

"That may be impossible, sir. We have no idea where he is or how to reach him."

"He's acting like a rogue agent using First World to back him. No one must ever associate him with us. Such a disclosure would seriously undermine our goals and credibility."

"What do you suggest?"

"We play the hidden card."

Chapter 8

Leon scrolled through the Internet document.

You are going to follow us into the life of a man to understand who we are, because one day you will also become one of us. His name is Paul Evans.

At times, we will be an illusion in his mind, and other times, the only reality he knows. I lie there in wait and grow. My surreal existence in his thoughts and dreams will become your trail.

We are inbred in humankind as a genetic code that cannot be broken, because we have no physical substance. We are dark energy, dark spirits. We live in dark space where human mortals cannot see us. Your technology cannot define us. We cannot be stopped, prevented, or eliminated. We are an integral function of life. We are spirit.

The man whose trail you follow will lead you to us.

Lawrence Livingston had to die, because of his attempt to reconcile all religions. There is only one true religion and we are its stewards.

I am a dark spirit, mortal and immortal. My name is Antonio Guzman. I was raised by Jesuit priests. I graduated from Georgetown University. Pearl is my mentor.

Leon recognized the behavioral symptoms of a psychopath. But because the killer was openly confronting him, he did not believe that what he was being told had any basis in truth or reality as to the killer's potential identity.

Leon knew that Guzman was a false name, but the deception of being raised by Jesuit priests as a child and subsequently attending Georgetown University might contain a hidden clue as to his true identity. The killer was leading him on.

For starters, Leon would investigate student archives of the university.

The task was staggering, but without some association or implication as to the killer's actual identity, finding and apprehending him would be impossible.

Leon waited for more, but the message ended. *I'm dealing with a classic psychopath*, he thought, *some deranged new age schizophrenic. The question is how he can be sending messages over the Internet and not be traced. He has all the symptoms of living in an imagined sordid dream world. Yet he and this other imagined one, Pearl, just murdered a man.*

The killer didn't perceive that anything was wrong with him. Leon believed the reference to Pearl was a fabrication. Sociopaths often assumed a double or triple identity to hide or repress their sense of paranoia. His goal was to enslave victims and exercise despotic control over every aspect of their lives until he could destroy them. The killer followed the pattern of selecting model individuals whom he could shame and humiliate. He was so out of touch with reality, that by degrading his victims, the killer sought to eliminate the hostile enemy within his own mind.

He clearly expressed an emotional need to justify his crimes and desired his victims' respect, gratitude, and even love. By his very act of murder, he was incapable of human attachment and he expressed a grandiose scheme of wanting to rule the world.

Leon associated Guzman's psychotic imaginings with clinical references. In Jungian psychology, the Shadow was the archetype that represented all that individuals consciously are not. A person's daytime persona or mask was normally polite and sociable, but aspects of the self were consciously hidden from other people. The hidden aspects were called the Shadow. They functioned outside a person's conscious awareness and control.

Leon had to analyze the personality from which the killer's profile emerged. He had to determine the characteristics by reading and interpreting the behavioral indicators and signs. The Shadow was a psychological component of every man, woman, and child. It often appeared as a sinister threatening presence in dreams. For individuals who became aberrant, they succumbed to the Shadow and allowed it to govern their lives.

Leon wondered if, after so many years of analyzing the Shadows of others, he was now being forced to confront his own.

The next morning, he met with Roland Pogue, a heavyset, young bespectacled, bushy-headed staff physicist from Great Britain, to clarify the nature and existence of dark energy.

"Dark energy is something I've never heard about before," said Leon. "My background is in medical science. The psychopathology of the killer is founded on his imaginings of the paranormal."

" Dark energy is a vacuum of space." said Roland. "Laboratory research has shown that what we think of as empty space actually contains virtual particles that move in and out of existence. The vacuum provides energy that can take the form of a negative gravity. The problem is that this vacuum-energy as calculated would be powerful enough to blow apart the universe. It may be that it's not constant and grows weaker over time.

"There is another theory called the fifth essence which proposes a repulsive field embedded in space, not unlike a gravitational or a magnetic field." He paused to make sure Leon understood him. "Under that hypothesis, the field was created in the beginning moments of the universe along with the other forces in nature, and now stretches across the universe like a spider web. As the universe expanded and cooled, gravity and quintessence or the fifth essence were competitive forces. Both fields weakened as the universe expanded, but ultimately quintessence became stronger than gravity and pushed the galaxies apart."

"This happened in the beginning," said Leon.

"Within the laws of physics in geologic time, yes."

"The name of the website is The Beginning."

"It's unusual that a website would be that selective, but as you have described the situation, the killer or killers are making themselves known to you."

"They are intending for me to follow them in some manner."

"Maybe they're using the website as a channeling medium, a digital way to communicate with you through your computer ."

Leon nodded. "That's a possibility."

"There is another aspect of dark energy related to dreams that has come out of the research."

"What is it?"

"It's rather involved in terms of the latest in quantum analysis," said Roland, "but it's premise is that humans are part of dark matter or dark energy as subconscious dreams or memory. There are models of quantum indeterminacy as the mechanism of human subconsciousness. It's a bit philosophical, but there are two theories to consider. The first is that our minds are an evolution of cosmic matter. The second is that indeterminate matter is what we experience and call our minds."

Roland swiveled his chair, leaned back with the weightiness of his knowledge, and continued. "The physiological process of mental activity involves mass and energy. The distribution of mass and energy can reach a significant gravitational threshold causing changes in the neurological structure of the human brain.

"The point is the structure of the universe may not be only physical. In the context of the mind in the structure of the brain, dark energy could be manifested as intangible attitude and negative aberrant or violent behavior, rather than something physical, and be linked to dark energy."

Leon absorbed the information. "So on the basis of what you've described, it's possible for my subconscious to be channeled and merged through dark energy with what is happening to another being and this becomes the source of my investigation."

"Based on mathematical models, it is possible."

"I have a hard time believing and accepting that."

"Most of us in scientific fields do," said Roland. "We work with theories, but you seem to be experiencing a phenomenon that goes beyond theory and becomes a kind of surreal reality."

"The merging and commingling of dreams," said Leon.

"The merging and commingling of physical existence with non-physical existence."

"It makes me wonder where this investigation is going to lead. The murder is real, but the circumstances that purport to define the killer are not. The profile is not clear."

"Well, as the investigation proceeds, if I can be of further assistance, please don't hesitate to call on me," said Roland.

"Thank you. I appreciate your input, even though it leaves unanswered questions."

Roland smiled as they rose from their chairs and shook hands. "Clarity can often be unattainable."

Chapter 9

Amy Jacobi intently watched the genetic analyzer recording images of DNA segments as they moved through a small tube. She was particularly interested in the spikes or peaks similar to an EKG chart. Twenty minutes later, the computer generated a picture of data. The numbers correlated to the DNA profile of whomever had deposited their semen on the St. Stephens Church Holy Bible.

Under the amplification of an electron microscope, she examined the structure of the DNA sample. What she saw she thought would have been physiologically impossible. A black spiral helix integrated with the original two appeared inconsistently throughout the sample. It twisted and choked the normal DNA structure much like a serpent would its victim. She wondered if this was a mutation or if the sample were somehow contaminated. She decided to try again. An hour later, she observed the same result.

She wanted to share her find with two other scientists to corroborate that what she was looking at actually existed. Then the realization came to her. She was looking at synthetic DNA. The semen wasn't human. It had been taken or produced from some other mammalian source.

The appearance of the black spiral strand challenged her scientific curiosity; but considering the source of the DNA sample and its symbolic association in defacing the Bible, it sent a chill of fear rippling along her spine. She did not believe in superstition and she was not a particularly religious person. In her study of genetics, she had come to appreciate and acknowledge the conceptualization of cellular life at the molecular level. In that sphere, she believed there had to have been some manner of origination, but not the mythological man-created God in scriptures. She was convinced that a sentient God-being took some other form. She was trained as a scientist in dealing with empirical evidence and principles. But what she had just seen through the eye of the electron microscope was not a figment of her imagination.

She rushed to the phone.

When he answered, Leon detected an emotional catch in her voice. "Leon, you need to come into the lab as soon as possible. This is not something I can describe over the phone. You have to see it under the microscope to understand it."

"The DNA profile?"

"It gives me the creeps."

"What is it?"

"The DNA structure has a black spiral strand. The characteristics indicate it was synthetically created. Under the circumstances, it gives credence to what could be a paranormal phenomenon, and I don't believe in that stuff. Yet, here I am including it in my analysis and it's the first thing I'm telling you on the phone."

"I'll be there in thirty minutes. They sent my wife a calling card intended for me." The twenty-four security surveillance he had ordered was in effect. Despite his assurance they were safe, the guards did little to abate his wife's and children's anxiety. "Just wanted to let me know. I'm bringing it to the lab along with a black silk ribbon used to wrap it. We'll see if we can trace it to a source."

"They sent you a pearl?"

"The very same."

"Then they know who we are. They know what we're doing."

"They shouldn't expect anything less. Obviously they're getting some perverse satisfaction from communicating with me. Eventually, we'll identify them or him. We still don't know if more than one killer was involved. Most likely it was a single individual. Serial killers don't normally work in pairs, but there's nothing normal about this. His description of himself is completely delusional."

When he arrived at the lab, Leon found Amy studying the screen projection of the DNA images from the electron microscope. "Well," she said without turning to greet him, "it's still there. Hasn't changed. Hasn't gone away." She spotted the third strand of the triple helix using the red beam of a laser pointer.

"Brings us a step closer," said Leon. "But I'm not sure to what. Here," he handed her two plastic bags, one containing the pearl and the second the black ribbon. "Put the ribbon under the scope."

Amy pulled on latex lab gloves and removed the ribbon from the bag with a pair of tweezers. She placed it on a slide and rotated the platform to a new position to view the object. The weave of the ribbon emerged on the screen.

"There's something written on it," said Amy. She changed the range and focal depth so that the letters became readable. "It's a website address. . . TheBeginning.com."

Leon left the forensic DNA center and rode an elevator up to the ninth floor dedicated to software and Information Technology intelligence and surveillance. Randy Newton, a short young bald man wearing a mustache and goatee waved at him from a massive computer station with a multitude of keyboards and flat screens. "Greetings, Leon. What brings you upstairs?"

"Hi, Randy, I need to have you check the origin of a website for me."

"What's the case?" Randy stuffed a handful of corn chips into his mouth with his right hand while his left traveled rapidly across a keyboard as through he were playing a musical instrument.

"You've probably seen it in the news. Reverend Livingston."

"Oh, yes, has caused quite a stir among religious sycophants. You have an address?"

"TheBeginning.com."

"Upper and lower case?"

"T and B."

Within a few moments, the galactic home page filled one of the large screens.

"Once upon a time in a galaxy far, far away," said Randy.

"Not far enough. Can you find out where this comes from?"

Randy's fingers danced over the clicking keys. "Trace in progress."

A multitude of data flashed and scrolled across the original image. The message came back "Origin Unknown."

"The system can't locate it," said Randy. "I'll need more time to work with it. If you don't mind my asking, why is this of particular interest?"

"More curiosity than anything else. Except for communications from the website. I'm not convinced, but I'm being pressed to consider the role that paranormal illusions are involved in the killer's methods."

"Gotcha."

"Call me."

"Give me ten minutes."

"I'll be down in the lab."

"Give my regards to Amy. Tell her I said she's a real fox."

"You should tell her that yourself."

"She isn't impressed with my intelligence or my body."

"Corn chips don't help with the second factor."

"No can do. I'm addicted to them. We're entitled to at least one vice."

Leon nodded and went back to the elevator. Upon returning to the lab, he found a large folder containing an initial draft of the CSI report at his desk.

"That just came in from document control," said Amy.

Leon began reading through the pages of detail in search of more clues that might lead to the identity of the killer. Thirty minutes later, he received a phone call from Randy.

"Nothing," Randy's flat tone of anger indicated his disgust. "Not a damn thing. Just come to a dead end, like all that space."

"There isn't any imprint of any kind and no satellite signal. I've checked them all. Sorry, Leon, this is professionally debilitating. It's like being temporarily castrated. I refuse to give up. I will keep trying."

"I appreciate your efforts, Randy. Thank you for the call."

"Any time."

Leon continued to read.

Late that night, he was awakened from a troubled sleep by another phone call. A man's deep voice he didn't recognize told him to go to his computer. He fumbled on his glasses and rolled out of bed.

"Who is it? Is it one of the kids?" asked Julie.

"No, I don't know who it is. Business. Go back to sleep." He careened down the hallway to his office. He did not remember that he had left the computer on. Maybe Julie had forgotten to turn it off. Tiny stars twinkled at him from the black void of the website home page TheBeginning.com. He brushed the wall light switch to the on position, walked to his leather executive chair and sat down. Nothing was happening on the screen. He jiggled the mouse slightly and a message slowly scrolled upwards from below the bottom frame.

I am your teacher. Follow my lead.

Leon's hand gripped the stress ball deep in his robe pocket. He could not bring himself to pull it out.

Chapter 10

As the bureau's information technology researcher, Randy Newton never surrendered to a challenge. He leaned forward like a pianist as his fingers raced over the clattering computer keyboard. He abruptly sat back to watch a blistering array of data and images explode and roll up onto the large flat screen.

"There it is," he said to Leon and Ed Berzinsky, who peered intently at the digital text and data. "Pearl is a code name for a terrorist network, not a person as far as we can tell."

"How come we've never heard of them?" asked Ed.

For a few moments, Randy did not reply. "Whoever they are or what they are could be a fabrication of the killer or maybe they've been around for a long time and we never made the connection. We speak of evil in the abstract, but it's not.

"Now the question is, why Paul Evans is their victim?" said Leon. "Other than his money and power, what does he have over anybody else? Why would these spirit terrorists want him?"

"What have you got on Paul Evans?" asked Ed.

Randy's fingers raced rapidly over the keyboard and seconds later, Paul Evans' image appeared on the screen in sharp resolution. As the analyst scrolled down, the three men read the data and information.

"Look at all the companies he owns," Ed commented.

"Acquisitions and divestitures," said Leon.

"But he's among the top ten corporate CEO's targeted for tax abuse. Yet no prosecution. Why you suppose that is? No whistle blower like with the others. Must be paying someone to keep quiet or knows the right people. Who's he work with?"

The First World Corporation. Randy clicked on the hyperlink.

"Look at that." Ed pointed to the DNA model logo on the screen.

"A triple helix," said Leon.

"What's that thing in the center?" Ed squinted at the image.

"A black pearl,"

"Isn't First World under investigation by the Justice Department for promoting tax abuse schemes?"

"Yes, but only based on allegations. There isn't any hard evidence," said Ed.

"Go to their website," said Leon.

Within a moment, the First World Corporation website appeared on the screen.

"It's well designed," said Randy. "Nothing appears to be unusual about it.

Look at their list of clients." Randy scrolled through the recognizable names of companies. "Wait a minute. What's this?"

He clicked on a website link. A black void filled the screen, but upon closer scrutiny, they could see what appeared to be amorphous forms surging about. Then a galaxy from outer space slowly faded in and gave them the visual sensation that they were traveling into infinity.

"This is pretty strange," said Randy. "Looks like some sort of intergalactic gateway, a black hole. There's been some research that claims a black hole could be a tunnel to another universe."

"What purpose does it serve being on their website?" asked Leon.

"It represents something significant for them. Time becomes space and space becomes time. You'd have to ask them to explain why it's there."

Leon hesitated to ask his next question. "I'm skeptical about paranormal activity, but can they relate to some form of psychic teleportation?"

"I'm the wrong guy to answer that," said Randy. "You need an astronomer."

"It does sound bizarre, but I was advised by someone I respect that I should keep an open mind," said Leon. "Don't disregard something just because we can't explain or don't understand it. Let's go back to Evans' profile."

Randy switched back to the previous file.

"Interesting," said Leon. "His wife has been an outpatient of the Chicago Franklin Psychiatric Hospital for extreme emotional depression. She attempted suicide."

"Think Evans drove her to it?" asked Ed

Leon shrugged. "Don't know enough about him yet."

"He has two children," observed Randy. "Both in California. "His son's a graduate student at UCLA and his daughter's been married for six years. Has two kids."

"Keeps her husband busy," said Ed.

"That reminds me," said Leon turning to Ed. "Is Reverend Livingston's wife still refusing to talk to us?"

"She's afraid something will happen to her and her children. She did say on the phone she really doesn't know anything about who would want to kill her husband and why, especially in such a brutal manner. She and her kids have a security team guarding them around the clock."

"Probably best not to push too hard," said Leon.

"She did offer one observation," said Ed.

"What's that?"

"She believes someone might have killed him because he was opposed to genetic research. She said he believed science had no business trying to create life through the use of stem cells."

"Might be a connection, but his attempts to reconcile different religions stands out as a more significant provocation," said Leon. "Consider the timing of his murder and the dismantling of the religious conference he had organized. There's something." Leon pointed to a segment on the screen. "Evans fired his first business partner after ten years and used their software technology to build his own empire."

"What happened to his partner?"

"Went bankrupt."

"Stay bankrupt?"

"Recovered. He seems to have provided the brains and product innovation."

"We need to talk to him. Could provide us some insight as to what started Evans down this road."

Randy entered Jim Owens' name. His photograph appeared at the beginning of a long biographical scroll.

نن

Chapter 11

From his parked car, Guzman traced Paul Evans' progress through the airline terminal to the American Airlines ticket counter. Paul had no knowledge that his attaché case, belt buckle, and cell phone contained tiny micro-chips that sent out a signal informing Guzman of his location via a satellite connection.

Guzman closed his slender laptop computer, left his car in the underground parking structure, and walked quickly to the terminal. As he traversed along the row of ticket counters to the American Airlines sector, he passed Paul going in the opposite direction toward the security check lines.

Guzman knew from tapping Paul's phone call to his son in California that they had arranged to meet in Great Falls, Montana. There was only one departing flight listed to Denver with a connection to Great Falls. Guzman purchased a one way ticket, then walked to security.

Paul was far ahead of him in the line. Guzman wanted only to keep him within sight. At the gate, he took a remote seat in a far corner and pretended to read a newspaper left by another passenger.

Paul was seated near the immediate boarding area. He rose quickly and was first in line when the agent announced access to the first class cabin. Guzman held a ticket placing him farther back in the main cabin. Now, he was inextricably attached to Paul Evans. There would be no escape.

* * *

Muscles bunched and rippled under the horse's glossy hide. The dark gray cutting horse pivoted and rolled back with smooth lunges always a nose ahead of the frustrated yearling calf trying to dodge back to the herd crowded against the far end of the corral.

Vince Macke concentrated on the horse's ears and direction of the snaking head. He tightened his buttocks against the saddle and his body swayed, leaning with the leaping rocking motion of the nimble-footed animal.

Vince raised Dandy from a colt and trained him as a champion cutting horse. The animal was quick and savvy and could work free of aid or signal from Vince. He even worked without a rider.

Gradually, they drove the yearling into a narrow chute. Perched on the high fence, Vince's younger brother, Willie, dropped a gate closed behind the animal. He prodded the calf forward into a smaller section of the chute and dropped a second gate so the calf stood in a tight pen with enough space to lie down, but not move forward or backward or turn around.

Willie's father, Luther Macke, reached through the bars and injected the contents of a large syringe into the animal's neck. The calf flinched and trembled as the tranquilizer and inoculation serum quickly spread through its system. Within seconds, his legs buckled and he collapsed against the rails, then slipped to the ground, losing a nit of reddish hide against the splintered gray wood.

Working quickly, Willie and his father maneuvered the young animal onto its back and splayed the calf's hind legs. Willie's rubber-gloved hand swabbed the exposed genital area with solution from a bucket of iodine. The acrid smell of dust and disinfectant made him sneeze.

Luther's scalpel cut and sliced into the connecting skin and tissue attaching the gonads. A small amount of blood gushed over his stained rubber gloves. The men held their breath a moment at the fetid bovine scent. Luther dropped the ragged organs into a metal container while Willie cauterized the wound.

They waited a few minutes for the steer's drowsiness to lift. Falling into the fence, the calf lumbered groggily to its feet. Willie opened the front gate and prodded it into the next corral where several other new steers stood recovering from the shock of potent anesthetic and the empty loss of their gonads. He closed the gate, looked back at Vince waiting in the other corral and waved to signal for the next calf.

Vince directed his horse at the clustered frightened yearling calves and the cutting process began again.

Joyce Macke strapped on her apron. Snug heeled boots and the tight security of tough denims linked her to the outdoors, to her men with their chaps and Stetsons and wading in the world of dust and sweat and rank animal smells. She worked in a continual cycle of preparing substantial food from meal to meal. Her men were her life. She could look out her kitchen window and see them framed, walking away from the house in the morning after breakfast. She would watch them among the flurry of animal movement in the fields and about the barn and corrals. She could hear their distant yells and whistles and the snorting, hoof thudding, bawling rush of horses and cattle. At the end of the long day, her men would return. Each day was a series of their comings and goings within the frame of her kitchen window. From her table they drew sustenance to continue the cycle.

Her boots sounded against the hardwood floor as she came from fixing the beds. She glanced at the wall clock in the kitchen. Everything in her house and in her life was in its time and place. Beginning with the rumble of Luther's morning flatulence, she clocked her day in a rhythmic pattern of domestic sights and sounds and smells from gray dawn to silver stars filling her window late at night.

Flush of toilet, slam of doors, rush of water, coughs, sneezing, nose blowings, gulps, swallows, grunts, eating noises, clink and clank of utensils, scraping of chairs, belches, shuffle of boots and the rustle of leather jackets had become familiar sounds to her over the years.

The thick odor of coffee, eggs, bacon, and hot biscuits hung in the kitchen air as Joyce served breakfast. Then came the next part of her routine, cleanup -- the scalding steam from running dish water, clink and clank of dishes and silverware in the sink, sharp ring of polished copper pots and pans as she washed them. And at last she thumped and pounded yeasty raw dough on the cutting board to prepare for her baking.

All throughout the day, the creaky squeezing tension of the opening and closing oven door gave birth to nose twitching provender from its hot womb. Her hand eased open the oven. "Pies could stand ten more minutes to brown the crust," she said silently to herself. Ten minutes gave her just enough time to get the mail. A time to escape the house into the air and sights and sounds and smells of the men.

She hung her apron on a curved metal hook where most of its black paint had rubbed away from years of supporting coats and hats. With the truck keys in hand, she walked out of the house, paused a moment on the running board to look toward the corrals, then stepped into the pickup cab and drove down the long lane toward the road. She liked the sensation of the vibrating truck responding to the pumping motions of her hands and feet, the chugging jolting machine power grinding beneath the floor, as the vehicle bounced over ruts that shook and rattled her out of her warm kitchen stupor.

She turned the truck around where the driveway widened to meet the road. Leaving the engine running, she climbed down from the cab and skirted the boggy ditch to reach the mailbox. When she had been a child, the small metal mailbox door was an opening to surprises. That someone unseen had been there, left a message or package or piece of mail from someone else far away had always been a source of pleasure and intrigue, an acknowledgment of herself and the family.

Even now, as a middle-aged woman, pulling open the mailbox door kindled her anticipation, for she ensured that it would be filled by sending away for countless magazines and catalogue subscriptions, and she inquired after advertisements for things she would never buy and could never afford.

Sifting through the stack of mail, she discovered a travel magazine she requested from a Great Falls agency. She paused to scan colorful photographs of the Italian Riviera with white yachts anchored in blue lagoons at the base of granite cliffs where villas perched with winding steps through lush hanging gardens.

Her imagination caused her pulse to quicken. Then she remembered the pies in her oven. She clambered into the pickup and roared back along the lane.

She pulled the pies from the oven and set them on the window ledge to cool. Separating her mail from the others, she distributed the rest at the table for her men. Twenty minutes later, Joyce opened the oven and removed a cookie sheet covered with crusty sourdough biscuits, which she scooped hot into a serving basket. On the stove, beef stew blistered and bubbled in a cast iron pot. She raised the lid for a final check, glanced at the clock and saw it was noon. Stepping outside the back door, she picked up an iron rod and whanged it with loud musicality inside the diameter of a dinner triangle.

Out at the corrals, the men glanced up from their work as the sound reverberated in the warm autumn air. Luther and Willie assisted a steer to its feet and prodded him into the holding corral. Vince dismounted from his horse, loosened the saddle cinch, then climbed through the fence and joined Luther and Willie walking to the sprawling wood and stone ranch house.

As the three men came through the door, the aroma of hot food smote them, purging the reek of animals and manured dust that clogged their senses. After hanging their hats on wall hooks, Luther and his sons trooped to the bathroom, washed, then returned to sit at the meal. When they had all been amply served, Joyce sat and ate with them.

"Salt," said Willie. Luther passed it.

They ate without conversation, giving full concentration to the eating, filling their tight visceral emptiness. When enough food had been consumed, they gave time and interest to their mail.

Vince opened a letter and stared at the stationery with a sudden intensity. Across the top, large boldface script spelled out

WYANDOTTE RANCH, INC. - TUCSON, ARIZONA

The WY brand was inscribed as a faded superimposed watermark filling the expensive rag sheet.

Luther stared at the letter out of curiosity; and when Vince finished reading and placed the letter on the table, he asked. "What's that?"

Vince looked at his father and a gloating smile grew in his piercing blue eyes. The wild applause and cheers of the grandstand crowd filled Vince's memory. A beautiful girl dressed in fancy sequined western garb was handing him a giant gold plated trophy and purple ribbon for best trainer and as the owner of the champion quarter horse stallion at the state fair.

The audience had given Vince a long, standing ovation. Dandy had performed in every stock horse event like no other they had ever seen. And as Vince rode out through the gate to the fanfare of drum rolls and trumpets, the most respected stockmen in the business had besieged him with offers and congratulations.

They had vied for his attention, thrusting cigars and business cards at him. He was a star, a professional's professional possessing an enviable talent. They had heaped expensive gifts upon him until he was forced to take an additional hotel room just to store the merchandise. For days, he had been lavishly wined and dined by the top ranch owners in the country.

At first, Luther had witnessed all the adulation for his son with great bursting pride. But his pride had quickly soured to abject fear that these other big important men would lure Vince away from him with their offers of fabulous money and the position of head trainer on corporate ranches.

Vince recognized his father's fear and baited him alone and in the company of Willie and Joyce and other men. He tortured his father with discussions of the offers, asking his opinion on the pros and cons of each, what decision he should make, again and again twisting the vindictive knife in Luther's heart to show how highly he was prized, valued, and adored.

Luther could only chomp and bristle with jealousy and anger. He vociferously reminded Vince that he owed his success and allegiance to his father. Other times, he would cringe away, because he had nothing more to offer his son.

In the end. Vince did not accept any of the offers. He returned home to his family with a new psychological tool, the threat of leaving, an unconscious emotional leverage that he might use to remind his parents that he had never been as loved as Willie.

Although Vince ruled and manipulated his parents, at twenty-nine he was still their child, still seeking to fill that other space in him that could never be filled so easily as his mother filled her mailbox with paper dreams, and her oven and his gut with food.

"Remember Wyandotte?" asked Vince. "Carl Wyandotte? Met him at the state fair last summer.

"Owns a big ranch in Tucson." Luther responded warily.

Vince nodded. "Still wants me as head trainer. Made the best offer yet."

Luther stopped chewing. He thought he had heard the end of talk about offers. "Let me see that."

Knowing the noises of the psychological game, the reason and the outcome, Joyce looked warily from Vince to Luther's sagging weathered face. With a beleaguered expression, Luther squinted at the letter Vince held just out of his father's reach.

Willie watched his brother and father while continuing to work his teeth with a wooden pick. He had seen and heard this by-play between Vince and Luther many times before and wondered why his father continually took the bait.

Vince handed the letter across the table. Luther snatched it and aggressively scanned its content. "He don't say nothin' about money."

"Says its open."

"When they say that, it means they're talkin' low money." Luther rattled the letter.

"Wyandotte is one of the biggest breeders in the country." Vince slightly rolled and cocked his head back at an imperious angle.

"That don't mean he pays high wages." Luther fumed. "How you suppose a man gets rich and stays rich?"

"You're so rich, you tell me?"

Joyce's coffee mug hit the table with a thud. "Vince, that was uncalled for."

"No. I ain't rich and probably never will be," said Luther. "But you keep it in the family. He keeps it in the family. That's how. And his family knows enough to hold it all together."

"I can name my price."

"Says who?" Luther hissed.

"Says Wyandotte."

"When?"

"State fair." Vince belched. "This is the second time. He liked what he saw. He wants me real bad."

"Sure," Willie joined the tease. "Wasn't a trainer there could touch you."

Luther snapped. "You keep outta this." Then glared at Vince with concern. Luther felt insecure, never certain, always off balance with this son who fed his gnawing anxiety. "You ain't really considerin' now. Not after all this time."

"Might be." Vince chewed a toothpick.

"He can't offer you nothin' to what you got here. We're your own flesh and blood. No one in the world cares for you strong as us. So why even think about leavin'?"

Vince held his father's angry frustrated expression with his own tinged with mockery. "I ain't said what I'm gonna do. But when I decide, it'll be my own business." He stared down his father, who glanced furtively at Joyce and Willie, embarrassed at his paternal weakness, then with rage at the letter clutched in his hand. "AAAAHHHHH!" He violently threw it to the floor.

Vince leaned back in his chair and watched with satisfaction as this last temperamental gesture of ritual infighting came to a close.

"We goin' into town tonight?" Joyce changed the subject. "I talked with Betty Halloran on the phone today. She and Deke will be at Brogan's."

Vince nodded. "Yeah, I'11 be seein' Regina there tonight."

Willie grinned. "If I don't show at Brogan's tonight, there's at least three girls I know who'll come out here lookin' for me."

"Ain't it great to be loved and adored." Vince's statement had an intended meaning that Willie did not catch, but that Joyce fully understood. She looked across the table at Willie.

Willie had inherited the color of his mother's hazel eyes. His features had a refinement about them that were almost perceptibly feminine in contrast to Vince's rugged looks. Joyce sometimes imagined that the spirit of her girl who had died during childbirth existed in Willie.

Willie had recently turned twenty-one. He was younger than Vince by eight years, a gap that would forever mark the hard times she and Luther had endured while building their ranch after they had been married.

They had very little money then. Their finances consisted largely of over-extended credit. At the time, Luther needed a hired hand more than he needed a wife. Joyce proved her worth in both respects. When Willie was born, Joyce experienced a sense of relief in no longer having to be her husband's hired hand.

Willie had come along with prosperity, a turn of fortune for Luther in the cattle business. Willie's appearance reflected their changed state of affairs. His beauty as a child crept into handsome young manhood. Some would call him pretty, but never to his face. He kept his wavy auburn hair carefully combed and cultivated thick sideburns.

For Joyce, her oldest son, Vince, would always be a living symbol of the early years after she and Luther were married. Vince was tall, lean, and hard in spirit, as well as in body. He had a cold unrelenting personality, devoid of warmth and affection for her and Luther.

During most of Vince's childhood, Joyce had been doing the work of a hired hand, and Vince had been left alone in the house for hours at a time. She had never been able to make up for her lack of attention and expression of love toward him. She regretted that she had not been more of a mother to him and she ultimately accepted his aloofness and spare filial respect as her due.

Willie allowed her to feel and act toward him in a maternal manner. When he was born, she had plunged her energies into domestic concerns to block out her sense of failure and disappointment about Vince. Although she had doted on Willie, she had attempted to draw Vince as an eight year old into her involvement with the new baby. Seeing how his mother acted with "Baby Brother" had alienated Vince even more. He saw the difference in how Willie was being treated in contrast to how he had been treated.

Vince's emotional suffering had been deep. He had started using his mother's feelings of guilt as a means to manipulate her. He showed a blatant preference for his father, who responded with a possessive kind of love and pride because his eldest son chose to emulate him.

Luther dominated the lives of both his sons, instilling his values with such authoritarian impression, Vince and Willie had never known the alternative of making personal choices and decisions. Everything they did was done their father's way. They came to think and express themselves like their father, who squelched any sign of individual expression from his sons the moment he detected it.

"We've spent enough time sittin' around here jawin," said Luther gruffly. He stood up from the table. "Let's get goin'. We've got work to do." He snatched his hat from its wall hook, crunched it on his head, and slammed out through the kitchen door.

As Vince rose to leave, the sharp tone of Joyce's voice stopped him. "Vince," she cautioned. "Go easy on him."

"He's never gone easy on me, or Willie. Where do you think we learned it? We're just like our old man." Vince reached for his hat and followed Willie out the door.

Willie had no argument with Vince's statement. Soon Willie would be springing his own surprise on Luther. Willie had his own plans to leave home. Unlike Vince, however, Willie had no internal need to taunt Luther with threats of breaking away. When Willie was ready to leave, he would just go, without looking back and with no regrets.

Joyce knew intuitively that, of her two sons, Willie had the intestinal fortitude to defy Luther by leaving to make a life of his own. She neither encouraged nor openly acknowledged the development of Willie's attitude. She knew that despite Luther's dominating influence on the lives of her sons, Willie had still grown up with the strength of his personality and self-esteem intact in contrast to Vince, who had been psychologically crippled by both herself and Luther.

She could look back now on their lives as a family and begin to understand the way they were today. There had been years when she understood very little about their behavior, only that they all just got through one day at a time.

She looked forward with anticipation to spending an evening at Brogan's tavern. Drinking at Brogan's wasn't much of a social life, but it was better than none. She picked up one of her travel brochures, the one with the photograph of the Italian Riviera and a white yacht anchored in an azure lagoon laced with reflective sunlight.

Chapter 12

Car headlights moved quickly uphill along the winding mountain road toward the small town in the distance. Inside the car Paul Evan's weary eyes shifted uneasily to the rearview mirror and saw the brief distant glow of high beams from another vehicle that had been steadily following, hanging back about a mile for the past two hours.

He glanced at his son, Matt, dozing against the door. A small gold earring winked at Paul through the young man's shoulder length blonde hair. He wished the boy's head rested against him, his father, instead of the frame and cold glass of the car door. Paul had wanted so much to embrace and hold him when they had met in Great Falls. Instead, they had shaken hands in a distant, polite, business-like manner.

The earring was a mocking bauble, one of the few eccentricities about his son he used to never understand or tolerate. The earring had once belonged to Matt's mother. Now, at this moment in their lives, the earring made no difference to Paul. It was only an ornament hanging on his son's earlobe. It no longer mattered to Paul how Matt looked, the style-cut of his hair or what he wore. Such concerns seemed insignificant to him now at this critical time in his life when he could not distinguish if he were mad or if a Satanic force was controlling him. Paul wanted to dispense with the small differences, like the earring, that had slowly, but with certainty thrust him apart from his son in the past and curtailed their communication with each other.

As they continued up the road to a higher elevation, the scent of ponderosa pine was carried on the cold wind that whistled through Paul's partially opened window. The scent triggered thoughts in Paul's mind of the mountain wilderness into which they were driving. In the days of the old frontier, a road would not have existed, only a trail traveled by rugged fur trappers, explorers, and mountain men.

As he looked at Matt again, such associations in his mind further diminished his concern with the once offensive earring. Even mountain men had worn earrings, like the Indians. Paul admitted to himself that the earring imbued Matt with the raw image of a mountain man. So did the drooping mustache and the brooding set of his son's blonde head in uneven sleep.

"In this place, at another time," thought Paul, "he could have been an army scout, a Buffalo Bill, a George Armstrong Custer."

Don't know why I ever let a little thing like that earring bother me so much. Paul silently conversed with himself. *It was so commonplace during frontier times, and pirates wore them too. Earrings worn by men are commonplace now. I guess what bothers me is the difference... what a man wearing an earring means now. If it's worn on the left ear though, I think it means you're not gay. At least that's what somebody told me it means. I could never ask Matt about that though. Don't have the guts. I really don't even want to know. If I did ask him, he'd probably tell me he is gay just to spite me. Laugh in my face. What have I done that has brought us to this impasse as a father and a son. I love him, but he doesn't know. Did he ever know? Did I ever tell him? Sure, plenty of times. Did I ever show him? I thought so. I tried. There never was any time. Then, one day he was gone, out of my life. My whole family was gone. I didn't care enough about them then. But now when it's too late to make reparations, I feel such an empty space in my life without them.* To his surprise, his face was wet with tears and he swallowed hard against the aching hollow sadness that rose in his throat.

He suddenly felt old next to his son. Their ages were thirty years apart. *Matt's not really a boy though, not anymore,* thought Paul. *I'11 still always think of him as a boy anyway. Shit. The way it could have been. Should have been. I want it back. I want to take it all back, to start over, to have my family again, to never have thought or desired the success I have now, to have never given in to Guzman's voice talking to me and writing the diary, to never have said yes to Guzman about paying for that success. He made me agree to all that has happened.*

Paul wiped his eyes with the back of his hand. *I hate thinking like this. I wish I could just clear all those thoughts out of my head forever. The night makes me depressed, feeling alone and moving through the night like a dream. My life is like a dream. I can't tell between my dreams and much of the real world anymore. Somehow, I have to.*

Peering through the bug-spattered windshield, his gaze followed the moving pool of his headlights. They rippled through the winding road which grudgingly parted like a dark brackish stream.

He felt gritty and fatigued from travel and worry. He needed a good night's sleep, one free of the nightmares that had plagued him for so long. So many years of horrible dreams. Now he felt he was just waking, here in the middle of the night on this snaking mountain road, with his son at his side.

He could hardly wait until he and Matt reached the next town. They would buy gas, check into a motel, then get something to eat. He felt tired, but he was hungry too.

A glance up at the rearview mirror confirmed that the other car was still following them. The headlights were still there, surging silently around a switchback curve somewhere below him, a brief flash, then gone in the darkness.

Paul didn't know if the driver of the other car was actually following them or if it was someone who just happened to be using the road at the same time. What he did not know was that Guzman traced his call to order airline tickets. Paul's most ardent wish was that Guzman existed only in his imagination. Paul decided he could deal with insanity, but there was no way he could escape the so-called Satanic powers of a real Antonio Guzman. Paul did not believe in any form of spiritualism. He believed that people who were practitioners were wackos and flakes.

Probably Guzman wasn't Satanic at all. *Maybe he's just some wacko stalking me.* The sudden thought gave rise to a breakthrough that provided Paul with a realistic option. Maybe the whole thing was a hoax, some kind of game. Or maybe someone was trying to ruin his business by destroying him. And whoever Guzman really was could already have murdered him. So something else was going on. As he conjectured, he kept coming back to his former partner, Jim Owens. But it couldn't be. Jim Owens didn't have the guts to hire someone to do this, especially if this were to be a contract killing.

Matt stirred in discomfort and woke. He stared at the dark shapes of trees the car passed in the night. He had been dreaming and he wasn't yet certain that what he saw was not a continuation of his sleep. He saw the scattered lights of the distant town against the far slope. After a time, he looked at his father, who was pleased that Matt had awakened. "We're almost there," said Paul. "Are you hungry?"

Matt nodded with a breathy yawn.

Paul leaned back in his seat and stretched his arms without letting go of the steering wheel. "I wonder if we'll find anything open at this hour way out in the sticks. Hate to have to settle for vending machine food. I can use a few stiff belts and a good hot meal. How about you?"

His son nodded. "If we don't find anything, we can always dip into the packs. There's plenty of trail mix.

"I need something more substantial," said Paul.

"How long have I been asleep?" asked Matt.

"Three hours."

"Whew. ." Matt stretched and yawned again.

"You were up late." His father grinned at him.

"So were you."

"I'm used to it," said Paul. "Even jet lag doesn't bother me after all these years." It thrilled him that they were having a friendly conversation.

His son rotated muscular shoulders, shrugging away the stiffness. "I should be able to get along on less sleep, but I can't. I just like to sleep."

"Wish I could sleep as easy," said Paul. "I never get enough anymore. Too many things on my mind. You need more sleep when you're young anyway. When I was your age..." His voice trailed off as, almost against his will, his thoughts returned again to the terrifying nightmares that incessantly haunted his sleep. His sleep was never gentle, clean, and refreshing. He felt so driven awake or asleep.

Even after he made the agreement with Antonio Guzman regarding his bogus contract with Satan, Paul had not experienced any change or relief in his sleep patterns. Even though he had agreed to pay the price, he was given no consolation. He was always paying the price.

"I get by on four or five hours sleep,' said Paul.

"Not enough for you. Shortens your life." said Matt. "Read it somewhere."

Paul thought how gladly he would shorten his own life for his son. He would rather this Guzman Satan character take him, kill him rather than this psychological hocus pocus and threat to take his son. Although he wanted to believe there wasn't any Satan in all this that was happening to him, Paul suspected that Guzman or someone who called himself Guzman might be more than a contract killer, a hit man who was toying with him. Under Guzman's influence, Paul had not been capable of thinking in such a way before. Now that he was trying to escape from Guzman, he felt he was purging himself of Guzman's existence in his life. If necessary, Paul knew he could sacrifice himself to save his son.

Paul shifted in the seat and repositioned his hands on the wheel. *If the dream has crossed over and become a reality, I'11 have to make a deal with Guzman*, he decided. *Take my life in exchange for my son's life. If I tell all this to Matt, he will probably think I'm insane. I wish I were insane. I hope I am. Pray to God I am. I'11 know soon enough. Maybe too soon.*

"There's some value in taking a vacation," Paul picked up on the conversation with Matt. "But when the work's there, it has to be done. Persistence is the key to success."

"Maybe your kind of success. It's not the way I measure mine." said Matt.

"How do you measure yours?"

"Not by the dollar and not by the clock." said Matt.

"How?" Paul was intrigued by his son's values.

"Personal satisfaction. Relationships. Observing life, appreciating it, taking part."

"I always thought I did that," said Paul.

"Maybe you do in your own way. But according to a different value system than mine. You asked me. That's what I have to say about the whole matter."

"But the business of doing business still has to be done."

"Depends on how important. There's work and then there are workaholics, if you follow me," said Matt.

Paul understood his son's reference. It was a not-so-subtle criticism of Paul's lifestyle. "With me, work has always been important. In retrospect it held too much importance, but I never would have become what I've become."

"We all have to make choices," Matt said diffidently.

"Unfortunately, in certain instances," Paul dropped the gear into low as they climbed a particularly steep grade.

His son looked at him.

Paul avoided his glance. "Sometimes."

"Mmh." Matt yawned again. His stomach grumbled. "Yeah, hear that. Hunger is sure one decision that's made for us."

"Here we are," said Paul. "Seems like we've been coming up this mountainside forever."

Entering the town, they drove slowly along the main street and pulled into the only service station. A heavyset attendant, whose name Andy was embroidered in faded red stitching across his jacket pocket, came from the garage out to their car. Paul rolled down the window. "Fill it up -- super unleaded."

While the tank was being filled, Andy cleaned the windshield.

A two ton stock truck pulled into the gas station and stopped on the opposite side of the tanks parallel to Paul and Matt's car.

Matt looked across the pumps at the truck driver, who was dressed like a rancher. A ruddy complexioned older man with shaggy white hair, he was lean and weathered, wrinkled skin sagging slightly between his chin and throat. Matt liked the man's broad leather hat with an owl feather stuck in the headed hatband. Matt also noticed a saddle horse and a mule in the trailer of the stake-bed truck.

Paul was inspecting the contents of his wallet in search of a few small bills to pay the gas station attendant. He had nothing less than a fifty. "Matt, you have anything smaller than a fifty? He might not have change."

Matt pulled his wallet from the back pocket of his jeans and handed it to his father.

Andy, the attendant, smiled across the space between the gas pumps at the old man in the truck. "Hi, Denham."   "Andy -- fill 'er up for me."

The attendant took a final swipe at Paul's car window, then went to fill the truck. "Where ya been this late hour?"

The old man, Denham, tipped back the rim of his hat. "Over at the Kirkland ranch in Honeylake Valley. Two mountain lions have been at their stock. Kirkland called me over there to see if I could get a shot at 'em or maybe track 'em down. I lost their trail."

"What are mountain lions doin' goin' after cows? Plenty of deer around this time of year." Andy adjusted the hose nozzle so that it would self-regulate the filling of the truck's large gas tank.

"Don't know," said Denham. "Cows don't run away as fast as deer. And cows are sweeter meat. Them two cats could be gettin' old and can't run down the deer. Cows are easy prey."

As he returned to Paul's car to collect the bills Paul held out to him through the open side window, Andy continued his conversation with the old hunter. "Think they'll come back?"

Denham nodded. "Most always do or go elsewhere looking for the same meal. Now they have a taste for domestic beef, those cats'll try for another kill."

Hearing the nature of the conversation between the hunter and the gas station attendant, Matt rolled down his window. "You say you hunt mountain lions?" He addressed the old man in the truck.

The hunter peered down from his truck cab at Matt's young face and nodded.

Matt's tone became caustic. "Yeah? Not many of 'em left, are there?"

"Not many."

Matt leaned slightly out through his open window. "Just like all the other gunslingers in this country, you're not happy unless you're out killing animals or people."

Denham's eyes glowed hotly.

Paul struck his son lightly on the arm. "There's no need to antagonize him! That was uncalled for."

"Aah! That's the only way anyone takes notice. He probably never heard of an extinct species."

"You should know better, Matt. You don't just drive into a strange town and start throwing insults."

Andy's face was puffed red with anger at Matt's remarks. The attendant's bulk loomed at the driver's window on Paul's side of the car. "That's sixteen fifty."

Paul quickly handed him the bills. "Thanks. Keep the change." Paul started the car engine. "Besides, he's obviously a professional hunter, not just someone out for sport."

"How can you tell, from your vast experience?" Matt's sarcastic tone sparked a slight flash of anger in Paul.

"Look at his outfit," Paul snapped. "You heard him. I know something about these people. I came from a small town. Not backwoods, but people like this. Never admitted it 'til now."

"You ashamed of where you came from?"

"No. Yes, I once was. I'm just being honest with myself. Still, you ought to show some consideration."

"Well," said Matt, "you're full of surprises."

"I am." Paul put the car in gear and pulled out of the service station. He and Matt missed the exchange and derogatory laughter shared between Denham and Andy about the two "flatlanders."

A few minutes later, the car that had been following Paul and Matt pulled into their vacated place at the gas pumps.

Matt's harangue at the old hunter had shattered the pure visage of pioneer and mountain man that Paul had earlier attributed to his son. Now Matt seemed to Paul more like a trouble-maker ranting against the establishment. As Paul pulled the car to a stop next to the motel office, he glimpsed Matt's earring reflecting the neon glow of the motel sign. It seemed to Paul that the earring had suddenly taken on a malicious aura.

Paul eased his stiff joints out of the car, stretched and breathed deeply of the cold mountain air. *I'11 sleep tonight*, he thought. *Aah, what of it. I shouldn't let Matt get to me like that. He has to flex his muscle to find out who he is. Family, rules, social convention, he has to test himself against all of it.* Paul walked to the office. *I was a radical once. Now, I represent tradition and the establishment.*

He opened the door to the motel office and stepped inside.

The tinkling noise of a bell hanging on the door brought a chunky country woman from inside the attached living quarters out into the office to see who had entered. Sniffling from her over-spiced cooking and nosy curiosity, she paused in the open doorway to look at Paul. He heard a blast of television noise carried from somewhere inside and he could smell a warm draught of beefy cooking odors through the open door.

The woman's molasses eyes took a full moment to assess him. "Evenin'," she said.

"Hello. I'd like two singles for one night."

She pushed an information card across the counter and glanced at the passenger outside. "Fill this out. We do have some cabins with double beds."

"Singles are fine."

She scanned Paul's outfit. "You and your wife up here to hunt?"

"Wife?" His brow furrowed. He looked out at the car. "Oh, no, ah, that's my son."

Her pointed pink tongue thrust against the back of her front teeth, then slipped outside to her upper lip. She gave a nod of disapproval. Again she glanced through the window, then back at Paul with a sharp crick of her neck and picked up the card. "Twenty-eight dollars, in advance."

Taking out his wallet, he handed her a fifty.

"Need change." Leaving the door open, she stepped back into the living room and mumbled a few words to her husband, who turned to look over the back of the couch with a suspicious scowl at Paul.

Paul smiled, then discreetly focused his eyes elsewhere in the office. *My wife*, he thought. *Matt's going to give me a complex. These people think we're a gay couple.*

The woman returned to the office from inside the house. The television program drew her husband's attention away from his appraisal of Paul standing uncomfortably at the counter.   The woman handed Paul his change. "Just passing through?" she asked inquisitively.

"In a manner of speaking. My son and I are on a short vacation. We're going to pack in for a week or so.

"Oh -" Again she glanced out the window. Her fat smooth jowls trembled with a nearly imperceptible quiver of disgust.

"Is there a place nearby we can get something to eat?" asked Paul.

"Brogan's down the street. It can get rough over there," she said pointedly.

Paul looked at her to explain what she meant by her statement. He was a little tired of her innuendo about his relationship with Matt.

"Not so far you can't walk," she said. "Open 'til two on Fridays. "She handed him a key. "Number four, straight back along this side."

"Thank you." As Paul opened the door, the car that had been following pulled in next to his own. Guzman stepped out. His body moved with a lethal catlike grace. He deliberately let Paul look into his eyes, then smiled, as he walked past into the office. There was a familiarity about the man that Paul could not immediately place.

Chapter 13

Paul went quickly to his car and slid in behind the wheel. He parked in front of unit number four. Leaving the backpacks in the trunk, he and Matt carried in small overnight bags.

Matt went straight to the bathroom. Paul lay on one of the musty smelling beds and looked about the spare room a moment. He closed his gritty eyes and listened to the long muffled splatter of his son's urine hitting the water in the toilet bowl. There was a moment of silence, followed by a metallic flush, then the rush of water in the sink. A few moments later, Matt came out of the bathroom. The toilet tank hissed behind him like an angry snake.

Paul opened his eyes. "There's a place to grab a bite down the street."

"Good, I can use a couple hamburgers."

With a weary groan, Paul sat up on the edge of the bed and rubbed his face. He stood and walked with a heavy tread into the bathroom.

A few minutes later, as Paul and Matt stepped outside of their motel unit, Paul noticed the second car parked three units down from their own. A light was on in the cabin. Two other units were already occupied with trucks parked in front.

Paul and Matt crossed the lot and walked along the narrow street. With a hint of winter in the air, the temperature was lower by twenty degrees at this high elevation. A thin frost glazed errant patches of dormant grass in the open spaces between buildings Paul and Matt passed as they walked along the main street of the town.

Matt recalled that during the past summer, he had hitch-hiked through several towns like this one in the Sierra Nevada foothills of Northern California, the goldrush country that still exhibited landmarks of the old frontier. Here also, in the Rockies, this town where he and his father walked retained the atmosphere of the Old West that had succumbed to the twentieth century, but still clung to its western traditions.

The architecture of the buildings had not changed much from the old days. But an occasional modern-looking house peered out from among patches of forest and powerlines hung in a loose network over the town.

Brogan's was the Friday night watering hole, the ritual gathering place for the ranchers and local mountain community. Paul and Matt walked past the trucks, cars, motorcycles, and four wheel drive vehicles that filled the gravel lot and were illuminated in the sleazy glow of cafe lights and colorful neon beer sign logos.

For a few moments, Paul and Matt stood unnoticed just inside the doorway. They squinted through the heavy smoke hanging like transparent shredded gray moss above the boisterous crowd. The conversational roar made the country and western music belting from a corner jukebox nearly incomprehensible.

Paul scanned the loggers, ranchers, and local businessmen with their wives and girlfriends, smoking, drinking, dancing, laughing and talking. One cowboy stumbled drunkenly from table to table. He leaned over a friend and clapped him on the shoulder. The friend said something about Paul and Matt, especially about Matt's earring and the odd cut of Matt's long hair. The drunken cowboy quickly went to another table and called attention to the couple standing in the doorway. A number of patrons were wedged shoulder to shoulder at the bar. Paul knew instantly that he and his son were out of their element. There was no room for them; and like the woman said at the motel office, Brogan's was a place where "it could get rough."

Paul's first impulse was to leave. Back at the motel room he and Matt could fix some peanut butter and jelly sandwiches. He felt Matt tug his arm and pull him into the crowd. The sudden move caught Paul off balance. He bounced off the shoulder of a hulking logger drinking a schooner of beer. Mumbling apologies that went unnoticed by the scowling red-bearded logger, Paul followed Matt in the direction of the bar.

At genteel cocktail parties and social gatherings, he had always stood out among the crowd and had been a leader in group conversations. People sharing his own urban sophistication had listened to him as the center of attention.

Now, here in this mountain tavern with its coarse social conventions, he had difficulty coping with the sudden wave of intimidation that swept over him. It bordered on fear. Exhausted, numbed by the assault of smoke and noise, he followed as Matt shoved deeper into the crowd toward an opening at the bar.

A girl's squeal pierced Paul's preoccupation with his own thoughts and impressions. The attention her comments drew to Paul and Matt stripped them of any anonymity they might have had.

"Oh, ain't he cute! He's got an earring! Look! He's got an earring!"

Paul's face flushed with embarrassment as he and Matt heard sporadic laughter and rumbles of derogation from people in the crowd who happened to take notice.

Paul thought angrily to himself, *the earring again, always that damn earring.*

His son ignored the remarks and shouldered past two ranch hands who had recently vacated seats at the bar. Paul straddled his stool with a feeling of unease. He sensed people's stares boring into his back. The stool was rickety. He grasped at the bar molding to steady himself and avoid toppling backwards. Drunk, he would have an excuse. Sober and ashamedly afraid, he had none.

Sitting on the bar stool to Paul's left, Vince Macke was talking to his girl friend, Regina. He only subliminally registered the shift in tone and undercurrent of conversation by a contingent of the crowd. He discerned the target of the crowd's gossip at the same moment he felt the clumsy nudge of Paul climbing on to the wobbling stool next to him.

Vince concentrated his attention on the level of the bourbon in his shot glass. He was also keenly aware of the hard sexy bigness of his girl friend, as she jettisoned smoke from red lips. Vince caught her sudden amused glance past him. The derogatory comments from the patrons behind him filtered into focus. He turned to look at Matt and glimpsed the flash of Matt's strange streaked blonde hair. Taking Matt for a woman, Vince saw the earring, mustache, and the young man's face. He turned back with a rigid flare of sarcasm at Regina, who smirked into her whiskey.

Further down the bar, the old hunter, Denham Hunsinger, was sitting with the sheriff and a few friends who were listening to Denham tell about the mountain lions that were preying on cattle in the local region. Upon seeing Paul and Matt at the bar, Denham changed his subject and related the incident of Matt's disrespectful comments toward him when he had pulled his truck in at the service station to buy gas. As Denham described what Matt had said to him, bitterness tinged the beery grins of the sheriff and his drinking buddies.

The waitress left off sharing a humorous exchange with Brogan, her bearded Irish boss, who owned the tavern. With an aloofness barely concealed by practiced courtesy, she sauntered along the bar to take Matt's and Paul's order.

"Have you decided what you want?" she asked.

Matt did not raise his eyes from his menu. "Couple of Coors. two hamburgers, fries, and coleslaw."

She looked up from her quick notation at Paul. Tension and emotional stress caused by his discomfort with being in the crowd and with the grinning hostility and speculation about Matt had diminished Paul's appetite. He had experienced the sensation once before as a junior executive making a marketing presentation to insensitive senior corporate staff. Feeling so ill at ease had never happened again until now.

Paul handed over his menu. "Beer and a hamburger, well done."

"Fries?"

"No."

"What kind of beer?"

"Ah, I don't know. Any kind. Bud." He hated beer. But ordering a scotch and soda might draw more verbal fire. What he really wanted was a tall cold glass of milk, the classic drink that prompted barroom challenges in the Old West.

Along the wall across the aisle from the bar, Luther and Joyce Macke were sitting at a table with their friends Betty and Deke Halloran. A fever of high spirits and alcoholic well-being flushed Luther Macke in the contagion of laughter at his table until he was blowing and snorting like a horse to catch his constricted breath.

Joyce Macke smoked a cigarette and quietly tolerated her husband's effusive amusement with the Hallorans'. She watched his shaggy gray head bobbing, twinkling eyes rolling drunkenly in their creased and wrinkled sockets. At such moments, he reminded her of a rodeo clown, face so red he didn't need theatrical makeup.

Joyce lifted her gaze beyond his laughing head and looked at her eldest son, Vince, seated at the bar next to his girl friend, Regina. Joyce liked Regina. She was a suitable choice for Vince. Regina reminded Joyce of herself when Joyce was thirty years younger, tough and raw-boned with a solid figure, good for straddling a horse, hard-fucking with her man, and bearing children. Secretly Joyce was pleased that Regina was attracted to Vince. Regina had Joyce's physical likeness.

Joyce's searching gaze roamed over the throng of barroom patrons to the low-lit gloom of another table and picked out Willie sitting with three girls.

Never just one girl for Willie, she thought. *Always at least two or three, petite pretty ones like the rodeo queens, the magazine cover girls.* She could not fault him on his preference. She had raised him not to be satisfied with his lot as the son of a rancher. She had secretly encouraged him with reading, praised his academic performance, planted in him the seeds of ambition beyond the confines and limitations of ranch life whose routines stifled her with each passing year. She would never escape. It was in Willie that she unconsciously vested her dreams.

Vince suddenly backed off from his stool and moved away from Regina. He stepped up behind the two men seated at Matt's right, draped his arms around their shoulders, and poked his head into their conversation. With calculated inaccuracy, he flicked the ash of his cigarette onto Matt's lap.

Matt stiffened, incensed at the deliberate gesture. As Matt brushed away the still hot flakes, Vince apologized for his clumsiness so that he could get a closer look at the older and younger man, whom the crowd assumed to be a gay couple. "Sorry," said Vince, "but you two're crowding me."

Paul avoided Vince's mocking stare and focused on his beer being served by the waitress. Matt did not look away. Vince stepped back to his own seat and carefully avoided touching Paul.

As Paul and Matt sipped their beers, Vince turned sideways on his bar stool to block out Paul. Vince's eyes screwed up in a derisive expression for Regina's benefit. He did not understand his impulse to want to smash the face of the long-haired blonde boy wearing the earring, except the boy looked soft and attractive and filled Vince's mind with disconcerting thoughts. He concentrated intently on Regina's eyes and thrusting breasts and the area of her crotch against her tight jeans.

The sly officiousness of the sheriff sitting at the far end of the bar gave Paul little confidence. The man rubbed shoulders with the good old boys. If push came to shove, the sheriff was likely to overlook the "horseplay."

It worried Paul that Matt could be goaded into a fight. Paul searched his memory of his son. *Where does he get his aggressiveness? Almost like he looks for a conflict, with me, with everybody. He dares someone to contradict him. But remember that time? What was it he called you? Dishonest.* Four years ago, he had bailed Matt out of a Los Angeles jail. Matt had refused to leave the cell, choosing to stay with his friends and undergo prosecution. The lenient judge had cited them for only disturbing the peace.

Matt had called his father a hypocrite, living behind a veneer of respectability, espousing tolerance, understanding, compromise and reason. In reality, Paul was a ruthless businessman who had also caused the disintegration of his family. Matt called Paul's values and behavior white collar dishonesty. It was as though Matt had to prove how different he was than his father. That Paul donated astronomical sums to politicians for favors, to public causes and non-profit institutions had never been compensation enough for Matt, who had lost all respect for his father. Over the years, Matt's social resistance had faded as he and his peers gained in adult experience. Still, the itch of anger was always there in Matt, something else in his thoughts, his chemistry, not requiring social injustice to cause it to flare up. Perhaps it was as Matt once said. He did not have the confidence, the understanding, the ability to express himself, to show the world "I am" apart from his father's millions about which Matt felt a deep hatred. So Matt expressed himself in a negative manner that was unmistakable.

Paul wanted to leave the bar. He and Matt could just take their hamburgers and fries with them. And in the clear light of morning when the crowd was gone, they could return to Brogan's and order a big breakfast, eggs, bacon, pancakes, the works. "Come on," said Paul. "Let's go."

Matt looked at him sharply. "What about the food?"

Paul shook his head. "We can take it with us. Let's avoid trouble."

"Trouble? I'm hungry, damn it, and I'm gonna eat. These cowboys aren't going to scare me off."

"Let's not argue," Paul assumed a reasoning tone of voice.

Matt looked firmly away and drank a slug of beer. Then the waitress was serving the hamburgers and it was too late to ask for a container. Paul did not want to precipitate a negative retort from the waitress either. Someone might decide to champion her cause.

The man who had checked into the motel after them entered the tavern.

Preoccupied with eating his hamburger, Paul did not notice him take the vacated seat at

the sweeping rim of the bar near the dance floor. But the man watched him.

Chapter 14

The record in the juke box ended. There was a lull until the next song, a slow number by Reba McEntire. Willie Macke pulled one of his three girls to her feet. His other two dates concealed their envy with nonchalance and a sudden preoccupation with cigarettes and beer. Their turn would come. Then Cheryl, the one who had squealed about Matt's earring, crushed her cigarette and announced to no one in general, "I'm gonna do it."

She went straight across the dance floor that was filling with couples and stopped behind Matt, who was in the process of wolfing down his hamburger. Thrusting out her slender hip, she tapped him on the shoulder.

He paused in mid bite, took a moment to swallow the food already in his mouth, then turned with a scowl that softened to an amused grin at the cute gum-chewing girl.

"So, you just gonna sit there eating a hamburger when a Reba McEntire song comes on?

I'm waitin' to dance. Your bein' a stranger don't bother me none."

"Somebody put you up to this?" Matt asked pointedly.

"Hey, blondie, if I didn't want to dance with you, I wouldn't be standin' here askin'."

Paul glanced over as Matt stepped down from his bar stool and placed an arm around the girl's slim waist. Cradling his beer in the other hand, Matt escorted her out onto the dance floor.

Paul detected the heavy odor of bourbon and acrid cigarette smoke on the breath of a passing man. The smell triggered an unease associated with simple virtues and barroom violence that quickened Paul's heart and made him tremble. Paul was not one to engage in physical violence. He feared getting hurt. He looked around with a sense of foreboding, trying to spot who had put the girl up to asking Matt to dance, but he saw no plotting menacing smiles. He could not prevent trouble if he didn't know where it would come from.

Maybe I'm overreacting, thought Paul. *The strain. the drive, God, I'm tired.* Then he saw the man who had just entered the bar watching him. The man's directness raised a cold sweat at the base of his back. Paul intuitively knew that this man must be Antonio Guzman.

Because he was exhausted, Paul wondered if his mind were playing tricks on him. How could Guzman possibly know where he and Matt had gone unless Guzman really was the professed agent of Satan, the contract killer, not someone Paul's imagination had concocted. But then surveillance technology could locate anybody anytime. Paul looked quickly away, searching out his son in the swaying throng. When he looked back again, the man's appearance did not seem so much like Guzman. *It's all in my mind*, thought Paul. *It's just that I'm tired. I'm seeing things that aren't really there.*

Out on the crowded dance floor Matt dipped and glided with Cheryl, holding her hand far outstretched in an exaggerated ballroom style. They moved with the quick rigid grace of the country and western waltz.

He tried to discover in her coquettish eyes why she had asked him to dance and realized instantly -- to draw attention to herself. He also justified to himself that she was intrigued by him like everyone else in the bar.

Matt had always found it easier to relate to women than to men. He was aware of their vulnerability. He was sympathetic, a good listener, and he was physically attractive to women.

He grinned at Cheryl. "Yeah, little honey, when push comes to shove, I can be a hell of a sexy dude."

Another couple jockeyed into position with the malicious intent of giving Matt a hard shove and throwing him off balance. Matt took their deliberately gauged momentum sharply in the back, causing him to stumble with Cheryl into Willie and his partner. Matt's can of beer tipped and spilled. The liquid darkened Willie's shirt. Willie turned with quick anger. As Matt attempted an apology, Willie lashed out, connecting with the side of Matt's face. Matt fell backwards into another couple, who laughed and cursed him, calling him a clumsy faggot.

Pushing away from them, Matt rushed Willie, separating him from his partner and driving him back. Their legs scissored across the floor as their hurtling bodies scattered other couples and crashed over a bottle strewn table, causing its occupants to fall and leap aside.

At the bar Paul looked for the sheriff to intervene, but the fight had instantly become the center of attention for the entire crowd, including the law and his cronies. They watched with intense spectator involvement the thud of fists against flesh, grunts of pain, clatter and stomp of heeled boots on the hard wooden floor, shatter of breaking glass, as Matt and Willie slugged it out and rolled over another table.

Above the struggle and the noise of the crowd, the raucous country and western waltz played on in strange contrast to the fight.

Standing up at his table, Luther Macke watched Willie with an idiotic grin of pride. He admired the bull-dogged toughness and spirit of his son. Joyce's face was pinched with worry.

On the other side of the room, Matt connected with a sudden strong right to Willie's eye and reversed the attack. Unable to see clearly, Willie opted for close quarter grappling and weakened rapidly under Matt's vicious assault with knees and fists. The raw smell of blood clung to them along with the odors of sweat, smoke, and beer. Then a sense of recognition crept forward in his mind and body that displaced his anger and connected with a similar impulse in his adversary. Willie was like him. He was one of the children of light.

Paul moved quickly down the length of the bar to the sheriff. "Will you please put a stop to that? There's no point in letting it go on."

The sheriff glanced at his friends, grinned and raised a beer to his lips. "Those boys ain't in no mood to listen. Be patient. They'll quit when they're good and ready."

Paul stepped away, shocked and angered more at his own impotence than at the sheriff's response. If Paul tried to stop the fight, he would only become embroiled in it. He could not place himself in such a position, a corporate president who engaged in barroom brawls. He was supposed to be a figure of respect and authority. In this situation the sheriff was the figure of authority. The sheriff carried more weight and he condoned the fight.

Part of it's Matt's fault, Paul tried to rationalize to himself. *We could have walked out of here. It's his own obstinacy that got him into this.* Paul was trembling and admitted to himself that he was afraid of physical harm and ashamed at his cowardice. And because he did not intervene, he despised himself even more for his excuses. Matt was his own flesh and blood. At that moment, he despised himself for having become the kind of man he was.

Overhearing the sheriff's statement to Paul, Vince dropped his cigarette, rubbed it out under his boot and strode out onto the dance floor to break up the fight. He pushed Matt and Willie apart and stood between them, preventing them from getting at each other, but they had ceased going at each other and were staring into each others' eyes.

"All right, that's enough! You're both tough shit! Let it go at that!"

"Get the hell outta there, Vince!" someone called from the side. "Let those fuckers fight!"

"You don't have to do me any favors," Matt rasped.

"I'm doin' you both a favor. It's over."

As Paul watched Vince break up the conflict, the sheriff brushed past him from behind and walked out onto the floor. The time had came to assert his legal authority before the crowd and he realized it.

"Well, looks like these boys have had enough," the sheriff intervened in a gruff social manner.

Paul left the bar and came over to them. The sheriff clapped him on the shoulder in a neutralizing gesture. "A little harmless fun, mister. Nobody the worse for wear. They're young. They can take it."

Holding a hand to his bleeding nose, Matt staggered past his father and the sheriff and hurried out the door. Paul offered Vince a grim ineffectual glance of appreciation and followed his son.

Paul hurried after Matt across the parking lot and along the street. He attempted to assist him, but Matt jerked sharply away.

Back inside Brogan's tavern, Vince helped his brother, Willie, to the men's room. Bleeding from the nose and mouth, Willie filled the sink with hot water and inspected his ruptured face in the mirror for cuts and bruises. His left eye was badly swollen. He wet several paper towels and dabbed away the mucousy strings of blood hanging from his nose. Vince leaned against the door frame. "You okay?"

"Yeah," Willie's voice was hoarse. "That fucker sure could fight."

Vince patted Willie on the shoulder, then left the men's room. Walking back through the tavern crowd, he passed his parents' table. Joyce reached out to grab Vince's arm and stop him. He leaned down.

"Willie okay?" she asked worried.

Vince nodded and returned to Regina at the bar. Regina said something close into his ear. He swallowed the rest of his drink, then maneuvered her through the crowd and out of the tavern.

Outside in the parking lot, they walked through the assemblage of vehicles to Regina's flashy red Ford Thunderbird. Vince held the passenger door open for Regina, then got in at the wheel. They drove from the parking lot and headed south out of town past the motel and service station.

At the motel, Paul grabbed one of the packs from the car, closed the trunk, then lugged the pack inside the motel room. Throwing the pack on a bed, he tore away the laces to get at the first aid kit, then went in to Matt, who was carefully washing his tender face at the bathroom sink.

"Let me help." said Paul.

Matt waved him away.

"Here, I'11 give you a hand."

"Isn't it a little late for that? Where the hell were you?" Matt grabbed the first aid kit from his father.

"Well, what the hell did you expect me to do? I don't know how to fight. It's not a skill I cared to cultivate." Paul clung to his point-of-view.

"Hey," Matt waved a bloodstained towel at him. "Did you see who stopped that fight?"

"You could have left when I said. You knew it was going to happen. You encouraged it."

"I didn't want that fight. But I would've thought you'd do something more than stand there like some numb nuts."

"Come on, Matt. Don't try to pull that. I've always given you my support where it counts. Don't distort this between us. A barroom brawl." He held his son's gaze in the mirror. "I tried to get the sheriff to do something."

Matt shot him a cutting sidewise glance loaded with sarcasm and continued treating his cuts and bruises.

"We didn't have to stay. We could have walked out of there long before it happened," said Paul.

Matt dropped the wet towel into the waste basket. "I don't let people push me around."

"You're just being bull-headed. Let's not start the trip out like this. We need to talk. We need to understand each other, to communicate, for God's sake."

"It was your idea to come up here. I didn't want to leave California and meet you out here."

"Please, Matt, not like this. Let's not have any arguments. It's pointless. You just blow up."

"And you don't?"

"All right, when anger is constructive; but nothing's accomplished when it's irrational, like tonight. I have so much on my mind I need to tell you."

"Save it. Will you? Just save it."

Paul resignedly accepted the deserved rebuke from his son. He was concerned that this incident might make it impossible for him to tell Matt the reason he had brought him into the mountains. Matt would only scoff at him.

Along the highway south of town. Vince slowed Regina's thunderbird to turn off onto a logging road that led back among the trees. The big car rocked and bounced along over deep ruts for a hundred yards, then stopped. Vince pushed a switch on the dash. The powerful headlight beams vanished, sucked away into the pitch darkness.

Touching and kissing in the small glow of the overhead interior light, Vince and Regina fumbled off their clothes, then caressed each other until Regina pulled a car blanket up off the floor and wrapped them in it against the cold.

She thrust her pendulous breasts against Vince's face and straddled him on the front seat. Several minutes later, they came, gasping, grunting, and clutching in a frenzy until they were quiet, collapsed in each others' arms.

Back at Brogan's tavern, Guzman had struck up a conversation with a rancher seated next to him. They suddenly laughed at one of Guzman's remarks. The rancher shook his head and took a draw of his cigarette. Guzman looked around at the crowd, then asked the man about the women there. After a moment of appraising looks at "the stock" the rancher nudged his arm, indicating that Guzman should follow him.

They picked up their drinks and moved through the noisy crowd to a table where two relatively unattractive women sat alone. The women shifted with sudden nervousness and anticipation at the prospect of the two men coming over to join them.

"Lila, Karen, how 'bout some company," the rancher towered over them with a flushed face and intimidating smile.

The women shrugged and moved over to make room for the men in the tight booth. Guzman slipped in next to Lila and offered his hand. "Name's Len Guzman. How do you do."

"Lila Stevenson. Haven't seen you before."

"I'm up here on a hunting trip."

"Oh," Lila blew cigarette smoke aside. "Where you from?"

"Back east. New York." His eyes passed quickly over the woman's fatty bulges accentuated by her jeans and breasts thrusting mountainously against the shiny fabric of her shirt. A trace of facial hair shadowed her upper lip and a small dark mole clung to her neck at the hinge of her jaw. Her eyes could have been attractive to Guzman, but they were dull and emotionless. She looked as though she had been disappointed with men too many times but was conditioned to the disappointment in exchange for temporary pleasure.

The rancher placed his arm around Karen's slender sympathetic shoulders in a quiet drunken huddle. They had been together many times before and carried a sexual understanding of each other not unlike a husband and wife in a long marriage. Guzman smiled at Lila. Her expression told him she was available and that she did not expect commitment. "Like to dance?" Guzman asked.

Out on the dance floor, Lila immediately pressed her body in close to Guzman's own. She liked his firm touch against the small of her back and the clean smell of his neck, like freshly laundered sheets.

After a while, Guzman and Lila quietly left the tavern. Taking her by the hand, he led her across the road and down a hill. The trees and underbrush screened out ambient light

from the town above.

As their eyes adjusted to the enclosing darkness, they came to a small clearing by a stream that reflected the moon and starlight and allowed them to clearly discern shapes and features. Guzman quickly stripped down, then turned to help Lila remove her clothes. Laughing self-consciously, she stepped out of her jeans that dropped and pooled about her ankles. "You're crazy," she said. "You've gotta be crazy. I've gotta be crazy for doin' this. At least it's different, but who in their right mind is gonna jump in that freezing water on a night like this. I mean I've heard of stimulation, but this?"

"My mentor made me swim in water, very cold water."

"Your mentor? Who was your mentor?"

"His name is Pearl."

"That's a strange damn name for a man. Where'd he get a name like that?"

"I gave him his name. It was the way he looked -- like a pearl."

Lila burst out laughing. "Yer jist givin' me a line of shit."

"Got so that in some ways I liked those cold swims. At least I got used to it. But then, I would do anything for him, my mentor. Have you ever made love in cold water before? You will soon discover it's a little like dying."

"Hell, no, it would pucker me shut. You're not talkin' about actually doin' it in the water. Come on. Let's leave this and go to the motel so we can enjoy it. I'm good for the whole night, but not out here lyin' on pine needles freezin' my tits off."

"You don't understand. The water is pure. It cleanses the act."

"What?" She stared at him and was sobered and suddenly unsure and afraid at his comment.

"We are not here by accident, but by design, Lila Stevenson."

"What the hell are you talkin' about? You one a them freako's from New York?"

"Come with me now. Enter the stream with me."

"Hey, I don't mind havin' a little fun, but that's enough of this shit. I'm goin' back."

Guzman shook his head. His grip held her wrists like steel bands as he pulled her into the freezing water.

"Oh, for Christ's sake! That's enough!" She struggled as his arms encircled her body crushing her against his own. She moaned in physical pain at the searing chill. Together they went under. She came up gasping and swearing. Guzman then forcefully guided her out onto the bank.

"You will soon be warm."

"Not here," she gasped. "I'm not gonna do it here. I'm freezing. You're crazy! Let go of me!"

Guzman clamped his mouth over her chattering teeth and forced her slowly to the ground. "It's okay, Lila. I will not harm you." His weight caused a spreading warmth to come over her. His long penis entered her with an ease she would not have thought possible. She closed her eyes at the intense heat seeping through her body like an internal hemorrhage. A sudden prickling sensation passed across the width of her throat. She attempted to struggle but could no longer move. Her brief flash of fear and panic quickly dissipated as she grew weaker and weaker at the rapid loss of blood, slipped into unconsciousness, then into death.

Guzman made a deep incision across Lila's abdomen and quickly disemboweled her. He then removed her ovaries. Holding them up to the moon, he chanted a prayer to Satan, the Lord of Darkness. Then, one by one, he placed her severed ovaries into his mouth and swallowed them. Reaching into a front pocket of his pants on the ground, he brought out a small soft leather pouch and from it, withdrew a medium sized pearl, which he placed in the palmed cup of Lila's motionless hand.

It was one o'clock in the morning when Vince and Regina returned to Brogans'. Vince bid Regina goodnight, then he went inside to discover his parents and Willie were ready to head for home. They said their goodnights to friends and walked out to the pickup truck.

Luther insisted on driving and Joyce wasn't in the mood to argue. Vince and Willie rode in the back among a few bales of hay and a canvas tarp. Willie slept.

As they left the town behind and drove on into the darkness, Luther nodded at the wheel. Joyce lit him a cigarette and watched carefully to see he did not doze.

At the Macke ranch, in a distant pasture far from the house, a female mountain lion hunched next to her mate and studied the dark shapes of the cattle herd that dotted the grassy meadow below. The lights were gone from the house across the valley and no smell of man came to the cats.

Still they watched and waited. The wind shifted and now carried the fetid scent of the cows. The two mountain lions stirred. Tails twitching with nervous jerks, the big cats crept down the slope to the fence line at the edge of the trees and waited, testing the cold air and choosing their victims.

A cow and her calf stood half asleep fifty yards away and were not aware of the cats, who began their stalk. The low feline shadows moved toward them in spurts and stops. The sudden lethal scent of the onrushing cats woke the cow's dull bovine brain. In fear and panic the cow plunged away snorting and kicking at the two phantoms until her calf's bleats of terror were silenced. Spindle legs thrashing, the calf thudded to the cold ground.

Fangs punctured the calf's jugular, filling the lions' red salivating mouths with hide, muscle and hot blood. The mountain lions' gaunt tawny flanks heaved and panted. The cats held the calf down until it ceased to struggle and died with jerks and twitches of finality.

The mother cow ranged in a hoarse confusion of long crying bellows. In grouped idiocy the herd watched the cats feed voraciously, jamming their faces into the hot steaming entrails of the calf.

A half hour later, the Macke's truck turned in at the mailbox and crunched along the gravel driveway the mile to the house. Luther parked near the barn.

The slam of the truck doors woke Willie and he stiffly climbed down after Vince. They stomped into the house through the rear door. A light came on in the kitchen windows.

Far out in the pasture, the mountain lions finished feeding on their second kill and with sated bellies moved off into the night.

Chapter 15

Paul and Matt woke at eight the next morning, checked out of the motel, and drove down the street to Brogans' where a few locals brooded over mugs of steaming black coffee and paid them no attention. The waitress brought them eggs, hotcakes, and thick slabs of bacon. Matt winced at the pain of chewing even soft food. He and his father avoided conversation.

As the waitress poured them second cups of coffee, the sheriff pulled up and parked close to the door. He entered and stared at Paul and Matt with eyes full of legal suspicion, then came over to their table and planted himself with authority creaking from his leather gunbelt.

"Mornin', gentlemen. Hope you ain't the worse for wear. I got me a problem. Maybe you can help. There was a man checked into the motel after you last night, then came in here. His name is Leonard Guzman. He never returned to his room. Bed wasn't slept in. His car's gone. He was last seen leavin' Brogans' with a woman by the name of Lila Stevenson. Both of 'em have disappeared. You know anything about the man or seen any sign of him?"

Paul stopped in mid-bite and swallowed hard. Guzman was here. Guzman was real. Paul didn't know where the first name Leonard entered into it, but that didn't matter. The diary wasn't just a fantasy. Matt's life was in danger. He now knew that he needed to confront Guzman alone and he had to use his own son to lure him into position. Without a weapon, he didn't know how he could kill him, but in some way he must. Trembling inside, he shook his head. "Never saw him before."

"Guess it's time to put together a search party. Checked Lila's place. Not there. No sign of anyone bein' there. Somethin' strange goin' on."

"Sorry we can't help you," said Paul, realizing that Guzman would probably kill Lila Stevenson, if he had not already done so.

The sheriff turned away with a grunt and took a corner table. When the waitress came over, he ordered apple pie and coffee and read the morning paper.

Matt sucked on a toothpick and walked outside to the car while Paul paid the check. A moment later, as he watched his father come through the door, an impulse of regret rose in him at what he had said back at the motel room. He did not want it this way between them, always this tension. He tried to focus on the feelings of openness and love he had experienced so strongly as a small child. The protective halo of childhood naivete had been excessively eroded by layers of reality. The psychological rubble of too many battle barricades cluttered the landscape of memory.

The positive feelings would not come.

He suddenly felt it would be awkward and embarrassing to apologize. From his father's perspective, perhaps an apology would even be taken as a sign of weakness. Maybe later, when they were in the mountains and had time to clear their minds, assess their feelings, and put away their pride, maybe then he could say he was sorry.

They drove out of town headed toward the high ranges.

"Hope we're right about the weather. Wouldn't want to get caught up here in an early storm," said Paul.

"We should be okay," said Matt. "Weather bureau's pretty accurate. Never let me down yet. I may have a job with them next year in California."

Paul tilted his head with a warm approving smile. "Well, good...definite?"

"No, just talked with them, testing the waters."

"My name carries a lot of weight in the media," said Paul. "Don't be afraid to use it to help you get the job."

"They don't know I'm your son. I didn't tell them. If they're going to hire me, then I want them to hire me, not your influence."

"But that's how business is done in the real world," said Paul. "Referrals and influence play an important role in getting what you want. Especially when it comes to hiring key people. I'm sure if they offer you a position, it will be on the basis of your own merit and capabilities."

"That and other recommendations. I haven't overlooked their necessity. But the names I'm using are known in the field. I need that kind of professional referral anyway. I hate going in cold on an interview. I don't feel intimidated, but I never developed interview skills."

"I can help you with that. There's nothing like being prepared to give you confidence."

"Oh, I have plenty of confidence," said Matt. "Sometimes it just comes out the wrong way. Defensive. I'm not a very positive person. At least that's the impression I give. If people turn me off, I turn them off."

"You get that from your mother. In the past, it often proved embarrassing at times in social situations."

"To her?"

"To me," said Paul.

"Well, some things need to be said without bullshitting."

"But there are ways to say them in a manner that has considerably more sophistication and, therefore, greater impact," Paul said.

"I suppose. To each his own, and her own," Matt discounted his father's statement.

Paul glanced out at the trim ranch they were passing in a broad green valley bordered by pine and gold leafed aspen. A line of blue-gray smoke rose from the house chimney, and a man on horseback rode among milling Hereford cattle in a corral near the barns. The sight of the ranch was abruptly cut off from the moving car by a wall of spruce as the car began to climb a steep grade.

By eleven o'clock, Paul and Matt turned off the narrow mountain highway at nine thousand feet elevation and followed an old little used logging road five miles back into a highland meadow. At the end of their jolting ride, they sat unmoving, drugged by travel, then climbed out of the car and stretched and yawned and shook the stiffness from their limbs.

They shivered in the sudden mountain chill. Matt opened the trunk and lifted out the packs and frames and leaned them against the rear bumper. He reached in for two down jackets and handed one to his father, who promptly pulled it on and zipped it closed.

Matt put on his own jacket, then carried one of the packs over to a log. Paul closed the trunk and brought over the second pack.

They sat on the ground and slid their arms into padded shoulder straps attached to the aluminum frames. Matt checked his pocket compass and gazed off toward the distant peaks. "You in good shape?"

"Not too bad. I've been playing tennis and jogging two or three times a week. But that's down at sea level," said Paul. "It's going to take a couple of days to get used to the air up here."

"Yeah, no sense pushing hard. No rush."

"Doctor say anything about your collapsed lung?" Paul recalled with concern.

"It's healed. I had the surgery. Won't happen again."

"Have you been swimming as much?" his father asked.

"Nearly. Collapsed lung's not all that uncommon. People can go right back to what they were doing," said Matt.

Paul nodded. "Nice, just sitting here."

"I know. But we're developing a good case of mountain inertia. Let's get started." Matt lurched to his feet and set off across the meadow.

Paul staggered up with some difficulty and followed, lagging behind, shrugging and adjusting his pack to a comfortable position. As they picked up a game trail at the edge of the forest, he found he was breathing hard early.

Matt glanced back and waited patiently for him to catch up, then set a slower pace as they followed the winding bank of a rushing stream.

Joyce Macke was just driving the pickup truck out from the house to get the morning paper. Seeing the sheriff's car approaching, she slowed and pulled aside and waited for him to stop. He looked up at her warm motherly face creased like a crusty biscuit fresh from the oven.

"Mornin', Sam," she greeted him. "What brings you out?"

"Mornin', Joyce, some night last night. How's Willie?"

"Few lumps and bruises. Every growin' boy gets 'em sometime."

"Yeah, they do that. Lila Stevenson disappeared last night."

"What?"

"Wasn't home when Beth called to check on her. She left Brogans' with a stranger. His car and bag are gone from the motel. No sign of him anywhere in town. Did Lila say anything to you about her whereabouts when she left?"

"We didn't talk none, just waved at each other. That poor woman has had a hard time of it. I sure hope nothin' bad has happened to her. It's a damn shame she's had to take to goin' with strange men. She's a wonderful woman. Her only fault is she lets men take advantage of her sweet good nature."

"Well, I'11 keep askin' around, but right now I'm stumped. Need to keep an eye out for the man she went with too. If he shows up without her, god damn."

"I'11 make some calls after I get the paper in."

"Thanks, Joyce, 'ppreciate it. Say hi to your men for me."

"I will." She waited for him to turn his patrol car around, then followed him out to the road. He gave her a honk as he headed back to town.

Chapter 16

As they drove over the Potomac River across the Key Bridge toward Georgetown University, Leon and Ed looked at the gray Gothic twin towers that spiraled skyward from the Lauinger Library and Healy Hall, campus landmarks of the venerated institution established in 1789 and founded in the Catholic faith and Jesuit tradition.

"Looks like a religious place," commented Ed.

"It is. There are layers of religious study and influence," said Leon. "I think our killer pointed us here for a reason but doesn't expect us to identify him. He has an extreme delusional religious purpose and agenda and is obviously consumed by it."

"Yup. Definitely a religious fanatic. Sure not the first to kill in the name of religion, but his methods are over the top. So you think he went here?"

"Could be. He says so. At first I thought it was a distraction, but more likely it's a hint. I read about the campus online. All Georgetown students are required to take courses in Philosophy and Theology, including the introductory Problem of God course or Introduction to Biblical Literature. There are upper-level courses in philosophy and theology. One of them is about the Jesuits and the church in the modern world."

"Didn't you say he told you on the internet that he was from South America somewhere?"

"According to his story, which I suspect could be pure fabrication, the killer claiming to be Antonio Guzman was raised by Jesuit priests and, as a student, matriculated in the Georgetown University system. We don't have enough clues to begin in reality. It's a guess. We're starting with Biblical associations and the killer's reference to genetics and dark energy quantum physics which narrows the field of search to the medical school."

Their appointment was scheduled for ten o'clock that morning with the Assistant to the President for Federal Relations.

"So, how much help you think we'll get from this guy we're seeing?" asked Ed.

"Hoping for the best," said Leon. "He's the liaison to the federal government for funded research programs and student affairs."

Leon and Ed found their way through the elegant burnished wood library to his office in Healy Hall.

Leon estimated Jacob Bruce to be in his early fifties, well preserved, athletic, judging from striking action photos of cross country bike racing on the credenza against his office wall. He greeted them in a calm business-like manner and invited them to sit in two comfortable chairs, while he took a third so the desk wasn't a barrier to their social proximity.

"Gentlemen, can I offer you coffee, juice, water?"

"I'm fine," said Leon. Ed shook his head.

"To business, how can I assist you?"

"You have likely seen the news regarding the murder of Reverend Livingston."

Jacob nodded. "A horrible and saddening spectacle. Obviously, your investigation has brought you here."

"We do have a search warrant," said Ed, handing Jacob the document.

Jacob briefly read the warrant. "Our resources are open to you."

"Judging from initial clues, there is a possibility that the killer could have been a student at Georgetown at one time," said Leon.

"That would be most unfortunate," said Jacob.

"Even if we are able to determine that he was a graduate, the problem is one of identity," said Leon. "The killer has created one or more alternative personae behind which he can freely operate undetected."

"What is the span of time you're considering?"

"As a reasonable estimate, within the last ten years."

"A multitude. What will you need?"

"Unlimited access to student archives for a controlled focused search on all male students. You see, the killer is playing a game with us. He has even contacted me directly on the internet like a blogger with blatant information about himself. It may not be real, but there is still a subconscious association, enough to analyze characteristics of his behavior. He stated that he graduated from this university. If that turns out to be true, then he is confident he can elude us regardless of how much we know or discover about him. He is extremely intelligent, but significantly disturbed, which makes him all the more dangerous."

"Are you willing to share his name, or at least the name he has given out to you?"

"We are unable to at this time."

"I fully understand. Will there be other law enforcement involved?"

"One who will come on-site, possibly two. We will need to download the archives and remove file copies to our lab."

"We can arrange a time or times with the registrar. Is there any other information you might need?"

"We do have a question regarding the metaphysical concept of dark energy. The killer claims to be a spirit derived from dark space or dark energy in the universe and that he is only one of many, located throughout the world to keep it in the social and political turmoil we are experiencing daily. I know this may sound far-fetched, but is there any study of such a spirit world taking place on this campus?"

Jacob squinted in thoughtful silence for several moments before answering.

"We do have an extensive curriculum in religious studies. Not the paranormal, however. As much as we profess faith in an all-encompassing higher being, there are many historical interpretations of what constitutes that being. This is manifested in the diversity of religions we have in the world.   The concepts and laws and value system are essentially and comparatively the same. Unfortunately the claim to exclusivity and accuracy of an interpretation creates a serious problem, as we can see from the various holy wars and social conflicts occurring in the world today. Religious diversity is not an issue for most religious scholars. However, it is for those committed to a particular faith with the unwillingness to acknowledge the validity of other belief systems."

"Religious fanatics," Ed said. He crossed his legs and got comfortable as though Jacob's story were just getting good.

Jacob shrugged. "This will sound strange coming from a man in my position, but there is no empirical evidence, and there never has been, that any of the anthropomorphic Gods in the various world religions actually exist.

They are based on stories and fables and chronologies. God in whatever form he may take is an invention of man, not the reverse."

"Well, that's a theory too, I suppose," Leon said, in a tone that suggested Jacob was headed in an unhelpful direction.

"As you can surmise, I'm an agnostic. I believe in the unproven possibility and I recognize the value of faith for the social well-being of populations needing the psychological comfort to grasp something in the face of a vast unexplainable void in time and space. This has been going on since man first worshipped the sun and the moon and spirits of nature. There is also no proof to counter the possible existence of spirits derived from dark energy. We just don't make a study of them." He paused. "Does that satisfactorily answer your question?"

"Satisfaction is the opposite of how I would describe it," said Leon. "But it does answer the question in a rather convoluted there is no answer way. From an investigative and scientific position, we don't believe that there is some spirit or a conspiratorial group wreaking havoc throughout the world. That's like blaming the Devil for causing conflicting and aberrant behavior which has a psychological premise."

"That's true," said Jacob, "but I've discovered it is worthwhile to keep an open mind regarding such phenomenon. We're a society dedicated to explaining life using empirical evidence. There is much we don't know that is beyond our intellectual reach."

"That is certainly acknowledged, Mr. Bruce. We're not ready to capitulate to that possibility. Perhaps after we have exhausted all other avenues and investigative resources available to us," said Leon.

"I would expect nothing less."

"We've researched a profile of the curriculum for a student who might major in molecular genetics. If we are able to determine several suspects, there might be a trail leading to his employment in the commercial or government sector. We've begun a covert investigation. Any referrals and available employment history would be helpful."

"That information is included in the archives. If you'll pardon my comment, as I recall, Reverend Livingston was an outspoken opponent of genetic research of any kind."

Leon nodded. "Yes."

"The information we have exchanged will not be expressed further in this office or outside of it."

"That would be deeply appreciated. We are at the very inception of trying to understand who the killer is and the reasons for his behavior."

"Gentlemen, I'm happy to be of service." Jacob rose and they shook hands. "One question – given the available technology, would it not be more efficient to directly download the files?"

"Even with security encryption, we don't want to risk the possibility of the killer gaining access to the files. He might have already. He possesses the most advanced IT knowledge and capabilities. Our people attest to that."

"When shall we expect your associate?"

"He'll arrive in a few minutes. We'll accompany him and there will be additional security. I would ask that you explain to the staff that they should remain calm and go about their normal routines. They are not under investigation. We request that your IT director provide us with access codes and passwords, however."

Jacob picked up his phone.

"Please don't mention our purpose in being here."

"Of course – discretion."

* * *

Randy Newton copied and transferred the student records database from Georgetown University into a mainframe system that would allow him to quickly locate an identity based on a particular search protocol. To narrow the field of potential choices based on Leon's input from his meeting with the Georgetown official, Randy established a descriptive baseline profile of the graduate program in molecular genetics.

Randy keyed in the name Guzman for attendance between the years 1985 through 2004, which produced a moderate list of 235 male and female students bearing that surname. There were no Antonio Guzmans in the group.

He next tried students from South America and came up with 173. Eighty-seven were males. No Antonio Guzman, but Randy opened their files regardless. The killer had chosen the alias for a specific reason or had randomly made the selection. Randy began looking for a subliminal connection or referent association by the sound and spelling of the name to no avail. So he modified his search based on country of origin.

As Antonio Guzman, the killer's internet message to Leon placed him in South America. Randy searched and read numerous files of South American students from various countries, but did not detect any clues that would lead him to electronically link into State Department and INS archives. He switched over to Argentina and the period of government repression and genocide during the years spanning 1976 to 1983 and known as The Dirty War. If the killer's story were true, he could have been a youth at that time . Twelve student Guzman surnames emerged bearing origination from Argentina with seven placing them as young boys during the period of The Dirty War.

In reviewing the file, Leon began to see the basis for the killer's Guzman persona and that it might conceivably be derived from experiences as a youth in Argentina when his family could have been murdered by a death squad. He asked Randy to send him the seven profiles. After reading the third one, he believed he had a suspect, Rodolfo Josnan.

Josnan's trail led from graduate work at Georgetown University to a series of short-lived positions at three different biomedical research companies. The fourth and last one caught Leon's attention in a big way. Josnan had been employed in the biomedical research division of a privately held company called Unicell, a division of the First World Corporation.

The CEO was Hiram Bean, known through the media to be a devout Christian.

"Look at this," he showed Ed Berzinsky the company profile. "Unicell does stem cell research, an opposing value system."

"Is there a connection?"

"Only that Rodolfo Josnan worked for them and is using the name Antonio Guzman as an alias."

"Looks like we need to pay Unicell a visit," said Ed.

Nursing a hangover, Ed dozed during most of the long tedious drive to upstate New York. Leon didn't wake him until they arrived at the forbidding windowless complex tucked back along a winding road through the forest. Unknown to them, strategically placed surveillance cameras monitored their approach. A uniformed guard stepped out of his kiosk as they slowed and stopped at the lowered gate. His grim countenance belied his cordial greeting.

"Can I help you gentlemen?"

Leon and Ed showed their badges. "We're from the FBI."

"Do you have an appointment?"

"No, we're here on an investigation?"

"Your names?" he recorded them with a body camera.

"Special Agents Leon Safullo and Ed Berzinsky."

"I'll let security know you're here. Someone will meet you in the lobby. Guest parking is near the entrance."

"Thank you."

The guard stepped back into the kiosk and raised the electronic gate.

"Tight security," said Ed, as they drove the remaining distance to the front of the building. "Place looks like a fortress. Think they'll let us in?"

"They don't have a choice," said Leon.

Hands pressed against their sidearms signaled the arrival of the FBI agents did not impress or intimidate the three lobby security guards. From their bulked up bodies and war-like expressions, Ed guessed they were mercenaries, guns for hire.

"Gentlemen, we're from the FBI." Leon and Ed showed their badges. Leon presented the warrant to a fourth guard standing behind a raised counter that housed phones, two computers, and other electronic gear.

"What is your purpose?" asked the fourth guard, returning the warrant to Leon.

"We want to speak with your human resources director," said Leon.

"I'll see if he's available." The fourth guard picked up the phone and pressed a button. "This is the front desk. Two agents from the FBI are here. They would like to speak with you." He listened for a few moments, nodded, then looked up at Leon and Ed. "Mr. Thomas says you should wait here and he'll come down and talk to you."

"Tell Mr. Thomas we want to see him in his office."

"They want to see you in your office," the guard said into the speaker. He listened, then hung up and motioned to two of the other guards to escort Leon and Ed.

With hands at the ready on their holstered guns, the two guards rode the elevator with them to the tenth floor and walked them to the HR director's office. They tried to crowd in after them until Ed ordered, "Wait outside." They reluctantly withdrew and hovered at the receptionist's desk. Their presence alarmed her. She excused herself and quickly departed.

Leon interpreted he HR director's defiant expression and entrenched position behind his desk as a sign he was a gatekeeper unwilling to cooperate.

"This is an intrusion," his harsh flat voice challenged them. "We conduct top secret research here. Despite your warrant, I cannot give you access to confidential information."

"You can be prosecuted for refusing to cooperate with a Federal investigation." Ed's menacing threat did not intimidate the confrontational director.

"I'm calling our attorney." He pressed a button on his phone. "Daryl, Mark, there are two FBI agents in my office demanding access to confidential files. . . They have a warrant." Clutching the phone like a hammer, he listened to the attorney's cryptic order, then asked the agents, "What is it you want to see?"

"We need information on a former employee, Rudolfo Josnan," said Leon.

Mark spoke into the receiver. "They want information on a former employee." He listened, then terminated the connection. "I can pull up his file and watch you read it. But you can have no further access to any other data."

"Now you're being helpful," said Ed.

The director turned the computer screen so they could view it. Ed and Leon sat on chairs in front of the desk. The director accessed the archived file of Rudolfo Josnan.

They learned that Josnan had been hired to develop new product concepts that met both business and customer needs in the area of stem cell applications. After eight months, he had been fired on suspicion of stealing embryonic tissue for use in a private clandestine lab, but management couldn't prove it. No forwarding address was available.

As they departed the building, Ed remarked, "Isn't Herr Direktor a piece of work."

"Check Josnan's social security number with the IRS. See if there's any history," said Leon. "Wait until we're in the car driving away. Use a secure connection."

Fifteen minutes later, Ed placed the call and identified himself. "I need an identity check on a social security number for a Rudolfo Josnan." He gave the number, then waited for several minutes. The IRS agent came back on the line. Ed's exasperation was unmistakable. "Nothing? Nothing at all? I'll get back to you if we need something more. Thanks."

"The name and number have been erased," said Ed. "No further record. That means this

Josnan/Guzman hacked into the system."

"That also means he created two false identities," said Leon, "Guzman and Pearl. We need to look into the First World Corporation. Why would Guzman be going after Paul Evans unless someone higher up ordered it. Evans' company is the Helix Corporation. It's a subsidiary of the First World Corporation."

They left the forest that shielded the Unicell building and made the long drive back to the city.

Upon returning to headquarters, Leon requested that research provide him with the information he sought.

An hour later, he was presented with a report that profiled the First World Corporation and its CEO, Hiram Bean.

"Here it is," he said to Ed, who sat with Leon at his office computer.

"First World has controlling interest in the Helix Corporation, Paul Evans' company. It's possible political pressure was brought against Evans. The dark energy religious ploy used by Guzman might be linked to the CEO, Hiram Bean. According to the media, he's a fundamentalist Christian. Let's follow the trail. Guzman murdered the liberal theologian, Reverend Lawrence Livingston, who promoted tolerance among all religions and espoused religious unity. What do you think?"

"Maybe Guzman is an enforcer working for Hiram Bean."

"That could be a connection, but we're operating in a gray area. It's only conjecture. We don't have the evidence," said Leon.

"Why would Bean want to take down Evans?" asked Ed.

"No answer to that, at least not yet."

"So we have to follow Paul Evans."
"Yes, but first we have to find him."

Chapter 17

Matt straightened from rummaging down inside his pack. His long shadow moved across the erratic flare of the cooking fire reflected against a boulder that sheltered the campsite from the chilling night wind.

Paul nudged his stocking feet closer to the circle of the fire's heat. He watched his son add another log to the flames and check a pot of boiling water. Pulling on a glove, Matt lifted the scalding pot and poured water into two large aluminum mugs. He returned the pot to its resting place on a flat rock near the fire, then stirred a tablespoon of instant coffee into each steaming cup. He handed one cup to his father. Being careful not to spill his own coffee, Matt settled down near him.

Paul sipped his coffee. The cup's hot metal rim burned his lips. He ignored the sensation and concentrated on the taste and warmth of the liquid, which cooled quickly at the high altitude. "Tastes good," he said. He felt secure in their choice of a campsite. It was sheltered from the night wind by tall pines and several large granite boulders. He felt as though he and Matt were safe in a different world now. He had a sense of having left the civilized world behind and of escaping from the satanic force that threatened to claim his son. Paul realized he must find a way to exorcise the dreams that haunted him. He must regain control of his mind and banish the disembodied voice that spoke to him in his sleep so that it never plagued him again.

"Your headache go away?" Matt inquired.

Paul nodded. "Aspirin helped. Doesn't the altitude affect you? "

"A Little. I feel some light-headedness is all."

Paul grinned. "The endurance of youth."

"I took some aspirin too."

"Ah ha!" Paul prompted a tired grin from Matt. He nudged a burning log with his foot. The log sent up a shower of sparks that were briefly reflected in the nearby stream where their image flowed out like luminescent orange snakes.

The two men sat silently, secure in each other's company. "Different up here," said Matt. "Time to think."

"Yes." Paul did not push for conversation. The things he had to tell Matt would come in time, when they were ready to be said.

"I'm sorry about last night," Matt's voice was low and quiet. "I really wasn't looking for that fight to happen. And then again, maybe I was. Have to admit I got into the swing of it. I'm basically a peace-loving man, but when push comes to shove --"

"When I was about ten years older than you are now," said Paul, "I suddenly came to a point in my life when I lost enthusiasm for nearly everything. I hadn't become the success I thought I'd be. I was very disillusioned with people, especially myself. So I rationalized it by telling myself I'd either grown too insensitive or else I really didn't know what I wanted anymore. I didn't know how to relate to anything or anyone anymore. But somehow, I did relate. Something strange happened in my mind. I was disappointed with the promise of life because it hadn't been met; and I grew disappointed with myself, because the world wouldn't allow me to become what I wanted to become."

Matt watched his father's face. "What did you want to become?"

"A successful entrepreneur."

"You are though," said Matt. "You became an entrepreneur. A successful one."

"Yes, but it's no longer what I want and it's too late for me to change."

"What would you want if you could start over?" his son asked.

"I would want to become the person I was, to succeed at that."

"Succeed -- is that what you mean by the promise of life?"

Paul nodded. "In a personal sense."

"So how do you feel about the promise of life now?"

"I'm still trying ," said Paul. I can't help driving on. I'11 always be trying to better myself."

Matt nodded. "That's how I feel."

"I don't blame you for fighting. I'm ashamed to admit it. I was afraid. I've been afraid a lot lately, for you."

"Why?" Matt looked at him with questioning surprise.

"I..." Paul could not meet his eyes. "There are different ways of fighting, I guess. In some cases, there may be nothing you can do to fight back. You just have to accept what happens. It was the town, the people. They're being forced out of existence by men like me, companies like mine. Not that town in particular, but others like them, all over the country, farmers, ranchers. I own a company that is strip mining the land for minerals. And I have the sanction and blessing of the United States Government."

"Another case of let's fuck America," said Matt.

"I suppose the romantic notion of rural life disappeared a long time ago."

"What?"

"The romantic notion of rural life. Or maybe that's all we have left, a romantic notion. Maybe rural life never was romantic. When Lyndon B. Johnson was President, I was invited to the White House among other corporate leaders. I remember one of his key advisors making a statement that represents the true corporate and government attitude. He said it was a mistake to go too far in trying to keep people on the farm when it didn't make sense economically.

The government had no moral obligation to patches of land."

"Translated meaning patches of people," said Matt.

"Well, power does reside with the urban population. Even though the memory of rural life is quaint, I think now it's worth preserving. Our whole society was founded on frontier virtues. We've even deified them, turned them into advertising icons for banks and cigarettes. Frontiers are different now. They're in the world of finance, high technology, defense, and aerospace."

"It's the milk everything for a buck mentality," said Matt.

"Yes, deification. It takes place in the media. The heroes change form, but the content remains the same. The westerner and the frontier spirit are a cultural myth -- the Marlboro myth. The cowboy is nothing but a folk hero, a cigarette advertisement. We invent our gods according to how we want to see ourselves."

"Then why are you concerned about strip mining? I'm seeing and hearing a side of you I never imagined possible."

"I suppose it's the last shred of that promise I once believed in -- the illusion of the promise, not the reality. Realities have faults and shortcomings. Illusions never do.

The tide has turned a little against federal hypocrisy. But the government interpretation of land restoration is based on balancing costs, not grasslands and woods and wildlife. Rehabilitation doesn't even mean restoration to them."

"Them?"

"The money, the power, which includes me." said Paul. He held the tip of a long red stick in the flames. Pungent pine smoke rose into the air. The crackling wood glowed hotly. "I think it's a mistake to try and deal with corporations like people. It can't be done. When it comes to fighting corporate power, people have everything working against them because they believe in credibility, trust, and honesty. When you're talking about megabucks, credibility, trust, and honesty are irrelevant."

The sudden scream of a cougar wailed to them out of the night. They sat up, chilled at the eerie cry.

"Is that a mountain lion?"

Matt nodded. "Probably the one that old hunter's after."

"Gives you the willies." Paul put another log on the fire.

"We'll never see him."

"That's what worries me. He'll sure see us. I know better. I know he won't come within miles of us, but still, that sound."

"Yeah, makes your hair stand on end," said Matt.

"It's a cold night. Hope this fire burns a long time. I'm all for turning in." said Paul.

"Yep. have to take a piss, first." Matt rose and walked away several yards into the surrounding rocks and brush.

Guzman had been following Paul Evans and Matt for most of the day. They did not know he was within a mile of where they had settled down for the night and that he could see the light of their fire.

Guzman relished the planning and arrangement of people's lives. His alternate personality, Pearl, told him "You're a genius at it. Your victims are totally ignorant of what is being done to them. They are unsuspecting and predictable, like laboratory mice moving toward or away from food or light or shadow according to their manipulated patterns of behavior. By tampering with people's minds, you control the outcome of their behavior. You create your own absolutes, an unwavering fate and the manner and moment of death. You are the freer of souls to capture their light."

He would face a challenging task during the next few days. He would draw the act together according to his design, create the psychic bits and pieces, then the physical

transformation and finally the capture of Matthew Evans' soul.

He contemplated his early experimental days. Under Pearl's guidance, he had chosen to alter the minds of certain victims for their impact and effect and to sharpen his skills. Pearl was always available to him, a constant companion with whom he could carry on involved philosophical discussions and plan the deaths of others.

Those individuals were people who were in positions of authority and power and could influence the chaos planned by the dark energy spirits.

He had caused an attractive young single woman, an attorney who was organizing a class action suit against Hiram Bean and the First World Corporation, to commit suicide, for no apparent reason, slitting her wrists with a razor.

Another victim was the Vice President of Sales at the pharmaceutical company, Unicell. The man could not be trusted to keep silent about the DNA triple helix discovery. Guzman caused him to die in a chemical explosion in the laboratory.

A third incident was the drunken hit and run death of a small boy by a security officer employed at First World. The officer was suspected of leaking information to the press about First World. The man had never been known to drink alcohol. His car fender had raked away the top of the boy's skull exposing the brain. Guzman and Hiram Bean considered the boy's death collateral damage.

As with thousands of others working in the shadow world of Hiram Bean's intelligence forces, his mission was to jolt small segments of society out of their smug complacency and destroy local security and traditions.

It took him several years to master mass psychic functions and the accompanying destruction through crowd hysteria. He fostered the notoriety attached to assassinations. Those who murdered prominent leaders, the prime movers, themselves became prime movers.

Another trend to which he frequently leant his talents was the disintegration of traditional American culture through the excesses of its own people. He preyed on the dying breed of illusionists, the men and women who espoused positive values and the common good and tried to live according to those values, including the tolerance of other faiths.

For Guzman, causing an unexplained death or disappearance was the greatest of all his achievements. Death was a hard act to follow. He smiled at his little joke. *If they don't meet the obligations of their contract, the cost is so much greater. And they have to pay anyway. There is no other choice.*

Pearl watched him. Steeped in drowsiness, the tremor of a stifled yawn quivered across Guzman's features.

His wandering memories drifted to a woman in his past. She was a shy, conservative member of the secretarial pool in the First World Corporation. She looked to be about thirty-six. It surprised him to learn that she was forty-four and a childless widow. Her clothes reflected propriety and taste with an occasional flare of color, stylish and complementary in effect to Guzman, a hint of caprice. She was warm, good-humored, even-tempered, and witty.

Following his initial instinct about her, Guzman found her altogether likable, someone who could satisfy his sexual cravings. For one year, she brightened his lonely bachelor existence. Then the day came when he decided he must terminate the relationship, because of what she learned about him, that he was from the spirit world, a missionary, an enforcer for Hiram Bean. He did this by entering her dreams and manipulating her state of consciousness through the alteration of visual and chemical impulses.

Overnight, she changed from the balanced person she had been to a woman of restless, unrestrained energy, charged with an enthusiasm that bordered on the psychotic. She wanted to do anything and everything. She took up parachute jumping and hang gliding, often executing her jumps in the nude. On her final jump, she deliberately failed to open her chute.

"Like Icarus," he told Pearl, "she strove to fly too high and the sun melted her wings, in this case her mind. You see, our lives are predetermined by limitations beyond our understanding, natural laws and the laws of the universe where the sun is no longer the eye of God."

"You're not a religious man," said Pearl.

"I am very religious," said Guzman. "I mention God only in a vernacular sense. He's nothing more than a mythical figure, just another pathetic attempt to explain ourselves and give meaning to our existence.

"I understand what you're saying. We've all had some taste of life's injustice," said Pearl.

"There's no such thing as injustice.

Pearl never objected to Guzman's cynicism. Guzman continued to call on her, but she did not want to feed on his philosophical bleakness and allow him to diminish splashes of color and light in her life. As he constantly dwelt on life and world events with a profound pessimism, she withdrew from him.

Guzman determined he would convince her with the ultimate truth in a direct manner. He called on her late one night at her apartment, shared a drink and some light conversation, then slit her throat with a razor sharp knife. As her blood pooled on the floor, he explained to her the rightness and necessity of his act.

It happened because as in the laws of the universe, it was preordained to happen, it must happen, and in fact, it did happen. Her life flowed out as the thought flowed in. He had lingered in her mind for only a moment, satisfied and justified by the absolute terror and despair in her eyes that faded and lamped out.

You have come a long way preying on your current victim," said Pearl. You intimately know his habits, his strengths and weaknesses. You have invaded his mind and distorted his memories by projection of his own will. Evans is one of your greatest successes, until his resistance. But then, knowing him so well, you expected he would renege on his agreement. In fact, you planned and looked forward to it.

"The world does not exist to cooperate," said Pearl. It feeds on and destroys itself. Man creates his own hell. He is his own guinea pig and will not survive his experiment in the world.

"That will be the final step, destroying the diversity of humanity."

Chapter 18

Luther and his two sons stood side by side smoking Marlboros as they leaned against the fence rail and stared idly at the few clustered calves remaining in the corral. Their heavy noon meal had left the men sated, for the moment not wanting to move. Content with the bulging weight of substantial food rumbling in their bellies, they half succumbed to the cloudy lethargy that threatened to drop a curtain of sleep behind their eyes.

Luther flicked his cigarette ash to the dust and watched it scatter before a slight thrust of wind. He still smarted from his clash with Vince the day before. This time he was not able to throw off the recurring twinge of insecurity. Some stronger impulse was working in his mind and he tried desperately to push the thought away.

He had seen another packet in the mail, the second part of Willie's extension course. The signs of his sons' potential leave-taking twice in one batch of mail were almost too much to bear.

He must fight off the influences, keep anymore from coming. The outside world kept creeping in, threatening to destroy the one he had made. He couldn't build high enough fences to keep it out and his own in.

He viewed their lives and affairs as property, things to be managed like cattle from season to season, from calving to feeding to branding to market. He would not acknowledge any complexity or threat to his simplistic philosophy.

He felt disadvantaged by his lack of ability to understand and cope and to express himself; so he would shout down alternatives, dominate them with rage and power that shadowed his impotence of human compassion and understanding, believing that by silencing them he would prove his rightness and his son's alternatives would go away.

Joyce, did not concern him. He had long ago established that their life was here in their work. There would be no vacations to exotic locales. There would be no vacations.

Joyce had rebelled only once, but the sharpness of his physical and emotional fury had killed the desire in her. He allowed the travel literature and magazines, harmless daydreams that did not threaten or touch him like Vince's insidious implications of leaving. Luther feared such influences from the outside world.

Luther was half certain he could control Vince just by playing his game, even though it profoundly disturbed him and reflected on his own stature in comparison to those other successful, powerful men who sought to draw away his son with offers of money and position.

But it was Willie, with his recent extension courses and quiet persistent study night after night that caused Luther greater feelings of insecurity. For if Willie should ever leave home, he knew Vince would follow just to save face. Nearing the end of his cigarette, he stared at it and spoke to his younger son. "Willie, Vince and me can finish these last ones. There's still about ten, fifteen head down the south pasture. Bring those on up and I figger we can get 'em all branded this afternoon."

Willie nodded, tossed away his cigarette butt, turned and walked to the barn.

His chestnut quarter horse mare watched him bring saddle and bridle to her stall. She nosed him roughly. Restless with anticipation to leave the barn, she thrust her head for the bit. He quickly slipped the bit into her mouth, then pulled the headstall of the bridle up over her ears.

He smoothed the wool saddle blanket across the mare's back, then lifted and carefully placed the heavy stock saddle on the blanket and tightened the cinch under and around her belly. She laid back her small fine pointed ears and switched her tail at the pressure of the cinch.

Willie opened the stall door and led her out of the barn. As he mounted, his weight barely hit the stirrup before the horse set out at a quick eager walk. She had been cooped up for two days and her gait was springy with energy.

Vince saw Willie coming. He opened and closed the pasture gate for him before returning to his own horse.

Luther climbed through the fence and ambled along the corridor of the branding chute to his station.

With the open field before her, Willie's mare immediately stepped into a last lope, shook her head with exuberance and leaped into a run. Willie followed her motion.

The cold wind smashing his face touched off the soreness in Willie's eye. He tucked his chin into his chest and pulled his hat low, letting the mare run and just going with the run, leaning forward slightly, setting his weight in the stirrups.

Her stride was clipped and snappy with thrusting leaps, a way of running from which she had derived her name, Frog. The name was hardly traditional for a horse, but she had her own style, her own power. Her stocky build and unique personality displayed a certain animal elegance and grace.

The thudding hoofbeats of her gallop matched the rhythm of a remembered song that throbbed a painful reminder in Willie's still swollen eye. He hunched his shoulders and cringed with regret and embarrassment at the thought of his barroom brawl at Brogan's.

It was not his inclination to fight. He had not wanted it, yet he had struck first, unthinking, impulsively, as though some thing or someone else controlled his mind. He had wanted desperately to stop, but felt pushed, forced from within to continue against his will. He wondered why.

It must have been the time and place, he thought, the time and place and the others, the shaping of his whole life to the smoke and the beer, the heeled boots, the plain talk and living up to the image of being a man.

I won't let it happen again, he thought. And then one day I'11 leave all this cowboying... just leave it all behind.

It wasn't the hair or even the earring. He had seen other men with long hair and earrings, hippie cowboys. You didn't dare look sidewise at them either.

The man he had fought was more ferocious than he. He had been grateful for Vince's intervention, breaking in like that and pulling them apart. But something had happened between him and the other boy. He had the sensation of being filled with a warm light that connected them. He had no idea what it was or where the feeling came from.

When the man and his son had entered Brogan's, Willie had disliked the smirking comments and laughter from the crowd. He had looked around and clearly seen and decided. These people were closed off, rigid, his people. He was one of them, the difference being he was not threatened by outward symbols of other values, norms other than their own, which were plain and human and good except for their intolerance.

He knew he could never live all his life in this mountain community and continue to be like them, their unacceptance of things foreign. He would leave and there would be no wavering about it like his brother.

His brother, Vince, was the epitome of these people, steeped in the life and credo of the modern macho westerner. His brother was the original Marlboro Man. They could put his picture up there on those billboards along the country's highways and in those magazine advertisements and he would belong there.

Far out ahead in the pasture the fifteen yearling calves grazed within a half mile radius. He sighted them through slitted wind wet eyes, drew the mare to a walk and began a slow gathering of the calves as he approached them.

At first glance, the dead cow and her calf could have been asleep, lying on their sides in the sun, which flashed in Willie's eyes and for a moment hid the evidence of their death. That the animals did not stir at his approach aroused Willie's curiosity. He pushed on and saw the scattered entrails, twisted necks and staring bovine eyes clotted with black flies and maggots. He stopped.

Two large crows hopped away and rose on reluctant wings, keeling back and forth with the heavy glut they had scavenged in their black bellies. An eye and optic nerve dangled from the dark beak of one of the birds.

Slowly, Willie dismounted and stared down at the carcasses. Glossy black buzzing flies swarmed up in a cloud of irritation at being disturbed at their feeding. Willie's nose twitched at the rising carrion smell. A sudden warm drowsiness seeped through him in the presence of the reality of death.

He sat on the ground near the carcasses. His hand loosely clutched the ends of the dangling leather reins. He had braided them several years ago. It had been a time consuming project accomplished sitting in front of the fire on long cold winter evenings. That was before his interest in the correspondence courses.

He yawned deeply and fully and saw the two deaths as casual acts of natural violence that did not shock him, a painted ritual of blowing tufts of red cow hide, the flies, the drying slime of the guts, the enormous crows like cowled creatures watching patiently from the edge of the trees waiting for him to leave.   The sense of death was timeless. It weighed him down.

A high distant hawk cast about the windy sky.

He wondered only vaguely what animal had killed them; but the conjecture was blurred, a haze and would not come clear.

Sensing he was being watched, he rose and led his horse away until he could no longer smell the raw odor of the dead animals. He slowly swung up onto the saddle, as though in a dream, glanced back one more time, then set out at a lope for the corrals and barn.

He felt thoughtful, unhurried. The sense of urgency eluded him. The scene had touched something in him. Again he yawned. He stiffened trembling against the chill that consumed him. He looked down at his hand clutching the reins. He could not control his palsied shaking.

With a sudden start of fear springing from his mind like a rabbit out of brush, he whirled the mare around to a halt and saw the scavenging crows swoop down from the nearby trees. In an instant, horse and rider turned and leaped at a flat out run for the corrals.

Vince and Luther looked up at Willie's running mare and wondered why there was such an urgency and unnecessary speed. They watched Willie's face as horse and rider pulled to a sliding halt just short of the fence.

Breathless, unable to speak for a moment, Willie stared at them. He loved their faces.

Sensing that something was terribly wrong, Luther slipped through the fence rails and came over. His hand rested kindly on his son's thigh; the other clutched the back of the mare's neck with anxiety. He was afraid to startle Willie out of his apparent trance.

"Pa." He saw Willie's lips part softly. The boy's head turned slowly up and back indicating the direction from where he had come, as though he were trying to remember what he had seen and what he was to say.

"What is it, son?"

Willie's eyes came to rest on him, studying him, searching his face as though trying to discover him for the first time.

Luther fought back a sudden impulse to weep, for he saw in the desperate expression Willie, his infant son, looking at him.   "Pa, somethin's been at the herd last night."

Luther nodded, understanding but not hearing the words, caught in the emotion of his infant son in those eyes. "You say somethin's been at the herd?"

Willie nodded. Vince drew close so that he would be able to hear what Willie was saying. Willie stared at him a moment, then back at his father. "There's a dead cow and her calf out there."

"How?"

"Animal...guts spilled all over."

Luther placed his left foot in Willie's loose stirrup and pulled himself up behind his son. Vince maneuvered his horse, Dandy, through the gate to join them. They rode at a gallop down the valley scattering the indifferent cows.

When they arrived at the dead animals, Luther slid from the mare's wide rump to the ground. Ignoring the raillery of the circling crows, he bent to examine the carcasses. He knew what had attacked the cows the moment he saw the jugular arteries torn from their ragged throats.

"Mountain lion."

Vince rode in close and looked down from his horse. "Cougar?"

Willie remained mounted a few yards away. As a reaction to the atmosphere of animal death, he felt himself slipping off into a sleep where he could see himself there on his horse watching Vince and his father examine the carcasses.

Luther rose and stared off toward the trees. "Yeah."

As Vince followed his gaze, cold lust rose in him, a sudden need to get down and pick up handfuls of entrails and hold them squishing through his fingers. He swallowed with a taut emptiness in his stomach that only a short while ago had bulged with a full meal.

He could see them out there waiting, the image of cats, lethal death, challenging, beckoning, calling to him. He itched to hunt and destroy them.

"Vince!" Luther's loud voice startled him.

He looked at his father.

"Get the rest of the herd in. I want 'em close to the house. Willie, ride in and tell mama to call Denham Hunsinger. Then bring my horse and some strychnine out here. We'll lace these carcasses." Willie wheeled his mare about and rode off at a gallop. Vince rode away to gather in the scattered grazing herd. Luther slowly walked about and studied the ground in the vicinity of the carcasses. With a surge of anger, he stared again toward the trees at yet another encroachment on his domain, only this time not from the civilization he so despised, but from the wild with only one law of survival and no complexities. There he could strike back and kill a clearly defined enemy in a personal conflict that would end with a physical death of the enemy. In some small way, the act would salvage him from his own slow spiritual dying.

Chapter 19

The match flared and briefly illuminated Denham's seamy face as he paused near the pickup truck to light his pipe. He jettisoned three bursts of smoke from the corner of his moist lips. The white puffs dissipated against the stars.

He looked back thoughtfully a moment at the dark rolling lumps of his stone house then climbed into the cab, started the cold knocking engine and headed out up the road toward the night tipped mountain peaks.

During his life, he had been married four times and fathered eighteen children. Looking back, the fact amazed him. He hadn't seen the last child in five years. Somehow, seeing his grown children again no longer mattered.

Their faces and personalities had begun to blur several years ago and he had even forgotten some of their names. Their making was done and past as far as whatever he had to do with it.

Although he had some vestige of paternal feeling for them, he had passed beyond them into the last phase of his own life. His concerns now were of a different nature, spiritual. *Hell,* he thought, *I might not even recognize a few of them if we met on the street.*

He hadn't discovered hunting and guide work as an occupation until he was twenty-six, discovered in the sense that what he had done before was no longer enough to sustain his restless energy, not enough to satisfy his hunger for something more.

He wondered what he had been moving toward all his life. There had been dreams and plans. Some had materialized. Most had fallen by the way. He wondered if his life had been nothing more than a rash of blundering impulses without reason or design, without purpose or even importance.

As he drove, his mind wandered over indiscriminate impressions of the moment -- the unusual nature of his meeting with Anna and their common-law marriage, -- the act of hunting, the hot ritual of killing and death that afterwards became such a cold natural part of things, and yet soured his soul.

Somewhere out there, on this night when he would lie in wait of the co-mingled spirit of life and death, maybe he would find what he sought. He felt drawn to an unseen force somewhere in the mountains, those cold wild dark tombs where he had often stared up at the universe of stars and trembled at their vast beauty and his own insignificance.

After driving for what seemed to Denham a long time, he saw the lights of the ranch house in the distance. The Macke mailbox shone with a dull metallic glare in his plunge of headlights, as the pickup turned in and bucked and see-sawed over the dips and ruts.

Slowing on the turn, the old truck chugged, wheels grinding noisily over the gravel, and moved with inevitable intent toward the long low shadow of the distant house.

Luther Macke was in the kitchen getting a drink of water. With his head tipped back causing an uncomfortable pressure against his larynx, Luther tucked his jaw down into his chest to relieve the hard sensation of water rushing down his throat. "Drinking water should not feel this way," he thought. He turned off the tap and listened. Filtering out the dim television noise from the living room, he recognized the sound of Denham's approaching pickup truck outside.

The headlights hit the windows with a startling brief flash and disappeared. The truck idled in the yard near the back door. Luther put down his glass and stepped outside.

Carrying his rifle and rolled tarp and sleeping bag, Denham appeared from behind the open driver's door. The two men stood in silent contemplation of the dark valley rolling out to the rise of the far slope.

"Come in for coffee?" asked Luther.

"No, I'11 get out there now," said Denham.

Luther nodded. Denham touched the rim of his hat with the rifle barrel and walked to the fence. He let himself through the gate and listened to the steady crunch of his boots on the crusted frost. His step carried him toward that force out there in the night.

From the porch, Luther watched the hunter's diminishing figure until it was well beyond the range of the house light, then he turned back inside to rejoin his family. Standing in the doorway, Luther watched Vince reading the latest issue of "Western Horseman" magazine, and Joyce knitting while she watched a television variety show.

Willie had been missing since supper. "He should have been there in the nest of the family, the youngest," thought Luther. He knew where Willie was and what he was doing.

"Too much now," thought Luther. "This is getting to be too damn much, night after night like that. What would it take to hold him there, to convince him he never had to go away? There must be a way to make Vince and Willie see as he did, make both of them see."

BASIC ELECTRONICS

The letters blurred. Willie adjusted the position of his desk lamp, rubbed his tired eyes, and again leaned over the page. Loosely clutching a pencil, he traced a schematic diagram with exactitude and jotted a few numerical figures. His mind wandered to plans, the trip he would take next month to Denver University, the inquiries, especially how far a bootstrap scholarship would carry him. Then he would serve four years in the army.

There would be new people, new ideas, new things that he had heard of, had a touch of during his six weeks in army reserve training that Luther had tried to prevent him from joining.

Willie had recoiled at what many of the enlisted college graduates had said, the blasphemy cutting away at his beliefs so that he shunned them. But weighing his own beliefs against what they said, he realized their derisive statements about the military held some value for him.

There had been one recruit in particular just ahead of him in the line at the barber shop. Willie had joined the laughter at the shearing of that student's shoulder length blonde locks. The barber had been especially vicious and the young man had winced at the bloody nicks. Willie saw him fight back tears.

When it was his own turn, he realized the tears were not of pain, but of humiliation at being shorn in such a manner and treated as a nonentity, an object of ridicule and abuse in the dehumanizing military machine.

They had ended up in the same unit for the duration of basic. What had intrigued Willie about him was his quiet strength and stoic manner. He seemed to possess endless endurance, excelling in all tests and phases of training.

The drill instructors called him "super trooper." Privately to Willie, he vehemently condemned the men and the society that had put them where they were.

Willie could not understand why "the professor," the tag given him by other recruits, put out so much energy when he carried such an explosive charge of hatred for the military. Then one day, Willie realized that was how his platoon mate survived. The professor feared being jailed in the stockade and worse, being handed a rifle and ordered to kill. Willie read that fear in his eyes.

Willie did not feel the same as The Professor. He accepted being in the army as part of becoming a man. But what he saw in The Professor made him question the value system. The Professor clung to his freedom of spirit in the only way possible for him.

Willie began to ask him about that other world of ideas, higher education, trying to discover where the different values came from, trying his own against them and finding his own inadequate.

He did not hear the door open behind him, as Luther slipped silently into the room. The voice at his shoulder made Willie jump.

"Good program comin' on," said Luther.

Willie glanced up and pushed back his chair. "Didn't hear you come in."

"Hell, don't know why you waste your time on this stuff. Not gonna do anything for you. Won't get you anywhere. You don't really like that stuff?" Luther shook his head in answer to his own rhetorical question. All them diagrams and fancy 'rithemetic."

"Yeah, I do like it. A lot."

"I don't see no son of mine goin' off and wearin' a tie, settin' behind a desk pushin' paper instead of on a horse punchin' cows. Especially when you got everything you ever wanted or needed right here."

"I'11 be wearin' a uniform for a while."

"Uniform? What the hell you talkin' about, boy? You ain't active military. You're in the reserves."

"The army's gonna pay for my education and then I have to pay them back with time, four years."

"Well, fuck me! Now I have heard everything! You're not gonna go out there and have your ass blown away. Not if I have any say. "

"First, I'11 go to college for four years, then the army. I won't be in the infantry and I'11 be an officer."

Luther looked up at the ceiling. "Lord give me strength."

Willie shifted uncomfortably. "I feel like I want to move on to something else, Pa. See some of the world."

"Now you sound like your mother. It's rubbed off on you. You wanna see some of the world, go gander at her god damn travel magazines. The pictures are always better than the real places. I been around. I know."

"I want to try new things for myself. The ranch is really for Vince anyhow. We all know that."

"No, no, where'd you ever get that idea? Did he plant that in your head? The ranch is for both of you. My pa once told me the most sacred thing you can leave your sons is the land. He tried and failed. I ain't failed and ain't about to. What you need now is to find yourself a good steady woman. That'll take care of your itchy feet soon enough. She'll give you kids and responsibility. That'll make you grow up quick and clean those crack-pot notions out of your skull. Hell, you should have been married two years ago, yes. And Vince, Jesus Christ, he should have been married ten years ago. Good woman'll settle you down all right. And you can build your house along the river, that place you like."

Willie shook his head. "I'11 be around another year yet. Give you plenty of time to find a good second hand."

"Don't want no second hand, god dammit! I want you! I want my son! I want both my boys! Why can't the two of you get that straight?" Luther suddenly smiled. "Now, who was that pretty Little blonde you was dancin' with t'other night, for instance?"

"Trixie?"

"Trixie, now there's a name for you. Bet she's all over you in bed. Never took her eyes off'n you once the whole night. Now that should tell you somethin' important."

Willie shrugged and grinned. "Tell's me she's got good taste."

Luther leaned down and placed his arm in position to wrestle. "Come on. Take on your old man." He grinned.

Willie hesitated, then with a slow grin, shoved the tools and writing materials aside. He planted his elbow as a pivot, clasped his father's hand and nodded to begin.

They applied pressure. The skin of their palms and fingers blanched with the intensity. Willie managed to hold against him for a full minute. Then inch by inch, Luther forced down and pinned his arm.

Luther released his grip and smiled broadly with a knowing wink. "That TV program's started by now. Come on and watch with us. Don't sit back here alone and hide away from your family. We want your company."

Willie reluctantly pushed back his chair. Out of respect, he stood and left the room with Luther, who glowed in triumph at his son's departing back.

Coming in from the hall, they sat with Joyce on the sprawling leather couch. Vince put aside his magazine to watch the show. Luther's eyes rolled slyly as he looked at his gathered family with satisfaction.

......*

The air was cold and clear, the sky brittle with stars. The somnolent cattle stood calmly in the corrals and pasture near the barns.

Far out in the fields, Denham lay prone on his tarp in the damp meadow grass coated with hoar frost. His breath steamed on the night air as he watched the line of trees and the expanse of grass between them and the cattle. He checked his rifle partially wrapped in the wool blanket and waited.

Chapter 20

Shortly after the end of the television program, Luther and Joyce went to bed. Luther was feeling horny and aggressively maneuvered Joyce out of her nightgown so that he could get on with intercourse. He tensed, ejaculated quickly and just as quickly went limp, but continued plunging against his wife hoping that the stimulation would make him hard again.

Joyce's acid stare went unnoticed at his contorted huffing and puffing in the dark. She objectively studied the dim form of his head and body as he grunted, half-compressed a bubble of gas, and shifted, seeking a more favorable position.

A sudden rush of irritation swept her like a flush of fever. She knew she would feel nothing, could feel nothing. "That's enough. That's enough! Okay?"

He prevailed, trying with a gasp. "Didn't happen for you yet. Keep going. I can do it."

Knowing how it would make him feel, she resisted the impulse to push him away, allowed him a few moments more. "That's enough, now! You don't have to!"

"How was it?" He hovered over her like a walrus sweating from his exertion.

"It was fine."

"You sure it was okay?"

"Yes." She tugged her leg pinned under his weight. "Did you like it?"

"Yeah, but I want to be sure it's okay for you too."

"I appreciate your concern. You're getting heavy on me." Joyce waited impatiently for him to move. Luther hesitated a moment, gathering his strength, then with an effort rolled off her, lying with a leaden arm slung across her breasts. The angle and weight were painful to her. She moved his arm down to her abdomen.

His semen streamed out of her, soaking into the sheets and mattress. She cursed silently. She would have to sleep on the greasy dampness. It was always on her side of the bed.

Her hand tore tufts of Kleenex from the box next to her pillow. She dabbed at the musky scented wetness pooling between her legs. She waited, clutching the Kleenex in her fist. "It's late. We should go to sleep."

A sigh expired from his lips. She glanced over to be sure he hadn't suddenly died on her. "You all right?"

"Just thinkin' about that damn Wyandotte and Vince not sayin' nothin'," his voice rasped close in her ear. His hot breath came with effort. "My boys don't show me no respect no more. Don't listen to me. Just go their god damn way." He rolled over onto his back. "I won't let 'em do this to me. I can't. Especially Vince. Willie I can handle, but Vince, never, can't. Even if I have to call Wyandotte myself and tell 'im Vince ain't interested, can't be bothered. Got hisself a position already and don't want to leave. I need Vince to run this spread. It's all natural to him -- raisin' stock, training horses. He's natural born to the life. He even talks their language. Never seen another like him. Never in all my days. And I have seen the best."

Joyce sifted his words through the dark silence, how much was idle threat, how much fact. "Don't call Wyandotte, whatever you do. Vince'll know and it'll make you look bad. Then he'll leave for sure."

"You wouldn't tell Vince!"

"No, of course I wouldn't tell him."

"And now Willie sayin' he'll be gone in another year. I don't understand it. What can be goin' on in their minds? Why do they even think about leavin'? Ain't I been good to them? Don't they know I love 'em?"

"You been good and they know it."

"You don't want to see 'em go, do you?"

"They're my boys too."

He remained silent for a few moments. "What's gonna happen when we get to be old?"

"We are old," said Joyce.

"I mean really old."

"There comes a time when you have to let them go," said Joyce. "For Vince it's long over due."

Luther sat up and stared at her. He held himself from striking her across the face.

At midnight, Vince lay sleepless, naked. His hand fondled and pulled at his swollen genitals. The other massaged his erect nipples. He suddenly rose from bed with a restless oath and padded quietly down the hall to his brother's room.

Willie lay in calm sleep, only subconsciously aware that the door slowly opened and that his brother peered in.

Vince felt immersed in the ritual sounds of dreaming. He listened to his brother's breathing in the hush of the night. Fighting his own guilt and desire. Vince shuddered in turmoil, stared at Willie's serene face, childlike, beautiful in sleep. Vince entered the room and bent over him like a parent would his child to be sure he was still breathing, had not died in the midst of a dream. Except for the steady serene rise and fall of Willie's abdomen, he appeared to be dead.

Vince had dreamt of his younger brother dying. Willie brutally murdered. His throat slashed. Vince had no idea why the dream occurred, but it disturbed him. He quietly withdrew, closing the door.

His long angry strides carried him back to his room. He hesitated near his bed, then lay down and stared at the ceiling. He fought for control, then released himself to tears that erupted from his wide eyes.

Exhaling a sudden rasping oath, he rolled with an abrupt jerk onto his side and, with an argumentative tug pulled the slipping blankets over his shoulders.

Out in the pasture, stiff from lying in one position, Denham sniffled and wiped away mucous that chilled, clinging to the hairs on the back of his hand. He shifted, unable to dispel the discomfort lodged in his hips. He watched and waited with the damp chill seeping into his old bones so that he had to swallow groans of minor agony. To divert his mind, he thought of the night and the meeting of Anna eight years ago.

Had it only been that long? It seems like years...many years...almost a lifetime... But there were things about her.

God, you might never have met her but for that lousy check. They called it a 'gold check.' What a laugh. Ten cents, supplemental income. What was it supposed to supplement, a gumball machine?

Hell, they took more 'n a hundred dollars a week out of what I earned for over thirty-five years. Livin' in that last pig sty of a place. Golden age of retirement, shit. 'Course I couldn't take any money out of the restaurant. That was all for the kids. Couldn't be any other way. Wouldn't want it to be. But still, things weren't the way they should have been. Could hardly buy groceries. Jumped the damn prices every time you turned around. Ten cents. Would have been embarrassed to walk into a bank with it. Ten cents. An insult to human nature. A God damn insult.

Tired of counting pennies then. Living in a trashy neighborhood, eating trashy food. Never thought it would turn out the way it did. I had to do it. Either that or end up in a flop house, or maybe an asylum. Damn well couldn't throw myself on the kids' mercy. Still had my pride. Same thing, sitting in a rocking chair feeding on memories. And so here I am. Old fart stickin' it out. Still got the yen for it. Still want the excitement, all stops out. Even die that way. Maybe even lookin' to. Won't be as nice a way to go as wrapped up in Anna's warm lovin' arms, but goddamn I've got to go soon.

Back then, had to take what I had and just leave. City monster eatin' up all I had. Banks. God, back in the old days, would've just gone right on in and robbed one of the sons-of-bitches. Even thought about it, a lot, in those days, standin' there waitin' for the lousy son-of-a-bitchin' clerk to count me out. Shit, didn't leave me with nothin', not even a damn dime.

What would I leave it for? Kids 'ud never see it. State would grab it all. What they got already though is more than enough, so. . . Done my duty by 'em as a father. No question about that. Old truck still holdin' up. Must be doin' somethin' right, or else, Lord, you're smilin' down at me. Just drive and see what I come to.

Must have been the plants hangin' in her windows. different shapes and sizes. The pots reminded me so much of Tessie, and the land around the house, way it was overgrown with fieldgrass and wildflowers, like I finally come home and knew it. My restin' place in life. Just waiting for the introduction.

She was drinkin' tea and I knew it was tea, herb tea. Woman like that don't drink coffee. Don't take nothin' foreign to her body, not with skin like that, high color in her cheeks like a flushed babe. She would drink wine though and allow me my Jack Daniels and beer. I ain't a drunk and she knew that.

Never know what a broke down truck'll bring you to. But here, somehow knowin', because you're lookin' for just that, like you've been there before maybe in a dream. The tea bag wet and heavy and her squeezin' it wrapping the string around it against the spoon. And she seein' you hot and thirsty out there in the shade across the road.

I must have looked like a tramp, me, but an old man and not overly proud, because in life it don't matter, and carin' people don't think about that, oldness. Just know my own pride in myself. And she smiled and nodded at my walkin' up and she's sayin'. 'Looks like you've come a long ways.'

"Truck broke down." I says. "Town far?"

"Three miles."

"Good distance to live away from a town. Hot, sun."

"Lemonade?" she asks. "Cold? Like some'"

I nodded.

"Come on up. Get in out of the sun."

Didn't have to ask twice. Didn't ask me in right off though. Either careful or shy. Both now that I know.

"Be right back," she says.

And I sat quick, tired, so tired. God, old legs throbbing. "Thank you. Thank you very much," I said.

She went in and I could hear the making, the clinking of ice and glasses; and she brought out the pitcher and glasses on a tray and I tossed one off fast, bitter-sweet good, stuck in my throat.

"Don't drink that too fast on a hot stomach," she warned, wifely, motherly. She sat on her rocker, took up her tea again and watched with that little smile like I was amusing to her, sayin' thanks and takin' another glass, only drinkin' that one slow, because she'd said to. I watched her to see she noticed I was takin' her advice, and I sure wasn't in no hurry to be leavin'.

Sitting there with her, at her feet, seemed so natural, like we'd both just been waiting for it to happen for many years and now we'd finally come to it in time.

Not wanting to frighten her but needing to know. You ask a question of a lone woman like I did and some think you're out to do 'em in. But you go careful about these things and there was almost a knowing without asking. But bein' me, I asked it anyway.

"You live alone?"

Her slow easy smile reminded me of sunlight spreading across a field. Everything about her was touched with light and entered into me and filled me with light. She was a kind and good-hearted woman who seemed to hold some special power. She nodded.

"I don't have a place." I said, and it was natural to say and my statement was accepted by her. "Had places before, but not now." I said. "Been married four times, rich and poor. Happy in both. Last social security check was ten cents. Not the main one, the supplement. Pulled up all my savings and all my roots, what there was, and there ain't much left when you're alone. Knew there was somethin' better in life, even at sixty-five and I set out to find it."

She looked at me a long time and I felt uncomfortable. Didn't want her to think I couldn't pull my own weight. But she surprised me and said, "It's nice to have company."

Nice to have company. That sunk in a long time, warm and deep and I had no desire to stand up and go my way. So wanting to stay, and not wanting to be too forward about it, I sat there tryin' to figure out how to let her know, even though knowin' that she knew. She played a little game. She was gonna make me earn the right. Could tell by the little smile about her mouth. But she had to ask my name. Made her do that part. My little side of the game.

"What's your name?" she finally did ask.

"Denham Hunsinger. Good name. Come from a worthy background. As I said, married, kids, made money, lost it, went through all that many times. Yours?"

"Anna Bischoff.."

"Lived here a long spell?"

She nodded. "Seven years. I came here after my husband died. The air is clean. The mountains are quiet. Darkness can't find me here."

We sat silent in respect of her memory. Then she said. "You won't find a place open to help you on Sunday."

"Didn't expect to and don't mind, seein' I'm in no hurry."

"The Ryersons' run a motel just in town." she said.

She was makin' it hard for me, so I said, "Don't care in particular for motels. Can sleep out. That's what I come up here for. Slept out a lot in my life. The ground and the stars are free."

"We pay a price for the ground too," she said.

Thought it strange her sayin' that, but it must have been somethin' of a struggle for her, wantin' a new relationship but still faithful to the memory of her husband. I admired that, but it left me uneasy as to my place there, and the situation, movin' further along than as it was, us sittin' there on the porch passin' time. But then we both feared that passin' time and she suddenly said, "If you're anything like I imagine, you like a good pork roast."

"Got to say I am partial to lean pork."

"Good." She stood up. "Then you'll stay for supper."

"Nothin' I'd like better, Anna."

Later, I soaked in a hot tub she run for me and put on some clean clothes from my bag. Anna poured me a whiskey and put out wine with dinner, and sweet old music and candle light and I was figuring on a night like I hadn't known in a good long time.

She was still full in the bosoms and let it show to me. She wore bracelets and earrings and talked light and happy about her sculpture and plants and pottery. Lookin' about, I began to realize from the style that most of the paintings on the walls had been done by her hand too.

The house was a warm solid place built of stone. Without sayin', neither of us wanted to be alone no more. But there was propriety to be observed at a time like this and you just don't rush things like jumpin' into bed, things that are important, feelings, even at our age, especially at our age. But she led me to bed. I didn't push for it, to my knowledge, but I didn't refuse nothin' either.

It was all so natural, like a place had been made and was waitin' for us to come bring the ends of our lives together.

We made warm sweet love and afterwards I slept like I hadn't done in a long time.

He felt his head nodding. A sense of change in things moved out there in the liquid night. The two mountain lions could have been shadows slinking toward him from the forest, starting somewhere, back for a caper. But there was never time to think.

He pumped off four fast shots with little aim. To Denham, the cats were dancing dark shapes in a dream and it wouldn't have mattered if he hit them or not. They whirled about, streaked back to the trees and were gone.

He woke with the noise of his own gunfire roaring in his ears and thought maybe it was only the noise that had kept him from trailing off into a death sleep. Sleep seemed to be pushing up there too much lately, warm-clouding his brain.

Far across the expanse of property behind Denham, lights came on in the house. The occupants had awakened at the sound of his gunfire.

Denham stood slowly. His muscles trembled with stiffness. He looked toward the trees where the cats had gone. Then he rolled up the tarp and bedroll and walked past the skittish cattle, whose inquisitive bovine stares followed him toward the house.

A light came on in the kitchen. He saw a flurry of shadows as the door swung open. Half-dressed, Luther and his sons stumbled out into the frosty night air and waited for Denham at the gate as he walked in.

"Did you get 'em?"

"Might have wounded one. Find out in the morning. Cold as a witches tit out there." Denham passed through the gate.

"Come on inside. Get something hot in you."

Blowing and muttering, shoulders hunched against the cold, the men lumbered to the house.

Joyce was already up in robe and slippers brewing coffee and frying eggs and sausage. She looked to the door at their shuffling entrance, then quickly set the table as they gathered around.

"What happened?"

"Gone. Run off," said Denham.

"Sit down, all of you," ordered Joyce. "Be ready here in a minute. Denham, you must he frozen."

Denham leaned his rifle against the wall, removed his hat and coat and joined the others, who, out of respect, waited until he had seated himself first.

Luther filled four small glasses from a quart bottle of bonded whiskey and handed the first to the older man. Denham drank it down in two swallows with a loud gasp. Luther refilled Denham's glass and placed the bottle within his easy reach. Denham tossed off the second glass, then refilled double. This time he drank slowly.

Vince drank and half refilled his own. "You get a close look at 'em?"

"Too dark for a close look."

"They look big?"

"They're big."

Vince nodded, satisfied, and drained his glass. "Sure like to get them cats."

Luther studied Denham's face. "How's the guide business?"

"Deer season comin' on.'Spect it'll pick up soon." He paused. "Didn't get out as much the past year. Feelin' old," he held out his arm, "and stiff."

"Not you. Lyin' out there on the cold ground don't help a body none. What do you make them cats'll do next? I'm not anxious to have 'em feed off my stock all winter."

"Oh, they're scared off all right. But now they got a good taste for fresh beefsteak. Beats mule deer." He drank a sparing sip. "Won't be around for a while though. Not 'til snowfall. Won't be much game in the high country then. That's when they'll come back. Follow the deer down."

"It'd be worth my while to go after 'em," said Luther. "Can't afford to lose any more stock. Pay you double the fee."

"Kin always use the money. But let's talk about it in the morning. You're a good friend and neighbor. Not as if I'd be haulin' some city dude up there to feel like a man and play at bein' Kit Carson."

He stared into his glass. "Haven't gone after a big cat in six years. Could be the last chance...last time for me. Time before, down in New Mexico. Used dogs. Four of 'em died in that one. Fierce, bloody. Won't use dogs this time. This time, different . .. go after 'em clean, stalk, quiet. In the morning, I'11 read sign. If there's blood, I know where they'll be headin'."

Joyce placed a large plate of eggs and sausages before him. He clutched his fork and dug in without waiting for the others. It was his privilege.

Joyce quickly served the others, poured mugs of steaming black coffee for all, set an apple pie at the center of the table, then seated herself.

Ravenous noises of chewing and swallowing replaced conversation. Denham finished first, cut a large hunk of pie and ate it quickly, washing it down with coffee.

The men rode out at dawn and searched the ground. Denham found a sporadic trail of faded fresh blood against white frost on the meadow grass.

"Hit one of 'em, all right. Not bad, but enough to send 'em runnin' for home." He turned to Luther, Vince, and Willie. "It's a three day ride to where they're goin'. I'11 head on back now and bring up my outfit. Be here at noon."

Luther grinned his appreciation.

Vince stared at the traces of blood leading away into the trees. Behind him, the others mounted their horses. As they started back across the pasture at a walk, he watched them a moment, then mounted slowly and followed.

Denham maneuvered his stake-bed truck so that he could unload the pack mules near the Macke corrals and barn. He climbed down from the truck cab, went around to the rear and lowered the tail gate. He positioned the ramp, then walked up into the truck.

The rancid ammoniac stench of urine rose sharply in his nostrils. The toe of his boot nudged a pile of fresh droppings steaming in the cold air.

Untying the lead rope, he faced the first mule and applied pressure through the lead and leather halter across her Roman nose. She backed intelligently out of the stock truck. Her hoofs pounded the wooden planks beneath the thin layer of soiled wet straw. She felt out each step, being sure of her footing, her large fuzzy gray ears cranking back and forth registering sounds of her progress.

"Come on, Babe," Denham spoke at her soft brown muzzle, applied steady pressure on the halter and pushed just above the brisket at the base of her thick neck.

She hesitated, farted explosively, then backed down the remaining distance on the ramp with a clatter of hoofs. Denham then led her over to the corral fence and tied her to the bars. He went back to the truck for the other two mules and his own saddle horse.

Vince helped him load the pack saddles on the three mules, then looped three quick diamond hitches in rapid succession, while Denham saddled and bridled his horse.

Her hands smelling of dish water, Joyce came out of the house to watch the men and their final preparations. Luther led his horse from the barn and handed the reins over to Vince.

"Need to take a last shit before we leave," said Luther. Squeezing his buttocks in anal agony against the extrusive threat of his bowels, he walked with quick jerky steps to the house.

As Denham saddled his horse, the gelding sucked air and expanded his ribs against the pressure of the wide hemp cinch. Denham walked him several steps about the yard forcing him to expel air, then pulled the leather the last few inches, executed the cinch knot through the metal ring, and dropped the wooden stirrup and saddle skirt back into their hanging position.

Joyce saw that Vince and Willie were tense and impatient from waiting for their father. A hunt was different than day to day routine. Excitement and the prospect of danger flared from their eyes. They were aroused, in a heat, all of them. She had known the look and what it contained many times before. The mannerisms, a man's gut-wrenching anticipation of sex, barely able to restrain himself hovering above a hot naked woman. Only this was something different, something more for them.

His bowels quivering, Luther squeezed and grunted, flexing his rectal sphincter like a camera lens. He decided the impulse to shit was mostly nerves, but that he needed that last moment of solace alone in his house, a moment to plan and think.

His mind groped. Somehow, somewhere on this hunt, he determined to find a way to seal the conflict with his sons. He needed the hunt, not so much to protect his cattle, but to protect himself, to bind his sons to him once and for all.

They all needed it, the foursome. It was the going off alone together of men without women, the sharing of experience, closing the emotional circle around a kill, an unspoken male bond of understanding. After that, nothing had to be said.

The others were mounted and waiting when he returned. He gave Joyce a perfunctory kiss good-bye, then swung up onto his horse.

Anxious to get away from her womanliness and aura of domesticity, the men set their horses out across the pasture at a brisk walk.

Joyce closed the gate and watched until the riders were small figures against the nearest valley slopes. Then she went into the house, poured a strong whiskey and changed for her trip to the city. Three or four days was not a long time. It was the getting away that mattered, seeing new places, doing new things, however small.

Her niece's children would be a year older now. She regretted not yet having grandchildren of her own. Still, she had her sons. Not the same, but with them grandchildren would happen late in life. Her sons had to find the right girls. And then, her grandchildren would have the world.

She locked the doors, took a final look around the empty ranch yard, then drove off in the pickup truck.

As she passed through town, a sudden light-heartedness bubbled up into her head. She had escaped. She was free. Rolling down the mountainside, she burst into song. Here, beyond the fences, with the open road ahead of her, she let it come forth.

Chapter 21

"I took him to JFK," explained Paul's chauffeur respectfully to Leon and Ed. "Since he didn't have any bags, I thought he might be meeting someone and asked if he wanted me to wait. But then he sometimes travels without luggage. He said, no, and told me just to take a couple of days off. Usually, he's more specific about when he wants me to be available. So that struck me as being a little strange."

"When he entered the building, what airline was it?" asked Ed.

"American."

"We've run a search on every airline, bus line and train. So he may have gone into the airport, but he never got on an airplane. We also checked out corporate jet services, nothing."

"Are you sure you actually saw him go inside the terminal?"

"Yes, I was standing beside the limousine and I watched him enter the building. I even waited ten minutes just to be sure."

"Obviously, he didn't leave from JFK. He didn't leave from anywhere of record, which is why we're concerned."

The chauffeur shifted his weight as though he were beginning to feel uncomfortable, suspecting that for some reason the two agents might not believe him. "I wish there was something more I could tell you, but that was the last time I saw him."

Leon smiled kindly and patted the man's arm to reassure him. "We don't question what you're telling us, Pat. We're trying to piece together in what manner he disappeared from the last time you saw him. It's possible that after you departed, he came back out and left the terminal by some other means."

"We suspect he might have been escorted out."

"You mean kidnapped?"

Ed nodded. "Did Mr. Evans employ a bodyguard?"

"Not as long as I've been driving for him." Pat smoothed back his springy red hair.

"Do you carry a weapon?"

"No, I'm not licensed and I've never been comfortable around guns," the middle-aged driver asserted firmly.

"How would you describe his behavior when you met him with the limousine?"

"He was anxious, in a hurry I think."

"Well, Pat, I don't think we have any more questions for now. If something else occurs, we'll get in touch with you."

"It's okay to leave?"

"Thank you. It's okay to leave." Leon stood and extended his hand. Pat gratefully grasped and shook it with visible relief.

Ed checked the list of Paul Evans' staff. He and Leon had questioned the five vice presidents who were Paul's direct reports and had not detected anything out of the ordinary in their responses nor could they shed any light on who or what competitor might want to either ransom or take Paul out of the picture.   Leon brought many years of experience as a profiler with the Investigative Support Unit in the field of criminal analysis, whereas Ed was recognized as being among the top field agents. He liked to get physical and he didn't mind showdowns.

Leon and Ed conducted the interviews in the executive conference room of Paul's office. Each person was advised that their comments were being recorded. The questioning of the Human Resources Manager and review of personnel files of employees who had been let go did not suggest personalities who would seek some form of retribution.

"We need to talk with Evans's secretary next," said Leon to Ed. "She should have the most knowledge about his personal and business life. You want to call her in? Tell her to bring a printout of his travel itinerary and meetings during the past year."

Ed stood from the conference table and stepped through a glass door to the outer office. He returned with her ten minutes later. Leon rose to meet her.

"Miss Porter, I'm Special Agent Leon Safullo." They shook hands across the table. "We have a few questions to ask about Paul Evans. We're investigating his disappearance."

"You requested these." She handed him the list of meetings.

"Yes, thank you. Please, have a seat."

After studying the list, he asked, "What can you tell us about this meeting he had on the day he disappeared? He met with Charles Rossman, Vice President of Acquisitions from the First World Corporation."

Nicole Porter studied the list for a moment, then leaned back in her chair. Leon noted her fashionable subdued business attire coupled with an aura of intelligence, efficiency and competence for which she was well compensated. Her luxurious brunette hair swept back from clean cool cover girl features that required no accents to highlight the natural beauty of a narrow slightly tipped nose bounded by rising cheek bones that pushed delicately against her pale skin. Aggressive blue almond shaped eyes assessed him. Given her knowledge and position, Leon knew she would be protective of her boss.

"Mr. Evans is not always consistent about having me take minutes. It depends on the nature of the meeting. Certainly I do at staff meetings, but others have a certain level of confidentiality that exclude my presence."

"Would you say that Mr. Evans is a secretive person, likes to operate from behind closed doors?"

"I don't understand what your question is leading to."

"Does answering the question make you feel uncomfortable?"

"No, I just need to know where you're going."

"Why is that, Miss Porter? Have you been instructed not to answer questions of this type?"

"I beg your pardon. I'm not trying to hide anything."

"I don't believe you are."

"It sounds like you're making an accusation," said Nicole.

"It's a simple question. Based on your experience as Mr. Evans's secretary, would you say that he's a secretive person."

"I don't know what I think has to do with anything."

"We're trying to arrive at a sense of who Paul Evans is. That knowledge and series of impressions allows us to create a profile that may contribute to the circumstances relating to his disappearance. His profile will also assist us in identifying other profiles that may be linked to him so that we can determine the causes of prospective interactions."

"He's no more secretive than any other CEO, as far as I know."

"Have you worked for other company presidents?"

"I've held three other positions."

"And how long have you worked for Paul?"

"I've worked for Mr. Evans for approximately seven years."

"Would you say, then, that you have some insight and understanding of his style, his methods and manner of conducting business?

"Yes."

Leon paused. He noticed that Berzinsky watched her with more than prescribed professional detachment. He was mentally undressing her.

"So, the meeting with Rossman."

"That was one of the confidential ones."

"There must have been some indicators. What does First World do? You coordinated the appointment."

"I believe they are a venture capital and acquisitions company."

"Did Mr. Evans seem to you to be upset after the meeting?"

"He exercises very good control over his emotions."

"Good control."

"When things go wrong, he takes a very objective approach to solving the problem."

"When things go wrong."

"Yes."

"Did you detect that something was wrong after Mr. Rossman's visit?"

"I don't know. I can't say. Mr. Evans remained in his office."

"Behind closed doors."

"Yes, behind closed doors."

"Did Mr. Rossman say anything to you?"

"Nothing, other than to introduce himself and present me with his business card."

"How would you characterize his demeanor at the time?"

"I suppose he was happy."

"Happy?"

"He came out of the office smiling."

"Did he say anything further to you?"

"It was late in the day. He wished me a good evening."

"Did Mr. Evans see you again or say anything to you?"

"He just told me over the intercom to take any messages and that he would be gone for a while. I notified his limousine driver that Mr. Evans was coming down."

"Did you actually see Mr. Evans leave?"

"No, he has a private elevator to the garage."

Leon was hoping she could describe his expression, any nonverbal movement or conduct, but she had not seen him.

"Do you ever speak with his wife?"

"Mr. Evans is separated from his wife."

"We understand that. Did you ever speak with her?"

"Only to put her calls through to Mr. Evans."

"Were there any recent conversations when she might have called him?"

"No, Mrs. Evans is hospitalized and is under psychiatric care. She doesn't call him."

"How long have they been separated?" asked Ed.

"Fifteen years."

Leon made a mental note of her quick response. "Have there been any incidents in the business, out of the ordinary of normal day-to-day activity?"

Nicole shook her head and offered a slight smile. "This is an office, gentlemen. A little crisis here or there is not out of the ordinary. We just take care of it. That's what we're paid to do."

"And I'm sure you do it very well," said Leon.

"Any further questions?"

"Oh, one or two," said Ed. "Based on our initial research regarding The Helix Corporation, Paul Evans partnership with Jim Owens was discontinued. That occurred about the time you joined the company. Did you also work for Mr. Owens?"

"Mr. Owens had his own secretary."

"Did you or the two of you attend staff meetings?"

"Yes, usually one of us. We would provide minutes to the other."

"What do you remember happened at the time of the breakup?"

Nicole remained silent and slumped back in her chair. Leon noticed that her eyes rolled to the right instead of to the left. She was inventing instead of remembering. Berzinsky's question had caught her off guard. They had something to pursue.

"I was not in the meeting," Nicole began.

"Do you remember who was?"

"The Board of Directors, Paul - er Mr. Evans, and Jim Owens."

"Do you remember hearing anything, any impressions either while they were in the conference room and when they came out?"

"Shouting -- I do remember shouting."

"Who was shouting?"

"Mr. Owens."

"Any words or phrases come to mind?"

"That was seven years ago."

"You're doing fine, Miss Porter. Was his voice raised in anger?"

"Yes, he was very angry."

"Did you see him when he came out of the conference room?"

"Yes."

"And?"

"He was crying."

"Crying?"

"Yes, crying in anger. Mr. Owens was a gentle trusting sort of guy. Real nice family man. He was also the brains of the company. He came up with the new product ideas. R&D guru. He was Vice President of Research and Development."

"Did he say anything to you or to his own secretary?"

"No, not a word. He walked out of the building and we never saw him or heard from him again."

Leon nodded.

"Did his secretary follow him?"

"Pardon?"

"Did she go with him to wherever he was working next?"

"No, she signed on with a temp agency. I never maintained contact with her."

"Were you aware of any tension between Mr. Owens and Mr. Evans before this incident? Arguments, disagreements?"

"I -" Nicole absently shook her head, "I would say their original friendship was -- eroding."

"Would you say they were good friends until the separation?"

"Yes, according to Mr. Evans."

"So Mr. Evans told you about their friendship?"

"Just somewhat."

"Here at the office?

"I don't really remember where. At a party once, over cocktails."

"Do you remember the conversation?"

"I think I had had a few too many martinis."

"Had Mr. Evans been drinking martinis?"

"I don't know what Mr. Evans drinks. I suppose."

"Do you keep his bar stocked?"

"You mean here, in the office?"

Ed nodded.

"I have it replenished if necessary. Cocktails are sometimes served to important visitors."

"Is Mr. Evans a heavy drinker?"

"What do you mean by heavy?"

"Does he drink a lot and often?"

"I've never seen him come to work with a hangover, if that's what you mean."

"You've never seen him drunk?"

"No, not really."

Leon posed the next question. "Have you ever seen him act in a manner that was not like his usual self, like being depressed or unusually stressed?"

"He managed his stress quite well. He didn't let situations get the better of him. He was a very good negotiator and basically he took charge and got whatever he wanted. It came easy for him, the times I saw him in meetings."

"You admired his skill."

"Respected and admired, yes."

"What was the nature of his social life?" asked Ed pointedly.

Nicole gave him a cold hard stare. She knew what information he was driving for, but it would not be forthcoming. "His social life was none of my business, Mr. Berzinsky. I made reservations for dinner and travel and such, but that's all."

"You went to parties with him occasionally."

"I went to company parties that we both happened to attend. I did not go with him. I was not his date, as I think you're alluding to. My business and social life are quite separate. And my social life and Mr. Evans' social life are quite separate, if you get my meaning."

Ed grinned. "I do, Miss Porter."

Ed glanced over at Leon. He had no further questions. "Miss Porter, we thank you for your cooperation. We have no more questions at the present time, but we will want to talk with you again."

"You know where to find me." She stood and walked out of the conference room back to her own private office and closed the door.

Ed turned off the tape recorder. "She 's a cool number. Does a pretty good acting job of not remembering."

"Well, we want her to be on our side," said Leon. "No point in pressing the wrong buttons."

"She has a couple of buttons I'd like to press."

"Ed, as a psychologist and your concerned friend, I have to say you are overly fixated on having sex with women other than your dear and loving and devoted wife."

"I have to say that you are exactly right." Ed grinned. "You charging by the minute or by the hour?"

Leon smiled and shook his head.

In her office, Nicole groped in a desk drawer for her valium. She knew what the agents were after, but she would never tell them.

In the beginning, Paul had seemed preoccupied, more like daydreaming, distracted and forgetful, not an unusual behavior for a middle-aged man. He was healthy enough, she knew from his medical report and from her personal relationship with him. He was a strong, active, and consistent sexual partner.

Then she noticed sudden displays of anger over trivial things, throwing tantrums like a frustrated child, sometimes shouting at her in accusatory tones

There was the time when Paul had acted crazy, bizarre crazy, two months ago when she had spent the weekend with him at his townhouse. Something about his computer. He woke up sweating, ranting and raving at something or someone who wasn't there. He had leaped out of bed and appeared to be struggling with someone who wasn't there. Afraid that in his deranged state he might become violent and assault her, she had slipped to the floor, grabbed her robe and run downstairs to the kitchen prepared to call the police. Then Paul had grown quiet.

She had cautiously crept back upstairs to look in on him. He was sitting naked on the edge of the bed and holding his downcast head in his hands. When she said his name, he had slowly looked up, his eyes sunken and haunted. She had gone to him and placed her arms around him, pulling his head to her breasts where the robe had fallen open, and she had rocked him like a child.

The next morning during breakfast, she mentioned that she thought he might need some counseling.

"You think I'm crazy? don't you," he said and sneered at her."

"No, Paul, I don't think you're crazy, but you're obviously troubled in some way, deeply troubled. Nightmares like you had are an indication."

"Nightmares? That wasn't a nightmare I had. That was real."

"What did you say?"

"It was him? You were in the room. Didn't you see him?"

"No, Paul, I didn't see anybody. Who are you talking about?"

He stared at her for several moments, then slowly shook his head. "Never mind. You're right. It was just a dream."

"Sometimes dreams can seem real. I know I've had dreams like that. But seriously."

"Ah, I'll be all right. Probably something I ate."

Frightened by the expression in his eyes, Nicole had stopped sleeping with him after that incident. He had grown resentful and distrusting, always working behind closed doors, no longer asking her into his office, communicating only through the intercom or by E-mail, even though she sat in the office on the other side of the wall.

Chapter 22

The unannounced appearance of two FBI agents waiting for Jim at his office when he returned from lunch precipitated an immediate onset of indigestion and heartburn. With nervous shrugs and a vacuous smile, his secretary handed him their business cards, which he studied for a considerably longer time than necessary to read their names and to understand what company they represented.

Noticing Jim's hesitation, Leon made a mental note of the buying time behavior and attributed it to either apprehension, confusion, or both. When the FBI called on you, something serious was afoot and you were either trying to figure out what the possible connection could be or you were hurriedly preparing your story while under extreme duress.

As Jim approached them with outstretched hand and a grin of concern, Ed and Leon rose in unison without smiling.

"Gentlemen," said Jim, "I understand you're here to see me. I'm Jim Owens, President of Genex."

Ed and Leon introduced themselves as they each shook his hand.

"Ah, would you please come into my office." He escorted them through his open door, motioned them to chairs at his mini-conference table, closed the door to shut out his secretary's curious stare, then remembered to ask, "Did my secretary offer you coffee or something to drink? Water?"

"She did," Ed responded, "but we're fine, thank you."

Jim remained standing awkwardly, apparently unsure of what to do or say next.

Ed picked up the cue. This was their show. "Please sit down, Jim. May we call you Jim?"

Jim half-lunged and collapsed his tall lanky body into one of the four chairs at the table. He would have preferred to take refuge in his executive chair behind his desk, but intuitively felt his visitors might interpret his move in the wrong way. They were in charge, no question about it. "Of course, of course, that's my name."

Too nervous, Leon thought. *Much too nervous. Go carefully here. We've got a rabbit surrounded.*

"We'd like to ask a few questions, Jim. Understand that we're only seeking information. This is not a formal investigation."

Jim nodded and swallowed hard. "I'll help you in any way I can. What is it about -- your coming here to see me?"

"Paul Evans." Ed and Leon watched his reaction closely.

Jim shifted tensely in his chair, back straight and taut, chin pressed down tightly as though to protect his throat. "I'm assuming you probably have done a little research before you came here, since you are mentioning the name of a man I clearly despise more than any in the world because of what he did to me. And I am speaking only in business terms, notwithstanding the emotional damage to my family. Obviously you know Evans and I were partners at one time and created a successful business."

"We're in luck," thought Leon. "He's a talker. Created. Uses terms like that. Means more than business to him, more than money involved. What you create is a child or like a child -- art, music, the joy of violins." In spite of the need to maintain professional distance and a degree of objectivity, Leon felt an instant liking and compassion for the man. He did not believe Jim's exhibited nervous behavior was caused by their positional authority, but by his deep-set anger. The mention of Paul Evans' name had had the effect of touching a match to the fuse of an explosive. The intensity of his hatred was significant, however. People killed over less.

"Something has happened to Mr. Evans," Leon continued.

Jim's eyebrows raised slightly with interest. "Yes?"

"He disappeared two days ago."

Jim continued to look attentively at the two men, but his thoughts were immediately miles away. Then it had happened. What he half-suspected might have been only a hoax, a con to get to some portion of his now freshly-earned millions, had actually happened. Logical. Why else would the FBI be sitting in his office? But what had happened to the guarantee of confidentiality? The assassin, Antonio Guzman, obviously an alias, whoever he was, had the money in his Swiss account. When Jim had checked, there was no electronic traceability and he had erased from his own system any traceable reference to even receiving and responding to the E-mail message.

The assassin knew that greed was not an issue with him. But he had been emotionally damaged to the extent that Paul Evans' untimely death was a desired outcome and the man knew that.

Jim had come across the E-mail message repeatedly one year ago. At first, he had ignored the immediate impulse it generated in him. But the message persisted, floating through his electronic mail until it had become a fixture in his thoughts. An intense curiosity had pulled him back to the strange message from Antonio Guzman.

Do you want to get rid of someone?
Antonio Guzman

There was someone he would like to get rid of -- someone who had nearly destroyed him, his family, and his career. In Jim's mind, he had always hoped that an opportunity would present itself by which he could take revenge, but he had only considered it in business terms.

Watching the dark digital letters appear on the blue computer screen, he had keyed in his response.

Yes.   What next?

Now, here the FBI sat in his office, the notorious suits. Jim would not have believed the FBI had nearly the technological capability that was commercially available. The government was too mired in bureaucracy, even the spooks. He knew. He had tried to market state-of-the-art software products and systems to them and his proposals had fallen on deaf eyes and ears. They still worked under outdated manual systems and archaic local networks. Their Field Office Information Management System was inadequate to the volume of data that required processing, mountains of paper growing taller. For all of the trillions of dollars that the government wasted, why didn't they flush a few down the electronics sewer pipeline. Jim was already way beyond point-and-click technology. His software devices provided users the capability to scan and enter data and generate documents through eye movement alone. He had developed artificial intelligence software. He was in the forefront of AI research. Paul Evans didn't have a product like that. Paul Evans was already obsolete. He had no imagination. Now, he was permanently archived. "The biggest mistake he ever made was in dumping me," thought Jim. "Let's just hope the biggest mistake I ever made wasn't dumping him." He refocused his attention on the present, the question being asked by Agent Berzinsky.

"Have you had any contact with him since the dissolution of your partnership?"

"Not a twit. My attorneys handled everything. I could not tolerate being in the same room, the same building, the same state with the man. So I moved far away. Far far away. I'm sorry you had to travel clear across the country to drop in on me."

Berzinsky appreciated Jim's sense of humor. Reminded Ed of himself.

"So, Jim, obviously there's no love lost between you and Paul Evans. Why we're here. He's gone," said Ed. "Disappeared without a trace. Nothing. Nada, as the homies say out here in Sunny California. You may be pleased to hear that bit of news."

"I guess that depends on the nature of his disappearance. I certainly don't wish him any harm. Maybe he ran off to Jamaica with one of his Playboy Bunny girlfriends. When he used to do that, he didn't leave a number where he could be reached. Paul was always first and foremost a pleasure seeker, a little known fact except by those of us who were close to him, especially his wife. You do know about his wife?"

"Yes, we do."

"Paul's trail of breadcrumbs of those he exploited and ruined is rather extensive. He's not a particularly nice human being."

"We're beginning to get the picture."

"In fact, he may have reached a point in his life where he's not all that pleased with himself and what he's done."

"How do you mean?"

"Age, growing older, enlightenment. Like you and me. We're about the same age. We arrived with many of the same influences and we probably share many of the same values."

"That's more than likely, Jim," said Leon. "That's why we're here. We feel this whole thing is about values."

"Now I know you're bullshitting me," Jim smiled. "You're here because you think I did something to Paul."

"Did you?"

"Oh, yes, sure, I personally whacked him because of what he did to me seven years ago. Excuse me, Agent Berzinsky and Agent Safullo. Paul did me the biggest favor of my life by firing me from what was then our company. Sure, I was angry and depressed, but I didn't go postal. I have realized more personal satisfaction and financial success than I ever could if we had stayed together. It didn't take me long to realize what baggage, what useless deadwood Paul was. He brought nothing to the table. He was a parasite like most of the big time CEO's are parasites living off the hard work and talent of others while they collect phenomenal salaries and perks for managing their companies into failure. They are rewarded by their Boards and the stockholders for doing so, laying thousands of people off as a substitute for effectively managing their companies. They don't know how to manage anything except their bank accounts. Excuse me. Let me retract that statement. They don't manage their money. Someone equally as criminal does it for them. As long as they get a short term return on their investment dividends, the board is satisfied.

"My company, gentlemen, is privately held. It is owned by its employees. We make decisions for the benefit of our customers and ourselves. We have an excellent quality management system to support those objectives. We do not answer to investors. The disappearance of Paul Evans means nothing to me. I left him behind in every way imaginable seven years ago, when I walked out of his office. Sure, I was mad. I was really pissed. But I got over it, because I walked away with everything he needed to make his business and his life whole. I have what he could not possibly have and can never reclaim. He squandered his opportunity, gentlemen. He blew away his family, his friends, his associates thinking that he would have greater and greater success. But do you know what he forgot to consider?" Jim was on his feet now, in a proselytizing mood, suddenly a lion pacing the room, not a cowering rabbit. He was in charge. "Do you know what he forgot to consider?"

"No, tell us."

"That life is short. Life ends. And what you do to yourself and with and to others matters deeply. I have to say, in one respect, I feel sorry for Paul, although I really don't feel sorry for him. He deserves whatever happens to him and I don't care if it's good or bad. His death would be irrelevant to me. He's nothing more than a fart in my past.

"You know, when I first saw you sitting out there in the waiting room and my secretary told me who you were, I didn't know what to think. But now, I'm really glad you came to see me. I'm glad to hear that Paul Evans has disappeared. And gentlemen, he has disappeared, because it is his destiny to disappear, just as eventually, you and I will."

Leon was more than a little impressed, but he continued to evaluate Jim Owens' performance that was not a performance. This was Jim Owens, the man, articulating his justifiable anger and reinforcing the values by which Leon himself lived. Jim Owens had nothing to hide. He was honest. He was clean. Yet there was a nagging doubt in Leon's mind. Some hidden impulse, some impression that did not come clear. Instinct perhaps, that Jim Owens might be lying but maybe it didn't really matter, because Leon could identify with and sympathize with him. But he mustn't do that. He must remain objective. The problem was, there was no evidence to be found here. If it existed, it was as invisible as an electron streaming through Jim Owens' futuristic software to some unknown realm where they all might be headed.

Leon posed a question. "Do you recall whether you observed any abrupt changes in his behavior before the separation?"

"Oh yes, very abrupt. It was almost as if Paul went to bed one night and woke up a different person. He was always driven, but in a friendly salesman sort of way. But suddenly, about a year before the incident, he basically turned his back on everybody who meant anything to him and decided he wanted to make money over anything else. I always knew there was an underlying element of greed with Paul, but what he did to me was totally unexpected. It was like he'd sold his soul to the devil to become the richest man in the world or something. He was single-minded about having power and control over everything.

"I had no interest in power and control. I just wanted to invent things. So I just handed it all over to him. My wife and I thought he was going through some kind of mid-life crisis, so we were tolerant in the beginning. But then his abusiveness was more than we felt we had to accept, even though he was an old friend. What especially embittered us was how he treated his wife and children, like there had always been another person inside of Paul, and now he was emerging."

Leon noted that this was the first mention of a radical change in Paul Evans' behavior, and it correlated with the separation from his business partner and ruination of his family. Neurotic episodes had all manner of origins. However, the sudden sustained abusiveness by someone who had been a loving concerned family man didn't fit the picture. Maybe Evans had undergone some sort of neurochemical change. His physiological system could create a wide variety of chemical agents or chemicals could have been introduced into his body.

"Did he use drugs?" Leon asked.

"No, not that I ever knew about. He didn't like to be out of control of himself or his situation. He wasn't a person you'd go out and get drunk with."

He could have had a thyroid problem, thought Leon, *which could lead to hyperactivity. Manic depressive behavior occurred predominately during middle age. Other characteristic behaviors Jim Owens described, especially the abrupt shift in personality, could have been related to a latent schizophrenia. The loss of affect or feeling for his family and friends was another indicator.*

It bothered Leon that he was beginning to question whether there was ultimately any purpose in what he was doing, any value. *Growing older*, he thought. *Maybe all this matters only when you're young and you're not looking to see what's on the other side. Life is short. Life ends. The joy of violins comes to an end. The joy of loving. He resolved that, as soon as he returned to the East Coast, he and Julie would take up ballroom dancing. While there's still time, for Christ's sake. While there's still time.*

After the agents departed, Jim poured himself a triple scotch and toasted what he assumed was probably Paul Evans' departed spirit. "Here's to you, you bastard, for making me the man I am today."

But the booze did not give him a sufficient comfort level. The two agents had not pressured him at all. They hadn't dug in going for details. Maybe they already had them. Maybe they already knew everything and they were just sizing him up. Maybe he shouldn't have answered that E-mail, committed the money to that Swiss account. He really didn't need to. It didn't gain him anything. He had everything that was important to him, a well-adjusted family, supportive, loving wife. With one exception, his children were making their trek through two different colleges. The third one would join them next year. Life was good. Life was sweet. Yet he had felt the need to bring the existence of Paul Evans to an end. And now he had. Paul Evans was gone. A blip on the screen of life, gone.

Chapter 23

From five hundred feet aloft the hawk saw the four horses and riders leading three pack mules move slowly up the rugged mountain slope like a small trail of ants. The rabbit he had been watching ceased nibbling lupine buds and bounded for cover among the rocks. The hawk would have to wait until the men and horses had passed, so the rabbit would again come out into the open. He screamed his hunger and frustration, caught a sudden updraught and rose three-hundred feet, tipped his wings and glided from view into the next valley.

Heavy revolvers and cartridge belts were slung about the riders' waists. The weight of the leather and hardware pressed their lean thighs that rolled down over the worn contours of the saddles.

The men rode with a smooth jerking motion from the small of the back. Their shoulders were slightly hunched and the Stetson hats set on their heads bobbed with rhythmic bird-like movements. The steady walking stride of the horses that carried the men was pleasant to ride.

The horses rattled their bits and chains, tongues rolling the metal bars with the whir of six-gun cylinders

The riders' knees fit snugly at the animals' rippling muscled shoulders. The strong equine rumps of the quarter horses flared widely behind, swinging slightly at each chink of hoof, as metal shoes struck against rocks that littered the trail.

The sweet acrid scent of horses and rising dust was snatched away by the wind, but the odor clung to the men's hands, skin, and clothes.

Sharp mucousy snorts from the horses punctuated the squeaks and groans of leather. Whisk tails slashed the air.

The riders moved gradually, imperceptibly up and up through timberline into low-lying scrub pine among great granite boulders that lay scattered like bleached prehistoric bones.

Woolly marmots whistled at their approach and crouched back in their maze of small caverns among the upheaval of rocks.

At sunset, the riders meandered down into a bowl shaped valley that provided good meadow grass for grazing the horses and mules.

Shortly, the ring of an ax echoed across the small lake, announcing the presence of the men. Luther staked out the animals. They lowered shaggy, winter-furring heads to crop the harsh browning grass laced with tiny blue and white flowers.

As Vince hacked at an old fallen tree near the camp, Willie gathered up the wood and carried it to a large cooking fireplace constructed of flat rocks. Luther added the logs to the young crackling flames, lay a grill over the top, then placed a blue metal coffee pot on to boil. Willie dropped another load of wood and walked back to Vince for more.

Denham measured out a quart of oats each into seven canvas feed bags. These he carried out to the horses and mules and fastened them on the animals.

From one of the packs, Luther drew pots and utensils and arranged them on a rock slab next to four aluminum cups. He then pulled out a large cut of smoked salt cured beef, a sack of sourdough, cans of beans, and a side of bacon.

He sliced meat into hot blistering dark beans, then broke off sections of sourdough for biscuits baked against the flat rocks.

Darkness enclosed the camp by the time they had finished their meal. They sat with full distended stomachs, exchanging farts and belches.

Vince added a large log to the fire and leaned back on his makeshift seat. Grouped, they stared at the flames. Heat flushed their faces and shadows wavered across their somber expressions of smoky fireside contentment.

Luther poured bourbon and passed the bottle to Vince, who filled his cup, passed the bottle to Willie, who first poured for Denham, then filled his own.

Denham set his aside and tamped strong tobacco into an ancient twisted buckhorn pipe. He touched the tip of a twig to the fire. Puffing intently, he lit the pipe.

The men sipped their whiskey and gazed into the flames, conjuring images, immersed in their camaraderie through silence. Willie sniffled and wiped his nose. Vince leisurely rolled and smoked a cigarette. Denham looked back at Luther and his sons sitting around the fire, and then beyond to the dark shapes of the grazing mules and horses. After a moment, he raised his eyes to the jagged peaks against the vast darkness of a cold starlit sky that he imagined was imperceptibly descending upon them.

Chapter 24

They pushed on, walking at an exceptionally fast pace, climbed to the top of the next pass and then made a long gradual descent into a small valley.

Weariness set in Paul's muscles. Stiff, he moved slowly. Now that he and Matt had stopped, the tension from the day's trek began to seep out of him.

Food and a fire warmed Paul and inclined him to conversation that weighed as heavily on his mind as the weariness in his body. He felt he must reveal the content of the diary to his son. Now was the time, what he had come for.

"It seems like -- we've never really talked much. I wish I had talked to you more when you were younger," said Paul. "I wanted to, but so many other things kept pressing in."

"I suppose I was too young."

"No," Paul shook his head. "I think maybe that was a growing place for you, and me. Only I didn't see it. Too wrapped up in -well, you know how it was."

"Yes." Matt stared off. "Do you think of mom?"

"Yes, often."

"I never thought I'd be able to talk about her with you," said Matt. "It's been hard for so long, so many years."

"I started having strange dreams," said Paul. "I didn't think anything of them at first, They kept coming back in a recurring pattern, and a voice would talk to me. Not like you and I are talking. The voice didn't speak words. It made sounds and I could feel what it was saying. It was such a strange feeling. I tried to shut it out. It got so bad I tried not to sleep. But then the voice grew louder, more insistent. I tried everything. exercise, drugs, booze, playing music all night. Nothing worked.

"Did you see a psychiatrist?"

"Almost. I was too embarrassed by the dreams, by what they told about me, I suppose. I didn't have any trouble interpreting them. I didn't need a psychiatrist to tell me who I am."

"I guess we know who you are,·" said Matt.

A note of nervousness crept into Paul's voice. "You're not going to accept my telling you this, but I am not responsible for your mother's breakdown. I did not drive her to it as you accused me."

"There was nobody else in the picture."

"Yes, there was, someone you didn't know about, but I'11 get to that."

"What the hell. What do you mean there was someone else? You trying to tell me you're not responsible because of some bad dreams you had?"

"Just hear me out. It did have to do with the dreams."

"Did they ever stop?" Matt asked.

Paul nodded. "Until a few nights ago. Back then, when you were still children, I would wake up screaming. Then the dreams did stop for a long time. Must have been nineteen, twenty years. I thought I was over whatever was persecuting me. I was wrong."

"Who was talking to you?"

His father hesitated. "I think it was a Satanic presence."

"Satanic presence?"

Paul nodded.

"You don't expect me to believe that."

Matt wasn't sure how to respond to his father's statement. He sensed there was something desperately wrong with him.

Paul stared into the fire. "He came to me. Night after night, he came to me in my dreams in various forms until I said yes."

"Sounds like you're having a mid-life crisis or whatever you're going through," Matt kept his voice calm and low.

"I wish it were only that."

"You're just not willing to face up to what you did to all of us. I don't mean this maliciously, but I think you're a very sick man. It sounds like you have some kind of mental illness. That's what's called being crazy, Dad. Now, I ask myself what I'm doing out here in the middle of nowhere with you. You should be where Mom is."

"But I have to explain," said Paul.

"You're crazy. You ruined out lives. What difference does it make?" Matt was angry, on his guard.

"A lot, to me...to clear myself with you. And - and to prepare you for what might happen." Paul looked away.

"To you?"

"No, to you." Paul could not face him.

"What are you talking about? Did you bring me out here thinking you would kill me?" Matt laughed. "I'm bigger and stronger than you now."

"Oh, for God's sakes no! If only I could take your place."

Alarms were going off in Matt's head at what he was hearing and witnessing. His eyes narrowed at his father's strange behavior.

"I sacrificed your mother, Jenny, and you that I would give you in exchange for the success I wanted. Only, I didn't know I had done that. They came to me and told me I had agreed, that I had a contract. But I didn't agree to anything."

"They? Who is the they you're talking about?"

"The First World Corporation. They're a major acquisitions and financial investment and accounting firm that bought my company. They kept me on as CEO. They've been," he hesitated, "making arrangements for me for a long time."

"Dad, you have a very sick distorted view of what is going on in your life. You should be talking to a psychiatrist, not out here in the wilderness with me. What the hell are we doing here?"

"I'm trying to find out what's real and what isn't -- the company, the money, Jim Owens, you and Jenny and your mother."

"That one's easy. You said it yourself. You exchanged us all for success. Satan had nothing to do with it. Your dreams were just a way of excusing yourself, trying to compensate."

"I deserve everything you say," Paul said before he shook his head in disagreement. "I thought I was rationalizing too, but it's not so. I'm afraid for you, and I'm so sorry for what I've done, for what I agreed to, for what I've dreamed. You can never know what a horror those dreams were."

Matt stared at his father's face glistening with tears of remorse.

"But it's not true," Paul whispered. "I did love you then. But the dreams, the dreams, what they did to me."

"Dreams come from your mind. You're accountable for your own behavior," Matt said sternly.

"I wish to God it could all be explained away so easily. But it can't. And I know I can't make you fully understand unless you have experienced it yourself. It was psychic torture."

"Dad, what do you take me for? There's only one person in our family who has even the remotest understanding of what psychic even means. Jenny has been studying it for years and it's basically horseshit new age black magic. It's whatever you carry around in your head. I'm sure there's some logical explanation for what you did. You need a psychiatrist to help you figure it out."

"When I was a boy, my father was always telling me that I had to become wealthy at any cost to be a success in life. He was a brutal man. He worked in a series of low paying blue collar jobs. I can't count the number of times he came home drunk and beat me and my mother, blaming us for his lot in life. You never met your grandmother, my mother, because she died at a young age. She committed suicide."

"You never told me this before."

"No, I didn't think it was suitable."

"Yet you drove mom to nearly the same thing."

"I never intended that to happen. You know I didn't."

"Maybe your dad didn't either," said Matt. "But he did. It happened."

"I never wanted to be like my father. I wanted to be as different as night and day."

"You were great when Jenny and I were little kids."

"I know. We can't go back but I want to try to become the person I was then."

"Better late than never, but the wounds are still there."

"I am sorry and regret what I did. Unfortunately, apologies are only words."

"They're still meaningful."

"Later, when I was in college, about your age, I had a friend, Cory Jameson, lived on an estate. He stood to inherit a great deal of money, which I wanted to tap in to. When he graduated, his trust would open up to him. Ten million. Can you imagine that? Ten million dollars for graduating from college. He didn't have to work a day of his life if he didn't want to. I wanted to make a good portion of that ten mil my own. I talked him into putting six into my company. Well, mine and Jim Owens. Jim the genius. All I needed was financing and an idea I could sell in the form of a product that would be big. Computers and software were the wave of the future.

"The reality is what got to your mother. The reality I created in your lives. She was so vulnerable, quick to feel hurt. I always had to be careful with her, what I did, what I said, the references I'd make. People tend to manipulate each other. That was her way, her defense against me."

They stared at the fire through a long silence

"I can probably never convince you that I love her."

His son remained inscrutable, his eyes never leaving the flames, offering his father nothing.

"It was always my intention to become one of the monopolies, and I did, buying out smaller companies left and right." Paul shifted to ease the pressure of his weight on his arm.

"The next ten years, building the business with Jim Owens, the late hours, I should have given more time to you and your sister, and to your mother. It's always easy to say, looking back, but things got worse instead of better between us. I became caught up in these forces beyond my control. I thought it didn't have to be that way, but it did. That's the way it happens and then the time is gone by and the damage is done.

"I had to go where I was going and didn't know how to stop. It was easier to submit to the voice in my dreams. It was a way to believe and justify everything I did. It allowed me the luxury to live with my choices.

"I lost your mother because of those things, not because I didn't love her."

Matt stared at his father for a long time. He saw him look away slowly, sadly, and felt a wrench of pity for him, coming home and finding his wife, slit wrists, bleeding all over the kitchen floor, his seven year old son screaming uncontrollably. With the blood and the screaming and the whiteness of her near death, he saw her as a sacrifice. In the dreams, they were all sacrificed, family, friends, to his success.

"Get out your laptop," said Paul.

"I was wondering why you asked me to bring it along. It's extra weight."

"I backed up some files on a thumb drive I have to show you."

"Why not at the motel or even the airport. You could have Emailed them to me and saved us all this trouble."

"No, I couldn't, and you'll understand when you see the contents. We needed to talk about other things first face to face."

Matt removed his laptop computer from its case and set it up on a large flat rock. Paul handed him the thumb drive. Matt inserted it into the drive and waited a few moments for the access window. He opened the drive and saw a series of thirty Microsoft Word files. From the touch pad, he maneuvered the cursor to the first file and clicked to open it. As the text appeared on the screen, he began to read and scroll down.

Through the diary you will clearly understand that I exist and what you must do for me. You will attempt to deny me what I am seeking, but to have what you desire, you cannot deny me.

I will talk to you in your dreams and you will believe that they are strange and awful dreams, because that is what you want to believe. But they are real and my voice speaking to you is real.

You cannot deny me. If you try to deny me, you will only deny yourself and you will suffer. The thoughts you think and the visions you will see are created by me, because of what I can do to your mind. My existence is in the dark energy of the universe where I can control your mind. So when you do and think things you would not normally do and think, you are not responsible for what happens. I am making it happen. You can blame it all on me. Such an arrangement makes you blameless and your soul very clean.

Every time we write in this diary together, you will come to learn more about me. The words here are yours. They come from within your thoughts, not from me. They represent who you are.

As a successful businessman, you know there's always a price to pay. More is what your life is all about and more is what you will receive.

People like yourself make agreements with us without ever really knowing what happened to them. They can have whatever they desire, and they eventually become one of us. Infiltrating people's minds is a kind of psychic espionage.

Think of me as a broker or middleman. Soon you will learn the nature of your contract. Now is not the time.

Matt looked at his father. "You wrote this, didn't you? This is just your sorry-ass attempt to explain your behavior and absolve yourself."

"No, no, that's not it at all. These files are just a small part of it."

"So, were you writing your autobiography, How I Became A Millionaire By Being An Asshole?"

"You have every right to be angry. Those events happened outside of my control."

"You expect me to believe you're possessed by some Satanic spirit from the dark spaces of the cosmos?"

"You know about dark spaces?"

"Of course, I'm a geologist. I've studied quantum physics. Dark energy is not a new concept. The research has just been recently published is all. But it's not considered to be a spiritual medium. What you're showing me here is nothing but a hoax. There are a lot of people who, shall we say, hold a grudge against you. Jim Owens, for instance. He's a software wizard. Given wireless technology, he could be sending you this by satellite and you've just added it to your personal baggage."

The firelight flickered over Paul's sullen features. "It can't be explained away so easily. This isn't an illusion. It's real."

"Not in my reality. Not in anybody's who's sane."

"That's why I brought us out here."

"Because you're insane?"

"To prove to myself that what I'm experiencing is imaginary."

"And how will you know that?"

"If Guzman doesn't come after us."

"You need to get help, Dad. We shouldn't be out here."

"Please, Matt, we'll know for sure in a few days."

"This is not how you deal with problems when you are a well person and obviously you are not. We should go back tomorrow morning."

"We can't. We have to find out."

"We? There's no we about this. I'm not living in your fantasy world. I don't want any part of it."

"Two days. Give me two more days."

"On one condition. You check yourself into a psychiatric hospital when you get back to New York."

"If I know that this is not real, I'll do that."

"People who are mentally ill can't tell the difference."

"I'll know. Believe me, I'll know."

"I don't believe you. I don't believe anything about you. You lost that right by what you did to us years ago."

"You will know too."

"Oh, great, I really have a need to know that some imaginary spook in your bad dreams isn't out to get me."

"You're in this with me. I'm trying to protect you."

"What am I going to know?" Matt's voice dripped with sarcasm.

"If Guzman doesn't come after us, then, yes, I'm crazy. But I know he's out there tracking us. I've seen him."

"Where have you seen him?"

"At the airport, in the bar, at the motel. You aren't safe."

"You're being paranoid. There is no spook out there. Safe from what?"

"From being taken."

"Being taken. Being taken where?"

"You have something he wants. He wants to possess you. He wants your spirit."

Matt stared at his father. "If Jenny would ever talk to you again, you should share this with her. Unbelievable." He rose and paced about to relieve his nervous anxiety. He wondered how dangerous his father might actually be. "She's into all this new age shit. But you're beyond that. If this weren't so serious, I'd laugh my ass off."

"You'll give me two days?"

Matt stopped pacing. "I should just walk out. But I want to make sure you get back."

"Thank you."

"For what?"

"For listening to me. For caring about me."

Matt returned to his computer and shut it down. He handed the thumb drive to his father. "You still want this? You'll need it to show your shrink."

"No, I don't need it."

With a backhand flip of his wrist, Matt hurled the thumb drive away into the surrounding darkness.

Chapter 25

Paul's groggy eyes peered out at the world. He had felt the same on mornings when he woke with a hangover, but here his head and vision were laden only with sleep, not the after effects of alcohol. It was a healthy awakening, breaking clear of sleep, sticky like a newborn chick from its fragile shell, welcoming the morning, welcoming life.

Frost coated the hard mountain ground and filmed the charred rocks and coals of the dead campfire.

Bundled deep in his sleeping bag, Matt's face was buried from the sensation of cold morning air.

Paul felt about for the stocking cap he had lost during the night. His hand clutched it and he quickly pulled it back over his matted sleep-churned hair.

Moving as Little as possible to avoid the penetrating chill, he further scanned the area and noticed that his son was not stirring. He looked with extreme irritation at the dead fire. His stiff fingers touched the dark nascent stubble of beard that bristled from his jaw, threatening to manifest an uncontained virile growth within a few days.

With a grunt and sudden burst of energy, he unzipped his sleeping bag, leaped to his cold reddened feet, and pulled on his socks and frozen hiking boots.

Wearing only insulated underwear, down jacket. and with boot laces flapping like stiff pasta, he rushed to the fire pit and snatched together a small pile of kindling. He frantically struck a match and held it to the kindling. It was wet from the frost and would not take. He wasted six matches in rapid succession.

Teeth chattering, shivering, cursing under his breath, he stood up and dashed away several yards, opened his fly and let loose a forceful piss. He shook violently with chills as his urine splattered and steamed across the frozen ground.

When he was finished, he raced back to the sleeping bag, kicked off his boots, crawled down inside the gut of the bag and huddled, shivering. He glared over at Matt, who still had not stirred.

When he had regained his body heat, Paul reached out and rummaged in his pack. His chapped hand came up with a distorted roll of toilet paper.

Remaining in his sleeping bag, he humped along like an unwieldy giant orange caterpillar to the edge of the dead fire. Tearing off several wads of paper, he structured a small kindling pyramid. His shaking hands struck a match and touched flame to the linty whiteness, which ignited and flared up catching the small twigs, then swept through the dry kindling. He added a few thin and medium logs as the fire began to take.

Bellowing laughter suddenly exploded from Matt's sleeping bag. Paul glanced back over his shoulder and saw his son peering out at him, gnome-like, from under a stocking cap, the sleeping bag pulled up snugly to his bewhiskered chin like a chrysalis.

"Have you been awake this whole time?"

"Yes, I was waiting for you to get the fire started. I'11 take my eggs scrambled and cream and sugar with my coffee."

"Ha! I can't believe it. That's a son's gratitude for you. I can remember rousting you out of bed to get ready for school when you were five and six years old. You curled up like a snail and I had to pull one leg and one arm out at a time to get your clothes on you, because you were too cold. And then I had to carry you to the breakfast table with your soft blanket and your stuffed teddy bear. You had a different stuffed animal every night. You rotated them. You must have had about five or ten stuffed animals.

Matt stared at him. "You remember that?"

"Of course. Those were some of the most frustrating and richest moments of my life. But you're an outdoorsman. You're a geologist. You're supposed to be an old hand at these things. You should be out here hustling about and I should be in a sleeping bag."

"That's why I'm letting you do it. So you can benefit from the first hand experience."

"Mmmph. ." Paul snorted loose a ball of mucous. The feeling of dirt and nature had already encrusted him inside and out. The odor of wood smoke clung to his hair and clothing and skin. The aftertaste of the previous night's supper coated his tongue making his breath malodorous even to himself. Crest toothpaste was not enough. He ardently desired to refresh his mouth, cleanse the grit from his pores and the black from under his fingernails.

"You remember." Matt raised his head slightly. "I'm glad you remember, because those are the good things I remember about you too. When I was just a Little kid, I loved you."

Paul struggled against sudden tears and turned his face. If Matt saw the tears, Paul felt he would have to make some excuse like smoke from the fire had gotten into his eyes.

I have always loved you. Paul needed to say it out loud, to tell him. But he could not look at him. Look at him, fool! He is your son. One day you will die, and as you pass away, you will regret that you did not look at your son and say, I love you. Say it like you did when Matt was a child. I love you very much into his ear with the clean warmth of his young hair smooth against your face, filling your senses with his marvelous being. He is a gift upon which no earthly value can be placed and you used him as a medium of exchange for personal success. So tell him. It may be the last opportunity, the last time.

"I love you very much," he said to his son.

"What?"

"I said, I love you very much."

"I love you very much too. You sure look funny all crouched there in your bag with that hat on."

"Well, you're not exactly a raving beauty yourself." said Paul. "Let me tell you, I thought my piss was gonna freeze and hold me stranded a few minutes ago."

"That's one of the dangers of camping out in the wilderness," said Matt. "Also one of the first lessons of survival. Never piss 'til the sun comes up."

Paul grinned and turned back to place more wood on the fire.

Remaining in his bag, Matt crawled in close. "How did you sleep?"

"I feel a Little stiff, but not bad. If only I wouldn't dream so much. Like I told you, I'm bothered by terrible horrible dreams. Have been for years."

"Well, the ground does get hard. I dream a lot too."

"What about breakfast?" asked Paul.

"Let's have pound cake and hot chocolate. Be enough to get us moving. We can snack later on trail mix," said Matt.

Paul smiled. His tongue scoured the morning mung from his gums. "Okay, I don't even want to get out of this bag though."

Matt wriggled forward. "You made the fire. I'11 do the breakfast."

"Who got the best of that bargain?"

"Do I look like a snail?" asked Matt.

"Out of its shell."

"You got that right.

Paul and Matt had been on the trail for two hours since breaking camp. The pack straps bit into Paul's shoulders with the pressure of live beasts. Paul could feel his arms and hands going numb from lack of circulation.

He leaned far forward, taking the weight of the pack across his upper back to ease the pressure. His taut pulse pounded like a stick on a thin membranous drum in his head. The odor of his sweat mingled with the smell of heat reflected from granite rock slides and trail dust and the acrid scent of pine resin.

He groaned from the fatigue that ravaged his leg muscles strung with jagged tension from the sharp climb. He breathed slowly, steadily, trying not to gasp on the dry air. He squinted up at his son's receding figure slowly clambering overhead like a tenacious hump-backed beetle through great granite boulders and jutting slabs. Paul waited for a full minute, then continued his dragging pace -- the slow motion stopped-in-time placing of one heavy dust coated boot before the other with a crunching roll of gravel, a rising brief puff of gray.

Through his harsh toil on a single slope, the forces of time and space and gravity struck his mind and body with the vast impenetrable power of the monolithic peaks and endless ranges of light. He was a mere insect struggling through this maze of rock. When he looked up, the blinding blue sky stung his swollen reddened eyes, forcing him to lower his head and blunder on.

A tormenting image filled his mind, seeing himself in a never ending hell in which, weighted down, he must climb this mountainside for eternity.

Finally, there was a leveling out to rough meadow grass fringed with wildflowers underfoot, a rivulet and marsh prolific with piping frogs and rising clouds of mosquitoes in quest of approaching flesh.

Matt waited, perched on a saddle of rock among large boulders that protected him from the raw salient wind that cut through the pass. Paul shrugged off his pack and eased down slowly. He closed his eyes to lessen the pounding pulse in his head and body. When he opened them, he saw the panorama, fluctuating blues, purples. and grays, an ocean of mountains like still silent waves with white clouds frothing and shadowing them from horizon to horizon. He looked at his son and was pleased with his own deep weariness and their being there together.

"Everything seems to move out there, like the sea," said Matt in reference to the view.

They rested only ten minutes so their muscles would not grow cold and stiffen, then they began the steep descent.

The trail zig-zagged down the face of a scree that dropped an abrupt five-hundred feet to a small lake and long narrow meadow.

As they traversed at sharp angles to the slope, with Matt again in the lead, their boots slipped on small pieces of loose shale that slithered away flinging off into space.

The angle and height and the steady rhythm of their downhill pace proved tiring and hypnotic and strained their concentration.

Suddenly, a large loose slab shot out from under Paul. He lost his balance and fell forward with a sharp cry. The bulk and weight of his pack carried him plummeting down the slope with Matt's scream and the wind rushing into his ears.

His head and shoulders snapped, jerked to a stop as abrupt as his fall. It took him a moment to realize his pack had caught and held on a corner of solidly entrenched granite. Shaken, cut and bruised, he hung suspended, afraid to move.

Matt frantically followed the trail down until he was as close above his father as he could get. "Dad! Can you hear me?"

"Yes," his weak shout raised on the wind. He feared if he spoke with any effort, he would dislodge himself.

"Don't try to move! Your pack is caught on a rock! That's all that's holding you!"

"Can you reach me?"

"Sit tight! I'm going to throw a rope down and pull you up!"

On a ridge two-hundred yards away, Guzman watched the precarious drama played out on the slope. He itched with frustration that he would he cheated out of his execution. He needed to have Paul alive or the taking of his son would provide Guzman with no satisfaction. There was no art, no skill or sophistication, no glory for Satan in such an accidental death.

If Paul's son could save him, that would enhance Guzman's prospect of taking Matt. His father would be so filled with relief at his good fortune, the next visitation of catastrophe would work upon his mind all the more.

Paul shouted up to Matt on the ledge above. "I can't look up. Can't turn my head enough."

"Don't try. You won't have to. You'll only jar yourself loose. I'11 drop the end of the rope right down next to you. All you have to do is grab it."

Matt shrugged off his pack and took out a long coil of climbing rope. He fastened one end of it around his waist with a bowline, then tossed the line in a snaking arc out over the slope. It slapped down next to Paul, who clutched it with both hands and took a few quick wraps.

"Go Slowly." Matt shouted. "Tie it around your waist. Use a bowline."

"A bowline, a bowline," Paul thought desperately. "God damn it, I can't remember how it goes. How does it go? All right, all right, think a minute. Clear your head."

"Dad, can you hear me? Can you move enough to do it?" "Yes!" Their voices bounced and echoed down the slick scree. "Around the waist. .slow...slow there." Paul silently walked himself through the steps of tying the nonslip knot. He threaded and pulled, feeling the nylon hemp slide over his buttocks. . "Now, the loop, over and under... Okay... The snake comes up out of the hole, goes around the tree, and back down the fucking hole. Tug. Good! Okay! Good!"

Sweat poured from his face, stinging his eyes. He blinked rapidly, tearing. The sun refracted in the tears and blinded him. He clung there. His blood raced with an abrasive surge. He did not want to believe he was hanging there and all this was happening.

For a moment, he began to panic, anticipating, expecting, preparing for the fall and hideous death. He choked on the rising scream in his throat. The sudden discomfort of his underwear clogging his anus restored him to a level of conscious awareness that he could control his panic.

"Did you do it?" Matt's voice broke through his panic.

"Yes !"

"Are you ready?"

Paul tugged gently on the rope to signal that he was.

"Okay, I've got you now!" said Matt. "You won't fall anymore! Listen! When you feel my tug on the rope, roll and start climbing! I won't let up, so just keep on coming!" Matt braced his boots against a solidly embedded rock and leaned back nearly flat on the slope. "Ready!   Go!"

The rope suddenly jerked taut, cutting into his waist. Paul twisted over and slowly inched his way up toward Matt. His boots slipped and kicked loose shale that shunted away with a dry rattle and crescendoed to an echoing clatter on and on for hundreds of feet below.

Strain knotted every fiber of Matt's body. He rocked back, pulled slowly, steadily, hand over hand. With unbelievable clarity he watched his father's face flushed with fear and exertion moving up toward him, hands and fingers rubbed raw by the life-saving rope. Then he was there near the edge. Matt grabbed him by the arm and hauled him the remaining distance. They lay gasping on the narrow trail.

"That's one hell of a sliding board," Paul's voice croaked in a hoarse whisper. "I'd sure hate to hit the bottom. For a while there, I didn't think I was going to make it."

"Did you think I wouldn't be able to hold on?" asked Matt.

"No, I knew you'd never let go. I thought I wouldn't have the strength. You couldn't have held me then."

"I had my end of the rope tied around my waist."

Paul stared at him. "We would have gone down together."

Matt grinned. "Knowing that insured I was going to hold on and pull you all the way up, even if you did let go. You don't think I could've gone back home without you?"

After what his son had said to him last night, the statement stunned Paul.

Matt's grin widened at his father's expression. "They'd cite me for negligence, parental abuse, not looking out for my old man."

Paul fought back tears and forced his face into a cracked smile to hide his emotion. "Well, as they said in the Old West, I owe you one, pardner."

"How do you feel?"

"Scared shitless," said Paul.

"Anything broken?"

"I don't think so."   "Good."

"I'd rather not move for a while though," Paul glanced down the long slope.

"Okay by me." said Matt.

They rested, two tiny human figures on the face of the massive slope.

Chapter 26

After he got over stepping on Julie's toes, Leon thought he might actually enjoy ballroom dancing, especially the sweeping extravaganza of Strauss waltzes and the intense passion and driving movements of Argentine tangos. But what he enjoyed most was seeing his wife's infusion of energy and wild child-like exuberance. How beautiful and wonderful she is, he thought. I am fortunate to be married to her. He was sorry they had not taken up dancing long ago. His legs and feet tired rapidly. In time, he thought. Just need to get into condition. Using muscles I didn't think I had.

They had expected to find a moderately sized dance studio with a bar and mirrors similar to where they had taken their daughters at a younger age for ballet and jazz and tap lessons. This studio was the result of a warehouse renovation including an oversized dance floor and an adjoining dancewear store and health drink bar.

Leon remembered the many hours he had sat with other moms and dads watching their daughters, and in some cases amazingly agile sons, perform incredible joint-popping complex combinations of moves and twists and turns matching rhythms from two black stereo speakers the height of a short man. The sitting area was just outside the dance floor and allowed parents to watch their leaping gamboling offspring through a long window. Leon didn't understand how the children could tolerate the high decibel level of the music that was played. He caught snatches of the blast when dancers would leave or enter the room chattering animatedly to each other wearing leotards and tights, often with a filmy silken skirt snugged at the waist.

The dancing tugged gently at his thoughts and was somehow associated with Jim Owens, an implication of family, as though Owens either knew or intuited that the disappearance of Paul Evans was linked to family relationships. Paul Evans had probably never sat with the other moms and dads and watched his daughter dance. There was a connection there someplace, but he couldn't determine the origin of the impulse.

In spite of himself, or because of himself and what he had seen and experienced of life during the past fifty-five years, Leon was at heart, a romantic. He championed good over evil, which was one of the reasons he had joined the FBI twenty-five years ago. He wasn't an enforcer, a controlling personality and never had been, never could be. But he understood human behavior.

The FBI needed people who understood, not just Ninja warriors who incapacitated aberrant characters by force of numbers, firepower, and technology. Leon did not carry a club. That was not his purpose in life. He possessed a deep appreciation for the expression of emotion, or affect as it was termed in his profession. Through that appreciation, he related to music and to dance and to visual arts. He especially related to the impressionist paintings of Gauguin, Monet and Van Gogh, what he termed soft visual emotions, subtle bursts of color.

Life is a dance, thought Leon, *a celebration. Julie, we are celebrating.*

Long before the written word could guarantee that traditions would be passed on and respected, it was song and dance that helped preserve continuity.

Leon sometimes thought he had been born out of synch, that he belonged back in early periods of history when romanticism flowered.

His favorite was the waltz. The waltz stood for freedom of expression and freedom of movement. Unlike more courtly dances, with their restricted steps and predetermined poses, the waltz allowed the performers to sweep around the dance floor, setting their own boundaries and responsible to nobody but their partners.

Leon thought that what might have become of Paul Evans happened because he never learned to dance.

Ed Berzinsky came away from the interview of Jim Owens with a disturbing thought. The Paul Evans that Owens described sounded a little like Ed himself, with the exception that Evans was a monster and wanted to become the richest man in the world and that he would sell his soul to the Devil to get what he wanted.

"I'm not that far gone," Ed spoke half to his image in the rearview mirror and half to Leon semi-dozing in the passenger seat, as they drove home from the airport the night after his and Leon's return from California. "I love my kids. And, actually, I love my wife, but I'm bored with her. Hell, not with her, with our relationship. It isn't exciting anymore. Everything ends. So why do we do anything? If it feels good, do it. If it feels bad, stop. End of story. Makes life easy. How's that for psychology, Leon?"

"Easy for you to say," mumbled Leon. "But you live with other people."

"I had a hard life when I was a kid, Leon. I grew up in a tough neighborhood. My dad was a bum, and with six kids to look out for, my mom didn't have time for me. I was the youngest. Mom had to work, so my oldest sister took care of me. But you know what? I still loved my mom more than my sister." He glanced over at Leon, who was sound asleep.

Later, when Ed arrived home, he opened a beer and while shuffling through the mail on the dining room table, noticed a book his ten year old daughter was reading for school, The Devil and Daniel Webster. He picked it up and began flipping through the pages, then sat down and earnestly read the slim sixty-one pages.

Set during the early American period, the story was about a farmer who was down on his luck and sold his soul to the Devil so conditions would change for him. Ultimately, there was a big legal debate between Daniel Webster, a lawyer and politician, and the Devil when the Devil came to take the farmer. Daniel Webster outsmarted the Devil in the end.

Ed wondered if Paul Evans in some secular way had sold his soul to the devil. At that moment, a thought hurtled through his brain as though he'd been delivered an electric shock. The glimpse had triggered his imagination. A case he and a team of investigators had worked on without success five years ago was thought to be the work of a serial killer. But they had not been able to come up with enough evidence to even identify a subject. The only consistent pattern was that all the victims in the sudden rash of deaths, were successful entrepreneurs, CEO's, and a few politicians. They had all died of apparent natural causes and the case was put to rest. The one underlying characteristic of the pattern which the team tried to analyze for a killer's signature was the abrupt change in behavior commented on by people who had known the individuals. That same characteristic was associated with Paul Evans. Ed did not think it was a coincidence. He and Leon had more to look into.

He finished off his beer and stared at the cover of his daughter's book. The hour was late. He was tired and he began to feel creepy.

Evans' secretary had mentioned something that stuck in his mind about Evans' last meeting before he disappeared. It was with someone from the First World Corporation. They masterminded some of the largest and most complex and sophisticated mergers and acquisitions.

"Imagination, Ed. Don't let it run away with you." He yawned, stood up and carried the empty beer bottle into the kitchen.

*   *   *

Droplets of sweat stood out on Jacob Woo's forehead, an expression of the anxiety he was trying desperately to contain at the unexpected visit from the two FBI agents. He was worried that he might be in trouble for breaking a law about which he was unaware. A U.S. citizen immigrant from Beijing, China, where paranoia was a way of life, he was conditioned to be fearful whenever he was confronted by government officials. The power they held could alter his existence with the invention of a crime he had not even committed. Because he had come from a communist country, an investigation by the FBI carried far greater implications for him than the reason they gave him for their appearance. There was always a hidden agenda.

Leon recognized Jacob's anxiety for what it was, but he and Ed did not say or do anything to relieve the man's tension. A little fear factor often resulted in more and better information, even unasked for information.

Clearly, the thin-haired bespectacled MIS manager was highly qualified and knowledgeable about information systems. He supervised a staff of six who were responsible for software and hardware system maintenance for a user base of over 300 employees. One young Chinese man and another middle-aged Caucasian were responsible for systems installation and repair. He had three programmers, two female and one male. Another female was dedicated to providing program support to the finance and purchasing departments.

"We need backup copies of all files generated by Mr. Evans during the past three years," Ed explained.

"They are archived in a vault in the basement," Jacob responded. "I can have someone bring them up. Maggie's responsible for backing up the system. We have a daily, weekly, and monthly procedure. Most electronic records are on hard drives."

"I'll go with her," said Ed, and followed Jacob into a neighboring office where he made his request of the thirtyish blue-eyed woman with burnt-red hair, who didn't utter a word the entire time Ed was with her on the elevator ride, in the vault, and on the return.

While they were gone, Leon pursued a line of questioning with Jacob intended to revisit any unusual behavior of Paul Evans that Jacob might have observed. The episode of the Satanic diary appearing in the CEO's Microsoft Word files was still vivid in Jacob's mind. He originally thought some hacker was fooling around creating the files. It was easy enough to do on the Internet once the password was determined. The company maintained a website and Paul Evans featured an email address on his business card.

"We had a strange occurrence," Jacob spoke in a halting manner, his English sprinkled with heavily inflected Chinese speech patterns. "Some hacker, we think, invaded Mr. Evans' system and created a bunch of messages that sounded like a Satan worshipper. We tried everything we could to block the sender, but nothing worked. Whoever it was had more technology than we have the capability to jam. It was even happening on his computer at home, but, of course, that system is linked to the office. What was really strange, even with wireless, was that even when we disconnected the power cords, the activity never ceased. I am afraid to think of what is happening. There is nothing normal about this."

"How do you mean?" asked Ed. "What activity?"

"The appearance and printing of the messages."

"And you backed up those files too?"

"Yes, everything."

"Do you recall how Mr. Evans was acting while all this was going on?" asked Leon.

"He was really stressed out and worried that someone could get into his personal files like that. He also wanted to be sure we didn't think he was losing his mind. But like I said, we thought it was a hacker."

"Did this - hacker - get into any other files besides Mr. Evans'?"

"No, the intrusion was localized. Then one day, it suddenly stopped."

"Did you read any of the messages?"

"A few, but that's when I thought it was all a hoax, except now I'm not so sure. Although I don't really believe in it, there seems to be something supernatural going on. What got me was that Mr. Evans took it all very seriously. He seemed to actually be afraid and he doesn't strike me as a man who would be afraid of anything. Then after that, he stopped worrying about them, at least as far as we were concerned."

"How long ago did these messages begin appearing?"

"About a year. The files are dated."

"How many people here in the company know about the messages?"

"Just my department and Mr. Evans' secretary.   We kept it very confidential."

"Thank you, Jacob. You have been helpful."

"If you need anything more, we're available."

Leon nodded.

Back at their own office, Leon found a phone message waiting for him from his SAG, Waterman, to call him the moment he came in.

"What do you suppose that is?" asked Ed.

"We're about to find out." Leon hit the speed dial. Waterman responded as though he had been waiting with his hand on the phone.

"Leon, I know you're getting close, but you'll have to pull back a little. I just got word that the First World Corporation is off limits to us in the investigation."

"Who told you that and why?"

"First World has a top secret link to the Government."

"To the Government or to the administration?"

"That's all I know and that's all I can tell you."

"Black Sea is not a secret. They're in the news."

"Black Sea has nothing to do with it."

"First World holds all the no bid construction contracts in the U.S. and the Middle East. That's no secret either and Black Sea is their private police force."

"This has nothing to do with that. Our new orders are to pursue Guzman, but do not attempt to penetrate the First World Corporation. If you do, you will be removed from the case."

"That's an extreme comment, Waterman. Sounds like a few power mongers are in charge."

"You work for the Government, Leon, and you take orders from me."

"I'm not confident you're watching my back. Being terminated does not sit well with me, Waterman, especially on behalf of special interest politics."

"This is not politics, Leon, just a simple order from the top. Follow it or you're out." The connection went dead.

"What was that about?" Berzinsky chewed on a Snickers bar.

"Micromanagement."

Ed and Leon downloaded and pulled up the long series of files, carefully reading page after page of what appeared to have been created by a psychotic mind. They then went back through the FBI's database for an Antonio Guzman and came up with a criminal who was doing time in a Texas prison.

"Not our man," said Ed. "Whoever set this up is not your garden variety. This could be the guy we were looking for five years ago when, what was it, ten prominent executives and politicians started dropping from some spreading terminal disease. There wasn't any signature like this though, a diary to make you think you're crazy. It was something else, a pearl. A pearl was left in the hand of the victim."

"There's your connection," said Leon.

While they waited for the transmission, Ed conjectured further. "Whoever's behind this knows his business enough to make it look like someone else is the serial killer. There's no traceability to any of our archives. But he's the kind of guy who could probably get into our pants and alter the data, maybe even delete himself. There's something very different about him, very special. He knows too damn much, including how to use the technology to make him invisible."

"So, what are you implying?"

"It's someone who can create the illusion of being a different person and knows all the characteristics."

"Sounds like you're thinking of someone on the inside."

"It's a strong possibility," said Ed. "It's someone who knows how to kill in a very lethal way and without leaving a trail. The only commonality in those deaths was the abrupt change in behavior, like you see when a suspect starts using heavy recreational drugs."

"When we searched his home, there wasn't any evidence of drugs."

"Doesn't matter. He might have been involved in the trade and pissed somebody off.

Based on that diary, there's someone else we'd better get in touch with, Evans' son. I'll call the Los Angeles office and they can follow-up."

The next morning, they received a call from the Los Angeles agent who had paid a visit to the apartment in Westwood near UCLA that Matt Evans shared with a roommate, a fellow graduate student. The information that Matt had gone to Montana to meet his father set Leon and Ed in motion.

Chapter 27

Denham knew the mountain lions could be holed up in one of several caves in a fifty mile radius. He saw the cats twice before on deer hunts. During the summer months, he returned and discovered their den. But soon after, they moved.

The following morning, he left the camp and found two distinct sets of prints in the lakeside mud among deer spore and read that they were shadowing a small herd.

He followed the deer for the rest of the morning until be located the herd's thicket near a heavily grazed abundant meadow well-trod with crisscrossing paths to a central watering place on the shore of a small lake bordering the meadow.

By not bringing in dogs, Denham anticipated the opportunity for a stakeout. A ring of large boulders at the base of the bowl of surrounding slopes narrowed the meadow into a natural arena with the lake blocking the main outlet down into the neighboring valley.

The deer had chosen a high place near timberline with adequate concealment and enough open space to make it difficult for natural predators to move in close without detection and surprise them. Denham saw this arrangement and knew the cats would have to expose themselves and make a running kill on the meadow. He returned to camp and explained the layout to the Mackes. They would move into position a few hours before dawn the next day and wait.

With an afternoon ahead of them and little to do but lie around camp, Luther and Denham broke out a deck of cards and played rummy and poker for loaded rounds.

Vince stripped off his clothes and waded into the lake. Whooping and splashing about in the chill waters, he shouted at his grinning brother.

"Come on in. Get the dirt and stink off you."

"Hell, I'm no fool. That's straight ice water. I can live with my dirt and stink."

"Then build up the fire. In about a minute, I'm comin' outta here like a shot."

Shaking his head, Willie walked back to the low fire and added several logs. As the flames crackled up through the pine bark to a height of three feet, Vince charged out of the water roaring like a buffalo and danced about the fire wildly waving his arms, slapping himself and whooping and howling like a naked savage.

His dick flopping against his thighs, he cold sprayed the two old men, leaped over their card game and sprinted out among the grazing horses and mules. He leaped bare-assed and bareback onto one of the mules, who proceeded to buck.

The other men roared with laughter at his exuberance and wild antics. "You're crazy," shouted Luther, holding his side pained with mirth. "You're god damn wild crazy."

Vince suddenly grunted and slipped off the outraged mule. Clutching his balls, he limped back to the lake and washed himself until the ache in his groin subsided. He returned to the fire and pulled on his clothes.

Willie sat tapping a stick against a rock. After a few moments, he rose and walked away.

"Where you goin'?"

"Take a short hike."

Vince nodded and contemplated the card game, decided against it and stretched out for a nap. "Damn mule's got a backbone like an ax."

Just killing time, Willie walked slowly past the mules and horses up a gentle rock studded slope to a flat low-lying saddle between two small peaks. Standing at the center, he gazed down into the adjacent valley.

Guzman had crept into position to study the camp from a high vantage point downwind from the horses and mules. He watched the young man leave the camp and walk up the slope to within a hundred yards of where he was hidden.

He counted four men. He could see the high powered rifles among the equipment. With the number of mules and horses, there was no mistaking it was a hunting party.

The site appeared comfortably established as a base camp. He did not see any hides or game. So they had only recently arrived and would likely go out after deer during the next few days.

The time was drawing near when he would take Paul Evans' son. The men in the hunting party below would play a part.

Early the next morning, like medieval apparitions, the deer moved through the predawn mist across the open meadow to drink at the lake. A doe lowered her head and wiggled her ears to clear off the gnats and flies. Her springing fawn ranged away from her, ran in erratic circles and returned with an energetic kick and twist of its hindquarters.

The lead buck tested the air. The two mountain lions that had been trailing the herd left him nervous. His caution kept the herd alive, and he was too seasoned to assume the herd had eluded the predators, although the other deer seemed calm and satisfied.

The valley created their sense of security, the seclusion of the thicket, the slopes and meadow and quiet lake. They were accustomed to their patterns in this location. Here they had never been molested. It was a place safe from fear.

The buck tensed and raised his head as though he sensed a change. His racks tilted to the left and he snorted. He detected a presence, though he had yet to give a warning. His nostrils flared, searching the wind. Ears twitched back, seeking suspicious sounds. The mountain lions fell behind, but hadn't been forgotten.

Rising trout dimpled the placid lake. The buck's head jerked up. His anxious snort resounded across the lake. The other deer came up, poised for flight, waiting. Droplets fell from their wet muzzles.

The buck sucked in air. He scanned the boulders and thickets, listened intently with nostrils flaring, sifting the familiar morning scents. Still he detected nothing. Then the stillness, the difference in the air came to him...the stillness. The morning birds were silent. He looked toward the dense brush at the edge of the meadow.

The male cougar sprang from the thicket and rushed the herd, which scattered in a stampede of terror. His mate waited a moment, then leaped from concealment at another location to head off the running deer. They whirled and doubled back and split into the thickets where they were slowed by the density of brush.

In fright and confusion, a doe ran for the lake. The two cats singled her out and went after her while the rest of the herd crashed away up the slope and over the rim.

She dodged and twisted in the frantic chase with bellowing rasping fear and death, striking thuds of sharp pointed hoofs. The mountain lions collided into her with a smack of bodies and dragged her to the ground with a tearing of hide and flesh.

The cats pulled her with their fangs sunk deep into her broken neck. They held and weighed her down, blood flowing into their mouths and into the cold earth. They finally released their hold, lay panting a moment, then rose and fed voraciously.

A volley of rifle fire exploded at them from the rocks. They leaped away, the female hit, blood coursing in sticky webs from a hole just behind her left shoulder. She ran after her mate and they were gone into the trees.

The men could hear the cats' rapid dash up the slope as a loud crackling swish through the underbrush. then sudden silence. The four men stood and walked down out of the boulders. They crossed the meadow along the lake shore and stared at the freshness of the kill. Flies gathered and fed on the blood.

Denham saw blood on the wet grass where the wounded female had left a distinct trail that would allow them to track her through the thickets.

"She's hit bad," said Denham. "Won't get far. Willie, go bring up the horses. Vince, I want you and Luther to back me up. Fan out going in."

Willie watched for a moment as the other three men cautiously approached and entered the thickets. He again looked at the carcass, then turned and walked quickly back toward the boulders and steep narrow trail out of the valley at the upper end of the lake.

He pulled at his underwear crawling up inside his anus. When they returned to camp, he vowed he would work up enough courage to bath in the cold lake. Grime clung to him like a second skin.

Among the trees, Luther, Vince, and Denham followed the blood trail spattered on rocks, darkening the grass and undergrowth. Clusters of large boulders crowded in among the dense foliage, providing many hiding places from which the cats could ambush.

The slope grew steep near the rim for a brief abrupt climb to the top. They stopped while Denham searched for more sign, worrying the cats might have circled back and could be coming up behind them. The others watched him scan the rocks and brush. A cold wind soughed through the pines. Death hung in the air. The men looked about in chilled isolation.

Denham continued. The others trailed him cautiously down the back slope among many more boulders and dense growth.

The cats suddenly appeared on a large granite mound just above and behind the three men. Blood streamed from the female's wound. She lay collapsed, her life flowing out.

Denham stopped, then Vince and Luther. A premonition was coming to Denham from a deep impulse in his mind, the sense, the sign, the moment, the meaning. But Denham could not see the slip, the passage of a soul energy into death. The impulse buzzed and clouded his brain. It was only in turning to find the slip that he saw the male cat crouch to spring at Vince and Luther.

He brought up his rifle and fired. Luther and Vince whirled, firing repeatedly. The male cat flashed away, gone in a brief tawny moment.

Screaming her agony and defiance, jerking at the deep penetration of slugs, the female slid through a wash of her gushing blood down the face of the boulder to the ground.

Concerned that the male might attempt another attack, Denham did not drop his caution, but covered the surrounding thickets.

When their trembling subsided, Luther and Vince examined the cat. She looked small in death.

Denham scouted around the uphill side of the boulder and discovered broken brush and fresh blood specks indicating the male had run angling away parallel to the slope. He followed the trail of kicked up humus and pine needles for several yards, until Luther came up behind him.

Denham stopped. "He's wounded. Not bad, but a Little. Won't stop him. Leavin' an easy trail. I'11 track him. When Willie gets here with the horses, take the female back to camp.

"You goin' alone?"

Denham nodded. They turned and walked back down the slope to Vince and the dead cat, again examined her and stood in awe, repulsed and nauseated at what they had done, yet hardening themselves in the manliness of the act, manifesting nothing of their emotions but a tough, humble acceptance.

Riding his own horse, leading the other three and one pack mule, Willie moved at a jog trot across the open meadow from the upper end of the lake and entered the trees. Maneuvering up the slope through the boulders, he met Vince walking down to meet him. "I heard shots. You get 'em?"

"The female." Vince took the mule and one of the horses. Willie followed him over the rim of the hill to Denham and Luther.

At the sight and smell of the dead cougar, the horses and mule balked and pulled back snorting with fear. Vince and Willie shouted and slapped them up with the reins to regain control. Two horses reared. Luther lunged to assist with the stomping milling animals. One fell over onto its back kicking and thrashing in the brush, intensifying its fear.

Denham waded into the melee to take his own horse and quickly lead him away up the hill to the trail of the male cat. He studied the ground ahead. The shouts of the men and fearful snorts and neighs of the horses reached him from down the slope. He moved on, following the tracks.

It was an hour before the Mackes could calm the animals enough to load the dead cat. She was heavy and left her strong smell and blood on the men.

The horses trembled and could not believe their sight over their smell. The small clearing reeked of cat musk and blood. The mule shit nervously and rolled its eyes back at the dead creature it carried, then followed the tug at its halter. The men mounted their horses and led the mule and its load away.

Connected by a rushing stream with many pools and waterfalls, a series of small lakes, like steps, extended the length of the valley.

Matt reclined in the shade and watched his father tying a fly to the end of a long section of nylon leader. Paul stuck the fly hook into the cork handle of the rod.

"I'm going to try the upper lakes. You coming?"

Matt's gaze wandered to the stream. "Think I'll just lie around here. Maybe swim, catch a little sun."

"How can you stand that water? It's freezing."

"It's not so bad once you're in. You can adjust to it in a few minutes."

"Maybe you can," said Paul. "Well, I'll be back in a few hours."

Matt nodded. He watched his father set off along the stream up a long gradual rock-strewn slope above to the next lake where he passed from sight.

A quarter mile from the Evans' camp, Guzman watched Paul make a leisurely climb up the terraced slopes to the farthest and highest lake, a great distance to return quickly and closed in by the terrain in such a manner that a shout, or even the report of a rifle from below would not reach him.

The uppermost lake dropped down into a shallow bowl. Paul whipped the line back and forth, then lightly set the fly out over the water. The area was a dead spot for traveling sound.

Back down near the Evans' campsite, never revealing himself, Guzman moved in slowly, patiently stalking Matt Evans.

Matt removed his clothes in a timeless sleepy manner. The wind touched his skin, raising a chill even in the warm direct sun. Standing naked by the stream at the edge of a pool below a small cascade, he braced himself for the cold entry, waded in up to his knees. Shivering, teeth chattering through grunts of shock, he splashed water over his chest, face, arms, back; then with a loud WHOOP plunged in and thrashed to the falls, letting it rain down upon him.

The Mackes' entered that same valley through a rocky cut slightly above the Evans' camp. Riding at a slow walk, Luther and Willie passed a bottle back to Vince, who led the skittish pack mule bearing the dead female cougar.

Vince took a slug of whiskey, then another. Willie slowed so his brother could hand forward the bottle, drank, rode up next to Luther and handed him the bottle.

Luther tipped it high to capture the last swallow, then tossed it away. For a moment, it arced and caught the sun in a spraying prism that exploded against the rocks. The men lurched with rag-doll drunkenness in their saddles.

Luther drew to a sudden halt on a slight rise of ground that overlooked the stream and campsite. Willie and Vince blundered into the rear of his horse.

"Will you look at that," said Luther.

They focused in the same direction

Lying on his stomach on a long flat boulder in the sun, Matt dozed, unaware of the men. At that angle and distance, his long blonde hair splayed over his back and shoulders and his slender waist and buttocks appeared to be those of "a woman," said Vince. Luther smiled. "Look at that nice white ass."

Eyes narrowed. Vince leaned forward. "She alone? Don't seem right for a woman to be out here alone."

"Don't see nobody else."

"Wonder what she's doin' way the hell up here all by herself," said Willie.

"Communing with nature, Willie Boy," Luther grunted and shifted, rubbing his expanding groin against the saddle pommel. "And nature is just about to pay her a call. Let's go down and say hello."

Guzman lay unmoving among the large rocks at the opposite side of the valley and watched the three men ride their horses at a walk down the slope to the campsite.

Matt lay sound asleep on his towel. The icy water had drained his strength. Now, in sleep, the sun slowly restored him.

The noise of the stream muffled the approach of the horses and riders. Then, one horse neighed. Matt jerked awake. He raised his head and saw the legs of the three horses and one mule close by, stared up further in recognition and surprise.

The three men were shocked and disappointed at the sight of the mustache and unshaven jaw that spoke with a deep voice. "Hello."

As Matt stood, he wrapped the towel around his waist. He stared at the dead cougar slung over the back of the mule, the rifles in saddle mounts, the thick leather gun belts jeweled with brass bullets. He grew increasingly aware of the men's ominous silence. They stared at him with mutual curious hostility.

Matt bobbed his head. "Hi, I'm Matt Evans. We've met."

Still silence, then the cruelty of Luther's voice cut through him. "First time I ever saw a woman with *cajones*."

Matt's guts jellied with fear at Willie's drunken giggle and Luther's malevolent grin. Vince smiled sheepishly with a good natured shake of his head.

Matt interpreted their expressions as an unmistakable threat. Trying not to show his alarm, he started toward the packs thirty yards away across an open space.

Luther suddenly spurred his horse to cut off Matt, who jumped aside to avoid being knocked down by the rush of the animal.

"Hey, what the hell you think you're doin'?"

He tried to dodge around the horse, but again Luther cut him off from reaching his clothes and forced him to back away toward the stream. He noticed that Vince and Willie watched their father with disapproving stares. He sought to assert himself to cover his fear.

"Hey, enough's enough. You got no right fuckin' around with me like this," yelled Matt.

"We don't fuck faggots, boy. We fuck wimmin."

Luther glanced over at his sons for encouragement and did not find it in their faces.

"Shit, move your horse's ass," Matt commanded.

"My horse don't like the way you talk about him, boy."

"Get the fuck outta my way, you faggoty old bastard."

Being called an old bastard stung Luther. Being called a faggot enraged him. "Nasty tongue you got there, boy. Need to do somethin' about that."

Matt shouted an angry appeal to Vince and Willie, who seemed immobilized by this spectacle. "Hey, come on. Make him stop. You've had your fun."

The earring and streaked long hair, the mustache and hard agonized features, like the college kid in the army basic training, broke through Willie's fog. "He's okay, pa. Let's leave him be."

Matt's eyes flicked to Willie with relief. Willie could identify with him, but Luther's words and unyielding manner killed hope of a reprieve.

"Whattaya mean, okay," Luther snarled. "He's a goddamn faggot."

Vince's cajoling authoritative voice crossed the space between them. "Come on, Pa. It was a good one on us. Laugh it off." Willie shouted to Matt. "We thought you was a woman lyin' down here alone. Got ourselves all hot and bothered for nothin'."

Willie's nervous laugh attempted to break the spell that held Luther in its grip. Luther's voice came from somewhere low and far away.

"Well, we ain't goin' yet. This cocksucker owes me and my horse an apology."

"Are you shittin' me? Jesus." Matt waved him away. "Get the hell outta here. We already played cowboy back in that bar."

"Come on, Pa," Vince barked. Let's go. Leave 'im alone."

"We ain't goin' anywhere 'til this prick-tease does what I tell 'im," said Luther.

Vince's voice commanded hard and cold. "I'm tellin' you, old man, leave him alone and get your ass down that trail."

Being called old man by his son further enraged Luther. He stared a moment at Vince and Willie, then suddenly lashed Matt across the face with his leather quirt raising a long red welt.

Matt stumbled back, putting his hand to the sharp sting. His towel fell away to the ground, leaving him naked.

Vince and Willie were angered and appalled at their father. They knew he really wanted to strike at them, his own sons. As he carried his act farther against Matt to regain his domination over them, he slid lower in their esteem.

Luther spurred his horse in a lunge against Matt, knocking him stunned to the ground. Luther challenged Vince with a powerful stare. He spoke aside, without looking at Matt. "Sister, before we leave, you're gonna crawl around here and kiss my horse's ass and tell 'im you're sorry."

"You're sick," Matt spit out.

Luther's gaze swiveled from Vince and bore ominously down on Matt. He noticed a camera placed out near one of the packs. With a quick dismount, he walked over, grabbed it, and returned to Matt, who feared to rise.

"Hey, you naked son-of-a-bitch, how'd you like to have your picture took?"

"God damn it," Vince persisted. "I'm talkin' to you."

Luther snapped pictures of Matt, angry, injured, humiliated on the ground. As Matt tried to rise, Luther planted his heavy heeled boot and sharp spur rowel on his chest and held him pinned to the ground."

"You're hurting me, god damn it."

"Awww, whatsamatter, Blondie, can't take it?"

Matt writhed under the increased pressure and needle prick of the spur that drew tiny bubbles of blood.

"Luther!" Vince bellowed his impotence.

"Come on, Pa!" Willie's desperate cry sang to him and glanced off his mind, a voice faint and distant.

"Let's get us a good one of your balls." In a sexual frenzy, Luther rapidly snapped pictures of Matt's genitals, then suddenly stopped, panting and sweating, climaxing with semen running wet and sticky down the inside of his leg. He looked up at his son's quiet sober faces staring down at him.

He could not meet their gaze and looked away with shame and fear at his behavior. Throwing the camera aside, he pulled his hunting knife from its sheath. The blade flashed downward at Matt.

Luther heard the click of a rifle. A bullet buzzed past his ear and ricocheted off the rocks.

"You touch him with that knife and I'11 blow your head off," said Vince.

Luther slowly looked up at him. "You wouldn't do that. I'm your father."

A second shell clicked into the chamber. Vince sighted down on his father's head. Luther suddenly knew real fear, that his son would not hesitate to kill him. Willie watched tensely, trying to control the shying mule.

"Get on your horse," ordered Vince. "We're going. Now."

Luther straightened and walked rigidly to his horse. He returned the knife to its sheath, then soberly mounted.

Tears streamed down Matt's soiled face. As he staggered to his feet, he picked up a sharp heavy rock and with a savage cry heaved it at Luther. It fell short and struck his horse across its face, gashing deeply and drawing blood. The horse reared, nearly toppling Luther backwards.

At the sight of the injury and streaming blood, in an impetuous moment of insanity, in one motion as his horse again reared staggering hind-legged with a high-pitched whistle of pain, Luther drew his rifle from its saddle scabbard one handed and fired at Matt.

The bullet passed through high toward his left shoulder. Matt screamed and fell, writhing, clutching at the wound, his hands and arms basted in blood.

"NOOOO!" Vince roared. "OH, JESUS CHRIST! YOU GOD DAMN BASTARD! OH, SHIT! OH MY GOD!"

The horses and mule reared and shied about violently, their hoofs beating a staccato of dust.

"WE GOTTA DO SOMETHING," Willie shouted. "WE GOTTA DO SOMETHING."

"YOU LOST YOUR MIND!" Vince roared, pulling his turning horse to a standstill. "HE'S BLEEDIN' TO DEATH!"

Surfacing from his momentary haze, Luther recovered enough to realize he must regain control of himself and the situation, control over his sons. "Shit, he don't need 'em anyway. He sighted on Matt's genitals."

Screaming, Vince leaped down from his horse. "MY GOD, YOU ARE SICK! WE GOTTA DO SOMETHIN' FOR HIM!"

Luther leveled his rifle now at Vince, who stopped dead in disbelief, staring up at his father and the rifle.

"Don't you touch 'im. He's gonna die anyway. Better him than you. We're gonna go now."

Bile rose into Willie's throat at the shock of what he was witnessing. He tried to hold it back and swallow, then suddenly leaned out of the saddle and vomited the whiskey sitting in his belly.

"I don't believe this," Vince's hoarse voice cracked. "I don't believe this is happening, not you."

Luther worked the rifle's lever action, loading a shell into the chamber. "So you'd kill your old man, would you? I said move. It was an accident. He shouldn't have throwed that rock. Look at Poco's eye."

Blood dripped from the gash across the animal's eye and forehead down his face. His nostrils snorted red bubbles.

Vince took a step toward him. "Luther, I'm talkin' to you."

"There ain't nothin' we can do for him. Now let's go."

Vince and Willie hesitated, afraid to move. They stared down at Matt, who was unconscious from pain and the rapid loss of blood. Uncertain of their father's sanity, they were afraid of him, afraid to go up against him.

Vince suddenly, quickly mounted his horse. With a final look at Matt and Luther, he bowed his head. Eyes hot with tears, he moved off.

Willie grabbed up the mule's trailing lead rope and followed them. He returned his rifle to its scabbard.

They crossed the stream at a gravel bar near the camp and rode at a gallop down the valley to escape the horror of what they had done.

Willie looked back once at Matt's diminishing body lying in the camp.

The dead cougar swayed and bounced on the back of the frenzied mule.

Chapter 28

Matt slowly regained consciousness. opened his eyes, looked down, and saw his blood flowing out of him. His hand clutched his towel in a feeble grasp and held it to the flesh wound. The bullet had glanced off the rock and had not penetrated.

"Dad." His voice was a weak whisper.

Losing the towel along the way, he half crawled, half dragged his weakened body to the stream. He eased into the rushing water that swept away his blood.

Momentarily revived by the cold shock, he let the current carry him to the opposite bank. He pulled himself out onto the grass, leaving a smeary trail of blood.

Watching from his hiding place, Guzman felt strangely moved and weakened. He saw the boy's father still peacefully fishing at the highest lake.

Guzman began to laugh, an uncontrolled emotional response to his own physical and psychological state. He laughed at the wind and the sky. He laughed at a column of ants trailing in and out of a small crater shaped hole. Then he stopped and removed his clothes and walked out to the stream.

Matt's vacant stare saw a naked man, liquid in form emerge from the stream, then

he reeled into unconsciousness at this strange apparition.

Guzman positioned his arms under Matt's body and easily lifted him. He carried him away across the meadow and disappeared into a grove of timber. There, near Guzman's clothing, he placed Matt on a soft natural bed of pine needles. He took bandages from his pack and dressed Matt's wound to staunch the flow of blood. Then he sat near him to wait for Paul's return.

Up at the highest lake. Paul landed his fifth trout and placed it on a cord stringer with the others. Pleased with the catch, he reeled in his line, gathered up the fish, and walked back along the shore to the lower end of the lake.

Descending the long gradual valley slope, he passed the other lakes in returning to the campsite. Coming in, he was surprised to discover that Matt was missing.

He called out, "Matt."

Scanning the area, he saw his son's clothes piled neatly on a rock near the packs. He looked toward the stream and saw the blood-stained towel and trail of drying blood over the ground. He dropped his fly rod and the stringer of fish and ran to the water. It was clear to the bottom.

He walked downstream along the bank, searching the water and stopped at three piles of horse droppings and a mosaic of hoof prints in the mud.

Frantic, he ran further dawn along the stream bank until he reached the gravel bar where the signs of the horses' crossing were evident. He stared hard at the water, here shallow enough that a body would not have been carried by the current beyond this point.

He waded the stream and climbed out on the opposite bank. He studied the tracks in the mud leading away across the meadow down the valley.

His hoarse cry lifted in the sunlight. "Matt. Matt."

Guzman watched and listened. "Your son is mine now," he said quietly. "Your son is mine."

The Mackes' climbed, thrashing their horses up the final slope and rode them stumbling into camp. The animals heaved, weaving straddle-legged, bleeding from the nose as saddles were loosened and pulled from their lather-soaked backs.

Vince dragged the dead cougar from the mule. Drawing his skinning knife, he slit her belly and disemboweled her, then quickly, angrily sliced and peeled and folded back the tawny hide leaving the raw red membranous muscle exposed.

Taking a hacksaw, he severed her head.

Willie turned away and retched, sobbing weakly at the finish.

Vince wedged the head and skin in a nearby tree, then dragged the guts and carcass far from the camp.

Only dimly aware of the skinning and choked retching, Luther sat and stared at the coals of the dead fire. Then after Vince had dragged away the carcass, he led the horses and mule into the meadow, staked them out and sobbed against the neck of his own horse.

Several miles from the base camp, Denham had caught only one glimpse of the male mountain lion slipping over the rim of a cliff, impassable to a man and a horse. It was always that way. The cats were elusive unless you waited and they came to you.

Even hunting with dogs, up here you could not run a cat to the ground or tree him. The terrain was too rugged, the air too thin.

A light-headedness softened his brain. Weakened, he sank to the ground at the feet of his patient horse, who breathed his stale, oat-scented breath snuffling down over the old man's head.

The horse nudged him to remind him of important practical things, of food and the comradeship of the other horses whom he had reluctantly left behind. His was a simple wisdom.

To his disgust and impatience, his master suddenly dozed on the ground. The horse waited as he was trained to do and did not fret. But he did nibble at nearby clumps of grass to ease the hollow rumble of hunger in his cavernous belly.

The storm had been brewing and cycling in for two days and now pushed its frontal warning clouds in great cumulo-nimbus pile-ups among the high promontories. The sudden blocking of the sun shattered the setting light in a brilliant corona of red-orange laser-like beams that struck the far peaks

Paul sensed the impending night. He lovingly gathered up his son's clothes and held them to him. Moaning with grief and disorientation, he sat on a rock as the night closed in around him.

At the Mackes' base camp, Willie sat apart from Vince and Luther and could not eat. Vince gorged ravenously. Luther ate reluctantly, holding small bits of food in his mouth for long periods, barely chewing.

The sky had grown ominously black. The wind tore at the flames with a rush.

The Mackes' saw Denham riding in slowly a half mile from the camp. Thunder rumbled among the peaks behind him.

Willie looked at his father. Indecision haunted Luther's eyes. He saw his son watching him and glanced away.

Vince's hard silence commanded them to say nothing. For a moment, his gaze locked with his brother -- a threat, a plea, a warning.

They watched Denham approach and enter the camp. His horse was eager with hunger. Denham slowly dismounted. The stiffness of age slowed his movements as he unsaddled and unbridled the animal and put on a rope and halter.

His eyes took in the head and hide of the female mountain lion. He poured grain into a feed bag and fastened it over his horse's snuffling nose. Then he walked to the fire, grabbed a plate and filled it with stew from the pot. Willie poured him a cup of coffee and placed several biscuits on his plate.

Denham ate slowly at first, then with increasing hunger, as though he had rediscovered food and life.

The others silently watched, quickly averted their eyes as he caught their collective glance. Chewing thoughtfully, he studied them, wondering at their somber mood, then turned his full attention to eating.

Vince looked at Willie, who turned away. I should have gone, he thought, should have gone long ago, the time I met Sylvie. Just walked away from here. Should have accepted Wyandotte's offer and we could've been married and gone on down to Tucson, her kid and all. It was the kid though, damn it. She got in the way. No, hell, it was me, my problem. The kid was all right. She was fine. I didn't really want to do it then. Wasn't ready. Hell, just plain didn't want to do it. That's all. What it amounts to. Admit it to yourself. Now it's too damn late

Vince had met Sylvie at his last big rodeo in Helena. She worked as a secretary on the program committee and they were introduced at a barbecue hosted by the rodeo association

They talked over his successes of the past week. She seemed nervous and awkward to him, laughing too much and inappropriately with shrugging shoulders and bobbing head. She was skinny, but had a nice face, dished nose, small mouth and chin. Braces winked out from her bottom teeth. A soft sympathetic Texas drawl flowered with her warm smile.

"You should hear my kid. All her friends have their own horses. Why can't I have a horse, mom? Same old story - money. But that doesn't make any difference, not to a ten year old."

"You married?" Vince asked her early in the conversation.

"Not anymore. Divorced three years ago. It was pretty awful. I won't burden you with it."

"Why not?" Vince leaned in close, interested in whatever she might have to say.

"We've just met and I hardly think you want to hear about my past marital problems," said Sylvie.

"You got me wrong then. I'd like to know more about you."

Her blue ryes deepened their intensity, judging his sincerity.

"Why don't we get out of here," he said.

Vince could not talk openly about his life to most people, but he felt secure with her, trusting her. Some things, as a man, he could not bring himself to reveal. When he was done, she told him he must get away, must finally leave home and make a life of his own

"It's a kind of dying," she said. "You're slowly suffocating out there. It's a trap, part of it your own making. I know what I'm talking about. I have a mother who refused to let go. Even after I was married, I depended on her. You know. I hung on. We fed off each other. I finally had to put miles between us. We had to separate our lives to go on cleanly. Do you know what I mean?"

He stayed with Sylvie two nights. On the third day, her daughter returned from visiting with a friend. Tamara hated her name, loved her father, and blamed herself for his leaving them.

She let Vince know at once what a wonderful man her father was, how nice he had been to her and how bad and awful she had been to him, always yelling, pouting, and demanding more things. Yet he had never raised his hand or voice against her.

When Vince offered to teach her how to ride, she melted in his arms. For a few hours during the days he was not in competition, he borrowed a steady old saddlehorse from a friend and the lessons commenced.

He feared he would be making a mistake. For the moment, it was sunshine and daisies. But what came later, six months, a year from then?

It also concerned him that he would be taking the leftovers of another man instead of starting out fresh on his own. The child worried him, her endless talking about her father and her unabashed comparisons between him and Vince. He wanted Sylvie without her child, but could not have one without the other. Tamara conspired to never allow them time alone. When Vince complained to Sylvie, she retaliated that it was none of his business how she raised her daughter and to stay out of it. He said he would do just that and walked out.

He received two letters from Sylvie, apologizing, asking him to come and see her. He did not reply. When the time came for him to leave home, he would not jump from the skillet into the fire.

But her memory stayed with him. So what if she didn't handle the kid the way he thought she should. What did he know about kids anyway. All he'd ever done was raise cows and horses. At least she understood me, like no other woman ever did. And I think I really love her. When we get out of this.

Suddenly, he felt the need of family, whole and complete, free of hate and blood and death. I should have gone, he thought. Maybe it's too late now. Coming to the end of everything, caught in our own loop. No way out for the old man, or us. Dying, maybe that's all we got left, dying.

At his camp Paul built up the fire slowly, twig by twig, bit by bit. He saw a vision in his imagination of his son's body lying close by. Matt's exposed face reflected the blow of the wind ravaged flames. The wavering movement mesmerized Paul. He stared hard, wanting desperately to hold the image of his son in the periphery of the flames.

The distant laughter of a small boy grew loud, faded in his mind. He heard Matt's childish voice calling, "Dad, hey Dad, look at me. Watch now. Okay, now see if you can find me."

They were playing hide 'n seek in Grampa Schultz's barn. So many places to hide, it was hard to tell from where his voice was coming. The perfume of fresh hay saturated the loft and made Paul feel drunk and heady with youth. Unshirted, he squirmed at the itch of sweat and chaff.

Hearing the thud of sneakers on the ground floor below, he smiled and moved quickly to the open loft door and looked down. Young Matt skidded to a halt in the dust and glanced up and saw him. With a squeal of laughter, he dashed back inside the barn.

Paul looked out across the yard. Smiling, Moya watched from the veranda. He raised his hand and she waved. Then he withdrew into the loft to stalk his son in the dusty filtered sunlight of their imagined world.

They picnicked and went rowing on the river. One warm sleepless summer night, he and Moya walked out into a. field with a blanket and made love while a thousand crickets sang to them, and several mosquitoes found them and left them with itching lumps in embarrassing places.

He cried with great sobs of despair, for the beautiful moments of his life were few and began and ended only in distorted memories.

The fire burned down to a pile of glowing coals. He sat vigil through the night and fell asleep just before dawn. When he woke, the coals were dead.

Rigid from lying in one position, he moved his arms slightly to restore circulation. His semi-comatose stare did not deviate from the black char that had been a dancing fire, memories.

After a long time, he rolled to his knees, then staggered up. He stood swaying slightly from the effort and shuffled to the edge of the stream. He planted himself on the long flat rock where Matt had lain and watched the sun appear over the peaks until the   golden shafts of warmth pierced him.

He slowly removed his clothes. Naked, unflinching at the numbing shock of freezing water, he entered the stream and rocked over in submersion, then surfaced with a gasp. His heart beat wildly.

Standing at midstream with the cold current tugging at his legs and groin, he stared with strength and rage down the valley as the sun rose at his back. He fully believed that whoever had been there on the horses had murdered his son. He would hunt them down.

Chapter 29

Paul hefted the pack to his back. With a quick shrug of his shoulders, he settled its bulky weight into position. At the sound of rolling thunder, he looked up toward the peaks. Wind-churned leaden clouds darkened the sunrise. Lightning cracked across the sky like an enormous whip of fire.

He steadily followed the trail down the valley in the direction of the Mackes' camp. From concealment, Guzman watched him go.

When Paul arrived at the camp, the Mackes were gone. He startled a raven poking about the dead fire. His eyes followed its flight, then, with unwavering intent, gazed further down the long valley to the next range that divided him from the departed hunters.

Snow began to fall in flurries whipped by the cold wind, driving it into the faces of the horses and men moving at a walk along the trail.

Willie suddenly pulled his horse off to the side. Sensing his intention to go back to the man wounded by their father, Vince stopped. As Willie attempted to urge his horse past, Vince cut him off and grabbed the other animal's reins close to the bit. He twisted the horse's head hard against the neck of his own horse. "Let go," Willie shouted.

Vince's commanding expression and his grip on the reins kept his brother in place. Willie's horse crowded against Dandy, who stood anchored against the other animal. The ears of Willie's mare flagged back and forth and her lips quivered nervously at this sudden punishment to her mouth by the jerking of the bit.

Fifty yards down the trail, Luther and Denham leading the pack mules stopped to look back. The older men could not hear what was being said between the two brothers. Denham recognized the signs of an altercation. He looked over at Luther, who avoided his glance. Denham realized that what was happening at that moment somehow related to the Mackes somber mood of the previous night.

His first thought was that they were having another of their notorious family arguments. But now Willie's sudden attempt to turn back and being prevented by Vince puzzled Denham.

Something had happened up there that he had not seen. Because of their silence, they were keeping knowledge of the incident from him. He suspected it related to him. He quelled his curiosity and the desire to ask Luther what was going on among them. He would discover his answers by listening and observance. Eventually, something they would say or something in their manner would tip him off.

Willie tried to force on but Vince held him back. Denham saw their postures of threat and warning against one another. Then Willie slumped in his saddle at something Vince said. After a moment, with Vince guardedly bringing up the rear, they returned to Luther and Denham.

The four men and the pack string straggled out along the trail as they continued making slow progress down the valley.

High among the peaks, the full force of the storm howled its release.

At noon, Paul paused only long enough for a cold meal and a brief rest. He did not build a fire. He had not yet seen the horses and men he was following, only periodic droppings and sunken hoof prints in the dust or gouged mud and turf at stream

crossings.

He judged they were at least two or three days from the nearest ranch or town and they would stop for the night. He would walk until he saw their fire.

While they stopped to make camp, he would gain on them during the next few hours of remaining daylight.

The storm concerned him. A driving blizzard would confuse his progress and obscure his vision. He might even walk right past them in the darkness.

He must proceed carefully, thinking out the terrain. A misstep could cause him a severe fall, a twisted ankle, a broken leg in the dark.

No mercy would be asked or given.

When darkness overcame him, he used his flashlight at short intervals to see where he was going through the wind-lashed snow.

He stopped at the top of a low rise. Below in another valley, a campfire flared like a small steadily glowing spark in the night.

Denham took a split log from the pile and placed it on the flames. He avoided looking at the Mackes leaning in close to draw warmth from the fire. His eye caught a point of light that was not a reflection of the fire from a rock nor a movement of one of the mules or horses.

A short distance up the slope, in the surrounding darkness and swirling snow, the tiny beam of a flashlight bobbed toward them. Denham knew at once that whatever had happened back up in the highest valley, the answer he sought was approaching with that light. "We got company."

The others looked at him, then followed his gaze. The progress of the light was slow, but steady. It seemed to hang suspended in the darkness, unmoving from time to time.

The Mackes glanced at each other with grave concern. Denham guardedly continued to watch the disembodied light draw closer and closer.

Still they could not see any person. They watched as though hypnotized as the light floated toward them out of the blackness.

Then suddenly it was there in the swirling snow. Paul Evans materialized out of the storm and the light was gone.

He stared at the four men around the fire. For several moments, no words were spoken. He stepped in close to the fire. "One hell of a night. Mind if I join you?"

The Mackes did not answer.

Denham noticed their expressions of guilt and suspicion. "Sit down," he said.

Paul removed his pack, set it aside and joined them at the fire. Luther, Vince, and Willie cast surreptitious glances at one another.

"Like some coffee?" Denham reached for a cup.

Paul nodded. "I can use it."

Denham poured the dark steaming liquid into the cup and handed it to him.

"Thanks." Paul warmed his hands around the cup and sipped the steaming brew.

Denham offered a half-empty bottle of whiskey.

Paul nodded. "That's what I really need." He poured a little into his coffee and handed the bottle back to Denham.

Peering over the rim of his cup. Paul drank slowly. He saw the Mackes staring at him with sullen curiosity. Denham finally spoke. "You were in Brogans' tavern a few nights back."

Paul nodded.

Denham grunted. "That other one was with you -- he your son?"

"Yes."

"I remember the fight." Denham shook his head slightly. "Wildcat, that one. He ain't with you." It was more a question than an observation.

"Well, you all saw him there. He and I didn't get along well. I thought we'd come up here and try to change that. He's hard to deal with. We had an argument the other day and he just took off on his own.

"So, tryin' to get reacquainted, sounds like," Denham studied his face

"Yes, it started off as a vacation. He was angry. I left him alone to think about things. I went off to do some fishing. When I came back, he was gone. I've been trying to find him since yesterday morning. I don't think he walked back to the road. He was headed deeper into the high country. Of course, he could have circled back. Maybe you've seen him."

Luther shook his head. "Nope, ain't seen nobody else up here until now."

"Well," said Paul, "I saw your fire here and thought it was my son's camp. The coffee's good. Thanks."

The falling snow settled over them like a shroud of silence. Denham bunched his shoulders against the chill and dampness. "First snow -- be a blanket on the ground come morning. Won't last."

"That's a relief," said Paul. "For a while there, I kept seeing myself trapped up here in a blizzard. I'm a city boy myself. Not used to this. Maybe my son had sense enough to walk out. I'm new at this sort of thing. He's the mountaineer. The only camping I've done has been in a motor home. It's hardly what you'd call camping." he continued, hoping to disarm their suspicion with his statements. He drank more coffee. "You men up here on a fishing trip or something?" He looked to the Mackes for a response. None came. He glanced at Denham, who said, "Hunting."

"Oh, that's right. It's deer season about now, isn't it? Never tried it myself. Any luck?"

"Ain't out for deer -- cougar." Denham pointed beyond the circle of firelight.

Through the falling snow Paul could barely discern the skin and grinning death mask of the female cougar hanging from a tree branch.

"I didn't know it was legal to hunt them."

"They was preyin' on stock," said Denham. "Pair of 'em. The other one is still out there."

"You must be local ranchers then," Paul scanned the inscrutable faces of Luther, Vince, and Willie. "You wouldn't think there'd be many people up in here this time of year, but I've met two other parties up here fishing in the last three days, one coming in and the other going out. We, my son and I passed them along the trail. It's nice to run into someone occasionally."

Paul finished his coffee. "Well, good." He handed the empty cup back to Denham. "That should keep me. It's been a long hard day." He rose. "I appreciate your hospitality.

Denham put the cup aside. "You ain't goin' on tonight, are you? "

"Well, I am concerned about getting back and finding my son."

Willie glanced sharply at Luther, who was now staring hard at Paul.

"You could break a leg or fall off a cliff tryin' to navigate them trails at night," said Denham, "and with a storm comin' on to boot. You'd do better to wait 'til daylight."

"I don't want to impose on you."

"In this part of the country we share a fire, Mister," said Denham. "You're welcome to sleep here."

Fearing a hidden motive behind the invitation, Paul hesitated. What mattered now was that he survive and escape so he could turn these killers in. As soon as there was an investigation he could easily identify them as the suspected murderers of his son.

He was worried that if he didn't accept their hospitality, they would know he suspected them. If they killed him, there would be no evidence

My God, he thought, it's written all over their faces. To not accept on a night like this would be the height of foolishness under the circumstances. Yet we sit here knowing what each other's thinking and something is holding us back. They know I'm here only to identify them. Paul wondered how he would get out of the situation alive.

Of the group he detected a difference in the old hunter. He did not show any tension like the other three men.

"Okay," said Paul. "Thanks. I'11 take you up on it." He wondered if he really had a choice in the matter anyway. "I'm Paul Evans."

"Denham Hunsinger," Denham gestured toward the Mackes. "Them's the Mackes -- Luther, Vince, and Willie."

Even though the Mackes did not respond, Paul gave them a polite nod.

Luther rose stiffly, stretched and yawned. "Better piss and turn in." He nudged Vince with his boot.

Paul turned away to open his pack. Willie stood. Denham remained seated and stared into the fire.

The Mackes walked away out of earshot of Paul and Denham. Standing shoulder to shoulder in the darkness, they opened their flies and pissed.

"He's lying." said Luther. "He knows we done it. There was two packs in their camp. He and his son was together."

Willie turned slightly away from the wind to prevent his urine from spraying against his legs. "You really think he suspects us?"

"Sure he does," said Vince. "He followed our trail all the way here. He knows."

"What about the other guy? Maybe he ain't dead."

Vince stared grimly into the night. "He sure as hell couldn't go anywhere after what Pa did to him.

"But just what if he isn't dead?" Willie persisted.

"He's dead," said Vince. "He couldn't survive that."

They finished in silence. One by one the sound of their urine hitting the hard ground faded.

"All right," said Luther, "so he's dead. We got his father to worry about now."

Vince savagely grabbed his arm. "We can't just go off and kill the man.

"What about Denham?" said Luther through clenched teeth. "He don't know what happened up there and we have to keep it that way."

Vince stared at his father in disbelief. "You've gone crazy, old man. Denham is our friend. There will be no more killing."

"He's already dying," said Luther. "His mind is going."

"Just put it out of your head. Let Denham be. I'11 handle the situation."

"That man," said Luther, "he walked into our camp cool as you please. He wanted to see us, wanted to see our faces."

Willie looked back at the hunched figures of Paul and Denham at the fire. "You think he'll try something on us?"

"Not here," said Luther, "not to hear him talk. Now he knows who we are, and Denham had to go and tell him our names. No, he won't do nothin' here. But if he gets out alive, he'll go to the sheriff. We can't let that happen."

"You can't kill him either," said Vince.

"Not so anybody would know he was killed."

"No." Vince squared off facing his father. "There's been one killing too many and you had no reason. I wish to God I could have stopped you."

Luther stared at his son for a long silence and, for the first time, he realized why he had shot the long-haired boy. In killing the boy, Luther had vented his hatred for Vince. Luther knew of those nights in the past when Vince had stood naked fondling himself at Willie's door.

"If he was still alive," said Luther, "his old man wouldn't have left him up there, not like that. So I'm tellin' you we can't let this man walk out."

"You can't kill him in cold blood either," said Vince. "There has to be another way."

"You know there ain't, unless you're meanin' I should turn myself in, take all the blame."

"I'm thinkin'," said Vince, "we should talk to the man. What happened could be seen by the law as an accident."

Luther leaned in close to Vince's face. "Are you sayin' I should turn myself in?"

"No, no, I'm not sayin' that at all." Vince knew he had to proceed carefully with Luther. His father was crazy. Saying the wrong thing to him might set him off and he would kill Paul Evans for sure.

"I sure hope not." said Luther, "'cause you and Willie are in this just as deep as me." He waited to let his comment sink in. "Just remember. I'm your father. That comes first -- above every damn thing else."

Luther looked at Willie, who trembled impotent with anger, then back at Vince. Quietly he said to Vince, "You may not have a plan, but I sure as hell do. All right, the man don't want to get caught in the storm. Let's say he does. Nobody's ever gonna find him. By spring, there won't be no sign of him.

Vince wondered from where in the depths of his father's soul this impulse for murder had sprung. "This is your business. Whatever happens, you'll have to answer for it."

"Sure, the way it's always been." Luther turned away.

Vince could not deny the stinging remark. Luther had always considered Willie the better extension of himself. Vince was his father's antagonist.

Luther could not live without his sons, so he had manipulated and controlled their lives to prevent them from becoming independent.

"Don't let Denham get wind of this," said Luther. He looked at his two sons, then turned away and walked back to the fire.

After a moment, Willie dropped his gaze and followed. Weighed down with morose thoughts about his father, Vince fell in behind. They passed Denham going out to check on the horses.

Removing his hiking boots, Paul watched the Mackes troop in from the surrounding darkness. They had been gone a long time. He knew much talk must have transpired, speculation about what to do about him.

"They figured out how they're going to kill me," he thought. Sitting quietly in his stocking feet with the snow drifting down about him, he watched the Mackes spread their bedrolls near the fire. "I need to be thinking about how I should kill them."

Denham walked in out of the whirling snow and darkness. He stared curiously at all of them until they grew aware of him. Luther stared back a challenge. Denham busied himself with his own bedroll. "Animals are okay. Moved 'em in closer to camp.

Denham did not understand what was happening among the four other men. He felt he was an outsider attempting to make a judgment and knowing nothing. He sensed death, perhaps the man's son. He stared at the face of the dead female cougar. "My days are filled with death," he thought. "Maybe that's all I can see anymore."

Denham noticed that Luther continued to watch him with a deranged expression. Denham ignored him, removed his boots, and climbed into his sleeping bag.

Through the aberrant screen of firelight, Paul watched them settle down to sleep. Half-hidden at the opening of his bedroll, his hand clutched a hunting knife. His eyes slowly raised beyond the fire. Out of the snow and darkness, he saw the death mask of the cougar overlooking them all.

Chapter 30

At the first light of dawn, Paul opened his eyes. He slowly raised his head and looked about the camp. The snow flurries had stopped. Everything was covered with a white powder. The fire was dead. The four other men in their bedrolls still lay unmoving, like corpses under nature's shroud. The wet sticky snow clung to the backs, manes, and tails of the horses and mules, who dozed in the nearby meadow.

Inside his sleeping bag, Paul's hand nudged the hunting knife that had fallen from his grasp during the night. He gripped the handle.

Quietly unzipping the bag so as not to awaken the other men, he sat up and stared at their inert forms. One by one he could kill them now while they slept, he thought. Instead, he put the knife in its sheath, then reached for his boots.

The laces were stiff with frost. He pulled each boot on slowly and wriggled his stocking feet against the cold enclosure of the frozen leather. His fingers worked the laces to make them pliable.

Kneeling at his pack, he rummaged for a small tin containing fishing flies. Selecting one of the colorful lures, he fastened it to the end of his fly line, then picked up the rod and reel and walked silently to the stream that cut across the meadow.

Soon, nine trout lay on the snow near where he was standing.

Denham was next to awaken. He shook the snow off his bedroll and looked through bleary eyes at the white world. He saw Paul cleaning the trout by the stream.

With a loud grunt that woke the others, Denham pulled on his boots and stomped about to keep warm. As he went off to relieve himself, he raised his hand in a morning greeting to Paul. Paul raised his knife, bloody from fish entrails.

After the last fish was gutted and washed in the cold rushing stream, Paul returned to camp with his stringer of trout and put them aside with the rod and reel.

Luther and Vince peered up out of their white cocoon's at Paul, who busied himself clearing the fire area. "Good morning," he said. "I'11 have a fire going in a few minutes."

Luther rose abruptly and turned his back to mask his irritation. Grumbling at the coldness and stiffness of his boots, he shuffled away to relieve himself.

From sleep-encrusted eyes, Vince watched Paul lay the base for a fire. The match flame ignited and blistered through a wad of dry wood pulp, then quickly spread and grew as Paul added kindling.

Denham returned and paused to admire the trout. "Nice catch there."

Paul nodded. He could detect only friendliness from the old hunter. He watched Denham warm his hands and feet at the fire.

Luther came back. He avoided looking at Paul and Denham and filled the animal's feedbags with grain. He carried them out to the mules and horses, who neighed at his approach and the scent of the grain.

Denham carried the coffee pot to the stream, filled it with water, then returned and set the pot on the fire. He hunkered down at one of the packs and took out a container of lard. Using his knife, he scooped a chunk of lard into a large iron skillet and placed the skillet over the fire. As the lard melted, he placed four of the trout into the hot skillet.

Vince staggered up out of his bedroll. Hopping and balancing on first one foot, then the other, he pulled on his boots. With a quick stride, he walked off to piss in the bushes.

Paul forced himself to grin at Willie, who moved shivering out of his bag and warmed his hands and feet at the fire. "It's a hell of a way to wake up in the morning, isn't it?" said Paul. Willie responded with an uncertain smile. "Yeah, yeah."

With two feedbags yet to be filled. Denham poured grain into the canvas containers, then carried them out to the remaining two horses, who tossed their heads and rolled their eyes with anxiety that they had not yet been fed.

Paul took a spatula from his pack and carefully turned the trout sizzling in the skillet.

When the other men had returned, Paul served everyone breakfast. Vince and Willie thanked him. Denham gave him a pat of appreciation on the shoulder. Luther said nothing. He took his plate with resentment that this man he planned to kill was so nicely serving him trout for breakfast.

Using their fingers to remove the backbone and ribs, the men ate quickly. Denham handed out cold biscuits left over from supper. They dipped the biscuits in hot black coffee laced with whiskey and sucked and chewed on the soggy dough.

An hour later, they broke camp. Denham and Vince packed the mules while Luther and Willie saddled the horses.

As Paul doused the fire with a pot of water, he noticed Willie looking at him as though he wanted to tell him something. He held Willie's gaze with an encouraging glance, but Willie ducked his head and continued to fasten the saddle cinch on one of the horses.

Paul rolled up his sleeping bag and tied it to his aluminum pack frame. He hoisted the pack to his back, then looked at the other four men. "Well, I'm on my way. Thanks for your hospitality."

They looked up from their preparations.

"Hope you don't have any more trouble with mountain lions," said Paul.

Denham raised his hand in farewell. "Have a good trip home. Hope you find your boy.

Paul nodded. Without a backward glance, he set out walking in the direction of a high pass at the other side of the wide valley. His boots left clear prints in the thin layer of snow.

Standing beside the mule he was packing, Vince watched over the withers of the animal as Paul's figure grew smaller in the distance. Vince pulled the rope taut he was fashioning into a diamond hitch to hold the packs on the mule.

Finally, all the packing was completed. They were ready to leave. Willie was the first to mount his horse. He shifted in his saddle and stared off in the direction Paul had gone. Paul was no longer in sight. The distant trees and granite slopes concealed him from view as though they had absorbed him into the rugged terrain.

The other three men mounted their horses. Followed by Luther and Denham and the three mules, Vince set out at the head of the column. Willie rode at the rear of the group.

Across the valley, halfway up to the pass, Paul stopped and looked back at the small train of riders and mules moving far off in the opposite direction from where he stood. Grimly he continued his climb. By the time he reached the top of the pass and looked back again, they were no longer in sight.

As Denham and the Mackes rode along at an easy walk, Willie held back at the rear of the column until the others progressed a few hundred yards ahead. Boulders and tall brush at a turn in the trail blocked him from view of Denham, Luther, and Vince. Willie suddenly turned his horse and headed back up the trail at a gallop in the direction from which they had come.

Farther along the down trail, Vince led the others on for a half hour before he chanced to look back and notice that Willie was missing. He stopped his horse. Luther's horse crowded him from behind. Denham and his horse and the mules came to a halt.

"What is it?" Luther grumbled at Vince.

"Willie's gone." Vince urged his horse back along the column past Luther. Denham, and the mules and stopped several yards beyond the last mule. He looked up the trail. Willie and his horse were nowhere in sight.

Luther left the column and rode up beside him. "What is it?"

"He went back," said Vince

"Why would he do that?" Luther felt a sudden inner tension.

"He's going to tell Evans what happened." Vince turned in his saddle and shouted to Denham. "We're going back and see what happened to Willie. Wait for us here."

Denham nodded and touched the brim of his hat in acknowledgment.

"Son-of-a-bitch," Luther muttered half under his breath. He and Vince set their horses at a lope back up the trail.

As he climbed down the slope to reenter the valley where he left the hunting party, Paul Evans suddenly stopped and jumped into a low pocket of ground. He looked intently across the broad sweep of the valley to where a horse and rider approached.

Although his mare was breathing hard, Willie continued to push her at a gallop the last mile to the deserted camp. He halted for a few moments to let her blow. Her breath steamed from flaring nostrils into the winter air.

Willie studied the clear trail of Paul's footprints in the snow. He looked up at the pass where Paul hiked out earlier that morning. Then he turned his horse and rode on at a jog trot in the opposite direction headed back up toward the higher valleys and mountain peaks where he and Vince and Luther had left Matt Evans to die.

As he watched the rider, Paul thought that he must be going back to the scene of the murder to destroy evidence. Paul rose from the low pocket of ground. Taking care not to be seen by Willie, he followed at a half-mile distance. He was hoping Willie would lead him to Matt's body.

Willie urged his horse up the steep rocky trail, and looked back down into the valley he was leaving behind to see if he were being followed. Paul reasoned that he must have sneaked away from his party and his paranoia meant that he knew they would come after him, once they discovered he was missing.

After a quick climb to the top of the trail, Willie and his horse passed from sight over the rim. Paul no longer had to remain hidden as he followed Willie's back trail. So he increased his walking pace and moved across open ledges without hesitation until he chanced to again look into the valley below. There he saw two more riders stop at the camp, Luther and Vince.

At the cold camp, Luther and Vince dismounted to search the tracks in the snow around the site and determine in which direction Willie had gone, for he clearly had not followed Paul Evans.

Vince finally discovered the hoof prints of Willie's horse headed up into the mountains. "Here. He must be going back for the body."

Vince and Luther remounted their horses and followed Willie's trail. Within a few hundred yards, they noticed the boot prints of Paul Evans intermingled with the hoof prints of Willie's horse.

"Look," said Vince. "Evans came back. Either he's after Willie or Willie's after him.

Luther pulled his rifle from its saddle mount and checked the load chamber.

Carrying the rifle balanced across the pommel of his saddle, he followed Vince closely up the steep trail.

Higher on the ridge, so that he would not leave any prints, Paul climbed across a slope of exposed granite that had not been covered by the snow. He concealed himself deep among a jumble of enormous boulders from where he could see Vince and Luther coming along the trail, but they could not see him. He settled down to wait.

Without moving, Paul watched the two men on their horses make the long slow climb. The horses' steel shoes slipped on the snow slick rocks in the trail, as the animals clambered and picked their way upward. They climbed for a half hour, then passed within fifty yards of where Paul lay hidden.

Paul could see the rifle balanced across the front of Luther's saddle.

By now several miles ahead, Willie stopped his horse on a rise that overlooked the stream and campsite where Luther had shot Matt Evans. Below, he saw the figure of a man moving about in the camp.

A single thought went through Willie's head. *Now who the hell is that?* He urged his horse down the slope past a grove of scrub pine and rode steadily toward the camp.

Guzman looked up and saw the rider approaching. He had not expected anyone to return. He glanced down at Matt sleeping in his bedroll near the fire. Matt was in a deep state of unconsciousness.

As the horse and rider came in, Guzman recognized Willie and wondered why he returned alone. Guzman worried that the others might not be far behind.

Willie pulled his horse to an abrupt halt and stared from Guzman to Matt lying on the ground. "Is he dead?" Willie asked.   "He was barely alive when I found him," said Guzman.

"Who are you?" Willie asked. "Where did you come from?"

"Does it matter?"

With uncontained excitement that Matt was still alive, Willie quickly dismounted from his horse and went to Matt. As he kneeled for a closer look at the sleeping face wreathed in blonde hair he did not see Guzman draw a hunting knife from its leather sheath strapped to his belt.

Guzman stepped in close behind Willie. He raised the knife high and brought it down with a strong swift plunge deep into Willie's back.

With a grunt of shock and pain, Willie arched forward and fell across Matt. Guzman's second stroke of the knife entered the base of Willie's brain near the top of his spine. Willie's body shuddered a moment, then was still. Guzman wiped the blood from the knife and returned it to its sheath. He then half-lifted and dragged Willie's body aside.

Hurrying to Matt, Guzman touched his face and Matt opened his eyes. Guzman said. "We must go now." He pulled back the top cover of the sleeping bag. Matt was fully clothed. Guzman supported him to a standing position. Through his blurred vision, Matt barely noticed the body of Willie Macke. He did not wonder at the riderless horse that grazed nearby. He listened only to Guzman, this stranger who had come out of nowhere and had saved his life. Matt wondered what had happened to his father.

Guzman hastily rolled and attached Matt's sleeping bag to his own pack frame.

Before leaving the camp, he scooped snow onto the fire. The hot coals sizzled and died. Guzman touched Matt's arm. "Come on." Guzman helped him along at a slow pace away from the camp. Matt stumbled as they crossed a stretch of rocks and exposed ground that did not have a coating of snow. Guzman made certain he and Matt did not leave any trace of footprints or trail for anyone to follow.

Guzman led Matt to their first hiding place among scrub pine and upended granite and boulders a few hundred yards from the camp. They removed their packs. Guzman told Matt to sleep. Then he watched the camp to see if anyone else would come there. He did not have long to wait.

Vince and Luther stopped their horses at the rim Willie had ascended earlier before arriving at the camp where he discovered Guzman with Matt. Across the valley in the distance, they saw Willie's riderless horse browsing on the stubbles of meadow grass that poked up through the thin layer of snow. There was no other movement or sign of Willie.

"I see his horse," said Vince, "but I don't see him."

Luther crowded his own horse on past Vince and took the lead as he recklessly plunged down the narrow trail. Vince followed.

By the time the two riders were on the flat, Luther had pulled ahead of Vince at a hard gallop. He rode into the dead camp a few moments before him. At their approach, Willie's horse raised her head from grazing and watched them.

Luther saw Willie lying face down on the cold earth. Small swatches of blood-stained snow clung to Willie's clothes from being dragged over the ground by Guzman.

With a hoarse cry, Luther dismounted from his horse and rushed to his son's still prostrate form. He fell to his knees and reached out a trembling hand, touching the oozing wounds in disbelief, as though the act of touching would make the knife strokes disappear. He gently rolled Willie over and probed his face and body for some sign of life.

"Willie." He tenderly touched Willie's sightless eyes. "Oh, my God. Willie." Luther shook with uncontrollable sobs.

Vince brought his horse to a halt near Luther's. He saw his father shaking as Luther knelt over Willie. A lump of sorrow tightened Vince's throat. He dismounted and came over to stand next to his murdered brother and Luther.

"He did this," Luther moaned through clenched teeth. "Evans did this. There's no stopping me now. I'm going to find him and kill him."

Vince stared at the knife wounds, then looked away at the stream near the camp. He gazed at the surrounding peaks and granite spires where powerful winds thrust storm clouds across the sky like dark chariots of death.

After a time, Luther raised his bowed head. His eyes were red and his face raw and streaked with tears. "We've got to find Evans. We've got to find him and kill him for this."

Vince scanned the camp perimeter and beyond, looking for a likely place where Paul Evans might be hiding. There were many such places.

He searched the ground for tracks, but the light snow in the immediate area of the camp had been despoiled by the horses' hoof prints as the animals milled about.

Clutching his rifle, Luther rose. "The son-of-a-bitch can't have gone too far. We have to get him. We have to hunt him down."

"There's been enough killing." Vince fought back tears.

Luther whirled to face Vince. "What's the matter with you? Willie's your own flesh and blood. Of course we've got to hunt the bastard down."

"You killed Evans' son," Vince's voice was hard with emotion. "There won't be any more killing. The law will take care of Evans. And we'll have to answer for what we did."

"What I did was an accident."

"It wasn't an accident," Vince shouted. "You murdered him in cold blood."

Luther stared at Vince. "You goin' up against me boy?" He raised his rifle. "This is the only answer."

"You gonna kill me too? You're crazy, old man. I should have left home a long time ago. So should have Willie."

"You're not gonna say nothin'," Luther menaced him. "We'll find Evans," he said with a sudden calm. "And when we do --" Luther did not finish. "What're you lookin' at."

"You." Vince felt lost and drained of energy. "You and me and Willie," he said slowly. "I should have left you long ago. It's too late now. It's too late."

"You're my son. You're gonna do what I tell you." Luther lowered his rifle. "Just like you always done."

As he looked at his father, for the moment, Vince could not decide whether he hated him or pitied him more. "Let's take Willie home."

Luther turned to look down again at the body of his youngest son. He placed his rifle aside against a large rock.

Vince knelt next to Willie, and, with Luther's help, positioned Willie's dead weight across his back and shoulders. He lifted Willie and carried him to his horse. Luther assisted Vince in positioning the body over the saddle and back of the horse. Then, using Willie's rope, they lashed him to the saddle so that he would not slide off.

Vince led Willie's horse over to where his own horse waited patiently. Luther went back to the rock to pick up his rifle. He began to walk about the deserted camp and search the ground.

"What are you doing:," Vince asked.

Without looking up, Luther answered, "Looking for tracks."

Vince mounted his horse. "We're going now. We're taking Willie home."

"No, we've got to find Evans first. I can't let him live after what he done."

Leading the horse with Willie's body swaying slightly at each step, Vince rode away at a walk.

Luther continued to search the ground near the camp perimeter, but couldn't find any tracks. He finally returned to his horse and mounted. He felt sick and feverish, as though his life were coming apart in fits and starts. Hunched over in his saddle, he rode slowly after his two sons.

Paul Evans moved from his hiding place and continued climbing up the trail to the low rim where he had last seen Vince and Luther Macke.

Remaining low so as not to expose himself against the sky, he ran the last few yards and dropped behind the cover of a thicket of scrub pine. A moment later and he would have been seen by the Mackes riding slowly from the flat back up to the rim.

Paul was only a few feet from the trail but the dense growth concealed him. He waited unmoving for what seemed a long time. Then be heard the chop of the horses' shod hooves as the animals bearing their riders neared the rim.

He chanced the slight movement of his head so that he could see something more than the horses' legs and hooves plodding past. The sight of Willie's body tied across the back of his horse startled Paul.

He immediately wondered how and why Willie had come to be dead. Willie had arrived at the camp well before Vince and Luther. Someone else had to have been there. It must have been Matt, he thought. It must have been.

Paul could barely contain his impatience while waiting for the horses and riders to pass back along the trail a sufficient distance so that he would not be seen when he broke cover.

He ran down from the rim onto the flat until the thin air and his lack of physical conditioning caused him to walk.

As he approached the deserted campsite, he called out, "Matt! Matt! It's Dad! They're gone! Where are you?"

He heard only the cold wind whistling down from the peaks. Calling Matt's name, he searched the nearby thickets, then ranged out farther from the camp to check behind clusters of boulders and within patches of conifers.

Standing in the gloom of a pine grove, as he pondered where next to look, he sensed a presence behind him. He whirled and a chill of fear prickled about his neck.

Guzman stood not more than ten feet away watching him. Paul recognized him as the man who had checked into the motel after him and walked into Brogans.

"What happened here?" Paul asked in a trembling voice. "Where is my son?"

"Your son is dead." Guzman's deep soothing voice seemed to come from a cavern.

"Where is he? Where is his body?"

"I saw them kill your son. I thought they would come back, so I hid his body.

"Then you killed their boy, the one they call Willie."

Guzman nodded. "He tried to kill me.

"Who are you anyway?" Paul feared the answer.

"I'm just passing through."

"Where is my son. I want to see for myself."

Guzman raised his arm in a gentle motion. Paul guardedly walked in the direction he gestured deeper in among the rocks and trees. Guzman walked close behind, guiding him by his presence.

As they came around a large boulder, Paul suddenly stopped. Guzman stepped aside and watched him and quietly waited.

Matt lay on the ground on a bed of pine needles. His eyes were closed. Paul noticed immediately that Matt's body did not show any sign of a wound.

"There was blood on the ground back at the camp," Paul said to Guzman.

"I cleaned him up. The wound was not serious."

Paul looked quickly over at Guzman. "You told me he was dead."

Guzman shrugged. "It's my way."

A chill rippled up Paul's spine at the man's words. He knelt beside his son and touched his face. "He feels cold, but he doesn't look dead -- the color in his face. Are you sure he's not dead?"

"He is -- to you."

A sinking weakness hit the pit of Paul's stomach. He raised his eyes and stared at Guzman. Paul whispered. "Who are you? "

A cold grin widened Guzman's lips. "You reneged on your agreement. You tried to keep him away from me. I'm here to collect his light, his soul. He is now mine."

"All those messages. You're not for real. You're just some sick bastard who has come into my life."

"Believe me when I tell you that I am the greatest reality in your life."

Paul was caught and held by the man's penetrating unblinking stare. He experienced a sudden shortness of breath. His skin grew cold and clammy. His heart beat wildly. The last thing he remembered was his doctor advising him about his blood pressure. Paul thought he was having a heart attack.

Guzman and the trees behind him slowly revolved, tilting as a strange dizziness overcame Paul. The light faded to black and he fell to the ground next to his son.

[Double Click To Add Text]

Chapter 31

Paul's eyes opened with great effort, as though they had been swollen shut. His head felt heavy when he tried to raise it. Then he realized the weight of his backpack held him down. He pushed himself up to a sitting position and looked around.

Matt and Guzman were gone. Paul knew that his encounter with Guzman had not been a dream, that Guzman was very real, flesh and blood real, and that through some insidious method, Guzman was destroying him. He did not know why. What was most important to him now was that Matt was still alive.

He wanted desperately to get his son back. He had to find Matt and somehow break Guzman's control over their lives.

He staggered to his feet and stood swaying in the gloom cast by the pines from overhead. Expecting to break clear of the trees and return to the clearing near the site where he and Matt had made camp, he began walking. Then stopped.

The valley did not look the same. He did not believe Guzman would have moved him. But Paul sensed this was the first time he had seen and entered the valley, that he had not been there before with his son. The sensation was a perceptual difference, for there was no physical change in the terrain. Paul felt that the memory of what had happened to Matt and to himself was slipping away. He could not remember why he had come up into the mountains or what he was doing there. The incident had escaped from his mind, leaving a blank, a sense of loss, a specific amnesia.

Not knowing in what direction he should go, he set off walking across the valley toward the nearest pass that could be sighted among the surrounding peaks. His laborious climb was a slow process up the steep, rock-strewn slope. He arrived winded and exhausted. Shrugging off his pack, he sank to the ground.

As his breathing returned to normal, he looked back the way he had come. A harsh wind blowing from an endless mass of rugged peaks and ranges struck his face. The slope to his left appeared to be too steep to ascend. He looked off to his right where the mountainside opened downward into a gorge one-thousand feet deep.

He rummaged in his pack and pulled out a geographical survey map and a compass. The wind tugged and rattled at the map as Paul spread it open on a flat rock, then attempted to align the drawn directional contours with his compass. The wavering compass needle settled, pointing north.

Confused, Paul stared at the lines on the map, then looked at the actual terrain that surrounded him. He could not relate the map to where he was.

As he turned to face a mountain peak on his left, a sharp gust of wind snatched up the map and lifted it with a wild rattle high into the air. The compass fell aside into a deep crevice among the boulders where Paul could not reach it.

Stumbling and falling over the rocks, he chased after the fluttering paper, then stopped as a powerful wind current swept the map out over the cliff and a downdraft rushed it into the gorge.

Shaken, Paul returned to his pack and closed and tied down the open flap he had loosened to reach inside for the map and compass.

Since there was no other way down from what he had thought was a pass, he traversed at an angle descending across the slope he had climbed for the past two hours. He headed for what appeared to be a second pass. When be reached that point, he looked down appalled.

The back slope of the pass dropped off at a precipitous angle for five hundred feet to a small barren lake surrounded by rockslides. Large granite slabs shingled the descent. Paul saw no evidence of even a game trail and the terrain beyond the lake rose further above timberline.

He was totally lost.

Angrily he lurched back down the slope into the bowl of the valley from where he had come after his encounter with Guzman. Alternately jogging and walking, he retraced his last three miles.

When he reached the valley floor, the terrain looked different to him than it had before. He took a guess at what he thought was the right direction and walked on.

Toward nightfall, he came to a narrow stream that rushed along the center of a gorge walled on three sides by enormous granite cliffs. Fatigue consumed Paul as he stumbled and crawled over rocks where the last vestige of a trail disappeared. Coming around a bend, be stopped in awe and desperation at the sight that confronted him.

The gorge ended in a blind canyon of high rugged cliffs down which a towering waterfall cascaded for several hundred feet. The steady roar of the falls filled his head.

He sat on a large rock and stared at the ground. He buried his face in his arms. His body heaved with sobs at the futility of his efforts to find his way out of the mountains. he also cried at the emptiness and the losses in his life.

He remained unmoving, dwarfed among the boulders against the backdrop of the falls and massive gray palisades. His desire to continue living ebbed away.

Shaking with chills and despair, he did not see the sun plunge into a building mass of clouds. The gorge engulfed him in the early shadow of night.

When the cold grew unbearable, he built a warming fire, crawled into his sleeping bag and listened to the rumble of rocks and gravel moved by the strong current in the stream bed nearby.

He stared at the liquid web of flames fanning and flowing through the network of glowing wood that was the base of his fire. The heat from the fire soothed him and the low steady throbbing of the stream lulled his mind.

Moya. He thought of a day long ago when he and his wife had been much younger. They had rented a small beach house along an isolated stretch of the coast. The house did not have a television, radio, or phone.

They had been married for only a short time. They had been very much in love then, before his mind had become contaminated with Guzman's satanic influence.

He recalled a moment when they had shared a bottle of red wine. The velvet soft wine had tasted whimsical. He had raised the bottle to his lips and held it there, not swallowing for a moment while he fixed his eyes on the radiant light of the sun reflected from the undulating sea. He watched the long smooth contours of the bottle slowly tip upwards as he drank.

When he lowered the bottle, Moya had shifted her body around on the blanket they shared and placed her head on his lap. She had looked up at him with her gentle smile as he carefully planted the bottle in the sand.

Moya had been wearing a cotton print dress that left her tan shoulders bare.

"You have magnificent shoulders," he had said to her.

At the end of a week, he and Moya had been reluctant to leave the beach house. He had wanted to take a few final snapshots of her. So she posed holding her large straw sun hat as warm sea breezes ruffled her hair. She smiled, but the expression in her eyes had been sad.

Paul had been anxious to move on. He had not understood why she walked so reluctantly to the car. He sensed she was emotionally withdrawn and remote from him.

"We have a lot of places to go yet," he had tried to perk up her spirits. "A lot of things to see."

She nodded solemnly. "But there was something special about this one, moments we spent here we can never have again."

He had placed his arm gently around her shoulders. "Well, at least we'll always remember it that way." He detected the wetness on her cheeks. "What's wrong? Why are you crying."

She did not answer.

The memory of the beach house faded, as Paul shifted in his sleeping bag to get closer to the campfire. "Now I know why she was crying," he thought. "We can only have those moments as a memory and we try to find them or make them happen again. But it's too late to recreate the moment after it's gone."

After a while, he fell asleep, then woke toward the middle of the night. The fire had burned down to only a few glowing coals. He panicked at the absence of the fire, the suddenness of the night around him, the looming trees, cliffs and boulders dark with haunting shapes, the heavy clouds that now roofed the gorge and concealed the moon and stars.

In a sudden panic, he crawled and scrambled to grab more wood and frantically built up the fire again to a roaring blaze.

He feared to look away from the firelight. He sensed something moving slowly toward him out of the night. He turned with a cry of terror and anguish into the blackness. He could see nothing. He bent over rigid and trembling, then slowly sank to the ground next to the fire.

A haunting memory, Guzman's words in the diary replayed themselves in his mind.

Florence Oakes is the perfect woman for you. She has the charm and social graces you need in a mate.

You and your wife are growing apart. You can do nothing about her psychological problems and emotional weakness. Florence is strong and vibrant. Her energy makes you feel young. She instills a strength and motivational drive in you that will help you achieve the success you desire.

Moya never was like that for you. She has an emotional debilitation that takes energy from you in a negative way. That is why you keep drawing away from her. You are perfectly justified in doing so. Moya will only hold you back and drag you down. Being with Florence is like flying free.

Now that the diary was gone and Paul had lost his son to a reality beyond comprehension, he suffered from such remorse that he would just as soon die there in the gorge rather than attempt to go on.

He did not know how he could possibly get his son back. Certainly he could not change the past and the damage he had done to his family.

Chapter 32

In heavily falling snow, Guzman and Matt followed the trail from above timberline taken by the Mackes. On foot, the two men would not catch up to the horses and riders, who were going the longest, but easiest route down from the barren peaks of the mountain range.

Guzman observed Matt walking at a steady pace a few steps ahead of him. Matt had Guzman worried. The drugs he had injected did not completely affect him. Although the young man trusted and depended on him, Guzman encountered an element of strength and resilience he had not figured would be there.

Guzman's plan was to destroy Paul by destroying his son. Paul's brain would be sufficiently ravaged by the drugs and mental stress and deterioration as to consume his psyche like a blackening cancer.

Guzman had extinguished *The Light,* the force of love, in many victims many times before. Even with his physical domination of Matt Evans through healing the minor gunshot wound and restoring him to life, Guzman had never met with such unconscious strength, conviction, and determination as in this young man whose soul he was responsible to deliver to Satan in a ritual sacrifice.

Such was the distortion of Guzman's mind.

Matt was unaware of the force of light within him that Guzman detected.

Having cared for Matt for two days, in his sick, twisted thinking, Guzman believed he had been exploring Matt's psychic terrain, the biochemical impulses that translated into a spiritual and emotional organism.

Guzman understood Matt's weaknesses, his hatred for his father and symbols and forces of power even remotely associated with Paul.

Guzman finally resolved he would have to turn the love that resided within Matt against his father. He would have to torture Matt into capitulation and ultimately the total acceptance of Satan as his Lord before freeing his soul.

With night approaching, Guzman ordered Matt to stop walking. He led the young man off to the side of the trail to a section of ground sheltered from the wind by an embankment.

Matt sank to the ground. He watched Guzman gather wood to make a fire. Matt felt weak from hunger and a strange emotional emptiness as though a section of his brain had been anaesthetized.

He wanted desperately to remove that blankness, a sense of being drugged so that he could not communicate. An occasional surge of will power peaked, then dropped back into his dark morass of mental confusion like a feeble green impulse on a wave form monitor.

He did not understand what had happened to him. He had only a distant memory of excruciating pain followed by blackness. He could not remember who he was, only that he was attached to Guzman by some form of mental umbilical cord.

Matt knew he still possessed his intelligence, but that it had somehow become clouded and repressed similar to a stroke victim or someone living in a semi-comatose state.

He wanted to tell Guzman to hurry with building the fire, that he was hungry. He opened his mouth to speak. He could not formulate sounds into words. He could only open his mouth and utter noises like a nonverbal child.

Guzman noticed Matt's discomfort. "I'll have this fire going soon and make your supper. Once we take care of the hunger in your belly, then we'll work on the hunger in your soul. Tonight, we will talk about who you will become."

Matt did not dislike Guzman. The man treated him kindly and Matt sensed that somehow Guzman had kept him from dying. But some impulse within Matt that he could not define resisted the meaning of what Guzman told him. Matt's image of the impulse was a quiescent glow deep within the mental recesses of his mind. He could no more grasp its function and existence than he could the pervasive emptiness that surrounded it.

Matt wondered why listening to Guzman talk was so easy while he himself could say nothing. Because of his state of mind and the need to feel oriented, he mentally focused on Guzman and listened to his words.

"You have come far in your life. Soon you will begin a journey beyond the realm of your imagination. Although outwardly for a while you will appear to be human, you will no longer be the person you are now. Your soul will be released and transformed. You will have a new name given you by Satan, who is your lord and god.

"Before you are ready for Satan, you must be prepared. Your mind must be cleansed of your past and of who you are now. There is a portion of your mind that is still light. Until that light is extinguished, you will continue to experience the discomfort and disorientation from which you now suffer

"You are taking an important step in your growth toward Satan. This phase is necessary to shed your sins of *The Light*, the love you possess." Under hypnosis, Matt had told him about *The Light* and its origin with his grandfather and how it united him with his sister.

"You will undergo a metamorphosis of the soul. Once *The Light* is gone, your soul will be cleansed and you will be ready to receive Satan as your lord. When your mind is dark, you will begin the process of rebirth into Satan's world.

"For now, concentrate on *The Light*. Listen to my words as we continue the journey to eliminate your past and who you are. As *The Light* grows smaller in your mind, you will know that you are changing."

As Guzman continued to talk to him in a gentle soothing tone, under the power of Guzman's suggestion, Matt began to re-experience in his mind significant incidents, moments, and impressions from his past.

He remembered when he was five years old. During one evening at bedtime, he and his father were making shadow figures against the wall illuminated by Matt's night light.

Paul was sitting on the floor and leaning against his son's bed. The blankets and sheets bad been pushed to the foot of the bed along with a disordered pile of stuffed animals.

Matt raised his hand and curled it into a fist. Paul helped him to position two fingers to look like the trunk of an elephant on the wall shadow. Matt was delighted with the result.

He could feel his father's arm about him, hear his breath, as Paul gently rested his cheek against Matt's small blond head.

"I can do it by myself. Watch," said Matt. His shadow effect was not the same without Paul's guiding hand. The trunk poked straight up into the air like rabbit ears.

"Move your hand sideways," said Paul, "so his trunk isn't sticking up in the air." Paul touched his arm.

"No, no, I can do it. I can do it," Matt's strident insistence caused Paul to quickly remove his hand from the boy's slender arm.

Paul's simple act of not interfering, of allowing him to make the elephant shadow figure himself was an incident Matt recalled with fondness. His father loved him and was allowing him to feel the pride of personal accomplishment without fatherly interference.

"You only have to show me once and then I know how," Matt had admonished his father.

Paul's tendency was to want to help and correct Matt's inexperienced fingers, not only in making shadow figures, but in tying Matt's shoes. He had finally learned to back off and watch and let his son learn through trial and error.

As a child, Matt had enjoyed playing scare games with Paul. He would say to his father, "Be a werewolf. Be a werewolf." Paul would oblige him with an exaggerated expression of werewolfishness until he reached Matt's threshold of fantasy and the boy cried out, "Stop. Stop, Daddy. That scares me."

Then Matt would grin and tell him, "Be Dracula." Paul would repeat the scare sequence until Matt cringed and shouted, "Stop. Stop now. You're scaring me."

Matt recalled how pleased he had felt that he had control of the situation and that his father respected his fantasies and real fears.

He insulated himself from Guzman by withdrawing deeper into *The Light* and further memories from childhood. He was floating inside *The Light's* bathing glow. In *The Light* he was a child again.

He remembered waking and looking out his bedroom window early one morning. He watched a gray cat relieve itself and cover its droppings with loose soil and dry leaves. Cats were interesting creatures.

Birds sang on the roof as the sun rose, illuminating the shape of his tricycle and other outdoor toys scattered about on a large patio.

His parents' alarm clock radio came on in their bedroom across the hall. Matt had fiddled with the dials the night before and the usual soothing classical music station was drowned out by ear-rending Heavy Metal rock music.

His father stumbled up out of bed with a harsh growl. "Who messed with the radio last night?"

Matt took a deep breath. He would surely never admit to playing with the dials. The radio dials were neat. Any buttons he could push or switch he could turn on and off were neat.

His mother was a curvaceous mound buried under the blankets. Her shoulder length blonde hair splayed over part of her attractive face. "Matt was in here before bedtime last night. He probably played with it. He must have changed the station."

Matt heard his father emit a combined grunt and mid-range sigh. He knew his father wouldn't get mad at him, but why did his mother have to say that?

He hated to make mistakes or get caught at doing something he shouldn't and be reprimanded by his parents. Being scolded almost always made him cry. He didn't like them to raise their voices at him.

Listening to his father take a shower, Matt stayed curled up in bed, then he suddenly remembered he wanted to shave with him. He threw back the covers, leaped out of bed and, still clutching his special cuddling baby blanket, raced across the hall and into his parents' bathroom.

His father was just stepping out of the shower. Matt watched him towel himself dry for a few moments. Someday he wanted to have hair growing on his arms and legs and chest like his father.

Matt's warm early relationship with his father remained strong in his memory, deep within *The Light* where Guzman could not reach him. He could hear Guzman talking to him, as they sat near the campfire, but Matt now had the control to either tune out Guzman's words or to listen, as it suited him. Matt wanted to stay out of the gray blankness and dwell inside the protective glow of *The Light*.

Another strong memory welled up like a giant bubble and floated in his mind. As the memory solidified from its surreal dream state, he saw his grandfather.

He and his grandfather had beached the canoe and were sitting on a sandbar. They were watching the effect of sunlight shining in the water where the current rippled across a peninsula of sand that extended from the shore.

"Hell is not a place where God puts us," his grandfather spoke. "It's a place where we put ourselves. The doors of hell, insofar as they have locks, they have locks on the inside."

The image of his grandfather faded. His sister, Jennifer, dissolved forward in his dream. She was standing at the edge of the river that flowed past his grandfather's farm. Matt was alone in the canoe his grandfather had given him.

Along that stretch of the river where it cut through the forest, Matt did not expect to see anyone. Because Jennifer blended with the foliage that grew along the bank, he had to look twice to discern her face and long blonde hair, as though she were a curious creature of the woods who had emerged to watch him drift past on the muddy current. She slowly raised her hand and waved.

Chapter 33

Denham rose at dawn and studied the storm clouds swollen with snow. "Could hit us by nightfall," he muttered to Vince, who was adding wood to the breakfast fire.

Agitated by the threat of the impending storm, Vince poured a cup of steaming coffee. He stepped back from the fire whose fresh smoke stung his eyes.

"Denham's right." Luther stared into the crackling flames. "And we still have to go back for Willie.

Vince stared at his father. Luther had lost touch with reality. "Willie is right here with us," said Vince. "He's dead."

Luther's mouth opened with an animal howl.

"When we die, we die, and that's the end of it," said Vince.

"No," said Luther. "He'll live in memory."

"Who's gonna remember? For how long?"

"Me. I'll remember." Luther stared at Willie's frozen corpse.

"You're already dead," said Vince. "You died with him."

Despite Luther's ranting tirades about the man who had killed his son, Denham was unclear how Willie had actually died. When he asked Vince, Vince shook his head and said he didn't want to talk about it.

Vince picked up his saddle and bedroll and walked out to the picketed horses. After he had finished saddling and bridling Dandy, he led his horse and Willie's horse into the camp.

He looked at Luther, who sat staring into the fire as though he were powerless to move. Vince saddled Willie's horse. Denham helped him lift Willie's stiff corpse over the animal's back. They lashed Willie to the saddle. By the time they had finished. Luther still had not moved.

Denham brought in Luther's horse. Vince quickly saddled and bridled the animal. "It's time to go," he said to Luther.

Denham poured the remains of the coffee on the fire. The sudden fumes and erratic smoke activated Luther, who slowly rose and went to his horse.

An hour later, the riders were descending a narrow winding game trail into a small valley that widened into a double bowl shape. The two sections of the valley each contained a small lake connected by a stream.

The terrain surrounding the valley dropped abruptly from bare exposed granite to a high mountain meadow. From dark clouds that draped the surrounding ridges, snow flurried down about the men and horses.

Denham rode in the lead. As they reached the valley floor, he stopped his horse and pointed ahead. A mile on at the other side of the valley, Paul Evan's tiny figure moved slowly toward them.

Denham, Vince, and Luther watched in silence. They were concealed by a dense stand of pine and several large boulders near the stream. They waited.

Stumbling, dragging his feet, Paul skirted the first lake, then followed the stream from the lower end at a diagonal across a grassy slope. From time to time, his hand passed across his dirty unshaven features. Glassy with disorientation his swollen eyes rolled as though he had lost control of them.

The sharp snort of Vince's horse caught Paul's attention. He shuddered to a halt and, with some difficulty, focused on the men and horses blocking the trail. He looked up at the riders.

"I know who killed them," Paul's voice cracked from stress and fatigue. "I saw him. He took my boy." Paul's wavering stare found Luther. "The man is still there, up there." Paul pointed toward the cloud-darkened peaks that rose at their backs. "He killed Willie. He killed your son."

As Luther dismounted from his horse, his eyes never left Paul's face. He pulled his rifle from the saddle and walked toward the man he believed had murdered his son. The rifle stock swept up smashing Paul in the face. Paul pitched away to the side with a grunt of pain. Blood rushed from his mouth and nose.

Luther slipped a knife from his belt, grabbed Paul by the hair and jerked his head back to cut his throat.

Denham quickly dismounted and, with a single stride, he kicked Luther's head. Luther fell back losing his hat and knife. His expression spit rage and disbelief. His hand reached for the Colt .45 slung from his gun belt.

The nervous lever action of Denham's rifle stopped him. Luther stared up past the dark barrel at the old man leaning in behind the sights. Luther looked savagely at Vince, who sadly watched the confrontation between the two old men.

"Well, ain't you gonna do somethin'?" Luther asked of his son.

Vince did not answer. He looked at his aging father, then slowly away past the corpse of his brother to the storm clouds moving in, roofing the valley.

For several moments, Paul felt dizzy and unable to rise. Blood flowed freely from his nose and mouth and dripped off his chin onto his clothes.

Denham helped him to his feet. "Can you walk? We have to get movin' before that storm catches us.

Paul turned away and stumbled on ahead of the others. The chilling wind froze the blood to his face like a mask.

Luther rolled over onto his hands and knees. He looked about and found his hat, which he returned to his head. Then he reached up and grabbed his saddle stirrup to steady himself as he staggered to a standing position. Staring at Denham with unconcealed hatred, he supported himself against his horse. He placed his left foot into the stirrup, grabbed the saddle horn, and with a heavy sluggish motion thrashed his body up onto the horse's back.

His face bloated with anger and resignation, Luther urged his horse on at a walk into the wind. He followed Willie's corpse swaying and bumping against the sides of the next horse in the line.

A row of tall peaks separated Matt and Guzman from the hunting party several miles away. Guzman was growing concerned that the impending snowstorm would trap him and Matt. They had another day's walk ahead of them before they would reach the road.

Matt realized that Guzman had not been able to eclipse *the light* within his subconscious mind. He had been able only to contain it and to prevent it from growing. The boundaries of *the light* pushed outward with diaphragmatic pulsations against Guzman's consuming mental darkness.

Guzman's concentration was drawn away from Matt to the arduous task of negotiating the narrow trail they climbed along the face of a slope that dropped sharply away hundreds of feet into a rocky canyon.

Sleet suddenly spit at them from the clouds. Matt followed several yards behind Guzman. An urge rose in him to rush Guzman and push him over the edge of the horizontal shelf, but his mind could not command his body to perform. Guzman still controlled him.

Before the storm struck them with full force, Guzman wanted to be clear of the open ledge and descending into the next valley where they could find shelter. He paused to look back over his shoulder at Matt, who was barely visible through the curtain of sleet.

Guzman had not counted on being hampered by a snowstorm. But there were some things over which he had no control.

*   *   *

Not far from Brogan's Tavern in the mountain town of Buck, the sheriff left his parked car and followed two young teenage boys down a densely forested slope to a rushing creek. The boys had come running to his office not more than fifteen minutes ago to describe what they had found while hunting squirrels.

The sheriff followed the youths along the bank of the stream to a place where the water widened into a calm pool protected by surrounding boulders.

For a moment, he stared up at the approaching snowstorm. High velocity winds were driving leaden gray and black clouds away from the peaks and over the town. Then he suddenly grew aware that the boys bad stopped a few yards ahead of him.

The boys stepped aside as the sheriff quickly came forward. He looked down at the frozen eviscerated corpse of Lila Stevenson. "Jesus Christ." He knelt down for a closer look at the wound. After several moments, he rose. "Whoever did this is a madman."

He turned to the boys. "That snow's gonna start falling any minute. There's a blanket up in my car. Will one of you get it. We need to carry her out of here."

The taller of the boys ran back along the creek bank, then made an abrupt turn up the slope to the road.

While he was waiting for the boy to return, the sheriff studied the area near the woman's bluish-tinged body for some sign that would help lead to the identification of her killer. He could not find any footprints, nothing left behind except a pearl clutched in the palm of her left hand.

A few minutes later, the tall boy, Biff, returned with the blanket. The sheriff positioned the blanket under Lila's inert form, then instructed the boys how to lift her legs using the blanket as a sling.

The sight of Lila's slashed vaginal area and abdomen soured whatever erotic fantasies the boys might have had about a woman's sexual apparatus.

At a word from the sheriff, they simultaneously lifted Lila in the blanket and carried her to a point where they could ascend the slope with the least difficulty. Her encased body swayed and bumped against the ground as they scrambled to maintain their footing in making the climb to the car.

When they reached the road, they lowered her body to the ground next to the car. From their nervous manner, the sheriff could tell the boys wanted to be on their way.

He quickly opened the back door of the car, then maneuvered Lila's head and shoulders onto the seat while the boys lifted and pushed her legs.

He thanked the boys, who nodded and walked away along the road. As he drove to his office, he radioed his deputy, who was several miles down the mountain on highway patrol.

"We have a homicide. Two boys found Lila Stevenson's body in the woods across the road from Brogan's. She was murdered."

The sheriff started linking together the pieces of his investigation beginning when he first attempted to locate the missing woman seven days ago. When he arrived at his office, he decided not to remove Lila's corpse from the car. He went inside and opened the file on his desk. Pat and Enid Mobley, who owned and managed the local motel had given him a detailed description of the man who registered as Antonio Guzman. Lila Stevenson had last been seen leaving Brogan's Tavern with Guzman.

Glancing out the window, he saw his deputy's car pull up outside. The sheriff picked up the phone and dialed the coroner's office. His call was answered on the third ring, as his deputy entered in search of the body.

"In the back seat of my car," the sheriff informed him.

The deputy quickly went outside to look, as the sheriff continued his conversation with the coroner.

Chapter 34

The storm raged, howling down from the dark shrouded peaks into the valleys. Rushing winds piled up massive drifts that blocked passes from the high country to the mid-range forests and plateaus.

Only minutes before the driving blizzard enveloped them, Paul, Vince, Denham and Luther crawled in among a cluster of pines and large boulders for shelter. The snow built up in a huge drift like a towering wave on the windward side and provided them additional protection from the direct blast.

The ripe smell of the horses cloistered in the thicket with the men was strong. Vince removed Willie's body from his horse and laid him out at the edge of the shelter. Luther helped Vince unsaddle the horses. Both men knew the animals would probably have to be sacrificed to the storm. Vince patted his horse, Dandy, on the neck. He did not relish the thought of having to put a bullet in the brain of this beautiful intelligent animal. A quick death for the animals was better than freezing and starvation or being ravaged by wolves.

Paul helped Vince gather wood for a fire. Soon a high reaching blaze illuminated and warmed the enclosure.

Holding his rifle across his lap, Denham sat slightly apart from Paul and Vince in a position where he could watch Luther. He knew that Luther had slipped over the edge of sanity and was unpredictable. Denham bit off a hunk of beef jerky and chewed slowly.

Luther stared vacuously at the warming flames, but once his glance wandered covetously to the rifle in Denham's lap.

Cupping half-melted snow in his hands, Paul cleansed the blood from his face. He held a ball of snow in his mouth to dull the pain from the blow Luther had struck with his rifle. He nodded in half sleep toward the fire

All four men crawled into their sleeping bags to keep from freezing. As sleep overcame them, Denham fought his fatigue and the delirium of fever. He hoped to fall only into a light doze and remain alert. But he was old now. The work and tension of the past few days had drained his energy. He sank into a deep abyss of sleep. In his erratic dreams, he saw his wife, Anna, and called out to her.

He suddenly snapped awake and stared into the flames. Paul was awakened by Denham's muttering and watched him. Denham's watery eyes slowly looked back at Paul.

"How far is it?" Denham's voice cracked.

Paul shook his head. "Don't know. Another day, maybe two. Are you all right?"

"What are we doing here?"

"We had to stop. The storm is too bad. We can't see where we're going or where we are."

"I'm holding you back," said Denham. "You can't carry me on, can you?"

Vince woke at Denham's words and watched him. "We'll make it old man. We'll all make it. Have to wait 'til the storm blows over is all."

Vince placed a lump of snow to melt in the depression of a rock near the fire. After the snow had turned to water, Paul held the small rock into position for Denham to drink the liquid.

"I feel weak, so weak," the old man whispered. "More."

Paul nodded, scooped up more snow and placed it on the rock near the fire.

"How could I tell her what I don't know myself," said Denham to no one in particular.

"What?" Paul stared at the old man.

Denham became clear again for a moment in his own mind. "Anna, my wife. She told me I shouldn't go. I didn't listen. Now, it's too late. Couldn't see. Chasing it. Chasing after death. Chasing it away. But all the time, it was right behind me, breathing down my neck."

Vince looked away from Denham. Consumed with his own discomfort, Paul eased back down to rest.

"It was the plants," said Denham, mumbling incoherently. "The plants in the windows. They was different shapes and sizes -- and the land around the house -- way it was overgrown with flowers like I finally come home."

Vince stared at Denham, then at Luther. He recognized in the two old men what he would one day become, crazy and senile. If he did not freeze and die in the storm, he vowed he would leave home and make a life for himself. He would accept Wyandotte's offer and go to Arizona to become Wyandotte's head trainer.

He noticed Luther's eyes open a slit and look back at him, then slowly close like the eyes of a heavy-lidded lizard.

Denham started up talking again in his delirium, remembering when he had first met Anna. His car had broken down in front of her house along the mountain road leading to Buck. He saw her sitting out on her porch on a rocker. He approached her.

"Hot, thirsty out there across the road," she said. "Looks like you come a long ways. Long ways. Come on up and set. Get out of the sun."

In his vision, Denham saw her pouring fresh lemonade. "Don't drink it too fast on a hot stomach," she said. "Yes, nice to have company." Denham gulped and opened his eyes. "I want to stay. I want to stay. Air's clean. Mountain's quiet. Not like the city. You have a warm house, made of stone. All so natural, like a place was made, waitin' for us to bring the ends together." Denham's head nodded. Snoring softly, he drifted off to sleep.

Paul looked over at Vince. For a moment, they held each other's haggard gaze. Vince yawned, a ferocious display of teeth. Then he lay back down and went to sleep.

Antonio Guzman had been searching for shelter before the storm came sweeping down on him and Matt Evans. Guzman discovered one of numerous small caves large enough for the two men to crawl inside and escape the cutting wind.

Guzman dragged in several rotted sections of fallen trees. He quickly built a fire and soon he and his reluctant disciple were warm and dry.

Matt stared at bits and pieces of fur and small bones from dead animals littered about. They were in the abandoned lair of some predator, fox, coyote, maybe a bear, possibly a mountain lion.

As a boy, he had seen the remains of small animals like this in caves and dens in the woods near his grandfather's farm. He had taken his younger sister, Jenny, to show her. When he told her how the fur and bones had gotten there, she had cried for the eaten animals.

"That's the way it is in the wilds," he had explained to her. "Some animals have to eat others to stay alive."

Jenny had wanted to go home after that, but first she had wanted to see *the light* that Matt had told her about.

They had gone back to the canoe and Matt had paddled them to the place where his grandfather had shown him *the light*.

"We have it inside us," he had told her. "Grampa told me that God is everywhere, and because we have the light inside us, God is inside us and nothing can hurt us anymore."

Jenny had nodded and stared at the shimmering spot in the water. Although Jenny could not fully understand or conceptualize the closeness she felt with her brother at that moment, Matt sensed the family love they shared and that *the light* bonded them.

As they passed through their childhood years, they often spoke of *the light* and made frequent visits to their backwater shrine to gaze into the reflective waters. *The light* became embedded in their souls and prepared them for what was to come. Matt suddenly attended to what Guzman was doing and saying.

Guzman was assembling the bones of the small animals in a pattern near the fire and seemed to be muttering to himself or to the animal remains or to someone who wasn't there. He removed his hunting knife from its sheath and passed it back and forth through the flames.

"Watch the blade. See how it shines and is purified by Satan's fire. Fire is the true light, not the reflection of sun on water. Fire consumes and allows your soul to go free. When I was a young boy, I was a freer of souls of animals such as these. Now I free human souls that were reincarnated from other animals and are only waiting for the final release. You and I each contain an animal's soul within us. I have the soul of a panther. What soul lives within you?"

Matt thought carefully before answering. He had always related to the stuffed rabbit given to him by his grandfather, so he said, "A rabbit. There was a dead rabbit that I cried for when I was a boy. I believe I have his soul."

"A rabbit is a small weak animal, like these," Guzman prodded the piles of bones with the hot blade of the knife. "The small and weak are prey to be eaten. Soon, I will set your soul free."

"Like the animals?"

"Like the animals."

"Are you going to kill me?"

"Yes."

"Now?"

"I detect fear in you. Why do you fear me? Why do you fear death? Death is a gift I give you, a gift to be embraced. But there is a purpose in your death. Your father must take part in it. So we must reunite with him. Once he knows that I have set your soul free, he will join you."

"Where is my father?"

"He is out there, in the storm, just as we are in the storm. There was a moment when I could have taken you both, but the time was not right. It was too soon. The arrangement must be precise, just as these bones fit together. We will meet your father again. You will draw him to us. The next time, the arrangements will be as they should. The next time, I promise you deliverance."

Matt watched the gleaming blade pass and turn through the flames as though it had a life of its own.

Concealed from the storm by the shelter of pines and boulders, Luther waited until he was certain that Paul, Vince, and Denham were asleep. He slowly opened his eyes and studied the somnolent forms of the other three men. With great caution, he leaned over past the fire and delicately placed a hand on Denham's rifle which had fallen from the old man's grasp.

The click of the bullet entering the chamber woke Paul. He rolled aside and out of the circle of firelight into the surrounding snow as the bullet intended for his head ricocheted off the frozen ground.

At the loud report of the rifle, Vince lunged upward and tried to grab the barrel. Luther staggered away scattering the coals of the fire and plunged the shelter into partial darkness.

With a loud grunt of effort, Luther broke away with the rifle and ran out into the storm. Vince pulled his sleeping bag free and went after him. He quickly returned.

"He's gone. I can't see him," said Vince. He looked across the coals of the fire at Paul and Denham. The old hunter had not stirred.

Outside the shelter Luther blundered about blinded by the force of the driving wind and sleet. Even in his crazed state of mind he realized he had made a mistake in leaving the enclosure of rocks and trees, and especially the fire. Whether he killed Paul Evans now or not no longer mattered. He felt his body physically dying from the extreme cold. He knew that if he were to live, he must get back to his sleeping bag and the life-giving heat of the fire but he couldn't find the shelter.

He had not gone more than a few steps away from the enclosure. He was certain of that. He couldn't discern the rocks, the trees, not a glimmer of firelight, nothing. A black void of howling wind and swirling snow encased him.

Hoping that Vince would hear, he fired the rifle into the air. He fired again and again, saw the brief spurt of flame from the barrel. Then the hammer clicked on an empty chamber.

"Vince," he shouted hoarsely. "Vince, help me. Help me." Staggering about, he slipped and fell, losing the rifle in the deep snow.

The snow was wet and icy, coating his hands and face. Having totally lost his sense of direction, he crawled and thrashed through the powder. Only by pure chance did he encounter a large boulder. He struck it with his shoulder and the side of his head. Edging along against the rock, he followed its contour. He stopped upon seeing the blinking coals from the scattered fire. He dragged his body forward and collapsed.

By dawn, the fury of the storm had not diminished. Paul and Vince woke stiff with cold and cramped muscles. Denham raised his head from his bedroll and looked outside. His old bleary eyes took in Paul.

"If he survived the night," said Vince, "he'll be out there waiting for you." He spoke to Paul without looking at him."

"I didn't kill his son," said Paul. "It was someone else. Someone else up here."

They listened to the howling wind.

"Tomorrow, we might get out under cover of the storm," said Vince. "Sounds like it's gettin' worse. If we don't leave in the morning, we won't get out alive. After we make it through the pass, it's nearly a day's walk to the nearest road. If the pass closes up..." He left the sentence unfinished. "Nearly a day's walk out to the road."

Chapter 35

Delbert James had been born and raised in Montana. Much of his adult life he had spent in major metropolitan centers of the United States on assigned duty for the FBI. During the first third of his long career, he worked in New York and Washington D.C. Then he had been reassigned to Los Angeles. Now, at age 60, he decidedly had had enough of big city life and his final duty before retirement had brought him home.

He and his wife lived in a rural outer suburb of Great Falls where the air was clean and the silence was only occasionally punctuated by the bark of their dog.

He routinely processed the request for information on the alleged disappearance of Paul Evans and electronically transmitted the data to agent Leon Safullo in New York. "No evidence of travel regarding victim. Will meet you at Great Falls Airport with winter gear. Major storm in area."

James considered there would be no further information requested by the New York office. In his own mind he had put the case to rest until that evening as he watched a local newscast. The lead story was about the bizarre murder of a woman in the mountain town of Buck. The sheriff of Buck and the coroner for that region both spoke during on-camera interviews and mentioned that the killer had left a pearl as his calling card. A composite drawing of the suspect, Antonio Guzman, with whom Lila Stevenson was last seen, appeared on the screen. The name Antonio Guzman provided by Ed Berzinsky was fresh in Delbert James' memory.

That a killer from New York must have been on the same flight as Paul Evans and had committed a ritualistic murder of a woman in Buck struck Delbert James as being more than a coincidence.

He quickly went to the phone and dialed information. A few minutes later, he was talking with the sheriff of Buck. James learned that Paul Evans and his son had stayed at the Buck motel and that Matt Evans had been involved in a fight at the local tavern. A conversation with the owners of the motel revealed that Paul Evans had commented he and his son were hiking into the back country. The sheriff had followed their car for several miles as they drove out of town.

James made the mental connection that Guzman was a serial killer and Paul Evans was a target. He finished his conversation with the sheriff, then immediately called Berzinsky and Safullo, who were in the air, to explain his conjecture.

A half hour later, the tall, soft-spoken, silver-haired James was speeding the forty miles to Great Falls to meet his fellow agents at the airport.

By ten o'clock, they were airborne in a helicopter rising through the cold night toward the mountains. Two black four-wheel drive vehicles bearing FBI plates set out at the same time to be available at the destination for ground transportation.

As a matter of habit, when Jenny Holme's husband came home from work, he greeted the children and played with them for a few minutes before turning on the evening television newscast.

The story of the strange murder of a woman in Buck, Montana had been picked up from local broadcast by network channels and was featured as a national news item.

At the mention of Montana, she dropped what she was doing and hurried into the living room to watch and listen.

An artist's composite rendering of Antonio Guzman as the suspected murderer of Lila Stevenson came on the screen.

Jenny stared at the drawing. There was something familiar about the man's face, not that she had seen him before. She recognized something behind the expression in his eyes in the drawing.

Then suddenly she knew. As a child she had seen that expression in her father's eyes as he had grown progressively worse in his relationship to her, Matt, and their mother.

The second key to Jenny's realization was when the journalist interviewed the coroner who had conducted the autopsy. He suspected that Lila Stevenson's death was a ritual murder by a Satanist or practitioner of the occult.

"I know what it is now," she said out loud. "Remember what I told you about how strange it was Dad wanting Matt to join him up there? Matt said he was acting strange and paranoid like there was something mentally wrong with him. That killer could be after him for some reason."

"That's nonsense. Who would want to kill Matt? Come on, Jenny. You're getting carried away with your psychic stuff."

"No, not Matt, our Dad. I'm telling you this is not a coincidence. I can feel it. And what if they're caught in that snow storm?"

She had never imposed her New Age preoccupation on her husband regarding her psychic ability, although she had used her healing power on him in a limited way to ease his mind during moments of stress. He would not be likely to understand or accept her suspicions about how Antonio Guzman might be linked to the disappearance of her father, the strange request for Matt to accompany him into the back country. Jeff Holmes would, however, listen to her concern about her brother being trapped in the storm. She didn't care what might happen to her father. Her brother was another issue. She believed they were linked by a special energy, a profound love shared as a result of their childhood experience together, a love realized by what their grandfather had given them, what he called *The Light*. She understood that the bond might only be a psychological mechanism that helped them to cope with their father's abuse and the emotional loss of their mother, but Jenny clung to the concept as her reality.

"I have to go there," she said.

"But why? For what purpose? There's nothing you can do."

"You just have to trust me. I can't explain why, at least not in a way --" she left her sentence unfinished.

"This is stupid, Jenny. What about the kids? I can't take off from work."

"I have to know when they find them whether Matt is dead or alive."

"And your dad?"

"I could care less about him."

"Whatever happens to Matt, you'll hear it over the news."

"This is something I feel very strongly about, Jeff. If he's alive, I need to be there with him."

"And what if he's dead?"

"Don't say that. Don't even think that. It only contributes to the negative possibility."

"What I think has nothing to do with what happens to your brother. I understand your concern, but the proper authorities are taking care of the matter. I'm concerned that if you go driving up into those mountains by yourself, something will happen to you. You're not used to driving on icy roads, let alone icy mountain roads."

"Nothing is going to happen to me. I will be all right."

"You know, Jenny, there are some things in life that are out of your hands. And you have to accept that. Just because you think you're projecting psychic signals doesn't mean it's anything more than your imagination."

"Without your ever knowing it, you have received my psychic signals, as you call them. You receive them every day. They are my love for you. They are your children's love for you. And they are your love for us. That's all this is about, Jeff. Nothing magical, no beads and crystals and wind chimes. You experience it every day and will continue to do so for as long as we are together. Now, do you understand? I'm going there simply because I care about my brother."

Duly reprimanded and feeling chagrined, Jeff remained silent.

"Annie will come over and take care of the kids until I return."

"I still don't understand what you think you can do up there."

"It's something between me and Matt and my father. Something is happening up there and they are going to need me."

"The searchers haven't even found them." Jeff was reluctant to say his next statement, but he did not want his wife to leave. "They might have been buried somewhere back up in there in an avalanche."

"I understand your concern, but I do have to go. This also has to do with my mother."

"Your mother? Now I am confused."

"I have to do this for her."

"Do what?" Jeff looked at her perplexed. "It would help if you'd explain what this has to do with your mother."

"I don't want you to mock me."

"Mock you? For God's sake." He switched off the television set. "I would never mock you."

Jenny looked away at their children playing with push toys on the family room floor. "All right. I'11 tell you. I have never been able to reach my mother, to connect with her since her attempted suicide. I tried to heal her, but I failed. I do not have the capability to heal someone whose life has been so devastated. If my mother were - normal - and she saw this on the news, she would go there. Since she can't, I am going for her. It's that simple."

"Okay, before I come off sounding liking a selfish asshole, I won't say anymore. All I can say it's a good thing one of us is practical."

"Yes, it is, Jeff, and I'm glad you're that one. I'm not practical. I'm romantic, like my mother."

"Just don't go goony on me."

"You have no idea how practical I am."

"Yeah, you're practical, for some things."

"I have to call the airline and get packed."

"Well, be sure you take the right kind of clothes. You're gonna freeze your ass out there."

Chapter 36

When he woke the next morning, Paul fought against the insistent pressure of his bladder to drive him out of the warm confines of his sleeping bag. He was stiff and cramped from lying on the cold ground. He raised his head slightly and looked around the shelter and noticed the fire was dead. He heard the horses stamping and snuffling nearby. The sharp sweet odor of their fresh droppings hung in the chill air. Outside the storm continued to rage and consume the enclosure with tall gaping drifts.

Paul barely remembered that Luther had crawled back into the shelter during the night. Although he feared Luther's craziness, he was glad the man had not frozen to death outside.

Paul struggled up out of his sleeping bag. Hugging himself for warmth, he gingerly stepped outside the protective circle of the shelter to relieve himself.

Vince was next to awaken. He lay still for a full minute listening to the force of the storm. He watched Paul return and sit back down on his sleeping bag. Vince's left leg and hip felt numb from the position he had slept on them all night. As he staggered to a standing position, the sudden pain of restored circulation coursed down his leg. He limped out of the enclosure to assess the condition of the storm.

He looked in all directions and did not see any break in the dark bellicose clouds or detect any lessening in the deluge of wind driven sleet and snow.

His piss steamed as it stained the snow yellow at his feet.

The increasing depth of the snow worried him. Forging a passage through it would be difficult except where it thinned out along the ridges. The horses would wallow and became trapped in the drifts. They would starve and freeze to death.

The men still had a long climb ahead of them to the pass before the final descent to the valley ten miles from the Macke ranch. Staying longer in the shelter would not do them any good. He turned and went back inside.

"Wake him," Vince said to Paul, who leaned over and gently shook Denham. Vince nudged Luther with his foot until his father stirred.

Luther groaned and propped himself up on one elbow. Bleary-eyed, he stared at the scuffed toe of Vince's boot.

"It's time to go," Vince said, then picked up his rifle, and walked slowly to the horses.

He placed the barrel opening against the head of Denham's horse. The sharp report of the rifle panicked the other animals who reared and shied, pulling at their tethers as the horse crumpled and thrashed to the ground.

Fully awake now, the other three men watched Vince as, one by one, he killed the horses and mules with a single shot each to the brain.

He saved his own horse, Dandy, for last. He placed his arms around the neck of his beloved animal and pressed his face into the muscular neck. After several moments, he stepped back, aimed the rifle muzzle at a spot just below and slightly behind Dandy's left ear, then pulled the trigger. The horse's head jerked away at the impact. His knees buckled and he went down with a great shudder.

Vince turned away and came back to the others. "It won't get any better. Let's go."

"What about Willie?" Luther implored. His haggard jowly bewhiskered face looked as though it had aged ten years.   Vince shook his head.

"We can't leave him," said Luther hoarsely.

"We'll come back for him." Vince picked up his bedroll and walked out into the storm.

The four men set out from the shelter and, with the blizzard crushing at their backs, made slow uneven progress through waist deep snow toward the nearly indiscernible slope. One thousand feet above, high winds blocked the pass with massive drifts.

The constant lunging through the snow required a physical effort that left the men gasping. They had to stop and rest every ten minutes. The needle sharp cold bit into their exposed faces with searing penetration and drained their bodies of energy.

When they arrived at the base of the slope. Vince uncoiled his lariat and passed sections of the rope back along the line of men. With freezing fingers fumbling and barely able to grasp the tightly woven hemp, each man looped the rope about his waist and tied it to his belt.

As they began the climb, they responded to the tug of the line to know in what direction to go, since each man was only a dark hulk to the man behind crawling like a snow encrusted beetle up the slope.

Their progress was barely discernible, only a few feet at a time. They were still more than they moved, curled into the snow, tucking their hands inside their coats for warmth, their faces nestled tightly against their raised shoulders as a shield against the blast.

Halfway up the slope, Vince discovered a small ridge where the wind had swept away most of the snow. A constantly shifting thin powder flowed across the granite surface which rose upward at a forty-five degree angle toward the pass. Following the incline of the ridge, they were able to climb more easily for a few hundred feet.

When they finally reached the pass, they collapsed from exhaustion. Their breath came in hoarse steaming gasps. As they lay there with the snow drifting over them, Vince knew they must continue to move or they would quickly succumb to sleep and death from freezing.

Vince raised his head from his shielding arms, then staggered to his feet. He pulled and tugged on the rope to get the others up. Then he led them to the edge of the descent and stopped with a quickening of his heart.

The storm had built up such a deep snow pack and the blizzard curtain was so intense, they could not see even the outline of a trail down.

Vince started walking and the others followed at the insistent tug on the rope. They immediately sank in up to their chests in a drift and then the whole side of the mountain began to move. The shifting plate of ice and snow sluiced downward bearing the four men with its increasing momentum.

The slide catapulted them over a ledge into space and tumbled them onto the next slope that fanned out at the base of the short drop.

Finally, they stopped rolling and falling. Vince located the others by pulling on the rope. One by one, no longer recognizable, they came floundering up out of the snow like subterranean creatures seeking light.

Vince continued the descent. Keeping tension on the rope that connected them, Paul stayed near him. When they reached the bottom of the descent two hours later, Luther, who had been at the end of the line, had disappeared.

Vince looked back up the slope, but the driving force of the wind and whirling dervishes of thick falling snow obliterated all visibility.

Half crawling, Vince, Paul, and Denham struggled to a stand of scrub pine. They dropped to the ground under the branches to rest.

Paul closed his eyes and immediately began to drift away into a deep sleep. Vince shook him awake and forced him to stand. "We have to keep moving," he said.

An hour later, as they crossed the white expanse of a broad valley. Vince suddenly stopped and pointed ahead to a small line cabin nearly buried under the snow.

Worn down by the extreme cold and fatigue, the three men continued. As they reached a point halfway to the cabin, the snow caved in beneath them and they fell from sight into a stream.

The icy water and rushing current terrified Paul into action. Calling on a reserve of energy he did not think he possessed, he thrashed in a frenzy to the opposite bank. A few yards downstream Vince was doing the same.

Paul felt the tug and drag of Denham's weight at the end of the rope. The old hunter had no more strength and the freezing water temperature was killing him.

Paul and Vince climbed out of the stream at the same time, then turned to assist Denham.

The water froze on their clothes and hair like translucent armor.

"Get him moving," Vince shouted. "Keep him moving."

Weaving and staggering, Paul and Vince supported the old man between them as they plowed on across the field of snow to the cabin.

Unable to get to the door, Vince scraped away the snow at one of the side windows and discovered it was boarded shut. With Paul's help he pulled and twisted at the boards. The frozen rotten wood and rusted fastenings came loose and the two men savagely tore them away.

Vince smashed the window with his foot, kicked out the jagged loose shards of glass and climbed through.

Paul assisted Denham through the opening into Vince's arms, then inserted one leg over the window ledge into the room and fell inside.

Except for the dim light from the broken window, the cabin was dark. Stumbling over a table and chairs, Vince ransacked the shelves in a frantic search for matches and found them among a few cans of food, pots, and pans.

He quickly grabbed handfuls of mattress stuffing from one of two cots. With frozen shaking hands, he lay the base for a fire in the small fireplace and added kindling handed to him by Paul. Vince struck and held the match to the stuffing. As the flames caught and spread, Vince added larger pieces of wood from a stack in the corner.

Paul and Vince quickly peeled off Denham's wet frozen clothes, then their own and crouched naked with Denham lying on the floor between them before the fire.

When they began to feel warm, Vince prepared hot soup from the rations on the shelf. They drank the brew slowly from scalding metal cups.

Vince piled more logs on the fire. Wrapped in wool blankets taken from the cots, the three men slept huddled together side by side on the floor. The flames roared and crackled and lay a spreading glow of heat over them for the night.

Driven by vengeance and a blankness of mind and body, Luther had deliberately released himself from the rope. He walked on late through the day and into the night with an unerring sense of the route home.

Chapter 37

Joyce Macke parted the curtain at the kitchen window and looked out into the night. Snow swirled from the black void through the framed cast of yellow light and away into the vortex of the storm. After a moment, she dropped the curtains back into their original position and looked at the clock on the wall.

The storm had continued without let up for two days and nights. Since the men had not returned by the second day, Joyce knew they had not been able to get out through the mountain passes in time.

Early that morning, she had contacted the sheriff to seek help. He had explained that he couldn't call in a helicopter search until the storm passed. He had assured her that her men would know how to survive until a rescue team could find them.

When she returned home from her brief trip to Helena, Joyce had been saddened to learn that Lila Stevenson had been murdered by a stranger who was just passing through town. Joyce had always sympathized with Lila and understood why she allowed herself to be exploited by men.

All Lila had ever wanted was for a man to love her and stay with her, to be steady with her. Lila had wanted some sense of romance, but she had never found it. Joyce

identified with Lila's emotional suffering, because Joyce had never had romance in her life either. Now, she accepted that, for her, romance was only a fantasy. She was incapable of turning it into reality.

Joyce went into the living room and walked over to the fireplace. She put a log on the already blazing fire and stared into the flames. The intense heat warmed her face.

She did not like being there alone. Not that she feared the night, but a sense of foreboding invaded her house as though in retribution for her desire to leave. Guilt blistered in her mind like an open sore. She felt that she was being punished for her sin.

She did not want to sleep alone and cold in her bed. So she brought a heavy quilt to the couch and wrapped herself in it before the fire.

After a while, the warmth of the fire and the quick upward swimming of flames licking at the charred logs lulled her to sleep. In the midst of her fitful doze, a knocking and scraping sound woke her.

At first she thought it was only the storm battering at the house, rattling the kitchen door. The noise grew louder and insistent. Keeping the quilt wrapped about her, she walked stocking-footed into the kitchen where she had left the light on. The door was shaking. Someone was pounding.

With a gasp she ran to the door, slipped the bolt, and pulled open the door. A frost covered figure fell into the room like some hoary monster out of the night.

"Luther!" Joyce cried out as a chilling blast of wind and snow swept into the room around her fallen husband. She Looked out into the howling storm expecting her two sons to follow. Finally realizing and accepting they were not there, she pushed the door closed against the force of the wind.

She quickly knelt beside Luther and turned him over onto his back. His face was red and raw, his lips a bluish pallor. His eyelids and lashes were encrusted with ice.

Grabbing him under the arms, she dragged him into the living room before the fire and struggled to remove his stiff frozen clothing.

As Luther sensed and responded to the heat of the fire, he opened his eyes and looked at her. His crazed unseeing expression frightened Joyce.

She pushed his clothing aside and wrapped him in the quilt. She ran to the kitchen cupboard for a cup and a bottle of whiskey. She returned, poured a small amount of whiskey into the cup, then held Luther's head upright and placed the cup to his chapped swollen lips.

The acrid whiskey fumes revived him. He sipped and swallowed the liquid which spread like a lava stream of fire down his throat and gullet into his stomach. He coughed and moaned and again opened his eyes. He began to shudder and tremble with convulsions.

Joyce put the cup aside and massaged Luther's arms and Legs to restore his circulation. From time to time, he muttered in delirium, and once he cried out; but Joyce could not discern any intelligible words.

Leaving him for a few moments, she ran back into the kitchen and turned the gas flame on under the tea kettle. She opened the top of the kettle and dropped two chicken bouillon cubes into the water. She returned to Luther and continued to massage his limbs while she waited for the water to boil.

When she heard the kettle begin to whistle, she grabbed the whiskey cup and went back to the kitchen. She filled the cup with steaming broth, then tempered it slightly with cold tap water so that Luther's lips and mouth would not be scalded.

This time when she raised his head so that he could drink, after a few small gulps of the restorative broth, he coughed and spoke in halting sentences.

"Out there. Still out there somewhere. Kill him. Find him and kill him."

"Luther," Joyce leaned in close to his reddened ear. "Luther, Vince and Willie, why aren't they with you?"

A moan of sadness escaped Luther. "Vince, don't know. Willie, dead."

A cold snake of fear slithered down into Joyce's bowels. Her Willie dead. "My Willie, my baby," she whispered. Her eyes burned with tears that reflected the firelight.

*   *   *

Across the white plain, gray smoke spiraled from the cabin chimney. Diamond-like mica flakes of powder snow skimmed and swirled before the wind with the ecstasy of light, a contradiction to the previous force of the storm and the heavy weight of snow that now fleeced the entire range of mountains in ponderous white.

Vince was the first to wake. Keeping his blanket wrapped around him, he stirred up the fire and added more wood until a fresh blaze crackled. Then he set a pot of water on to boil to make tea.

In Paul's last few moments of a dream he was thawing back to life from a frozen state. As the heat of the fire touched his face, he woke and slowly sat up on the old tick mattress.

Vince glanced at him, then busied himself with getting dressed.

"How far is it from here?" asked Paul.

"Five miles out to the road. Another eight or so into town," said Vince. "Road is easier walkin' than tryin' for the ranch."

Vince pulled on his still cold boots, then noticed that Denham had not stirred. He leaned down from his chair and nudged Denham. "Hey, old man, time to wake."

The old hunter did not move. Vince dropped down to his knees and pulled back Denham's blanket. He leaned in closer and could not detect any breathing. He placed his head against Denham's chest and listened for a heartbeat, then slowly straightened. "He's dead." Vince covered the old man's face with the blanket.

When he and Guzman crawled out of the cave, the brilliance of the sun flashed off the snow nearly blinding Matt. Guzman noticed that Matt raised his hand to shield his eyes. The difficulty of seeing would create a greater dependency. Guzman turned his back and rummaged in his pack for a pair of sunglasses. After he had put them on, he looked around to tell Matt to walk ahead of him, but Matt was gone.

Guzman leaped to his feet and quickly scanned the area. "Matt! Matt! Where are you? You cannot hide from me."

Thinking he might have crawled back into the cave to escape the glare, Guzman searched inside. He began to panic. Perhaps Matt was not actually under his control, as Guzman believed. But where could he have vanished so quickly. "I should have thought to look." He went outside. A line of fresh footprints led to the edge of a short precipice that fanned out into a steep slope. "I didn't notice the tracks, because I would never have believed he would jump."

Three hundred yards below, he saw movement. Matt's diminishing figure blended with the trees.

"We may not wait for your father to be reunited with you." Grabbing up his pack, Guzman negotiated along the edge and determined that Matt had landed safely in deep snow, although the initial drop was fifty feet. Guzman heaved the pack and watched it plummet to near where he planned to land. Then he walked back ten yards to get a running start, turned and charged the edge. He catapulted out into cold space and controlled his hurtling downward position to land feet first in the deep snow with an explosion of white powder. Recovering his pack, he set off following the tracks that broke the virgin surface.

Matt had seen Guzman sail out over the edge of the cliff and realized that he could not physically outlast or outdistance his captor in an arduous pursuit. He would have to find a place to hide, but how and where. Once Matt's tracks came to an end, Guzman would know that he was in the area, unless the tracks ended where Guzman could not possibly follow. If he could make it appear that he had taken his own life, Matt believed he might stand a chance of escape.

A thick stand of pine forest blocked Matt from Guzman's view. Matt slung along through the snow that dragged at his legs, impeding his progress. Within minutes, he came to the edge of another cliff. Only this one was a sheer drop of one-thousand feet, a fall that no one could survive, despite the blanket of snow.

Taking care to step into the holes he had created in the snow only facing forward, Matt back tracked to a stand of exposed boulders that afforded him the opportunity to climb over them out of sight. He buried himself in the snow under concealing low-hanging boughs and remained silent and unmoving.

Thirty minutes later, Guzman came out of the trees and followed Matt's trail to the edge of the second precipice. The view down over the edge was too far to see a body that had fallen from so great a height. Yet Guzman did not believe that Matt would have been so driven to jump. He had been trying to escape. But then death was a form of escape.

"You cannot cheat me," he thought. "You cannot escape me. You cannot refuse my gift to you."

Guzman turned and looked back at his companion prints that paralleled Matt's. He retraced their steps to the stand of boulders, turned again and looked back toward the edge. Maybe he had underestimated the fortitude of Matt to take his own life. Maybe he, Guzman, had mentally pushed him over the edge. If so, in a way, he could still take credit for the young man's death. It was then he noticed the slight wet imprint of a boot halfway up the side of the exposed face of the largest boulder.

Drawing his knife, Guzman cautiously circled the perimeter of Matt's sanctuary and entered it from behind. He lifted the low sweeping bough enough to see the snow had been disturbed where Matt had concealed himself.

"You cannot escape," he said, "until I set you free. Come out now," he commanded.

After a moment, Matt struggled up out of his snow tomb. Brushing himself off, he stood and came over to Guzman. The knife blade flashed and came to rest against the side of Matt's neck. A slight pressure would penetrate the skin and severe his carotid artery.

"It is good that you desire the end of your life. You will have it soon."

He motioned for Matt to walk on ahead of him. They retraced their steps through the trees back to the first cliff, then traversed the base until they reached a slope that allowed them to climb up to the trail.

Chapter 38

The sheriff returned from an inspection of road conditions below the town where a slide had been reported. He had radioed for a plow and the snow had been cleared. The call had caused him to miss his usual mid-morning coffee. Also, he wanted to be around the television people in the event there was a breakthrough on the helicopter search for the lost men. He had discovered he liked those cameras looming at him with their magic eyes and the microphone thrust at him to catch his important words.

He parked among the news media cars and vans outside Brogan's tavern and entered. A reporter called out to him, "Any new developments, sheriff?"

"Nothing yet. Choppers are still out there."

Taking a seat at the bar, he removed his hat and sat a few chairs down from the driver of a giant logging truck that had been forced to stop in the town when the storm hit. He had been stranded for two days and was anxious to move on. The waitress came over to the sheriff. "Coffee?"

He nodded. "And a good hunk of hot apple pie. And put a piece of cheese on that."

The driver finished his coffee and turned to the sheriff. "That slide down the road been cleared yet?"

"Yep, 'bout fifteen minutes ago."

The driver nodded, left a quarter tip and walked outside down the street to where the giant truck was parked near the motel and service station. He climbed in and, with some difficulty, started the cold engine. It coughed to life with a tractor roar.

While he was waiting for the engine to warm up, he lit a cigarette and watched an attractive young woman get out of her car at the service station and talk to the attendant while he put gas in the tank of her rented car.

Jenny Holmes had waited down the road two hours for the slide to be cleared, and now she was asking the station attendant where she could get something to eat.

She went to use the restroom, returned to the car and paid the attendant for the gas, then drove away slowly along the icy street to Brogan's. The chains on the car tires clanked rhythmically as she increased the car's speed slightly until she saw the tavern whose roof was topped with snow.

She pulled into the parking lot next to the sheriff's car. Her stomach constricted with hunger. She had been driving since before dawn without having eaten any breakfast.

She walked from the car past icicles that hung like long pointed daggers from the eaves.

Upon entering the warm tavern, she looked about the room occupied mostly by a few journalists and news media crews. One of the television reporters, John Morley, she recognized from the news broadcast she had seen. He was huddled with an assistant going over a script for another brief segment that would be videotaped that morning in front of Brogan's.

Jenny took a seat at a corner table where she could inconspicuously watch the media people. After a few minutes, three of the technical crew members went out to their van and began setting up reflectors, a camera, and sound recording equipment.

The waitress came over to Jenny and offered her a menu. "Good morning. Coffee?"

"Thank you." Jenny quickly perused the menu and was ready to order by the time the waitress returned with a mug of black coffee. Jenny poured a little cream from an aluminum pitcher on her table.

The waitress jotted the coffee down on her order pad and looked at Jenny expectantly.

"I'l1 have the hotcakes and sausages and two eggs scrambled. Also a small glass of orange juice," said Jenny.

The waitress finished writing the order, said, "Thank you," and went back behind the bar to the kitchen.

While she was waiting for her food to arrive, Jenny watched the activity of the television crew outside. A pickup truck coming down from an elevation above the town turned right into the area where the crew was setting up. With curses and sharp cries at the driver, the crew members leaped aside. The truck stopped near the sheriff's car and Luther Macke stepped out of the cab. He reached back inside to a rack mount and pulled out a Winchester repeating rifle. The sight of the rifle immediately silenced the crew. Carrying the rifle in one hand, Luther entered the tavern.

When the sheriff saw him, he slid off the bar stool with an elated expression. "Luther, you made it. You're back."

Luther's entrance and the sheriff's remarks caught the attention of John Morley and his female assistant who both rose and came over to them.

"Is he one of the men who was caught up there in the storm?" John Morley asked.

Luther gave the stranger a menacing stare.

The sheriff nodded. "This is Luther Macke. He and his sons were up in the back country on a hunting party." Then to Luther he said, "Maybe Joyce told you. We're looking for the man who murdered Lila Stevenson. FBI's here lookin' for him too. They think he's a hit man with the Mafia or something. Remember them two boys was in here from back east? The one with an earring got in a fight with your Willie? FBI thinks the killer's out to get one of 'em."

"Willie's dead," said Luther in a flat emotionless voice.

"What?" The sheriff's eyes narrowed into a squint.

"He was killed by the man who was in here with his boy. That's why I'm here now. I'm waiting for him." Luther emphasized his point by gripping his rifle with a sharp thrust at the floor.

"Where's Vince and Denham?" the sheriff asked with concern. "Did they get back?"

"Don't know. We separated."

"Luther. I've got to talk to you about this. You need to tell me what happened up there."

John Morley interrupted. "Mr. Macke, it's important we get this story to the public right away. My crew is setting up outside right now. Sheriff, you can question him on camera and we'll record everything."

The sheriff shifted uncomfortably. He liked the thought of being filmed, but was concerned about the law in this matter before making the details public, since now his friend, a local was involved. "I think maybe Luther and me need to talk in private first."

"I ain't talkin' to you and I ain't talkin' to this asshole with a camera. I come here to wait and that's all I'm gonna do." Luther roughly pushed between them and headed for an empty table.

With John Morley hounding him, the sheriff followed Luther. He was worried about the rifle and Luther obviously had information he needed for his investigation.

"Sheriff," said John Morley, "You have to understand the importance of getting this story as it unfolds. This man is the key. I can explain so he'll understand how taping the interview can be helpful to him, as well. Remember what I told you yesterday about the power of the media."

Luther suddenly whirled and leveled the rifle at John Morley's gut. "Get the fuck away from me before I blow you away."

John Morley halted in mid stride. Then with a catch of excitement in his voice, he ordered his assistant, "Jane, get the crew in here with a camera and sound mic. This is fantastic."

The young woman turned and rushed outside.

"Luther," the sheriff said gingerly, now fully realizing his friend's extremity. "Give me the gun. There ain't' gonna be any camera yet," he said to John Morley. "I'd advise you to go outside and let me handle this. I'11 talk to you afterwards."

The crew suddenly came bursting through the door. Luther took one look at the camera riding the operator's shoulder, brought up the rifle and fired. The bullet's impact smashed the lens and the camera spun off the operator's shoulder as the man leaped away. The rest of the crew dropped to the floor.

The sheriff grabbed the rifle barrel with both hands and forced it high over Luther's head. His knee came up with a sharp blow to Luther's groin and he quickly wrested the gun away from him as Luther doubled over in pain.

Behind the sheriff, John Morley was shouting excitedly to the crew, "Get a backup camera quick. I want to capture all this. That fucking lowlife."

"I'm sorry, Luther," the sheriff slapped a pair of handcuffs on the troubled man. "I'm gonna have to arrest you and lock you up."

"Wait, sheriff," shouted John Morley, "It'll take us only a minute to get another camera ready."

"If you would have done like I told you, none of this would 've happened. You're damn lucky you didn't get killed, or one of them. Now, get out of the way." The sheriff walked his grimacing prisoner past John Morley and the trembling camera operator, who was lifting his smashed equipment from the floor.

A crew member respectfully held the door open as the sheriff escorted Luther out to his patrol car. He put Luther in the back seat behind the screen, then got in at the wheel. A few moments later they were driving down the snow-encrusted main street to the jail.

Back at Brogan's, sitting unnoticed at her table, Jenny Holmes contemplated the altercation she had just seen and heard. The feeling she had experienced when she first saw the newscast and the composite drawing of Antonio Guzman were now confirmed by what the raving old man, Luther Macke, had said. She knew she had made the right decision to come there.

The waitress brought her breakfast and Jenny dug in ravenously.

At the jail, the sheriff finished locking Luther in a cell, then pulled up a wooden chair and sat facing him through the bars. "I know you're in a bad way, old friend; but the rifle was a mistake. Whatever happened up there, you need to tell me about it. Sure that newscaster is an asshole. Don't worry. I won't let him get to you. It's me that has to keep up appearances with them around. You're better off in here anyway 'til this is worked out. But what you can tell me can help."

Luther stared at him and remained silent.

"Well, old man, when you're ready." The sheriff stood and moved his chair back against the wall. "I'11 call Joyce and let her know what happened." He went to his desk and picked up the phone.

On the road five miles above the town, a snowplow crept along like a giant yellow insect against the mountain slope. With a steady roar it scooped aside the deep drifts and cleared a white channel walled by continuous banks of hard-packed snow.

Perched inside his cab on top of the tractor, the driver suddenly throttled down the engine and stared through the window befogged by his warm breath at two men who appeared out of the snow and trees ahead.

He radioed to the driver in a road maintenance truck following the plow a few hundred yards behind. Within moments, the truck pulled up alongside the plow. The drivers of both vehicles stepped down to greet the two snow-covered men stumbling toward them.

Paul and Vince were too exhausted to say much of anything as they climbed into the truck. The driver quickly poured them coffee from a large thermos. The hot brew and the heat inside the cab warmed them.

The driver backed the truck, turned it around, and headed for town.

Upon Vince's request, the driver stopped at Brogan's. At first, Paul's and Vince's entry into the tavern went relatively unnoticed, as though they were two locals just stopping in for coffee and a meal. They took seats side by side at the bar.

The waitress came over to greet them with a hearty grin. "Welcome back, Vince. Bet you didn't know you were a celebrity." She nodded toward the media people who occupied several tables.

"We need hot food and plenty of it," said Vince.

"You've got the works comin' right up." The waitress hurried to the kitchen.

Outside, the driver of the maintenance truck finished talking to one of the media technicians, who came into the tavern, paused a moment to look at Vince and Paul sitting at the bar, then walked across the room to John Morley. Leaning over the table, be spoke quietly to the journalist.

"That's him, Paul Evans. A road maintenance driver just brought them in."

"Get a camera and sound in here fast."

Everyone at the table pushed back their chairs and rushed to action. Waving his clipboard at the crew to hurry, John Morley stood and walked with slow steady steps over to Paul and Vince.

Several days growth of a beard and the bulky winter clothing her father wore did not conceal his identity from Jenny. Knowing that he would be distracted by the media and not wanting to become involved herself, she chose to wait before going to talk to him.

She watched John Morley introduce himself to her father. A moment later, the first camera, sound, and lighting crew came awkwardly through the door with their equipment. As other reporters and their crews realized what was happening, they scrambled to bring in their equipment and join the process of capturing the news story.

Shaking his head, Vince refused to look at the cameras and would not respond to the barrage of questions about his father and brother from the crowd that hovered around them at the bar.

Sipping at his coffee, Paul's statements were clipped about what had happened, where his son was, about a hit man, about a woman who was murdered, about the FBI. The arrival of food was a relief. "I'm hungry," he said. "Just let me eat. I'11 talk later."

The cameras continued to film him and Vince while they ate hotcakes, sausages, eggs, and fried potatoes. During the lull in the interview, John Morley recited his commentary at one of the cameras about the arrival of Paul Evans and Vince Macke and that now two murders were related to the incident of Paul Evan's disappearance with his son, who had not yet been found, but, according to Paul Evans, was possibly still alive. Evans also claimed that no attempt had been made on his life.

Paul could not tell them the truth. The media people and everyone who saw him on a television screen would think he was insane. He had no way to prove who Guzman really was.

As he ate, he tried his best to block out the presence of the cameras, lights, and microphones recording his every move and sound. Their intrusion caused him to feel persecuted and self-conscious, penetrating and recording his guilt for all the world to see.

He wanted his son back. He did not know what to do. He did not know what to say to them. He did not want to say anything.

Joyce Macke stepped out onto her back porch, shaded her eyes against the sun and looked up at the two helicopters as they passed overhead and navigated up the valley toward steep mountain terrain.

You're too late, she thought. *You're too late for my boy. Find Vince. Find him. Don't let him die out there.*

She went back inside and paced about the kitchen, jerked a chair away from the table, but could not sit down. She rammed her body against the sink counter and leaned and pressed until the pain against her abdomen became unbearable as she tried to recall the pain of their birth.

At the distant rotary thumping of approaching jet helicopters, Guzman stopped suddenly and Matt, eyes downcast as he plodded after him in the deep snow, stumbled into his back. "Wait." Guzman looked up at the sky, but his view of the long valley before them was eclipsed by a forest of tall pines. The search helicopters would come upon them within minutes, and Guzman did not want to be found.

Matt followed his gaze and listened to the sound. A glimmer of hope clicked into his mind that he would soon have an opportunity to escape Guzman's influence and power over him.

"Quick, into the trees," Guzman ordered him. "We don't want them to see us."

"But why?" Matt held back. "We need help."

Guzman roughly grabbed his arm. "We don't need help. We don't want anyone to find us."

"But I don't think I can walk anymore." Matt sagged.

Guzman slapped him across the face and Matt went down. Droplets of blood stained the snow where his mouth was cut. He made no effort to move. The sound of the helicopters was drawing closer, shattering the mountain stillness.

"Get up!" Guzman's vehement command sliced through the cold air. "Now!"

Matt did not move. Guzman reached down with both hands and raised Matt to his feet with a savage jerk. "You will not get out of this. Believe me. You and your father are going to die. Now move." He shoved Matt along ahead of him until they were hidden deep within the gloom of the trees.

Moments later, the two helicopters filled the sky with their sound and cast giant moving shadows over the vast field of snow. Maintaining an altitude of one-thousand feet and a distance of a quarter mile between them, they maneuvered toward the head of the twenty mile valley and in among the peaks.

"We'll keep moving," said Guzman, "but stay within the trees."

"How will we get back? I'm too tired to walk much further."

"You can and will walk as far and for as long as I tell you," said Guzman, staring into his eyes. Matt lost the sense of his immediate consciousness, as

Guzman's power of hypnotic suggestion was reinforced. "I can and will walk as far and for as long as you tell me."

"There's a ranch a few miles farther down the valley. I remember seeing it from the road when I was following you and your father into the high country. We'll get a vehicle there."

As they pushed on, the going was a little easier, since the snow was not as deep under the trees as in the open central valley.

Matt focused on the scent of pine and the throbbing pain at the corner of his swollen upper lip.

The five man FBI investigative and support team set up their command center in a vacant lot a few blocks from the sheriff's office. The communications van contained the latest radio, video, and surveillance device technology. Wearing a headset and mic, Sam Mulkern, a young agent with a stylish crewcut, maintained radio contact with the pilots and Agent Delbert James combing the back country in the two search helicopters. The lead pilot, Dan Fisher, fed him frequent information as to their location and visuals. So far, the only possibility of a recovery had turned out to be two foraging deer. Although, they had seen other tracks across fields of clean snow, they assumed they could have been made by wildlife or stray cattle.

Berzinsky and Safullo were more than a little peeved at the local sheriff's lack of cooperation and his tendency to want to put on a show for the media crews. They had witnessed Luther Macke's reaction to one news team's attempt to interview him. Shortly after Luther's arrest, they had gone to observe him in his jail cell, and determined they would not be able to derive any reliable information from the man, who appeared to be demented.

Later that afternoon, they saw the sheriff's car speed past the command post with flashing lights headed in the direction of Brogan's tavern, shortly after a giant snowplow chugged through town. They conjectured whether he were responding to a call regarding a road condition or if there were some additional development in the situation that he wasn't ready to share with them. Assuming the latter, they climbed into one of the four black FBI off-road vehicles and followed. Arriving at Brogan's several minutes later, they discovered they could not get anywhere near Paul Evans because of the crowding media. They decided not to push back the news teams, but to wait for a more opportune moment to get to Evans. They did, however, move in to where they could observe him. Other than obvious hunger, exhaustion, and some nasty facial wounds, he would be able to answer their questions later; but for now, he refused to respond to any questions the clamoring insensitive reporters hurled at him.

The other man, Vince, the cowboy, also wolfed down his food and ignored the clamoring media people, waving them away. They watched the sheriff with arms widespread encouraging the reporters to step back and give the survivors room to take care of their immediate needs.

Berzinsky and Safullo would also want to question Vince Macke, but after a short conference with the sheriff, he rose and departed with the local law enforcement officer to go see his father, Luther Macke, at the jail.

"We need to get control of the situation," said Berzinsky. He spoke into his radio phone. "Sam, we need crowd control over here. Send Hawkins and Lewis. Any more from James?"

"Nothing yet," "Evans came in. "So we're going to stay with him, protect him from the sharks. Let us know immediately if James makes contact with Evans' son and the suspect."   "Ten-four."

Chapter 39

At the jail, Vince also found Joyce sitting on a wooden chair outside the cell watching her husband, who was staring at the wall.

Vince went to his mother and placed an arm around her shoulders. She stood up from her chair and he embraced her, holding her close against him. She cried over the loss of Willie and over Luther's deranged behavior. And she cried, because for the first time in thirty years, Vince held and comforted her in a gesture of love she had never known from him and never expected to have.

Guzman and Matt had not heard the choppers for quite some time. They stood at the edge of a stand of trees and gazed across a two mile expanse of snow-covered pasture toward the house, barns, and corrals of the Macke ranch. "Okay," said Guzman, "let's go. If we encounter anyone at the house, you are to say nothing. I will do the talking." Matt nodded slightly that he understood. They left the shelter of the trees and set out into the pasture where Hereford cattle stood about as though immobilized by the storm and watched the two men pass.

As Guzman and Matt drew closer to the outbuildings, Guzman noticed a single vehicle, a stakebed truck parked near the barn. The cab and windows were encrusted with snow. A tarp sagged in the rear under the weight of windblown snow that had drifted high over the side of the main barn. A wisp of gray smoke spiraled from the chimney at the house, which indicated to Guzman that someone would be inside.

When they reached the house, they stopped at the back porch and Guzman tried the door. It was unlocked. He entered with Matt following close behind to escape the cold and to seek the warmth and domestic smells of the kitchen. Guzman paused to detect any noise or indication of the whereabouts of an occupant. He drew his knife and, keeping it hidden at the side of his leg, moved on to the hall. Matt remained standing at the kitchen table.

After a quick search of the house, Guzman determined that no one was there. Joyce had departed an hour before to go into town after the sheriff called to tell her that Luther was in jail.

"There's nobody here," said Guzman, returning to the kitchen. "We'll get some food then go out and take the truck. We should be able to just drive through that town without being noticed. Once we're out of these mountains, I'll be making other plans for you and your father."

Guzman found a stack of folded grocery bags in a pantry closet, then rummaged about in the refrigerator and the cupboards for nonperishable items that they could eat and drink while they drove. He noticed keys hanging on a peg board near the back door and grabbed them on the way out. Matt had not moved.

"We're leaving now," said Guzman.

"I have to go to the bathroom. Can I go to the bathroom."

Guzman hesitated, considering whether this might be another ruse. "All right, we'll both go." He escorted Matt down the hall to where the bathroom door was open. "You first." Guzman watched Matt position himself in front of the toilet and urinate, an activity that required a full three minutes. Guzman grew impatient. He knew that by being in the house, they were in a precarious situation and could be discovered at any time. He was anxious to get on the road.

The massive expanse of glacial snow covered peaks dwarfed the two Bell Ranger helicopters that alternately rose and dropped scouring the slopes in search of movement. The glistening white fields of snow reflected laser bursts of sunlight as the searchers made their sweep through one pass and down into the next valley.

After he finished relieving himself, while Matt stood by, they stepped out the back door of the house and started walking toward the truck about fifty yards across the ranch yard when they heard the returning helicopters.

"Run," shouted Guzman. "Run! Move! Get in the truck! Now!"

Matt staggered and stumbled slightly ahead of Guzman. He could hear the steadily increasing whacking thumping noise of the choppers, as they swept along down the valley directly toward the ranch.

The pilot of the lead helicopter was the first to see the two human figures. He radioed back to the FBI agent, Delbert James, and the pilot in the following chopper that he had spotted two men. James radioed to Sam Mulkhern, who was on the ground at the command post in Buck. Sam, in turn, passed the message along to Berzinsky and Safullo at Brogan's. Within a few seconds, the pilots of both helicopters and Delbert James could see the figures of two men running from the ranch house toward the barn. "Over there," said James. "We'll hover. Dan, you set down there in the yard. Wonder who they are and why they're makin' a run for it."

As they were climbing into the truck, Guzman and Matt watched the lead helicopter make a vertical descent to within twenty-five yards of where they sat in the truck cab covered with snow.

"Can't get far when they can't see through the windows. Somethin' strange goin' on here," James commented into the radio. "Be careful there, Dan. Don't know what we've got here yet."

The cockpit door opened and Dan, the pilot, waved and cut the engine, then stepped out of the cockpit to the ground and walked over to the truck.

Guzman returned the wave, then spoke to Matt. "When we get back, you will continue to listen to me and do as I say. You know nothing about your father. I saved you from dying. I'm your friend and you want to go with me."

"Either of you Matt Evans?" the pilot asked, still in radio contact with James, who was listening overhead with an open channel to the command post.

"Matt Evans is right here with me," said Guzman.

"And your name, sir?"

"Arnold Turman."

"Mr. Turman, would you and Mr. Evans please step out of the truck and come with me. Mr. Evans is now under the jurisdiction of the Federal Bureau of Investigation." The pilot showed his badge.

As they left the truck cab, Matt stared into Guzman's eyes. He felt a slight lifting of the shadow in his mind as though a pressure were being slowly and steadily released from his brain. He sensed that his original fluency of speech had returned, but that Guzman controlled the words he could say. Floundering in Guzman's tracks through the snow, he followed him and the accompanying pilot to the waiting helicopter.

The second helicopter continued to hover one hundred feet above and to the left of the craft on the ground picking up the suspect, who identified himself as Arnold Turman, and Matt Evans. James radioed ahead to notify Berzinsky and Safullo to assist in making the arrest when they landed.

The sheriff had been standing near Berzinsky when he received the call from Sam Mulkhern at the command post. He heard Berzinsky tell Safullo, "They found them. They're bringing them in." To Agents Hawkins and Lewis, he snapped an order, "Get these people back. As soon as the choppers hit the ground, we're making an arrest."

The sheriff wasted no time in telling the media people what was going to happen. Attention was shifted from Paul Evans inside the tavern to setting up cameras and other equipment outside on the main street where the helicopters were expected to land.

Back in Brogan's, with the exodus of the media crews outside to the street, Paul Evans thought he had finally been left alone. For a few moments. he rested his head in his hands. Then he heard the light footsteps of someone approaching him. The person stopped next to him. Paul's eyes traveled upwards from her tennis shoes, which struck him as an anachronism at that time in that place, over her blue insulated nylon jacket, to her face.

"Jenny." he whispered. "Jenny." He reached out to touch her, but she pulled away with a vindictive look.

"I'm here for Matt," she said. "Not for you."

The distant staccato throbbing of approaching helicopters reached them. Paul stared into his daughter's luminous blue eyes. "You know." he said softly. "Don't you? You know."

She nodded. He again reached for her and she stepped away. He followed her outside as the sound of the helicopters grew louder until they were hovering directly overhead.

The helicopter that carried Matt Evans and Antonio Guzman was the first to descend.

Looking down. Guzman saw the cameras and media people and the sheriff. He had not anticipated a reception like this. The crowd worried him. Then, at the outer edge of the gathering, he saw Paul Evans standing near a young woman, who in some way resembled Matt. Her features and blonde coloring were similar.

In an instant. Guzman realized he could not let the helicopter land. Evans would identify him as the suspected killer of the boy, Willie. With automatic weapons clearly visible, five FBI agents were moving toward the helicopter as it dropped lower and lower.

Guzman drew his hunting knife and pressed it against the pilot's throat. The pilot recoiled, sending a shudder through the controls and set the helicopter to swaying. "Pull up," Guzman ordered him. "Pull up."

The pilot started to speak into his helmet mic, but immediately stopped as the pressure of the blade increased and drew a fine line of blood.

"Don't try to tell them what you're doing. Cut radio contact - now."

The pilot did as he was told.

The crowd was surprised and perplexed as the helicopter slowly rose again and pulled away. In the second helicopter, Delbert James and the pilot tried desperately to get a response from the first pilot. They could only follow until the voice of the first pilot crackled through warning them that he was being hi-jacked and they were not to follow. The radio went dead and the second helicopter immediately dropped behind.

As the first helicopter pulled away, the pilot said to Guzman, "I'm not going to try anything. You can take the knife away. Just tell me where you want to go."

Matt was watching and listening now. He didn't understand why Guzman had threatened the pilot, or why they had not landed back at the town.

"Where are we going?" he asked.

Guzman turned to him in surprise. He recognized that Matt was cogent and clear in his thinking and perceptions. The drug had worn off. Now Matt presented an additional danger to Guzman.

Matt could see the concern in Guzman's eyes. He realized he must not arouse Guzman's suspicions. He must play out the situation with duplicity.

"Are we going home?" he asked.

Guzman studied him closely. Maybe he had been mistaken. Maybe the young man was still under his power.

"Yes, we're going home."

"For a while. I was feeling so strange," said Matt. "Thank you for saving my life."

Guzman did not respond. He looked out ahead in the direction the pilot was flying them. "I want you to crash the plane," he told the pilot.

"What? You must be crazy."

"Land where I tell you and we'll make it look like a crash."

"What good will that do you? We're being tracked by radar. They'll find you wherever we go down."

"Just do as I tell you." Guzman studied the rugged terrain and settled on a deep rocky canyon with sufficient clearance at the bottom for the helicopter to land.

"There's no place to go."

"The canyon. Down in the canyon."

The pilot carefully maneuvered the helicopter in a steep descent between two slopes. The skids came to rest on the uneven boulder-strewn ground in such a way that the airframe leaned over to one side. The pilot quickly killed the engine so the rotor blades wouldn't shear off against the rocks. In that instant, Guzman slashed the man's throat. Blood splattered the cockpit window. Guzman pressed the knife against Matt's ribs. "Get out."

Horrified, Matt opened the door and stepped down out of the cockpit. Guzman followed quickly. "Turn around."

Again, trembling, Matt obeyed.

"Pick up a rock - something you can handle."

Matt stooped and lifted a rock about the size of a man's head.

"Now, over here," said Guzman. "Smash the fuel line." He pointed so that Matt could not miss its location. "Go ahead. Smash it."

Matt raised the rock and brought it down with enough force to damage the fuel line and a section of the tail frame. Fuel gushed out over the rocks and soaked into the snow-covered ground.

Matt suddenly turned and hurled the rock at Guzman, hitting him a square blow on the shoulder, causing him to drop the knife. Matt scrambled away. As Guzman picked up the knife and chased after him, his foot glanced off a rock slick with fuel and he fell heavily. He tried to stand. but he could not put any weight on his right ankle.

"Matt, come back. Help me. You must help me," he shouted.

Matt stopped a short distance away and watched him. He could see that Guzman's clothes were soaked with fuel, darkened down one side.

Reaching into his pocket, he pulled out a small khaki green, plastic cylinder - a waterproof match box. Slowly, he walked back toward Guzman, whose head bobbed in two desperate nods of encouragement. A painful smile spread across his face, then froze in a mask of fear. His eyes transfixed on Matt's hands, which had opened the container and removed a wooden kitchen match.

"No!" Guzman tried to hobble toward him. He reached out his hand. "No! Don't do this. No! I beg you!"

Matt stooped and scratched the match against a rock. The sulfurous head burst into flame.

"No!" Guzman screamed. "No!"

Matt dropped the burning match into a rivulet of fuel. then turned and ran as he envisioned Guzman exploding into a human torch screaming and clawing at the air in a macabre dance of death. But Matt's persistence of vision and wishful image were not accurate. At the first sight of the match, Guzman had grabbed his pack and leaped and scrambled away. Matt was running in the opposite direction as the match fell and ignited the line of fuel. Guzman buried himself in a deep snow drift behind a boulder a moment before the explosion rocked the valley.

Instantaneously, the stream of leaking fuel leaped skyward as a ragged wall of fire. The enclosing walls of the canyon magnified the explosion and the echoes reverberated long after the final blast shattered and melted down the cockpit.

Delbert James was on the radio phone to Great Falls calling for an interception when the escaping helicopter appeared to plunge into a slope further down the mountain.

"There's something wrong. They're going to crash," the pilot with James shouted.

Several minutes later, the muffled throb of the explosion and echoes reached the town and dark smoke plumed into the air.

Paul turned at the wail of lament rising to a scream that came from Jenny, who flailed her arms and head from side to side. He started to go to her, but she would not let him come near.

Leon and Berzinsky scrambled into their car. Spinning tires gained momentary traction on a spot of exposed asphalt, as the two agents headed out of town in the direction of the crash.

Pandemonium broke out among the media crews, who grabbed up cables and equipment and rushed to their four wheel drive mobile units. With the exception of a pickup truck driven by a teenage boy accompanied by a friend, the local townspeople continued to stand about Brogan's parking lot and speculated on what had happened. A few went inside the tavern for coffee or whiskey to warm them.

Suddenly dizzy and weak, Paul turned away from Jenny and followed members of the crowd into the tavern. He sat in the first chair he encountered. Whatever energy remained in him drained from his body. Staring out the window at his daughter moaning and thrashing about, he saw again what he had seen his wife do many years ago in emotional distress caused by his actions. Now his daughter was holding him to blame for the loss of her brother. He wished he had died back up in the mountains rather than this. Jenny seemed to be frozen in time. Paul began to quietly and uncontrollably cry, as a swelling knot of sadness rose from his heart and lodged behind his eyes.

The sheriff preceded the paramedics and media crews closing in behind him in the slalom ride down the snow-slick road. He didn't understand what was happening to his town. People he had known all his life were going strange on him, and the bizarre murder of Lila Stevenson overshadowed it all. He was not a superstitious man, but he sensed that an evil force or influence from the corrupt world beyond the remote idyllic seclusion of his town had swept through and decimated their complacent existence.

Matt raised his head to look from behind a protecting boulder. There was no evidence of Guzman or the pilot. He watched the flames consume the helicopter until it looked like the threadbare skeletal shell of a giant insect. As the oily black smoke bellowed into the sky from the charred metal he moved away from his shelter, then trudged and clawed through the boulders up the long slope of the canyon.

Slipping and sliding, he floundered at an angle across the snow-covered embankment. Upon reaching the road, he was shaking with fatigue. His wound had re-opened from his exertions and had begun to bleed, increasing his exhaustion. The harsh wind and chill air forced him to the ground. He lay trembling at the side of the road.

As though in a dream, he heard the crunching tires approach him, but he did not have the strength to turn his head, and the concerned voices of men hurrying to attend to him. He saw cameras and microphones thrust at him. He could not respond to their questions.

Matt felt himself being wrapped in blankets and placed on a stretcher, then lifted into the ambulance, heard doors slamming shut, saw the blurred figure of a paramedic bending over him checking his vital signs and fitting an oxygen mask over his mouth and nose. He began to breathe more easily. A needle pricked the back of his hand. Overcome by drowsiness, he slept.

With the sheriff stumbling through the drifts not far behind, Berzinsky and Leon climbed down the slope and followed Matt's back trail through the deep snow to the site of the wreckage. Only one set of footprints led away from the blackened mass. Nothing gave evidence that Guzman and the pilot had even existed.

The intensity of the heat and the choking smoke kept the three men at a distance. They would have to investigate later after the metal had cooled allowing them to sift through the remains.

As they returned to the road, they heard the voices of the media crews above whipped away by the wind. Ignoring John Morley's insistent questions, they stamped their feet to clear the snow from their boots and climbed back into their cars.

The sheriff offered, "Ain't nothin' left of 'em." He stepped into his car and slammed the door.

John Morley conferred with his assistants as to whether they should pursue the paramedics or stay with the agents, whose car was receding up the road between a partially exposed granite wall on one side and snow-coated spruce and pines on the other. They opted for the latter choice, repacked their equipment in the mobile unit, and followed the sheriff's vehicle.

Leon and Berzinsky found Paul in the tavern on the verge of collapse. "He needs medical attention," said Berzinsky. "We'll take him down to Great Falls. Listen. Your son walked away from that crash, if it was one. The paramedics have him. He's enroute to the hospital in Great Falls where we're about to take you."

"He's alive?"

"Yes, in a state of severe shock, but alive."

Leon spoke to Vince aside, but Vince declined his offer, said he was okay and had things to tend to at home.

Leon and Berzinsky walked Paul out to their car. As they passed Jenny's rented four wheel drive Isuzu Rodeo, Paul had to look away from the hate and depression she projected from her eyes. "Wait," he said, "Wait. Please tell my daughter about Matt, that he's alive and where he's being taken so she can go see him."

Berzinsky nodded and stepped over to the driver's side. He motioned for Jenny to lower the window, then explained what had recently transpired. "You can follow us down, if you'd like."

Jenny nodded and started the engine.

The sheriff conferred with Vince about Luther's incarceration. Then they drove over to the jail to get Joyce and Luther, who mumbled incoherently as they assisted him from the cell to the car.

An hour later, they arrived at the ranch and made slow progress between the drifts from the distant road. When they reached the house, the sheriff and Vince supported Luther inside. They placed him in his chair before the fire. Vince pulled a second chair over and sat next to him.

The sheriff followed Joyce into the kitchen to briefly explain what he would have to do next, while she poured coffee. Then, not wanting to intrude on their privacy, he left them to their sorrow and reconciliation and drove back to town.

Chapter 40

Paul woke disoriented in a hospital bed. For a moment, he wondered if he had been dreaming the events of the past week, but the reality returned to him in a rush.

He knew that Matt was alive and that Guzman had been incinerated, according to the FBI agents. They could only conjecture how that had happened and how Matt had survived until they talked with him. Paul had slept most of the way during the long drive down out of the mountains; but upon their arrival, he had insisted on seeing his son.

Separately, Jenny had also gone into Matt's room where he slept under heavy sedation. His wound had been examined and treated. An IV pack provided him nutrition and a periodic flow of antibiotics.

A nurse came into Paul's room to check on him. Seeing that he was awake, she crossed to his bedside. "Good morning, Mr. Evans, how did you sleep?"

"Okay, I guess. I feel much better than when I came in."

She timed his pulse against the second hand of her watch. "Looks like you'll survive."

Paul grinned. "You don't know how much of an understatement that is."

She smiled in return. "Feel like some breakfast?"

"Sure, I'm hungry."

"That's a good sign."

"I'd like to know how my son's doing, Matt Evans. He's in room 32."

"While I arrange for your breakfast, I'll check on him. But he was stable during the night."

"Thank you. I appreciate it."

"The two of you have become celebrities. The media has been trying to get in here since early this morning. But the doctor says no interviews just yet. Your FBI friends are waiting to talk with you too."

Paul nodded, then timidly asked, "Is my daughter out there somewhere?"

"She's visiting with your son."

"Is he awake?"

"Barely, still pretty groggy from the medication."

"Well, just, I guess, just don't disturb them. They're very close. Always were, growing up. She came here for him."

The nurse smiled and nodded. "Be back in ten minutes."

"Thank you."

Down the hall in room 32, Jenny sat next to her brother and held his hand. He opened his eyes for an instant and saw her blurred features. "Jen, that you, or am I dreaming?" His mouth felt like it was filled with cotton and his tongue swollen.

"I'm here. I'm for real."

"I dreamed about you when I was up there," he mumbled. "You were standing on the riverbank where Grandpa used to take us to see *the light*. You kept me alive, even though you were a dream. I stayed focused on *the light* and I didn't die. He couldn't control my mind -- the man who took me. No matter what he did to me."

Jenny watched her beloved brother through her tears. "It's okay, Matt. It's okay. You don't have to talk now. You can tell me later."

He nodded slowly. "Later. Later." His eyes closed and he drifted off into sleep. He dreamed of himself and his sister paddling quietly along in their grandfather's green canoe in a place where light played and reflected in the water.

Paul resigned himself to the fact he would never regain the lost relationship with his daughter, and he accepted that. He didn't know where or how to begin to cope with his conflicting emotions of elation and remorse, but he was clear in his mind that he was neither insane nor possessed. He knew that apologies were meaningless, yet they were all he had to offer at the moment. He also knew he would be making some changes in his life, but he didn't know what they would be.

He had irreparably damaged his family. Doctors had told him that the likelihood of his wife, Moya's recovery was beyond the realm of possibility. However, he would try to visit her, if the doctors didn't think her seeing him would drive her deeper into her depression and escape from the world. Both Matt and Jenny had gone to see her from time to time and she had barely responded to them. They had not been certain she even recognized them. Jenny believed the medication might have been a factor.

Paul understood that nothing he could do or say would ever reconcile him with Jim Owens. Paul had left a trail of ruin that he could never restore. The realization saddened him deeply. He would in some other way move on in his life, perhaps not so radically changed, but at least rendering a semblance of kindness to those he encountered.

*   *   *

Even though he'd lived in the mountains all his life and was accustomed to the hardships and danger of hazardous road conditions, Wes Herndon still felt the locking tension in his neck, arms, and shoulders as he gripped the wheel of his Ford pickup and steered down into the inky black canyons of the mountain night.

A contractor for forty years, Wes had worked on a number of civil engineering projects in the area, including improvements along the winding highway, so he was familiar with its twists and turns. But headlights casting ahead into a heavy blanket of snow altered familiar shapes and created the impression of hurtling into an endless void.

For an instant, he couldn't be certain what the dark shape was lying sprawled across the icy tract of road. Slowing, he thought it might be a deer that had been hit by another vehicle. Upon closer inspection, he saw that it was a man, and stopped abruptly. The high beams fully illuminated the still figure.

Setting the brake, Wes stepped down out of the truck and cautiously approached the man, who was dressed in mountaineering gear. He bent down for a closer look, bringing his face close to that of the fallen man to see if he could detect any life signs.

The hunting knife materialized out of the periphery of the night and sliced deeply into the side of his neck. He fell back with a gasp. Gouts of blood raced from his carotid artery, soaking into his clothes, and, as he collapsed, flowed from him in reddish black pools onto the road.

Guzman immediately rolled away to avoid getting the blood on him, sprang to his feet and stepped around the dying man. He walked a few yards off the road to retrieve his pack. which he placed in the truck bed. He then returned to the body and dragged it to the edge of a steep slope on the downside of the road where he shoved it deep into thick snow-encrusted brush well-hidden from sight.

Three hours later, two blocks from the Great Falls Municipal Hospital, Guzman placed a call from a pay phone at a 7-Eleven convenience store to inquire if he might speak with either Paul or Matt Evans. He was informed that calls could not be put through after ten o'clock, but that he could try again in the morning at eight. The operator confirmed that Paul and Matt Evans had been admitted that day. Guzman hung up the receiver and stared down the dimly illuminated street toward the hospital a few blocks away. Somewhere among the upper stories where lights shone in a random pattern from numerous windows, he would once again find his prey; and this time, they both would die.

Leaving the 7-Eleven, he drove the stolen truck to the hospital and left it in a dark distant corner of the parking lot. He was quite familiar with hospital operations from his past forays into their labs for various blood, bacterial, and viral specimens. So once he gained access and scanned a posted floor plan or a directory, he would begin his maneuver to locate and close-in on his victims.

As he approached the front entrance, he saw a young woman coming across the lobby from the elevators toward the glass doors. Her features bore a strong resemblance to the face of Matt Evans. Guzman immediately assumed she must be Matt's sister. It was too late for him to turn away, since they approached the doors from opposite sides at the same instant; but there was no way for her to know him or recognize him. However, her momentary hesitation and the catching of each other's glance as they passed through the doors moving in their separate directions raised a flicker of concern. He continued to the elevators, pressed the down button, and waited. He noticed that two security cameras scanned the lobby and that he had probably been seen by a night guard in the surveillance center when he entered the building from the parking lot.

Continuing out into the parking lot, Jenny Holmes engaged the source of her sudden tingle of fear, an instinctive response to the recognizable expression she had detected in that brief passing glance. She was certain she had seen the man before, but could not immediately recall where or under what circumstances. Perhaps among the crowd at the small town up in the mountains. He was dressed for local outdoor weather, hiking boots, black down jacket and a black knit ski cap. That he walked with a slight limp did not seem significant to her. Climbing into her rented car, she probed her subconscious for an image that would link that expression to an identity. Nothing materialized, but the emotion lingered like an ominous malaise.

Guzman noticed from the hospital directory that the cafeteria was located in the basement. He knew that typically other support facilities such as laundry, maintenance and medical supplies were inventoried in these subterranean rooms. As he stepped out of the elevator and walked along the hall, he passed a directional sign indicating the way to the morgue. No surveillance cameras were mounted in the halls.

Clad in green scrubs, a few female medical personnel passed him enroute to their appointed tasks on other floors. He paused to glance into the cafeteria, which was deserted except for a young Asian male intern intently reading a medical book and sipping hot tea. He did not notice Guzman, who checked for any others in the now empty hallway, then moved quickly to the room labeled *Laundry*.

Peering through the window, he determined that nobody was inside. He pushed through the double doors and hesitated, listening to the surge of five commercial washing machines and the thunk of three industrial dryers at the far side of the large area half occupied by canvas laundry baskets, two gleaming metal folding tables, and a large iron press, as well as two hand irons and ironing boards along a side wall. The activity of the machines indicated to Guzman that an attendant would likely return soon, giving him little time. He grabbed an extra large smock to fit over his jacket, pants, booties, cap, and a surgeon's mask from among the neatly folded piles on one of the long tables.

Returning to the door, he peered out through the window and saw the laundry room attendant, a young Hispanic woman approaching garbed in green and humming a song. She pushed a canvas laundry cart filled with soiled items ahead of her through the double doors. The momentum of the cart flung the doors back sufficiently to conceal Guzman flattened against the wall, as the attendant continued down the central aisle toward the machines.

Given the monotony of noise in the room and her preoccupation with pushing the cart and with her attention on auto-pilot, the attendant did not notice the man's figure follow the swing of the door back into its closed position, as he slipped out into the hall.

Guzman rushed to the nearest restroom, found it unoccupied, and locked himself in one of four commodes where he quickly donned the medical clothing, including the surgeons mask which covered the lower half of his face. His identity fully concealed, he left the restroom and went further down the hall to a door labeled *Supply Room*. It was unlocked. He entered and looked about for an attendant. None was in sight.

He stepped around the end of the distribution counter and searched frantically along storage aisles and cupboards filled with medical paraphernalia until he came to a container of IV Packs. He selected two, whose contents were labeled glucose, a package of regulator flow tubes and two packs of sterilized insertion needles, which he dropped into the right pocket of his smock. He also selected a sterile hypodermic syringe and needle package which joined the other pocketed items. From among the several hundred in-vitro and pharmaceutical products, he removed three vials of methadone, which injected intravenously in overdose would cause lethal respiratory depression, cardiac arrest, and death.

Snatching a stethoscope, he slung it around his neck. All he lacked to complete his disguise was a plastic name tag. He found a half dozen clustered on the supply clerk's desk. He pinned one to his smock with the last name of Blumenthal, R.N., then exited the supply room.

Returning to the elevator, he read the designated floor directory indicating the various wings and corresponding wards. By the process of elimination, he determined Paul and Matt would be on one of two floors in the East Wing. He pressed the button for level five and ascended.

At the fifth floor, he held the elevator door in the open position and cautiously looked out to determine where the nurse's station was located. To his satisfaction, thirty yards down the hall, he could see the night duty nurse seated with her back facing him. He moved along quickly and silently from room to room, peering in at the lumpish sleeping patients bathed in dim bluish illumination. He continually checked the nurse to see if she changed her position, but she did not move and was not aware of his being there in the hall, until the moment a plastic catheter seized and wrapped around her throat like an invisible snake. She choked and thrashed and her eyes bulged as Guzman steadily increased the strangulation until the nurse ceased to move. He positioned her head on her arms resting on the desk top so that she appeared to be sleeping. Then he looked at her patient location chart.

Jenny had removed her motel room key from her purse and was about to insert it into the door lock when the image, an accumulation of fragments and impressions, materialized in her mind. The face of the man she had seen entering the hospital resembled the composite drawing shown on the news broadcast when she was back in California.

"Oh my God." She spun about at her low utterance, stepped to her car parked only a few feet in front of her motel room, and fumbled with the key, which she dropped while attempting to unlock the driver's side door. Grasping for it on the cold asphalt, she accidentally kicked it under the vehicle and had to drop to her hands and knees to locate it. Swearing under her breath, she leaped up and opened the door, jammed her body behind the wheel, and started the engine before closing the door. Her heart raced and thumped erratically and tension surged like an electric jolt to her solar plexus causing a cramp that nearly rendered her unable to move. Moments later, she reached out and grabbed the handle, slamming the door. Turning on the headlights, she threw the gear into reverse, rocketing the car halfway across the parking lot, then re-shifted and roared out over the curb with a crunching jolt and sped down the street back in the direction of the hospital.

No longer needing the pretense of the IV packs, Guzman left them on the floor at the nurse's station and went directly to the room where Matt Evans peacefully slept. He removed the syringe and hypodermic from the pocket of his smock and affixed the needle. He then brought out the vials of methadone and carefully filled the syringe with a lethal dosage. While drawing fluid from the third vial, he heard footsteps running along the hall in the direction of the room and heard a woman's voice shouting, "Matt, Matt, wake up! He's here! Wake up! Maaaatttt!"

Jenny exploded into the room, saw Guzman bent over her brother, preparing to make the injection, rushed at him with a savage cry, colliding into him causing him to drop the brimming syringe on the floor. She leaped on his staggering frame, wrapped her legs around his middle, grasped him around the neck with her left arm and beat at his head with her other fist. Guzman reached back and up, grabbed her by the hair and jerked downward with such force that she released him and plummeted to the floor. Guzman whirled and kicked her in the face and ribs, sending her in a rolling sprawl across the floor. She screamed, "Matt, Matt!"

Matt opened his eyes and tried to focus in the strange light. He sat up abruptly, but fell back dizzy and light-headed from the medication.

Several rooms down the hall, Paul was pulled from his dreams by the sound of his daughter's voice screaming, calling for him over and over again, "Dad! Dad! Dad!" For a moment, he thought her voice was part of his dream. He suddenly snapped awake and rolled to a sitting position, now fully hearing the screams coming from down the hall.

Jenny covered her head with her arms and rolled away from the brutal kicks. Blood spurted from her nose and sprayed with the spittle of her screams. She felt something hard and cylindrical on the floor press against her broken rib, the syringe and needle. She clutched it like a dagger and her hand lunged upward thrusting the weapon deep into Guzman's inner thigh where it intersected his groin.

With a grunt of pain and surprise, he staggered back and clawed at the penetrating needle, breaking it off at the attachment point, leaving the needle embedded in his flesh. It had pierced a branch of the inferior vena cava, a vein that carried the methadone in the bloodstream directly to his heart. Guzman began to feel the effect of the drug instantly.

Jenny saw him reach through the opening of his smock and draw out the knife. He staggered and weaved across the room toward the bed. With great effort and pain from her broken rib, she rose up from the floor, and charged him again. She reached out with both hands to clutch away his arm, as it began its descent. The blade missed her brother's body by inches and plunged into the mattress. Guzman's other fist swung at her, lightly striking the side of her head. She dropped to her knees but refused to let go of his weakening arm, exerting a downward pressure so that he had difficulty pulling the knife free, as his strength drained from him under the influence of the lethal drug.

Jenny's head lifted. Her mouth opened. Blood-lined teeth like a savage animal crunched the bones of his wrist. With a sharp cry, he jerked away, leaving the knife in the mattress. Jenny grabbed the handle and pulled out the knife. On her knees, she went after Guzman, slashing at his legs, ripping through cloth and flesh, drawing blood. She reached up for a higher target and buried the blade deep in his abdomen slicing into his spleen.

With his respiratory system shutting down from the methadone and the room beginning to spin, Guzman stumbled past Jenny, who crouched gasping on the floor, and staggered out into the hall toward the elevator.

Paul collided with Guzman and clutched him with clawed hands, then whirled him around to dash his face, pound his skull into the floor. Guzman was still stronger and more ferocious than Paul, soporific from a pain killer. Two quick blows sent Paul careening against the far wall opposite the elevator. With blood pouring from his mouth, Paul watched the elevator door close Guzman from his sight.

Bracing himself against the wall, Paul struggled to his feet and ran to the exit stairs. Throwing open the door, he leaped and careened down the five circuitous flights not knowing where he would come out, but fearing that Guzman would reach the ground floor ahead of him.

Paul burst through the stairwell door several yards to the right of the elevators near the hospital entrance. The lobby was deserted. Paul raced across and thrust open both the glass entrance doors with a single sweep that seemed slowed and immobilized in time. He ran out into the parking lot, but to himself, seemed not to be moving at all, lifting his pajamaed legs high treading the air.

He saw Guzman in a far dark corner of the parking lot climbing into a pickup truck. But Guzman was also moving slowly. Paul saw the door close, heard the engine start, saw the truck pull away, weaving sluggishly across the mostly empty lot and out into the street, gone.

Paul stood gasping, bare-foot, shirtless in the cold night, watching the receding red tail-lights of the truck.

The sensation of dying corresponded to a sharp pain and slowing of Guzman's heart. In his final moments, the prayer he had raised to the Lord as a child passed through his mind.

The truck's stilled headlights cut into the blackness of the city night reflected back from a storefront window. The street lamps overhead cast disconcerting shadows that created the sensation for Antonio Guzman, that he was floating in dark water that consumed him until he became an amorphous shape undulating through time and space with other like forms.

Leon and Ed Berzinsky waited outside Paul Evans's hospital room until the attending nurse had finished checking his vitals. She told Paul that he had visitors. Curious as to who would come to see him, the appearance of the two FBI agents startled him. He wondered if they were there to arrest him for some past crime. His anxiety fled after they introduced themselves and explained their purpose.

"We've been trying to find you for over a week," said Leon.

"We talked with your daughter," said Berzinsky. "She's a brave young woman. She saved your son's life."

"Your son isn't quite able yet to understand what happened to him," said Leon. "He said a dark spirit had taken him, but he had fought against it and was back. He wasn't aware that his sister saved him from being killed. He's suffering from severe trauma and PTSD. From what we've learned about him, he's a strong young man. I'm confident he'll recover. Obviously, under medication, he's experiencing confusion about his abduction. Once we identified the killer, we were only able to track him by following both of you. In fact, he pointed us to you. We're aware of his Internet communications and understand how they terrified and affected you. What we would like to determine is how real the dark spirit he claimed to be is to you."

"What do you mean by claimed to be?"

"He died when the truck he was driving to get away crashed and exploded," said Berzinsky. "He was immolated. Nothing remained of him."

"He was real. His existence will haunt me for the rest of my life."

"We understand. You've also undergone significant trauma," said Leon.

"It isn't just trauma," said Paul. "He came after my son and me. He was real."

"We appreciate you sharing your thoughts," said Leon. "Your reunion with your son and daughter is a happy one." Leon and Ed rose from their bedside chairs and each shook Paul's hand. "Thank you, Mr. Evans. We wish you and your family the very best."

"He was real."

Leon and Ed departed. They did not speak until they were in the hospital lobby.

"What do you think?" asked Leon.

"I believe him."

"I believe that in his mind the spirit was real."

"That's all we can ask for," said Berzinsky.

Epilogue

When Leon arrived home, Julie greeted him at the door with a warm hug and kiss. "Hello, lover, welcome home."

"Mmmh, I should go away and come home more often."

"Have I got a surprise for you -- actually two surprises." She helped him move his luggage from the foyer into the house.

"Well, I always like a pleasant surprise. I hope it is pleasant after what I've seen and

"That's the first one. I've been following your story on the news."

"It's not my story, thank God. What incredible misery those people have gone through. But now they've returned to their original lives, hopefully for the better. I talked at some length with Evans and his children. They seemed to have come to some point of reconciliation as a result of their experience, but they were reluctant to talk about the past. I can't blame them. I would want to get on with life too."

"Well, I saved all the newspapers and most of the newscasts for you."

"Why in the world did you do that?"

"It's a milestone in your career."

"Julie, you don't understand. In this kind of sordid work, I don't want any memorabilia hanging around. That's baggage I want to lose at the station. I want to return to a healthy normal life." The lingering knowledge that the highest level of the U.S. Government was involved with the First World Corporation belied that there was a paranormal force fueling world chaos. He wanted to believe that political and economic catastrophes were perpetrated by men, not dark spirits, but what he had seen and experienced raised a nodule of doubt and uncertainty in his mind. Whether imagined or real, he could not deny the existence of the spirit world and its influence on the shadow of human personality.

"Mmh, well," said Julie, "I'll just tuck them away somewhere in a box."

"The trash is where they belong."

"Oh, Leo, Leo, Leo, there is value in reading and keeping the news. It's history in the making."

Leon shook his head. "What's the other surprise? I can hardly wait," his nose wrinkled with a dour expression.

"This one you're going to like. I guarantee." She picked up an envelope from the kitchen counter and waved it aloft. "These, my dear, are tickets to the land, or I should say lands, islands to be specific, of romance and enchantment."

"Tickets?"

"You need a vacation. We're leaving tomorrow to go on a two week Mediterranean cruise. Life is short. You need to taste some of its pleasures. Here, look at this brochure. Feast your eyes on that feast." She thrust a four color brochure at him bursting with sumptuous photographs of food, shipboard entertainment, idyllic island scenes and azure seas. "We'll also be touring Italy. I want to see the art in Florence at the Uffizi, especially The Birth of Venus. We can visit your brother. Eat great food, drink lots of wine. Whets your appetite. Doesn't it?"

"My cholesterol level went up just looking at it."

"You don't worry about such things on a trip like that. Besides, you're going to be dancing so much, you'll burn off all the fat and calories."

"Can I unpack first?"

"No, you are just going to replenish your socks and underwear and throw in a swimsuit and your summer togs. I already have your tux ready."

"You should have been a psychologist. You're able to get people to do things even if they're not sure they want to do them."

"I am a psychologist, Leon. I'm married to you."

Leon noticed Sigmund eyeing the bulge in his left pocket. Leon pulled out the stress ball and tossed it to the dog, who caught it expertly in midair. He thoroughly mushed it around in his mouth, then dropped it in a pool of slobbery drool on the floor.

"Why aren't you running off and hiding it?" asked Leon.

His wife chuckled. "It's because you willingly gave it to him, you goofus. He hides only the ones he steals from you. He's really a smart pooch, Leon."

"Oh."

*   *   *

Hiram Bean intently watched John Morley's newscast   Paul Evans was stating on-camera that he planned to sell his interests in the Helix Corporation and resign as CEO. Hiram immediately got on the phone to the First World Corporation chairman of the board and told him the time had come to take over the Helix Corporation. They didn't have to concern themselves any further with Paul Evans. He would issue a warning to Evans that if he shared any information with the FBI, his family would pay the ultimate price. Hiram was sure the threat of being investigated by the Justice Department and spending the rest of his life in prison would buy Paul Evans' silence.

The information that Antonio Guzman had been annihilated in a car explosion ensured there would be no fear of his traceability to First World. Guzman was at that moment sitting next to him, having evolved into the form of another human, Simonetta Vespucci, an exquisitely beautiful blonde woman with a different name, life history, and persona, who would soon be given an assignment. Together, they watched the giant floor to ceiling plasma wall screen where the ethereal shapes of two other nude women evolved twisting and turning from the roiling void of darkness.

Hiram would enjoin himself with these women as their guiding spirit, Pearl, and continue unconstrained in his preparations for a new world order enforced by the faceless agents of darkness. His plans included the FBI profiler, Leon Safullo, whose struggle to disbelieve validated their existence.

*   *   *

Jeff Holmes had received a call from his wife two days ago. She had explained that her brother, Matt, was safe and would be released from the hospital on Friday and that she planned to fly back to California with him. She didn't mention her father other than that he had survived the ordeal. So Jeff was surprised when the phone rang Friday morning and he answered to hear the voice of Paul Evans at the other end of the line.

"Jeff, this is Paul Evans."

"Yes? Is Jenny on her way back?"

"No, there was an incident."

"What are you talking about?" Jeff reached down to rub his son's tousled head.

"Is that Mommy?" the boy asked. "Can I talk to her?"

Jeff shook his head.

"I want to talk to Mommy."

Paul cleared his throat. "Things didn't happen the way everybody thought. The killer escaped the crash. He came here to the hospital last night."

"What happened to Jenny?"

"She's right here with me. She fought off the killer and saved Matt's life."

"What? Jenny's not a fighter."

"There's another side to her none of us knew about." Paul grinned at his daughter, whose face was partially wrapped in bandages. He was standing next to her hospital bed.

"Why are you calling?"

"She has a sore jaw, but she wants to talk to you. I'm handing her the phone."

"Jeff."

"Jenny, what happened? Are you all right?"

"I'll be fine," she mumbled. "I have to stay here in the hospital a few days. I have a broken rib and a broken nose."

"Jesus Christ. Your dad said you stopped the killer. You could have been killed yourself."

"I'm okay, Jeff. We're all going to make it. How are the children?"

"They miss their mommy."

"I miss them too. Give them special hugs and kisses for me."

"I will do that. I miss you. If anything happened to you...." Jeff left his sentence unfinished.

"I'm going to go now. It hurts to talk."

"I love you, Jenny. We love you."

"I love you too."

"Give the phone back to your dad."

"Okay, bye."

"Bye." Jeff waited a moment until Paul came on the line again. "Listen, Evans, I don't know what the details are, but if anything more serious happened to Jenny, you wouldn't have to worry about the killer. I'd come after you myself. I want you to know I was against her going out there in the first place. She did it for her brother, not for you. She has never forgiven you. You need to know that."

"I understand. At least for the moment, we're somewhat on speaking terms. What happened here can't erase the past. I have to accept that."

"You're never going to see your grandchildren, Evans. Your name is never mentioned in this house. They don't even know who you are."

Paul remained silent, saddened, as he watched over his daughter, who had closed her eyes. Later, when she was awake, he told her of his conversation with her husband. "I'm surprised he really isn't much like you."

"What do you mean?"

"Forgiving, I guess."

"Oh, he'll get over it. You and your grandchildren will get to know each other very well."

"What about Mom? So many years have gone by, but I need to do something for her."

"Actually, she has a head start on you. I plan to have her moved out to California to be close to me."

"Then you've talked to her. How is she?"

"She's, shall we say improving. It's like she's waking up from a long sleep."

"You and Matt have something special about you. I'm not sure where it comes from."

"Actually, Dad, we are who we are because of you and Mom."

"I don't understand."

"You remember that year Matt and I went to stay with Grandfather on his farm, after Mom had her breakdown and you left us?"

"Well, in some way."

"Grandfather helped us cope with what was happening to you and Mom and to us."

"What did he do?"

Jenny closed her eyes again, but she wasn't resting, she was remembering.

how they went out across the expansive back lawn and entered a woods by one of many trails that criss-crossed the farm. Their grandfather's polished knotty walking stick intrigued Matthew. Before they had gone far, he selected a suitable bare dead branch for himself, and Jenny searched and discovered one appropriate to her size so she could be like them.

Bird calls fluted the silence. The crunch of twigs and leaves underfoot skittered rabbits out of their path through the underbrush. Emerging from the trees into an open field, they spooked a covey of quail whose diminishing rattle-thunder of wings left the boy and his sister trembling.

They crossed the meadow and hit a downward slant in the terrain that brought them to a concealed backwater of a placid river. A green fiber-glass canoe was tied to the branch of a tree at the water's edge. Their grandfather instructed them how to safely enter the canoe and situate themselves in the bow and at the center. With a strong thrust they shot away from the bank into the copperish current. Matthew tried his paddle. With a few pointers, he was soon pulling rhythmically through the water.

The old man and his grandchildren maneuvered along a tributary, startling sleepy mud turtles. Matt and his sister listened to the plops of frogs diving from sight.

A long blue dragonfly hovered for a shimmering moment in advance of the bow, then vanished. Spider-legged water bugs skimmed the surface barely out of the canoe's gliding path.

After a time, their grandfather removed his paddle from the water and rested it in front of him across the gunnels. Matt followed his example.

The canoe drifted at rest in the quiet water that captured and held the sunlight streaming down through the branches that arched like a natural cathedral overhead.

"This is my church," their grandfather said. "This is where I come to meditate and pray. The light you see in the water is everything you see around you and think about and feel in your life, the good and the bad."

He paused and watched them staring at the sparkling play of the light in the gentle wavelets. "I want you to always remember that you have that light within you. The light is love. It is forgiveness. It is meaning and understanding.

Regardless of what happens to you in your lifetime, no one can ever take the light from you. It can only be given willingly."

The children turned to look at him. The boy's eyes were filled with tears. He crawled back in the canoe into his grandfather's arms. His sister clambered after him. Their grandfather held them and together they looked at the light.

*   *   *

The Rocky Mountain jay hopped to a lower branch of the pine from which it had been surveying the open area near the frothing rushing stream. It preened its gray feathers for a moment, then suddenly swooped out low over the boulders to the metallic object that had attracted his eye.

Checking to be sure there were no competitors for the prize, he attempted to grab the object in his strong beak, but it was firmly attached to a thick strip of leather and would not come free despite his repeated attempts to jerk at it. With a squawk of frustration, he leaped to the nearest alternative, tufts of hair that he could use in the construction of a new nest. The hair came free with ease and he busily gathered several strands and clamped them in his beak. A thudding sound from up across the clearing reached him, followed by the creak of leather and jingle of metal. The jay leaped into the air and flashed back to the safety of its tree to watch the approaching horse and rider leading a pack mule.

The rest of the winter had been hard to endure at the Macke ranch. Despite the efforts of Joyce and Vince to rekindle Luther's interest in continuing day to day activities, he would only sit and stare into the fire, drinking himself into incoherent delirium. Vince single-handedly went about the chores and maintenance of the animals, fallen fences, and building repairs. From time to time, Joyce left her kitchen and came out to help him, revisiting the hard work of her early days, before her boys had become men.

There wasn't any more talk of Vince leaving to work in Arizona. He found within himself that he could not desert his mother and leave her with an invalid husband. He mentioned that he would hire another hand to help with the calving when winter broke. He said he would need two for the haying later in the summer. And in his mentioning these plans, Joyce knew that he would not be leaving her, and that this was a manifestation of his love.

At the first spring thaw, as he had promised Joyce and Luther, Vince rode back up into the mountains where Willie had died to retrieve whatever might remain of his brother. But he knew he could not bring home what he found.

Willie had been taken back by nature, eaten by large and small animals, and his skeleton picked clean by birds and insects. Shreds of clothing still clung to his bones and a few tufts of what had been his beautiful blonde head.

Vince dismounted from his horse and held in his grief. He knew death for what it truly was and he could only hope that Willie's laughing young *light* spirit was at peace.

About the Author

Author and retired business and management consultant within a wide range of industries throughout the country, Rob resides with his wife in Southern California.

He is a graduate of the University of California, Santa Barbara and of the University of California, Los Angeles with Bachelor's and Masters of Fine Arts Degrees. He is a recipient of the Samuel Goldwyn and Donald Davis Literary Awards and has also worked in advertising, corporate communications, and media production.

An affinity for family and generations pervades his novels.

His works are literary and genre fiction that address the nature and importance of personal integrity.

Book Club Discussion Topics

The premise for the Black Spiral Series urban fantasy is that black spiral DNA is man's genetic link to the origin of dark energy in the universe.

The Black Spiral four volume series is a continuous paranormal thriller of deception, illusion, and a fantasy of bizarre murders that defy explanation. It is also a philosophical and psychological exploration of the origin, evolution, and existence of aberrant characters, criminals, and psychopathic behaviors.

Dark energy is scientifically real. It does exist and is researched, studied, and documented by physicists.

When the atoms of a substance are disturbed, such as in a metal or in a biological form, the death of an animal or a human, all the atoms of that substance begin to vibrate and the energy radiates outward and escapes just as a vapor dissipates into the medium of air from boiling water. It becomes dark energy.

That malevolent spirits reside in these dark spaces of the universe is the premise for the series.

Vividly drawn characters desperately try to escape and are forced to combat the tyranny of the spiritual mastermind who has infused dark energy into contemporary populations like an insidious cancer that invades every level of human society.

In the first book, A SEASON OF SONS, a family decimated by the invasion struggles to regain a sense of normalcy.

The year is 2012. While investigating the heinous death of a prominent evangelist, FBI agent, Leon Safullo is unable to identify the killer through traditional methods of forensic analysis. Simultaneously, Leon learns of the sudden disappearance of Paul Evans, CEO of a major corporation.

Leon is a pragmatic realist whose career is based on interpreting symptoms of aberrant human behavior. The killer contacts Leon with the purpose of challenging the validity of his investigation. Leon perceives the threatening direct communication as a masquerade using digital technology, but fears for the safety of his wife and adult daughter.

How does aging influence Leon's character, his perspective about life and death and his incredulity regarding the existence of paranormal beings? Does his disbelief interfere with the investigation?

What is the significance and influence of religious beliefs in the characters' lives?

With the help of an illusionary alter ego named Pearl, Antonio Guzman claims to be a macabre combination of man and spirit, who has infiltrated society as a normal human being. He uses advanced technology combined with microbiology, drugs, and hypnosis to invade his victim's minds and manipulate their unconscious desires. Guzman is in search of "candidates" to possess and convert those who embody "the perfect light."

Why does Guzman/Pearl select Paul Evans as a preferred target? Once a considerate and responsible husband and father, Paul has fashioned his life according to how he believes others perceive him, which exposes him to the influence of corporate greed, destroys the life of his business partner, and damages his own family. How does Guzman/Pearl manipulate him?

How does Guzman break down Paul's resistance to acknowledging that dark powers have created his success, and now those powers want Paul's only son, Matt, in a Faustian exchange. Matt and his sister, Jenny, possess the resistant strain of "Perfect Light." What does "the light" symbolize? Is it a reality or a delusional fantasy? Struggling to reclaim shreds of his identity incrementally taken and possessed by Guzman, Paul and his son flee into a mountain wilderness.

How does the relationship of the rancher, Luther Macke, and his sons, Vince and Willie, compare with Paul and his son, Matt? What are the similarities? The differences? What incidents bring the two families into conflict?

How are women treated and depicted in the story? Leon's wife? Paul's wife and daughter? Luther's wife? What are their roles in relationship to the men? How do they respond to the ways they are treated?

In the midst of a violent winter storm in the remote Rocky Mountains, Paul and Matt fight for survival against the forces of darkness whose sole objective is to possess them and extinguish the light wherever and in whomever it may exist.

What is the unfolding evidence and trail of mayhem and murder that force Leon to confront his disbelief in paranormal forces as something more than the imagination and projections of a psychopathic killer. Does the experience change Leon? Does the experience change Paul? If so, in what ways?

Tell-Tale would like to thank you for your purchase. If you enjoyed this work of fiction, please let the author know by leaving a favorable online review. If you would like to read other works by this or other fine TT authors, please visit our website:

www.tell-talepublishing.com